W9-BOO-022

Also by Santa Montefiore

The French Gardener
Sea of Lost Love
The Gypsy Madonna
Last Voyage of the Valentina

The Perfect Happiness

SANTA MONTEFIORE

A TOUCHSTONE BOOK
Published by Simon & Schuster
New York   London   Toronto   Sydney

Touchstone
A Division of Simon & Schuster, Inc.
1230 Avenue of the Americas
New York, NY 10020

First Touchstone trade paperback edition June 2010

TOUCHSTONE and colophon are registered trademarks
of Simon & Schuster, Inc.

For information about special discounts for bulk purchases,
please contact Simon & Schuster Special Sales at
1-866-506-1949 or business@simonandschuster.com.

The Simon & Schuster Speakers Bureau can bring authors to
your live event. For more information or to book an event contact
the Simon & Schuster Speakers Bureau at 1-866-248-3049 or
visit our website at www.simonspeakers.com.

Manufactured in the United States of America

10 9 8 7 6 5 4 3 2 1

Library of Congress Cataloging-in-Publication Data
Montefiore, Santa.
    The perfect happiness / Santa Montefiore.
        p.   cm.
    I. Title.
    PR6113.O544P47 2010
    823'.92—dc22   2010011937

ISBN 978-1-4391-8346-5
ISBN 978-1-4391-8347-2 (ebook)

To the girls:

Amanda, Jane, Julie, Trilbey, and Sam

Prologue

The human spirit is a kaleidoscope of millions of tiny mirrors, reflecting a whole spectrum of colors, depending on where the light falls. It is multifaceted and limitless in its potential. Yet within this intricate hall of mirrors, some surfaces never get a chance to shine but lie in darkness, ignored.

We may never completely realize our capacity to love. We may never flower to our full bloom. But sometimes, something happens in our lives to give us a glimpse of what we could become were we to allow that light to find those dark and secret surfaces of our soul. Then, we realize we have wings and always have done . . .

In Search of the Perfect Happiness

PART ONE

Desire

I

The happiness of your life depends on the quality of your
thoughts.   *In Search of the Perfect Happiness*

Angelica Lariviere pulled on a pair of Spanx and looked at
herself from all angles in the luxurious bathroom designed
especially for her by Smallbone of Devizes. Mirrors encased
the bath on three sides and opposite, above the two basins
where Dyptique candles burned and perfumes adorned pale
marble surfaces in pretty glass bottles. Angelica loved beautiful
things: sunlight shining through a dew-encrusted cobweb,
mist over a mirrored lake, an antique glass chandelier, birds
in the magnolia tree, stars, a pregnant moon, Paris, perfume,
the melancholy tones of a cello, candlelight, the stirring bleak-
ness of a winter heath, snow. More exquisite than reality was
her imagination. As elaborate as an enchanted garden, her
dreams spilled onto the pages of her fantasy children's novels,

where life had no limitations and beauty could be manifested at will. Most of all, Angelica loved love, for nothing was more beautiful than that.

As she mused on the swift passing of time, her thoughts lingered on that first kiss in Paris, beneath the streetlamp on the Place de la Madeleine. Olivier would never kiss her like that again, and she'd never feel the intoxicating sensation of a hundred tiny bees' wings tickling the walls of her belly. Not that he didn't kiss her—just that a husband's kiss is different from a lover's. A first encounter can never be repeated. Marriage, children, and domesticity had deepened their affection for each other but, at the same time, stolen something of their magic, leaving them as familiar as siblings. She felt a wave of nostalgia for that precious moment, and a little wistful that so intense a love would never be experienced again.

It was then that eight-year-old Joe wandered in, clean and flushed in his pajamas, and his eyes widened in horror at the sight of her. "Yuck!" he exclaimed, screwing up his face. "Not *those* again!"

Angelica picked up her wineglass and scrunched her tousled blond hair between her fingers.

"Sorry, sweetie, tonight I need my big pants," she told him, taking a sip of chilled Sauvignon. "It's Big Pants or Big Tummy, and I know which I prefer."

"Daddy doesn't like them, either."

"That's because Frenchmen appreciate beautiful underwear." She thought of the drawer of exquisite Calvin Klein lingerie she never opened, preferring to wear simple cotton underwear from Marks & Spencer, and felt sad that after two children and a decade of marriage she had given up trying to be sexy. She slipped on her black Prada dress. "Better?" she asked, striking a pose and smiling at him coquettishly.

"Phew!" he sighed melodramatically. She crouched down to kiss him. "You smell nice," he added.

"That's better. Remember, if you want to be popular with the girls, only ever tell them they look beautiful. Good training to get a wife someday."

"I'm never going to marry anyone." He put his arms around her and rested his head on her shoulder.

"Oh, you'll change your mind when you're bigger."

"No, I won't. I want to be with *you* forever."

Angelica's eyes welled with emotion. "Oh, darling, that's the nicest thing you've ever said." *Who needs magic when I have you!* "Give me the Full Joe." He pressed himself against her with a giggle. "That's so nice!"

"Can I watch *Ant Bully* now?"

"Go on then." She watched him grab the television control and climb into her bed. He shouted for his sister to join him, and Angelica heard six-year-old Isabel hurry across the landing.

She turned back to the mirror and wiped away a smudge of mascara. *That boy is going to break hearts one day,* she thought. She stood back and appraised herself. *Not bad, thanks to the Spanx.* She actually looked quite slim. On a wave of enthusiasm, she hurried into the custom-made dressing room and reached for a vintage black belt with a pretty gold buckle in the shape of a butterfly she had found in the Portobello market. Back in front of the mirror she put it on, slipped into open-toed black stilettos, and admired the transformation.

Joe and Isabel chattered on the bed, their voices erupting into the uninhibited laughter exclusive to small children. The door opened and Olivier strode in with the insouciance of a man used to being the dominant power in the house.

"It smells like a bordello!" He turned up the lights. "The children should be in bed."

"They *are* in bed—*our* bed." She laughed. "Hello, darling."

He scowled and blew out the candles, knowing that she would forget. "I see you've got a glass of wine. I could do with a drink myself."

"Bad day?"

Olivier took off his tie. "It's a difficult time. The mood in the City is very depressed." He went into the dressing room and slipped his jacket onto a hanger. "Did you pick up my dry cleaning? I want to wear my Gucci jacket tonight."

Angelica flushed. "I forgot. Sorry."

"*Merde!* Sometimes I wonder what goes on in that cotton wool head of yours."

"There's a whole world in here, beyond the cotton wool, of course." She tapped her temple, trying to be upbeat. "I get paid to imagine."

"You remember the plots of those fantasy novels of yours, but you don't remember to pick up my dry cleaning. You still haven't collected my trousers from the tailor, and I asked you weeks ago. If you had my job, we'd be broke!"

"Which is why I don't have your job. Look, I'm sorry."

"Don't apologize. I'm obviously not a priority."

"Darling, don't be angry, please. We're going out to dinner, it'll be fun. You'll forget about the City and your Gucci jacket." She walked up behind him and put her arms around his waist. "You *know* you're my priority."

"Then be an angel and get me a drink—and put the children to bed. The summer holiday is too long. When do they go back?"

"Thursday."

He sniffed irritably. "Not a moment too soon." He stepped out of his trousers and hung them up carefully. Olivier was meticulously tidy. "I'm going to take a shower."

"So, how do I look?"

Olivier glanced at her as he removed the gold-crested cuff links from his shirt. "Why the belt?"

"Fashion, darling!"

"Why would you want to emphasize the widest part of you?"

Angelica stared in astonishment. "The widest part of me?"

He chuckled and kissed her neck. "You always look beautiful, Angelica."

She watched him remove his shirt and toss the cuff links into the leather box on the trouser press. Though slightly built and not very tall, Olivier was an attractive man. He was athletic, playing regular games of tennis at Queen's, or running off his excess energy around Hyde Park when one of his four couldn't make it. He was typically Gallic, with thick brown hair swept off his face in waves and smooth olive skin that never paled, even in winter. His features were fine, his nose long and aristocratic, his eyes a startling cornflower blue against lustrous black lashes. It was his mouth that had first attracted her to him, the way it curled at one corner. Now it took a lot to make it curl at all. He wore his clothes with the panache of a true Parisian, paying special attention to his shoes, which were always polished, and his suits, which were always beautifully tailored. Appearances were important to Olivier, and he spared no expense at Turnbull & Asser and Gucci. He liked to look good and he liked *her* to look good, too.

With the help of Sunny, the housekeeper, Angelica put the children to bed and served her husband whiskey on the rocks as he came out of the shower smelling of sandalwood. He didn't notice that she had removed the belt, replacing it in the drawer along with her joy. She no longer felt like going out to dinner, even though Scarlet was one of her closest friends. She felt like a sack of flour.

As she reached for her handbag, her mobile telephone bleeped with a message. **Please come quickly. I need you. X Kate.** Angelica's heart lurched. Kate was in trouble, again! She looked at her watch. Kate lived in Thurloe Square, on the way to Scarlet's house in Chelsea. If she was quick, she could jump in a cab and meet Olivier there.

Olivier's reaction was predictable. He sighed grumpily and swore, clipping his words to emphasize his annoyance. "She is such a drama queen! And you run to her like a lady-in-waiting who cannot see that without her drama the queen is not a queen at all."

"She's fragile. She's obviously in a state."

"She spends her whole life in a state."

"It's not her fault that Pete is having an affair."

"I sympathize. If I were married to her, I'd have an affair, too."

"I hope that's not a threat."

"Not to you, my angel. The very fact that we are opposites is good for my soul. I am material, you are ethereal." He laughed, pleased with his analysis. "Go on then, I'll meet you there. But don't be later than eight-thirty. I'll let them know that you are dealing with a crisis. No doubt your fellow lady-in-waiting will understand!" he added, referring to Scarlet. "Though, I'm sure she won't want you to be late for dinner." As she left the room, he noticed her handbag, thrown carelessly on the bed with her lip gloss and compact. "Angel, you cannot pay the cab without your purse!" he called impatiently. She rushed back, gathered it all up, and hurried out again.

Angelica wrapped her pashmina around her shoulders and hailed a cab on Kensington Church Street. It was a chilly night for September. Gray clouds filled the sky like porridge, and the evenings were now setting in early. Some trees were even beginning to turn orange. The streets were bustling with people having returned from their summer holidays for the start of the school term. The traffic was heavier, too, slowing down to near gridlock opposite Kensington Palace. She was grateful to be going in the opposite direction.

The cabbie interrupted her thoughts with glum comments on the lack of sunshine, the misery of yet another wet summer. "Global warming," he said gloomily. "Still, Boris is mayor and Cameron will sweep Brown down the proverbial drain. It's not all bad."

He dropped her off outside Kate's white terraced house where two bay trees stood on either side of the shiny pink door like sentinels. She rang the bell. From inside came the sound track of *Mamma Mia* and voices. She tried to peep in, but the curtains were drawn. Maybe the text message was old and she was interrupting a dinner party.

Finally, the door opened, and Kate appeared in a cashmere dressing gown, a bottle of Chardonnay in one hand, cigarette in the other. Her face was tearstained, mascara smeared over blotchy skin, her spiky brown hair pulled off her face with an Hermès scarf. She looked like a little girl in her wretchedness.

"Oh, Angelica, thank you for coming. You're a real friend."

She wasn't the only real friend. There in the sitting room sat Letizia and Candace, apparently as bewildered as she was.

"What's going on?" Angelica hissed as Letizia enveloped her in a cloud of Fracas.

"Not sure, darling," she replied, her Italian accent curling seductively around her words like a soft cat's tail. "Your guess is as good as mine!"

"Where are the children?"

"With her mother."

"And Pete?"

"In Moscow."

"Lucky."

"*Esatto,* darling. No man likes to see a woman in tears, especially if they are shed for him."

"Let me get you a drink," said Kate, wandering unsteadily out of the room.

Angelica sank into a chair. "If I'd known you two were here,

I wouldn't have bothered. Olivier will be furious if I'm late for dinner."

"You think that's bad?" said Candace, raising a perfectly shaped eyebrow. "I'm meant to be at the theater."

"You're so good to her," said Letizia.

"No, I'm a schmuck!" A born-and-bred New Yorker, Candace never minced her words. "I've texted Harry that I'll meet him in the interval. He's so mad, he hasn't replied. If I continue like this, he'll divorce me."

"She looks so thin," said Letizia, sliding her green eyes towards the hall. "Like she hasn't eaten a carbohydrate in weeks. I'm a little jealous, actually."

"Misery," quipped Candace. "They should sell it by the bottle."

"Has Pete left her, do you think?" Angelica asked.

"Of *course* not. They're *addicted* to each other. They make each other *equally* miserable." Candace glanced impatiently at her pretty pink nails. "What's she doing in there, treading the grapes?"

"This is going to be a long night; I just know it," sighed Letizia.

At last Kate returned with the bottle of wine. "Couldn't find the bottle opener," she said with a drunken giggle, dragging on her cigarette. "You're probably wondering why you're all here."

"It's your birthday and we've all forgotten!"

Letizia shot Candace a look. "What's happened?" she asked kindly, patting the sofa. Kate sat down with a sigh.

Candace took the bottle from her and twisted off the cap. "I think I need a little fortification."

"I'm late," Kate stated darkly.

"Honey, we're *all* late," said Candace.

"Not for the theater. *Late* late." She gave a meaningful look.

"Oh, *that* kind of late. Well, that's a surprise!" Candace

continued. "I thought you two were at each other's throats, not in each other's pants!"

"Have you done a test?" Angelica asked.

"No, that's why I invited you all around. I need the moral support to do it."

"You haven't done a test?" Angelica was annoyed. If it turned out to be negative, what was the point of dragging them all out tonight?

"So, you have another child, what's so bad about that?" asked Candace, pouring herself some wine.

"Yes, another child will bond you back together again. There's nothing more romantic, darling," Letizia purred encouragingly.

Kate shook her head, her eyes welling with tears. "Not in this case." She bit her bottom lip. "If I'm pregnant, I don't know whose it is."

"Have I missed something?" asked Candace, stunned.

"You're not the only one," said Angelica. All three women looked at Kate.

"I had a one-night stand. It was a mistake. Pete was with The Haggis, and I was in despair. I'm an idiot. Now look at me. I'm a wreck. To think I'm a model. No one will employ me now except those ugly agencies."

"In this state? I think you'd be lucky to be employed at all," said Candace, teasing her gently.

"It was only once, and now I'm going to be punished for the rest of my life."

"So, who is he?"

"I can't tell you. I'm too ashamed."

Angelica narrowed her eyes, considering possible candidates. Letizia put her arm around Kate's skinny shoulder and gave her a reassuring squeeze, enveloping her in pale cashmere and perfume.

Candace looked at her watch. "I don't mean to be rude

here, but Jeremy Irons isn't going to wait for me to turn up to Act Two. Can we move this along, please?"

"Sorry, Candace, you're really good to me." Kate sat up, bracing herself for the moment of truth.

"Have you got the kit?" Letizia asked. "There is no better time than the present."

Kate pointed to four boxes on a side table. "Just in case . . . you know . . ."

"Sure, they lie all the time!" said Candace, striding over to get them for her. "Come on, Kate. Let's get you upstairs."

Letizia fetched her a glass from the kitchen, Candace handed her the tests, Angelica helped her up the stairs and pushed her into her en suite bathroom.

"Right, give it your best shot!" said Candace, throwing herself onto Kate's super-king-size sleigh bed. She ran her hand over the brown furry bedspread. "This is nice."

"Who do you think it is?" Angelica hissed.

"Must be Ralph Lauren," said Candace.

"No, not the bedspread. Her *lover*?"

"Oh, well . . ."

"Robbie?" Letizia suggested.

"Robbie who?"

"Her trainer!"

"Oh no! That's such a cliché! She'd have told us if it was him." Candace waved her hand dismissively. "It'll be someone we all know. *One of us*."

"I can't pee! I'm too nervous!" Kate wailed from the bathroom.

"Run the tap," Letizia suggested.

"I'll kill her if this is all a false alarm," said Candace.

Angelica glanced at her watch. "Not if Olivier gets here first. It's eight-thirty!"

"Is it coming?"

There was a long pause, then finally a shriek. "Now I can't stop! Help, the glass is too small!"

They all waited without uttering another word. Kate poked her head around the door. "Are you still here?"

"Of course we're still here. It's not like we've got anything better to do!" said Candace.

"Well? What does it say?" Letizia asked anxiously.

"I haven't done it yet. I'm too scared." She emerged with the glass.

"Oh really! Too much information!" Candace cried, hiding her eyes.

"You must all have a test," insisted Kate, handing them each a box.

"This is insane!" But Candace took one anyway and opened it.

Letizia threw her empty box on the bed. "I'm confident it will be negative. What are we looking for?"

"Were you born yesterday? A blue stripe," said Candace. "And you're going to have to look at mine for me."

"This takes me back a few years!" said Angelica, studying the device with nostalgia. "I should have had another one."

"You can have mine," groaned Kate.

"Don't say that, darling. You might not even be pregnant." Letizia was a natural optimist.

"Let's see," said Angelica. "All together now."

"Oh Lord, can I do this with my eyes closed?" said Candace.

"You're making more of a fuss than me," said Kate.

"That's simply not possible!" said Candace.

The four women dipped the sticks into Kate's urine. "I think I'm going to be sick," moaned Kate.

"*You're* going to be sick. At least it's *your* wee!" Candace grimaced.

Angelica pulled hers out and watched as the little window turned blue. She felt a wave of pity for her friend. "But it's *your* baby, Kate," she said quietly.

They all stared at their tests. Then they all stared at Kate.

"Any negatives?" Letizia asked hopefully. They all shook their heads.

Kate sank onto the bed. "Hell! What am I going to do?"

"What do you *want* to do?" asked Letizia, sitting beside her and putting her arm around her again.

"You don't know how hard I've worked for this stomach," she exclaimed, then burst into tears. "Now I know, I can't even have a fucking cigarette or a glass of wine. I might as well enroll in a convent!"

"It's a little late for that!" said Candace.

Kate put her hand on her belly. "If I could be sure it was Pete's, it wouldn't be so bad, would it? But what if it's not Pete's. I mean, he'll *know*. Men always know. Babies always look like their fathers, don't they?"

"Not always," said Letizia.

"Oh, they always do. That way the fathers don't eat them," Candace retorted.

"You don't have to make your mind up now, Kate," said Angelica, aware that she was now running very late indeed. "Think about it for a few days."

Kate ran her rheumy eyes over Angelica's dress. "You need a belt," she said with a sniff.

"I put one on and Olivier said I was emphasizing the widest part of me."

For a moment Kate was drawn out of herself. "He said what?"

"I hope you cut off his balls!" said Candace.

"No, I took off the belt."

"You sop! What are you? A doormat?" Candace laughed fondly. "What are we going to do with you?"

"I think I need a new body."

Letizia sighed. "No, darling, you just need a new husband."

Kate managed to stagger over to her chest of drawers and pulled out a belt. "Don't argue with me. I'm dangerous when drunk." She slipped it around Angelica's waist. "This is *not* the widest part of you, whatever Olivier says. You look fabulous!"

"You really do," agreed Letizia. "Olivier should be ashamed of himself. You should have married an Italian. They love curvaceous women."

"The widest part of you, my ass! His ego's so wide he can barely make it out the door! Tell him that and see how he likes it." Candace smiled at her affectionately. "Go knock 'em dead!"

"Now we've sorted you out, let's talk about me," said Kate.

Candace gave her a big hug. "Angelica's right. Sit on it for a few days. Call me in the morning. Letizia will put you to bed."

"You're leaving?" said Kate in a small voice.

"*I'm* not," said Letizia, stepping in dutifully.

Candace beckoned Angelica with a brisk wave. "Come on, honey, we're out of here."

Angelica put her arms around Kate, whose face crumpled like a child being left at boarding school. "I'll call you in the morning—if I'm still alive!"

"Thank you for coming, you two. I really appreciate your support."

"I know," cried Candace as she hurried down the stairs. "We expect huge rewards in heaven! Birkin bags and Louboutin shoes by the truckload—in every color!"

"What a mess!" Angelica sighed as they stepped onto the pavement.

"This time it really *is* a mess," agreed Candace. "Where do you have to go?"

"Cadogan Square."

"I'll take you." She summoned her driver with a wave. The glossy black Mercedes pulled out into the street.

"But you're late for the theater."

"I'll say I crept in at the back—what's the difference? He's mad already. Anyway, you know what? I've seen enough theater for one night."

"You think she's acting?"

"Her whole life is theater, God love her. And we do love her, don't we!"

As they climbed into the car, Kate's front door flew open and Letizia hurried down the steps waving Angelica's bag.

"Oh Lord!" Angelica sighed. "Not again!"

"If your brain wasn't in your head, you'd be leaving it all over the city," said Candace.

"You sound like Olivier."

"No, honey. Olivier doesn't think you *have* a brain!"

2

Buddha says that pain or suffering arises through desire or craving and that to be free of pain we need to cut the bonds of desire.   *In Search of the Perfect Happiness*

Angelica arrived to find the dinner had already begun. She was led by a young man in a black Nehru jacket through the candlelit hall to the dining room, where the sound of chatter and clinking glasses rose into the lily-scented air. When she entered, those she knew called out and waved, teasing her for being late. She dared not catch Olivier's eye; it was enough that she could sense his staring at her furiously from the far end of the table. The hostess in tight leather trousers and shiny black boots was more forgiving. She leapt up and strode around the table to embrace Angelica affectionately, wrists jingling with bracelets and bangles.

"Hi, doll. I got a text from Kate but couldn't leave the house." Scarlet lowered her voice. "Is she okay?"

"I'll fill you in later. Long story. But she's alive!"

"Well, that's something. You look like you could do with a drink?"

"I've already had one."

"Then have another. You're as pale as a pancake. I'll get Olivier suitably wasted. He'll be love's young dream by dessert!"

"Thanks, Scarlet. Right now he's a grumpy old nightmare!"

Olivier was now in conversation with the ravishing Caterina Tintello. There was nothing that lifted his mood as surely as a beautiful woman.

"Now, you've got the delicious Jack Meyer from South Africa on your right—give that husband of yours something important to worry about—and my slightly less delicious husband on your left."

"Oh, Scarlet, William is very delicious!"

"Well, he is to me, I suppose, but Jack's delicious to everyone. Now, let me introduce you."

Scarlet tapped Jack on the shoulder. He said something to Stash Helm, the vivacious woman on his right, then stood up politely, towering over them like a bear. Angelica felt her spirits jolt back to life, recharged by his big shaggy head and wide, infectious smile as he grinned down at her appreciatively. She smiled back, the tension melting away in the warmth of his handshake.

"Jack, meet Angelica Lariviere. Jack's a notorious flirt," Scarlet teased. "Don't say I didn't warn you."

"While the cat's away . . ." he replied, without taking his eyes off her. Angelica was enchanted by the humorous twinkle behind his glasses.

"There's no keeping this dog on the porch," Scarlet added with a chuckle.

"Some dogs aren't made for porches," said Angelica.

"You seem to know a lot about dogs."

"She knows a lot about everything. Angelica's an author, a very successful one, too! Jack loves books. That's why I put you next to each other."

Scarlet returned to her place, and Jack pulled out Angelica's chair.

"You smell of oranges," he said.

"Is it overpowering?"

"No. It's delightful."

She basked in his accent. It wasn't strong, but she could feel the sun and smell the rich red soil in those gently clipped vowels.

He sat down and scrutinized her. "You seem familiar," he murmured.

She shook her head and looked away, disarmed by the intimacy of his gaze. "I don't think so."

"We haven't met before?"

"Definitely not."

He laughed it off and spread his napkin on his knee. "Funny, I feel I know you. A past life, perhaps."

Before Angelica could respond, William turned to greet her on her left. Reluctantly, she swung around to kiss him, hearing Jack resume his conversation with Stash. "You look well," William commented, running his eyes over the glow Jack had just ignited. "Where have you spent the summer?" William was reserved in that cool, phlegmatic way for which upper-class Englishmen are notorious. Angelica had known him and Scarlet for years: they were part of the London social scene, and Scarlet had become one of her inner circle of friends. However, as fond of him as she was, right now Angelica wished she could turn away and talk to Jack.

She was aware of every movement he made and most of William's conversation went unheard. The first course was eaten, the plates taken away, and, although Jack passed her only a few comments about the food or the wine, she felt they were isolated from the rest of the guests on a little island of their own, acutely conscious of each other. She could feel his arm against hers, and it was warm and strangely familiar. Neither moved away, and she wondered whether he, too, was aware of it. She could hear his voice, the foreign way he articulated his words, but having to respond convincingly to William made it impossible to tune in to what he said. His laugh was infectious, and she laughed herself, deliberately feigning amusement at something William had said. Her host felt witty, growing uncharacteristically animated as a result of her encouragement.

Finally, with reluctance, William turned to Hester Berridge, a buxom, rosy-cheeked Englishwoman who bred horses in Suffolk while her husband worked at the Tate. Angelica was cast adrift for a moment while Jack continued to talk to Stash. She sat back and sipped her wine, the sense of anticipation causing her stomach to fizz. She glanced at her husband, who was still deep in conversation with Caterina. Their heads were almost touching, and he was grinning roguishly. He had once looked at her like that, before they had married and their conversations had been dragged into a more domestic domain. He threw his head back and they laughed together. Angelica didn't mind—Olivier was always better company after a good flirt.

"So, now I get to talk to the authoress," said Jack, turning his heavy gaze on her as if she was the only woman in the room he wanted to talk to. She noticed the deep lines around his mouth and across his temples, slicing through his rough and weathered skin as he smiled, and felt something she hadn't felt in a very long time: the stirring of tiny bees' wings in her stomach. "What sort of books do you write?"

"Fantasy novels for children. Probably not your thing, unless you're into sorcery and time travel."

"I'm definitely into those. I love Tolkien, and I've read all the Harry Potters. I suppose I'm just a big kid."

"Most men are. The only thing that changes as they grow up is the cost of their toys." He laughed and the crow's feet deepened across his temples. "They're a bit of fun, that's all," she added modestly.

"Children's books are far harder to write than adult fiction."

"I think I'm just too fanciful to stick to reality."

"Which writer is your role model?"

"I'd hate to sound like I'm comparing myself to the greats. But I suppose I aspire to be Philip Pullman in the same way a painter aspires to be Michelangelo!"

"It's good to aim high. If you focus hard enough on your goal, I'm sure you'll get there. Philip Pullman's a genius. Your imagination must be exceedingly fertile."

"You have no idea." She laughed. "I get lost in there sometimes."

"I'd like to get lost in there, too. Real life is way too real most of the time."

"Oh, I don't think it's a place for a man like you."

"Why not?"

"Far too fluffy. You have to swim through an awful lot of cotton wool to get to it."

"I'm a good swimmer." He smiled, running his eyes over her features appreciatively. "What name do you write under?"

"Angelica Garner. My maiden name."

"I'll look out for your books. I need a good book for the journey home."

She blushed with pleasure. "So, what do you read?"

"While I'm on the porch?"

"While you're on the porch."

"Lots, simultaneously. I have books in every room of the house. I like mystery, adventure, love."

She raised her eyebrows. "Love?"

"I have a strong feminine side." He pulled a soppy face.

"Now that surprises me."

"Why? A book without love is like a desert without flowers." His gaze grew intense. "What is more important in life than love? It's what it's all about. Why we're all here, and, when we go, it's all we take with us."

"Well, I agree with you, of course." She was stunned by the emotion in his words.

"I'm a frustrated writer," he confessed sheepishly, playing

with his spoon. "Never had anything published, though. Not for want of trying."

"What have you written?"

"Rubbish, clearly."

"I don't believe that."

"I'm Jack of all trades, master of none."

"What are the other trades, besides writing?"

"There was a time in my youth when I wanted to be a pop star." He pulled a face, anticipating her amusement. "I had long shaggy hair and leather trousers and smoked joints while I strummed my guitar. Now I make wine."

"Not a poet then." He gave her a quizzical look. " 'A book without love is like a desert without flowers.' "

He laughed and shook his head. "Just a hopeless old romantic."

She watched him help himself to food, admiring the leonine strength in his profile, the big, pawlike quality to his hands, the very male ruggedness of his skin—so unlike Olivier's polished European glamour—and wished the night could go on forever.

"Do you have a vineyard in South Africa?"

"How well do you know South Africa?"

"I've never been."

He looked surprised. "Then you must come. I own a beautiful vineyard called Rosenbosch in Franschhoek. You would love it. You can set your next novel there."

"I need something to inspire me. I'm growing tired of what I do. Right now I'm considering doing something a little different."

"Which is?"

She hesitated. Olivier teased her about her fascination with the esoteric; she didn't want to look foolish in front of Jack. "I'm not sure I'm ready to discuss it," she replied, embarrassed.

"A love story?"

"No."

"Murder mystery?"

"No."

"Erotica?"

She laughed throatily. "Not yet."

"I'm determined to find out. I'm a Scorpio: once I set my heart on something, there's no stopping me." His gaze was too intense: she had to look away.

"I'm not even sure how I'm going to do it, if at all. Olivier thinks it's too ambitious."

"That's not very supportive."

"But it's honest. Olivier is very honest." She looked down at her belt and sucked in her stomach.

"He must be proud of your writing, though."

"Of course he is," she replied, but even she could detect the lie in her voice. Olivier didn't think there was much of a challenge in writing for children; she rather hoped she'd prove him wrong with her new idea.

"Is he the good-looking Frenchman over there?" He nodded in Olivier's direction.

"That's the one."

"Does that dog stay on the porch?"

"I think so. He does a lot of barking, though."

"Dogs need to bark, makes us feel butch."

"Give them long leads and they generally don't stray farther than the edge of the porch. If it's a big porch, which Olivier's is."

"Lucky Olivier."

"I know. It's the biggest porch in London."

He frowned. "No, he's lucky to be married to the most beautiful girl in London."

Angelica laughed and looked down at her plate. "Scarlet's right—you're an incorrigible flirt."

"Not at all, my bark is bigger than my bite. But you *are* very beautiful." She dismissed his comment with a toss of her hair, but he continued without taking his eyes off her. "I like sensual women. Women with big hearts. Passionate women."

"Like your wife," she teased.

"Exactly, like my wife." But his eyes twinkled again with mischief, and Angelica smiled into her glass.

"So, what's the new subject?"

"I can't discuss it with you."

"That's where you're wrong. I'm the perfect person to discuss it with, because you don't know me. I won't judge you, because I don't know you, either. In fact, I am the only person here you *can* discuss it with." He replenished her wineglass and sat back in his chair expectantly.

"You're very persistent."

"When I know what I want."

"All right." The wine had made her reckless. "I'm not sure I want to continue writing children's books that are simply good adventure stories. I want to explore the deeper meaning of life. Perhaps add another layer, like a parable, for me as much as for my reader. I want to find the elusive happiness we're all searching for." She stopped his interrupting by raising her hand and continuing at great speed, wishing she'd never begun. "Before you laugh at me, I want to add that I've read all those self-help and esoteric books. I know all the clichés. We *all* know those. The secret is putting them into practice in a practical way. We can't all become hermits and meditate in distant caves. There must be a way of finding heavenly peace while living in the material world. I just feel there's more to life than living it mechanically. There, I've said it. Now it's your cue to laugh."

He let her finish, then nodded gravely. "I'm not laughing. It's probably the best idea you've ever had."

Her face lit up at his unexpected approval. "You really think so?"

"Absolutely. Everyone is driven by a desire to be happy."

"Yet so many people are miserable."

"The secret you're looking for is love."

"Well, I know that much."

"Then you don't need to write the book."

"It's not that simple. Pure, unconditional love is near impossible."

"No, it isn't. You feel it for your children, don't you?"

"Well, do I? Of course I'd kill for them and die for them. But I'm not sure it's completely unselfish. I need them. That's ego driven, isn't it? I mean, it might be better for them to go to boarding school, but I can't bear to be parted from them, so they'll go to London schools. That's *conditional* love, isn't it? True happiness comes from loving *unconditionally*—and I don't just mean our own children, I mean everyone."

"Well, I do see there's a problem there. I find most people intolerable."

"You see? Jesus loved everyone unconditionally. All the great teachers and avatars preached unselfish, absolute, unreserved love. The kind of love that loves no matter what. Impossible for we less spiritual creatures." She grinned at him playfully. "I certainly don't love Olivier unconditionally."

He laughed and glanced across the table at Olivier, now in animated conversation with Scarlet. "So what are the conditions?"

"They're too many to list. We don't have all night."

"Which is a great pity." He turned his eyes on her again and lowered his voice. "Loving your husband is dependent on how he makes *you* feel. So you love him on condition that he makes you feel alive, beautiful, and valued." She was surprised by the wisdom in this analysis—Olivier wouldn't even discuss such a subject. "If he ceases to make you feel good about yourself, you will cease to love him. You might not leave him, but the essence of your love will change."

"You're so right. Olivier has the power to make me feel good about myself or bad about myself. His love can wound me or uplift me. Unconditional love would love him no matter what, even if he didn't love me at all."

"Pure love loves even the hand that strikes it."

"I couldn't love like that."

He leaned towards her conspiratorially, and she felt the flame of his charisma as if his body were made of fire. "I think it's a great idea."

"You're very sweet to say so."

"You should have been called Sage, not Angelica."

She laughed in astonishment. "Most people don't know that Angelica is an herb."

"I'm a countryman. I know my herbs, flowers, shrubs, and trees. I know my birds, too. I love nature with a passion. I can't be in a city for too long, the concrete depresses me."

"I love nature, too. I just don't spend enough time in it."

"I suppose the park doesn't quite satisfy."

"No, it doesn't. But I grew up in Norfolk. My parents still live there. It's beautiful, by an estuary. There are all sorts of birds on the beach."

"Ah, Norfolk, the bird-watching capital of Britain."

"How do you know that?"

"Because I love birds and I've been to Norfolk. I remember thousands of geese in winter, marsh harriers, bearded tits, avocets, terns, and the odd bittern."

"You're joking!"

He grinned, pleased that he was able to impress her. "Don't they have the most wonderful names!"

"You recognize all of those?"

"Of course. As I said, I know my birds."

"You really do."

"Come to South Africa. We have all sorts of exotic breeds there: the little malachite kingfisher with her electric-blue plumage and the cheeky hoopoe who calls 'poop poop poop' across the garden."

"Wow, you're a fount of information. How come you're so wise about life and nature?"

"If you love nature, you automatically ask yourself the big questions. You're constantly faced with the death and rebirth of trees and flowers. And when you gaze over vast distances, that prompts you to think of your own mortality and makes you feel very insignificant."

"I'm going to wipe the dust off my binoculars!"

"I'm glad I've inspired you."

She sipped her wine thoughtfully. "You've *really* inspired me, Jack, and not just in the feathered department. I'm going to try to add a deeper layer to my books. I'm going to search for the perfect happiness."

"You should. I'm not just saying so because I find you attractive. Most people go through life as if they were blind, mechanically, as you say, without ever questioning what it all means. Trust me, I ask myself that question every day." His face darkened as if a sad thought had passed through his mind. "We're all going to die. I'd like to find out what I'm doing here before I go. I'd certainly like my last years to be happy ones." He drained his glass, which was promptly filled by a hovering waiter.

"Let's talk about something happy. Tell me about your children?"

So Jack told her about Lucy, Elizabeth, and Sophie: the three jewels in his crown.

"I bet they've got you well wrapped round their little fingers."

He laughed as he thought about their wheedling and manipulating. "They're young women now. Even Lucy, who's just fifteen, is going on twenty-one. It's hard for a father like me. I want to wrap them in pink candyfloss and hold on to their innocence. I'm a terrible old rogue, so I suspect all the young men in their lives of the worst intentions."

"Judging them by your own standards."

"Exactly. I keep a shotgun under my pillow, and woe betide anyone who lays a dirty hand on one of my girls."

"It's going to happen, you know."

"Oh, it already has. Elizabeth is eighteen and has a boy-friend at Stellenbosch University. Sophie is sixteen, and who knows what mischief she's already got up to. Lucy's a knock-out, and I can see a knowing shadow in her eyes. She's tasted the fruit of good and evil, I'd bet my life on it. There's nothing I can do."

"Children come through us, but they don't belong to us."

"That is a hard lesson for me to learn."

"For all of us. Mine are still little, but Olivier will find it hard, especially with our daughter."

"You never forget what they were like as little girls. In spite of their makeup and grown-up clothes, they're still the same underneath. And they don't know how naïve they are. They think they know everything. I want to stand at the helm of their lives and steer them through the mines." Angelica felt a wave of tenderness. She, too, wanted to steer Isabel and Joe through the mines. "When you find the secret of happiness, let me know."

"You, Jack, shall be the very first person I tell."

After dinner Olivier remained at the table with Caterina and a few others while the rest of the guests adjourned to the sitting room, where a fire burned in the grate.

"Isn't it a little early for fires?" asked Hester, flopping onto the sofa.

"It's been the most miserable summer on record," Scarlet replied, lighting a cigarette. "I've spent the last month in Italy, and I'm really feeling the cold. You horsey people never feel the cold."

"It's all that rolling around in the hay," said Hester, laughing huskily.

"Do you really get up to all that?"

"As much as one can without frightening the horses," Hester replied, glancing at her husband, who was standing by the window talking to Stash.

"I'd expect you to be burning up in those leather trousers," said Angelica, joining Hester on the sofa.

Scarlet gave her a hand. "See, I'm as cold as a fish! I have terrible circulation."

"You could eat more. You're so skinny, you have no insulation," said Angelica.

"Thank you for the compliment!" Scarlet puffed out a ring of smoke.

"I'd happily give you some of mine!"

"At our age, women have to choose between their faces and their figures," said Hester, who had clearly chosen her face.

"So they say, but if my arse expands, my misery pulls my face down, so I choose my figure, every time. A little nip here or tuck there will take care of the face. As it is, I'm so riddled with Botox I can only just pull a smile."

"I've sacrificed my figure by default, and it's done nothing for my face," said Angelica, noticing Jack talking to William in the library.

"Oh, I'd love your face, Angelica," said Scarlet, warming her bottom at the fire. "We'd all love to look as wholesome as you. Trouble is, no amount of makeup can disguise my unscrupulous past."

"Oh, I don't think I look wholesome!"

"You do, like a field of golden wheat. You look like a fresh bun just out of the oven. In fact, I'm surprised you haven't been discovered to star in a Hovis advert."

They all laughed, and Angelica caught Jack's eye as he turned to see what was amusing them. His attention was like sunshine, and she basked in the delicious warmth of it.

Coffee and tea were brought in on a tray, and William and Jack joined the group in front of the fire. Angelica tried to behave naturally, but her whole body tingled with a pleasure as unfamiliar as the taste of a long-forgotten fruit. Jack's smile was contagious. His hair, the color of wet hay, fell over his forehead until he pushed it back into shaggy waves like a lion's mane. She admired the generous width of his face, his dark eyebrows that knitted together when he frowned, and his almond-shaped eyes that seemed to see the humor in every-thing. He dominated the party, his comments wittier than everyone else's, his charisma brighter, and everyone laughed at everything he said.

"Jack, why don't you play something?" Scarlet asked, light-ing another cigarette. Scarlet was classically trained and never missed an opportunity to show off her talent. "Because if you don't, I will."

Jack needed no encouragement. "Bring me a glass of red wine, and I'll play anything you want." He went into the li-brary and sat on the piano stool. The baby grand, a wedding present to Scarlet from William, was covered in silver photo frames and a large vase of tuberose. If Jack had impressed Angelica during dinner, it was as nothing compared to the sight of him at the piano. He began with jazz, his fingers dancing deftly over the keys, his powerful body moving in time with such grace and confidence it was as if the piano were an extension of him. Then he played their requests, and they all sang the songs of the Beatles, Abba, and Billy Joel. An-gelica joined in, blushing each time he caught her eye, hoping he couldn't hear her pitiful effort. Whether he did or not, he seemed to smile for her alone.

When Olivier sauntered in with Caterina and declared that it was time to go home, she was disappointed. There was no point trying to persuade him to stay. Once Olivier had made up his mind to go there was no changing it. He looked pointedly at his watch, indicating his impatience with a brisk toss of his head.

Angelica said her good-byes. When she got to Jack, he took her hand and kissed her on both cheeks. "Come to South Africa. You might discover the secret you're looking for riding across the veld."

"You don't give up, do you?"

"Life is short." He pleaded with his eyes.

She laughed and removed her hand. "It's been fun meeting you and I loved your piano playing. You're not Jack of all trades, you're Jack, master of music. You have a wonderful gift."

She could tell he was disappointed at her departure, and she was flattered. She hadn't received such attention in years. She couldn't wait to tell Candace.

Olivier was in a good mood. He didn't mention her tardiness nor ask about Kate, and she didn't volunteer any information.

"What a great evening," he said, opening the car door and climbing in. "Scarlet always gives good parties."

"She's a pro at throwing people together and leaving them to get on with it. There are always new people, which is fun."

"What was that South African like?" he asked. "He looked a bit pleased with himself, if you ask me."

"Charming, actually."

"I bet. He's the sort of man who's strong on charm and weak on brains. I suppose girls like that rugged Clint Eastwood appeal."

"He was amazing on the piano. You should have joined us."

"I didn't think you liked singing."

"I do. I just have a terrible voice. How was Caterina?"

He grinned. "Caterina is a naughty monkey."

Angelica was relieved to change the subject. She didn't want to discuss Jack with her husband. "You've met your match with her."

"She's an atrocious flirt. Her husband should keep an eye on her."

"Nothing wrong with a flirt."

"It's different for a man."

"In what way?" Angelica bristled.

"I'm afraid there are double standards. A woman flirting in front of her husband is humiliating."

"Oh, and it's not humiliating for a man to flirt in front of his wife?"

"It's different."

"Says who?"

He turned into Gloucester Road. "Boys will be boys. It means nothing. I flirted with Caterina, but she knows I am devoted to you. Whereas if you flirt with a man, he assumes you're not happy with your husband and that you are looking for an affair."

"You're so wrong!"

"Did you mind my flirting with Caterina?"

"Not at all, but that's because I'm not possessive. I trust you."

"And you are right to."

"Are you saying that you wouldn't trust *me*?"

"Yes." He put his hand on her knee. "If you flirted with another man like I flirted with Caterina, I'd be crushed like a grape under your foot."

"You're ridiculous."

"No, just a hypocrite. Unlike you, I am very possessive, and my heart is very tender." She laughed. "The South African flirted with you, naturally. I would be surprised if he didn't. You are a good-looking woman, Angelica. But did you assume he is unhappy with his wife?"

"Of course not."

"But if you had flirted with him, he would have assumed you were unhappy with me."

"I didn't flirt with him," she said quickly.

He stopped at the traffic lights at the bottom of Kensington Church Street. "I would never accuse you of that, *mon ange*. But don't think I wasn't watching you."

She wanted to say that he was too busy watching Caterina, but she bit her tongue. Caterina had done her a service.

As luck would have it, Olivier found a parking place a few yards from their house in Brunswick Gardens, beneath a leafy cherry tree that had not yet begun to turn. Angelica hurried up to the front door and waited for Olivier to join her with the key. She smiled as she thought of Jack and how close she had come to getting into trouble with her husband. There was nothing wrong with a flirt, she thought blithely. She felt more alive than she had in years. Perhaps the secret of happiness was in living dangerously. But how to make that feeling last?

3

Thinking positively will attract positive things into your
life.   *In Search of the Perfect Happiness*

The following morning Angelica was awoken by the children climbing into her bed. Olivier had risen early to go to
work, turning on the light and waking her up, but once he
had gone she had drifted back to sleep and into Jack's big
embrace. She had felt a warm sense of belonging there, like
a ship docking after a long time at sea. The children's voices
seemed distant, like gulls in a faraway sky, and she yearned
to remain in those strong, protective arms. But the cries had
grown into loud squawks, forcing her back into the present,
where Joe and Isabel were fighting over the television control.

Sleepily, she took over and chose *Tom and Jerry* for them,
then lay back on the pillow to savor the remaining traces
of her dream. It was a new feeling to fancy someone. Since
meeting Olivier in Paris in her mid-twenties she had had eyes
only for him. Sure, he could be difficult and demanding, like
a petulant child who expects his every whim to be indulged
and sulks when he feels unappreciated, but she had always
been dazzled by him. He had the power to send her spirits
soaring and, as so often happens with mercurial men, the
same power to pull her down. Her attraction to him had never
waned, and she had always relished his touch, even though it
was rare these days.

Jack had made her feel attractive in a way Olivier no longer could. There was nothing like the first spark of desire. She had forgotten the magnetic pull of another human being, the invisible force that held her attention wherever he was in the room, the sense of loss when he was out of sight. Those bees in the pit of her belly that made it impossible to eat or sleep. It had been a decade since Olivier had made her tremble with nerves. Her meeting with Jack was like an invigorating wind sweeping through her sails, shaking them out, reminding her that she was still attractive.

She breakfasted with the children, a dance in her step, an Abba tune on her lips. Then they skipped off to play in the garden, leaving her alone with her thoughts. She sat in front of the newspaper, a cup of tea in her hands, lost in the sunlight flooding the kitchen. It didn't matter if she never saw him again: he had caused something to shift inside her and now everything looked more radiant.

She jumped when the telephone rang at nine. It was Candace. "Hey, Angelica, you're still alive!"

"Oh God, I'm more alive than ever."

"So you had a fight, then made up in the most degenerate way possible."

"No." She sighed dreamily. "I fell in love last night."

"I get a feeling this isn't about Olivier."

"You're right. It was nothing more than an innocent flirt, but God, I feel fantastic this morning."

"Who was he?"

"Some friend of Scarlet and William's from South Africa."

"Sounds interesting."

"It's just that I haven't fancied anyone in years, and I'd forgotten how good it feels."

"Did Olivier suspect?"

"No, he was too busy flirting with Caterina Tintello."

"Oh, that old reptile. She's anyone's!"

"Well, he was welcome to her. She diverted his attention, so I had Jack all to myself. God, he's attractive. Scarlet warned me, and she's absolutely right, he's bad news, but . . ."

"But?"

"There's nothing wrong with a harmless flirt."

"After that belt comment I'd say it's what Olivier deserves!"

"He doesn't think before he speaks. He's so French."

"Well, honey, I'm glad you've realized you've still got it. It won't do Olivier any harm. He takes you for granted. I'm not saying you need to do anything drastic, but a little flirt every now and then will remind him that if he doesn't play his cards right, you might find someone else who does."

"What about you? Has Harry forgiven you?"

"I told him I'd been at the back for the whole second half. Fortunately, I heard a couple of old biddies discussing it in the ladies' room afterwards and just repeated their opinions."

"Have you heard from Kate?"

"Yes, she rang at dawn, God love her. I was fast asleep!" She growled a laugh. "Pete gets back tonight, so she's got to pull herself together. I suggested we all meet up for lunch at Cipriani tomorrow to console ourselves after the kids have gone back to school. I know most mothers long for the end of the summer vacation, but I'm going to be bereft. I'm dreading it."

"She might listen to some advice."

"Not old Groundhog! Oh, she'll listen as if her life depends on it, but the minute you walk out that door she's forgotten all the wise words you've given her and is off to make the same mistakes all over again. I have more success reasoning with my dog."

"What's she going to do?"

"I know what she *should* do."

"Which is?"

"Get rid of it."

"She'll never do that."

"God will understand."

"Hers won't."

"It's better than the alternative. If Pete finds out it's not his, he'll leave her. Period. I'd hate to have to support her through a divorce. Besides, I don't think she'd survive it. She's very fragile."

"But what if the baby comes out looking like someone else?"

"Depends who that someone else is."

"Any ideas?"

"No, but I'm working on it. Whose shoulder does she cry on?"

"Not *my* husband's, at least. Olivier finds her intolerable."

"But it could be anyone else's!"

"I'd better call her."

"Then bring the kids over for lunch."

Angelica went upstairs to dress. She put on a CD, and the throaty voice of Amy Winehouse filled the house. Sunshine flooded her bathroom, bouncing playfully off the marble and mirrors, a rare sunny day in what had been the very grayest of summers. She knew she should start on a new book, but continuing in the same mold didn't inspire her at all, and today, she felt wildly free from care. Perhaps she didn't have it in her to write any more novels. Five was a decent number, after all, and they had done pretty well. She hadn't hit the big time, but they sold all over the world, and she had broken into America with the last one, which was based in Arizona. Her latest, *The Silk Serpent*, was due out in March, and her publicist was trying to get her to go and promote it in Australia. She was big in Oz, apparently. Perhaps she should quit while ahead and float about having lunches with her girlfriends and pondering the meaning of life. Olivier didn't like her working anyway. He made no secret of the fact that she was a wife and mother first and that her writing was merely a hobby. But what would she do if she didn't write? Candace was busy with her charities; Letizia was a contributing editor for *Vogue;* Scarlet ran her own PR company, Bright Scarlet Communications; and Kate modeled, for catalogues mostly. Writing was the only thing Angelica was good at. She brushed her doubts away. Today, she was free of care. Jack's memory hadn't faded, and when she looked in the mirror she saw an attractive, sensual woman, Spanx or no Spanx!

She slipped out of her nightie and opened her underwear drawer, where the neat rows of matching Calvin Klein lace panties and bras lay unused. With a shiver of guilty pleasure she chose a set in ivory. So, she didn't have the lean, slender figure of her youth, but she was undeniably All Woman. Riding on the crest of this most enthusiastic of waves, she decided to join Candace's Pilates class in Notting Hill. It was about time she took a grip, and David Higgins's classes promised quick results. Candace was blessed with height and the long legs of a racehorse, but she insisted her flat stomach and sculpted waist were down to David's rigorous regime. Angelica would never be tall like Candace and no miracle could lengthen her legs, but she could tone up and lose weight. Not for Olivier, not even for Jack, but for herself. The handsome South African had inspired her to get in shape.

She pulled on a pair of jeans, pink trainers, and a floral blouse from Paul & Joe, leaving her unruly hair to fall over her shoulders in shiny curls. She felt the underwear clinging to her skin and smiled at her own daring, as if she were wearing it especially for Jack to take off.

Before leaving the house she telephoned Kate, who sounded a lot better in spite of her hangover. "Candace asked me for lunch today as well," Kate said, "but Mum is bringing the children back and having lunch with me here. I have an idea, which I'll share with you tomorrow at Cipriani." Angelica wished she'd share the identity of the Other Man. "Thank you for coming over yesterday. You didn't get into too much trouble with Olivier, I hope?"

"No, he was fine," she lied.

"He knows how much I need you. I don't know what I'd do without all my friends."

Without an audience there'd be no play, thought Angelica cynically. "That's what friends are for," she said. "To pick you up when you fall."

"I've fallen very hard this time."

"Nothing you can't cope with."

"I'm not sure, this time. I think I've really gone and blown it!"

"No, you haven't. These things are sent to make us stronger."

"Would it make me stronger to lose Pete . . . and the children?"

"You're not going to lose anyone. Look, you said you had a plan."

"Yes, I do." The strength returned to Kate's voice.

"Hold that thought until tomorrow, then we can all discuss it over a glass of wine and a delicious meal." She forgot that Kate didn't eat.

"Okay, thank you again, Angelica. I owe you one."

Angelica put down the telephone and wondered what it was that compelled them all to buzz around Kate like worker bees around the queen. Was it her vulnerability that inspired them all to look after her? Or her charm, of which she had an inordinate amount? How could someone like Kate be taught the art of happiness—or even the art of serenity?

• • •

Angelica spent the morning in Harrods buying shoes for the children and picking up the uniforms she had ordered in July but forgotten all about. Efficient mothers, like Candace and Letizia, had complete winter sets in the right sizes by June, all name-taped and folded in the children's cupboards for the beginning of the autumn term. They returned to London from the South of France or the Hamptons with nothing more than the odd haircut to organize. Angelica, on the other hand, squeezed all the back-to-school tasks into the week before term started, dragging the children around town in a fever to buy the long list of things they required. They'd return from each shopping trip armed with toys that Angelica had been too weak to deny them. Every year she cursed her lack of organization, but every year it was the same last-minute rush.

She arrived late for lunch at Candace's, the boot of the car filled with shiny green Harrods bags. Candace lived in leafy Notting Hill, where the pavements were wide and tree lined, and shiny Mercedes and BMW four-by-fours were parked among Porsches and the odd Aston Martin. Her silver Great Dane greeted them at the door, alongside the Filipina maid in a pink-and-white uniform. Candace's children scampered upstairs excitedly to hide, followed by Joe and Isabel, who hurried past their mother to chase after them. Candace was on the telephone in the immaculately weeded garden, lying on a sun lounger, a glass of fruit juice on the table with the October issue of American *Vogue*. When she saw her friend, she waved. "Isn't this glorious!" She pushed her Dior sunglasses to the top of her head, sweeping her thick hair off her face.

"I see you're making the most of it," said Angelica, descending the steps to join her.

"It'll rain tomorrow." Candace had the sleek brown skin of her Latina mother and the pale green eyes of her father, a stunning combination that enhanced her fine features. "Come and join me. How hungry are the kids?"

"They've all disappeared upstairs."

"Great, let's lie out a little longer. They'll come down when they want to eat."

"Mine had doughnuts in Harrods."

"Did you get everything done?"

"Just about." Angelica dropped her handbag to the grass, ignoring the lip gloss that rolled out, and flopped onto the lounger beside Candace. "I spoke to Kate. She says she has a plan."

"I wonder what that could be?" Candace laughed dismissively. "I'm not holding my breath. You do realize we've got nine months of this soap opera?" Candace sipped her juice. "Ringside seats."

"Why do we all flock around her? What is it that makes her so compelling?"

"Because our lives would be dreadfully dull without her little dramas to entertain us." Candace grinned mischievously. "Why don't *you* have a little drama for a change?"

"My life is very drama free, thank God."

"It was until last night."

"Where it began and ended."

"It just shows that you're ripe for an affair."

"Oh really, Candace, the sun has gone to your head."

"No, I'm just putting it out there."

"Well, pull it back in again, fast! You think I have time for an affair?"

"What? Too busy, like JFK, Lloyd George, and Clinton?"

Angelica laughed. "You think I'd risk all that I have for a fling?"

"That's the fun of it, apparently. The risk, the excitement."

"I prefer sitting in the audience watching Kate's life spiraling out of control. I couldn't live like that—it's exhausting."

"You'd be surprised how many women have affairs at our age. Ten years of marriage, bored of the monotonous plod,

plod of their daily lives. Then some handsome, dashing stranger walks in and ignites a flame they thought had died."

"The flame Olivier ignited all those years ago is still burning strong, I assure you."

"I hope so. But you felt the frisson of attraction last night, didn't you?"

"Yes, I did. But I can leave it at that. I really don't care if I never see him again."

"But there might be another Jack around the corner. You're on receive. I'll bet there have been countless Jacks in the last ten years, but you haven't noticed them because you haven't been on receive. It doesn't mean you don't love Olivier, just that you are ready for a little excitement. Just warning you to be careful."

"You sound like you're speaking from experience."

"I have the knowledge but not the experience. I just observe what goes on around me. I don't know what it is about me, but people confide in me. Look at you. I'll bet you haven't told Kate, Scarlet, or Letizia about last night."

"You're right. I haven't told anyone."

"There you go. I'm the keeper of secrets, the sacred vault."

"You should be the one writing the book."

"How's that going by the way?"

"It's not."

Candace put her glasses back on and curled her glossy lips into a smile. "All you need is a little inspiration."

That evening Angelica and Olivier had dinner alone together in the kitchen. Angelica had cooked a root vegetable soup and Thai noodles with ginger, but not even his favorite dish could raise her husband's spirits. He told her about his day, his fear that the City was on the brink of collapse, speculating that thousands of jobs were under threat. The financial world was about to implode, and Olivier was right in the middle of it. He looked gray and tired.

"I've got a sore throat," he added gravely, as if that was the worst thing to befall him. "I had it this morning when I woke up."

"Have you taken anything for it?"

He shrugged helplessly. "Only aspirin."

"You should gargle with TCP."

"I can't abide the taste of that stuff. I'll have an inhalation and sleep in the spare room."

"You don't have to do that."

"If I can't sleep I want to watch television."

"Take Night Nurse, that'll knock you out."

"And make me feel drugged in the morning." He took a spoonful of soup. "This is very soothing."

"Good."

"I'm sure I'll feel better in the morning. I can't afford to take time off work at the moment."

"Oh, you'll be fine after a good night's sleep."

"I don't know . . . these things tend to linger."

Angelica recalled the times she had been nearly incapacitated with flu and still managed to look after the children. She grinned into her bowl. Throughout history, men had fought bloody battles with incredible acts of bravery, and yet nothing could slay a man more surely than a sore throat.

Olivier retreated to the spare room after fumigating the kitchen with his Karvol inhalation. Angelica had a bath, lighting candles and scenting the water with aromatherapy oils. She lay back and closed her eyes, letting her mind wander wherever it chose, reining it in when Jack's face surfaced and his arms spread wide to hold her. It was still early when she climbed into bed. She didn't have the will to read—other people's books just reminded her of her current lack of imagination—so she put on a DVD instead. An old movie, one of her favorites: *Falling in Love,* with Meryl Streep and Robert De Niro. She had seen it countless times but still managed to cry when they found each other on the train at the end.

She switched off the light and lay in the semidarkness listening to the distant drone of cars and the sudden roar of a motorbike as it sped up Bayswater Road. The bed was large, and she felt small lying there, alone. When the children were younger, they'd pad across the landing to climb in beside her. She had relished those nights snuggled up against their warm little bodies, listening to the reassuring rise and fall of their breathing. Now the children slept soundly down the corridor, and Olivier was wallowing in self-pity in the spare room upstairs. Tonight, there was no one to hold but in her dreams.

4

If you love yourself, you open yourself up to being loved in return.   *In Search of the Perfect Happiness*

The following morning Angelica woke the children early for their first day back at school. They had spent the whole summer going to bed late and waking up at eight, so she had to open their curtains and stroke their faces, coaxing them out of their deep sleep with gentle words of encouragement. They lay inert, their warm bodies curled up beneath their duvets, their pale faces buried into their pillows. She felt sorry for them. There was nothing pleasant about being woken for school, even if it was the most luxurious in London.

Isabel rolled over and stretched like a cat, blinking in the weak light of a gray day. Joe staggered into the bathroom, where he hovered dangerously by the loo, eyes half closed, barely aware of his aim. Angelica rushed to steady him so that he didn't wee all over the floor.

Once awake, they recovered quickly, rushing about with excitement, throwing their pillows at each other while Angelica struggled to get them washed and dressed. She knew how important it was for them to look polished for their new class teachers. She hadn't expected them to be concerned about *her*.

"Mummy, I hope you're not going to wear *that* into school," said Joe.

Angelica looked down at her wide-leg jeans and trainers. "What's wrong with what I'm wearing?"

"All the other mothers will look cool. You look like you haven't tried."

Angelica was mortified. Her jeans weren't *any* old pair, but Hudson's most fashionable, and her trainers were shiny new silver ones. "What do you think, Isabel?"

"I want you to wear your big shoes." She meant the new Tory Burch platforms Letizia had brought back from America.

"Well, if you really mind, I'll change."

"Zeus's mummy's very cool," said Joe.

Angelica couldn't disagree. Jenna Elrich was famously glamorous, if somewhat overdone in Angelica's opinion. She was one of those girls who wore cream in midwinter, real fur, a lot of big gold jewelry, and oversized sunglasses even when there was no sun.

"She *is* cool, Joe darling, but I'll never be as cool as her. I haven't the time to spend my mornings being blow-dried at Richard Ward."

Joe wasn't listening: he was too busy sneaking his favorite Power Ranger toys into his backpack. Angelica changed into a pair of J Brand jeans, the brown platforms Isabel had requested, and a Burberry khaki jacket.

When Joe saw her, he nodded his approval. "That's better," he said.

She threw on a gold Yves Saint Laurent necklace for good measure and wondered whether other mothers were dictated to by their children.

The scene at the school gates was pandemonium. The road was partially blocked by shiny chauffeur-driven cars. One or two bodyguards with important-looking devices plugged into their ears trailed their small charges, while handsome fathers in suits and long-legged Prada-clad mothers, with straightened blond hair and suntans, tried to control their excited children as they greeted their friends and gossiped on the pavement. The air was thick with perfume and voices and the odd irritated mutter from a local trying to get to Kensington Gardens to walk his dog. Angelica lived close enough to school to walk and stopped to chat to those she knew on the way.

They shook hands with the headmistress, who remarked how much they had grown and how much the sun had bleached their hair. "We spent the summer with Olivier's family in Provence," Angelica told her, aware that it sounded far more glamorous than it really was. The women in his family were a coven of grumpy, dissatisfied witches bent on making everyone around them as miserable as they were. The only consolation was his father, who was dashing and charming, with old-fashioned manners and a dry, cynical wit that made her laugh, mostly at his wife's and daughters' expense.

She was happy to find Candace and Letizia in the hall, talking to Scarlet. When she saw her, Scarlet grabbed her arm exuberantly. "You have a fan, Angelica!"

"She has many fans," Candace interjected.

"Sure, but this one's very smitten."

"Who is he?" Letizia asked.

"A devilishly handsome South African I put her next to at dinner. I didn't notice that you two had hit it off."

Angelica blushed and tossed her hair casually. "He was fun."

"Well, he thinks you're gorgeous! He called to tell me what a rare and special woman you are. Duh! Tell me something I don't know!"

"I hope he knows she's married," said Letizia.

"He's married, too, but it doesn't stop his flirting as if he were single." Scarlet laughed huskily. "You know, I was in

Clapham yesterday seeing my acupuncturist, and I spotted him knocking on a little door at the end of the street. He looked really nervous. I was about to shout out and wave, but knowing him as I do, and what a terrible old rogue he is, I left him to his business."

"A lover perhaps?" asked Candace.

"Without doubt," Scarlet agreed. Angelica was surprised to feel the twist of jealousy in her gut. Scarlet continued, "He might be badly behaved, but he's very attractive."

"He wasn't badly behaved with me," Angelica retorted nonchalantly. "He just flirted a little."

"I hope Olivier noticed," said Scarlet. "It would do him good to swallow some of his own medicine."

The four of them took the children to their new classes. None of them looked as immaculate as Candace's children, with their perfectly ironed uniforms and polished shoes, their hair shining like silk. When it came to saying good-bye, Candace bent down and hugged them as if they were embarking on a long voyage rather than a short day at school. "I hate leaving them," she said, her eyes glittering with tears as they walked back down the corridor.

"They love it here," said Angelica.

"Oh, I know *they* do, but what about me? I'm a wreck."

Angelica laughed at the absurdity of such a suggestion. Candace, with her manicured nails, sleek hair, and beautiful face was nowhere near a wreck. She looked typically pristine in skinny jeans and flat shoes, an olive cashmere vest worn over a crisp white shirt. Her beloved Birkin handbag hung on her arm, almost eclipsing the enormous diamond ring Harry had bought her on his last business trip to Hong Kong. Angelica doubted Candace's children had ever criticized *her* choice of clothes. "They'll be out in less than seven hours."

"I know, but the first day is always hard. I hate the emptiness in the house. All I can hear is the scuffle of feet as Florencia goes up and down the stairs to clean and Ralph lies in his basket sulking because the children aren't there to play with him. Thank God we're having lunch somewhere nice today. I don't think I could bear being at home on my own watching the clock."

"I'm going to get to my desk, finally," said Angelica, wondering what she was going to do there.

"I'm going shopping. Screw the credit crunch!"

"I would say the credit crunch demands it. There's no point adding to the misery by denying the shopgirls their commission."

"I'm so glad you see it that way. I thought I'd pop into Harvey Nichols—fancy a little wander around the first floor?"

"Much as I'd love to, I'd better try to do something. Besides, I haven't checked my e-mails in weeks."

They made their way through the throng of parents to the street, where Candace was met by her chauffeur. She climbed into the front seat and waved a bejeweled hand at Angelica. "See you later," she shouted, already pressing her telephone to her ear.

Angelica turned towards home, imagining Joe and Isabel settling into their new classes, when a voice shouted at her from the other side of the street. It was Jenna Elrich. Her heart sank. Jenna held her son's hand and crossed the road without a glance at the Range Rover that had to brake suddenly to let her pass. "How are you?" she asked.

"I'm great," said Angelica, taking in the big hair and giant sunglasses that made her look like an insect. She was tanned the color of her Gucci handbag, but her face had the remains of a frosty beauty.

"How's Joe?"

"Thrilled to be back."

"Zeus didn't want to come to school today. I had to drag

him out of bed complaining. *'Mais Maman, je ne veux pas aller a l'école!'* Isn't that right, Zeus?" Angelica was startled by such pretentiousness. Her own children had a French father, but she wouldn't dream of showing off so shamelessly.

"Oh, he'll be fine when he gets inside. Miss Emma's incredibly sweet."

"We've had such a busy summer. I'm exhausted. We've just finished the house in Mustique, but there are terrible delays on the chalet in Gstaad. I've told John that if they don't finish it by Christmas, I don't want it. Then Jennifer got sick and had to be flown back to London, so I had to have the children on my own for two weeks in Biarritz without a nanny! Imagine the horror of it! So now I'm interviewing for a new nanny, if you hear of anyone who's looking."

"I'll keep my ear to the ground."

"Well, I'd better get on, or Zeus will be the last boy to arrive, and that won't be a good way to start the new year." Then as an afterthought, she added, "You look great, by the way. I wish I could do that tousled, just-got-out-of bed look, but I always end up looking polished." Angelica watched her stride off in her leather boots and big coat and hoped she'd boil to death in the heat of the school building. *Tousled, just got out of bed!* she thought indignantly, marching up the road. *If there's one woman I can't abide, it's Jenna Elrich.*

At last she sat down at her desk in her office at the top of the house overlooking the garden. With its pale walls and New England furniture, leafy plants and bookshelves, it was her little sanctuary, where Olivier couldn't complain about the scented candles and her choice of music, a room of her very own where she could meditate without disturbance and dream without distraction. With a sigh of pleasure she sat in her chair and switched on the computer. It had been a long summer away, and it felt good to be back. While the computer was starting up she lit a candle and switched on her iPod.

The sight of the seventy e-mails was alarming at first, but after scanning the list she realized that most were spam and could be swiftly deleted. There was one from her agent, Claudia Hemmingway, and a couple from her editor in New York. She replied briefly, skipping the ones from friends asking them for dinner and printing out long epistles to read later. Then her eyes caught sight of a familiar name: Jack Meyer. With a rush of curiosity she clicked on his name. How on earth had he found her?

Dear Sage, I hope you don't mind my writing to you. I've been thinking about the idea for your book (which I think is great, by the way). I'm back in Rosenbosch now. It's spring. The air is infused with the smell of flowers and camphor. I love this time of year: everything is new and exciting. I think you should come out—it would really inspire you. I enjoyed meeting you in London very much. I love your Web site by the way, though there aren't enough pictures of you and the ones that are there are not as beautiful as the real woman. From Dog Safely on Porch

She stared at the words in amusement. What a devil to have taken the trouble to find her Web site. He knew she was married. Judging by his adventures in Clapham, he obviously got a kick out of living dangerously. She read it again, dwelling on the best bits. She could hear his voice in her head, the lilt of his accent, his gravelly tone, and she smiled. She could imagine the Dutch vineyard of Rosenbosch settled beneath a bright blue sky, surrounded by camphor trees and budding flowers, and visualized his lying on the grass with a pair of binoculars, watching the birds.

So, what to do? It would be rude not to reply. After all, there was nothing wrong in lighthearted e-mailing. Wasn't it possible for two married people to be friends? Wasn't it presumptuous to assume he wanted to sleep with her? He hadn't overstepped the mark at dinner, and she hadn't encouraged him. She looked at the date: he had sent it yesterday. With a mounting sense of guilty pleasure, she placed her fingers over the keys and pressed Reply.

> Dear Dog on Porch, Thank you so much for your e-mail. It's nice to hear from you. I'm sitting at my desk pondering my new idea, but feel blocked and uninspired—if you come up with any gems, do send them. I need all the help I can get! How heavenly to be enjoying spring. We're in autumn as you know, and it's only going to get bleaker! Oh for sun and the smell of camphor! Rosenbosch sounds delightful. Olivier and I would love to visit you there one day.

She crinkled her nose at the mention of her husband. *That's very childish,* she thought, and swiftly deleted it.

> Rosenbosch sounds delightful. Would love to see the porch! It must be as big as Olivier's. Sage

She read it over a few times. It wasn't flirtatious; she didn't want him to think that she fancied him. Her finger hovered a moment over the Send icon. *What harm can it do to have a cyber friend?* She pressed the key and watched the message disappear off her screen, suffering a sudden, though fleeting, stab of regret.

She imagined his receiving it. Would he write back immediately? She waited a moment, staring at the screen, expecting to hear the ping of a new message, but none came. Finally, she clicked out and went into Word, opening a new blank document on the screen.

There was nothing more disconcerting than a blank document with nothing to write on it. So she typed the working title: *In Search of the Perfect Happiness* by Angelica Garner, then played around with the typeface, settling on large flowery letters in pink. This took up a few minutes, during which time she listened for the ping of an incoming message.

After writing down as many ideas as she could think of on the big subject of Life, she picked up the telephone and called Candace. Her friend was in the McQueen department at Harvey Nichols.

"He's e-mailed me," she stated simply. "He found me through my Web site."

"Oh my God! What did he say?"

"I'll read it to you."

"Wait, I have to sit down. Wait, wait, wait! Oh, for a chair . . . Don't they have anywhere to sit in here? What about the old or disabled, or simply demented like me! Okay, I'm sitting down, fire away."

Angelica read her the e-mail.

"He's mad about you."

"Do you think so?"

"Of course. The fact that he went to the trouble to find you speaks for itself."

"He's just being friendly."

"You're just being naïve."

"I've written back."

"You're crazy!"

"There's nothing wrong with a little cyber chatting. After all, it's very presumptuous of me to assume that he wants to get into my knickers."

"No, it's not, it's intelligent. I told you, you're ripe for an affair."

"I'm not going to have an affair."

"Look, they always start like this. A little chatting, a little flirting, then it's lunch . . ."

"He lives in South Africa."

"He was in London. Trust me, Angelica, he'll ask you to lunch. Would you tell Olivier?"

"Sure."

"No, you wouldn't. Are you going to tell him about this e-mail? Of course not. It'll be your little secret, and you'll love every minute of having one. Every time Olivier loses his temper or gets grumpy or whatever, you'll have your little secret to smile about."

"Are you suggesting I shouldn't e-mail him?"

"No, I'm just warning you. Keep him at a distance. Don't write anything you wouldn't want your husband to read and don't ever, ever write an e-mail under the influence of alcohol!"

"You know your stuff."

"Like I said, I'm the sacred vault."

"Well, Sacred Vault, I'll call you if he e-mails back."

"Honey, it's not a question of if but when."

Angelica checked her e-mails once more before leaving to meet the girls for lunch, but there was only spam offering her discounted Viagra. The sun had come out, shining through a break in the clouds, and Angelica turned her face to it, wondering whether it was shining on Jack, too, safely on his porch.

She wasn't the last to arrive at Cipriani. Candace, Letizia, and Scarlet sat discussing Kate over Bellinis.

"Darling, we've ordered you one," said Letizia, reaching out to greet her.

"Guess who I bumped into this morning?" Angelica said, kissing Candace and Scarlet in turn.

"Who?"

"The ghastly Jenna Elrich." She sat down next to Letizia

and recounted how Jenna had imitated her son speaking to her in French. "It was so pretentious," she complained.

"You know what? You should have replied like this," said Candace, clearing her throat. "'Why, that's so funny, Jenna, because Isabel woke up this morning and said *"Mama, tengo ganas de ir al colegio,"* then Joe piped up: *"Anch'io voglio andare a scuola!"*'" She pulled a face, clearly pleased with herself.

"Brava!" Letizia declared in delight.

"Now *you're* showing off." Angelica laughed.

"I'm a natural linguist," said Candace. "What can I say?"

Angelica leaned into the table. "You know what else she said? That she wishes she could have my tousled hair that looks like I've just got out of bed and haven't bothered to brush it, but every time she tries she just ends up looking perfect and polished."

"And plastic," Scarlet added.

"How rude!" said Letizia.

"I think she's hilarious." Candace laughed. "She's barely able to say a sentence without bigging herself up. If she mentions a man, he fancies her; if she mentions a woman, she's jealous of her; if she pays you a compliment, it's a backhanded one designed to pull you down. She came for dinner once and complimented me on my 'quaint country cooking.'"

"I find her infuriating," grumbled Angelica.

"Don't worry, darling. She'd kill for your tousled locks," said Letizia.

"No, she'd like your marriage," said Candace. "Hers is a deeply unhappy one, and that's the core of her bitterness."

"Last year she admitted to me that she was well past forty, but she's clearly forgotten, because she keeps referring to the approaching 'Big Four O' and asking what she should do to celebrate," said Scarlet.

"Correct her," Candace suggested. "Honey, it's the Big *Five* O!"

"Her husband works at Lehman's. I don't think she'll be doing anything to celebrate," said Angelica.

"Maybe selling her vast collection of shoes and handbags," said Letizia.

"The Birkins are fakes," said Candace. "Believe me, I *know*."

At that moment, Kate strode into the restaurant in a knitted minidress and boots, her eyes hidden behind big Chanel sunglasses. Every eye turned as she looked around for her friends, then waved vigorously when she saw them. Women envied her lithe body and striking face, and men sensed something wanton that women did not. She weaved through the whispering tables like an enchanting snake, savoring the attention.

"Sorry I'm late." She blew them all kisses. "It's just been one of those mornings." She flopped into a chair, dropping her Anya handbag to the floor. "I need a drink."

"I didn't think you were drinking," said Letizia.

"I'm not meant to be, but one little teeny weeny Bellini won't hurt the baby." She smiled at the waiter, who blushed.

"So Pete got back last night. Did you tell him?" Candace asked.

"No. I'm too scared."

"So what's your big idea?" Angelica asked.

"I'm going to wing it."

"You're not going to get rid of it?" Candace was astonished.

"I can't."

"It's only a teeny weeny bundle of cells."

"I know, Candace, but still it's a life. I've always been anti-abortion. There's a child in here." She touched her belly.

"Not that you'd know," said Letizia.

"It's smaller than mine," Angelica observed.

"Not for long," said Candace. "Angelica's joining my Pilates class."

Scarlet grinned at her. "Make sure you have a pedicure first—that David is delicious."

"Trust me, that's the last thing on your mind when you're trussed up, in agony, and sweating like a pig."

"You don't sweat, Candace, for sure!" Letizia laughed.

"Of course she doesn't," replied Scarlet. "She glows like a princess, of the Park Avenue variety."

The waiter came with Kate's Bellini. She took a sip and smiled. "That's better. You see, I was thinking, my lover has similar coloring to Pete, so hopefully, unless there are any hideous kickbacks from previous generations, the baby will look enough like Pete to fool him."

"That's optimistic," said Candace.

"It happens all the time," said Scarlet. "Apparently a vast percentage of children in this country do not belong to their fathers."

"I think you should come clean," Letizia advised.

"And risk losing Pete?" asked Angelica.

"Is he worth keeping?" Candace asked. "What's your lover like?"

"Not the marrying type," said Kate.

"Already married?"

Kate shook her head. "I can't say. I haven't told him about the baby, and I'm not going to. To be honest, he's rather embarrassed about the whole thing. As far as we're both concerned, it never happened."

Candace growled, "There's someone in there who says it did." She pointed a manicured nail at Kate's stomach.

Kate grinned. "But he's not telling."

"Not *yet*," said Angelica.

At half-past three they picked up the children from school, standing in a huddle discussing Jenna Elrich, who was barking into her telephone in French to one of her staff. When she got the children home, Angelica went upstairs to check her e-mails. Never before had she been so eager to read them. With an expectant grin she clicked on her mail. There was one from her agent suggesting lunch—and one from Jack Meyer.

Dear Sage, Your e-mail is the most exciting thing to happen to a poor old dog lying on the porch, bored and neglected! I can hear your voice in your sentences and your laugh, as I imagine you must have laughed when you suggested that my porch is as big as Olivier's. If Olivier is clever, he won't require a big porch, but lie next to you in complete bliss on a porch the length of his nose to his wagging tail. (Wagging, I stress, because he's married to you!) As for my ideas, I'm putting them together for you, looking back over my life and experiences. It's not ready yet. Perhaps I'll give it to you when you come out to South Africa, which I hope you will, very soon!
From Dog on Porch

5

Search for the beauty in everything because it's there if
you look hard enough.   *In Search of the Perfect Happiness*

Angelica stared at Jack's e-mail, a mischievous smile playing
guiltily about her lips. She knew she shouldn't be encouraging him. But the chance of their meeting again was very
slim. He lived a safe distance away in South Africa. Even
if he came to London, she'd never be able to explain away
lunch, and she certainly wouldn't dare go behind Olivier's
back. She'd be sure to bump into someone they knew and
be found out. She toyed with these ideas for amusement, for
the sheer pleasure of the impossible dream.

With a recklessness that was quite out of character, she
wrote a reply.

Dear Dog on Porch, I think the first secret to happiness is
acceptance. Isn't the desire to have what one can't have the
root of our unrest? Sage

Pleased, she pressed Send without hesitation. She waited a
while for a reply. She'd have to go down to the playroom in
a moment to beg, bribe, and coerce her children into doing
their homework, but she was reluctant to tear herself away
from the computer. Just as she was about to get up, the telephone rang. It was her agent, Claudia Hemmingway.

"Hi there, Angelica. How's the writing going?"

"It's great," she lied. "Just began today."

"Fabulous. Can't wait to read the first draft."

"Don't hold your breath. I won't have anything for you until after Christmas."

"That's okay, so long as you're pushing on. Listen, I think we should have lunch. There are a few proposals I want to discuss with you."

"Nice proposals?"

"*I* think so." She paused. "I haven't seen you all summer. Let's say it's time to regroup."

"Oh God, you're going to try to persuade me to go to Australia again."

"I promised I wouldn't."

"I can't leave the children for that long—you know that."

"And I totally understand; it's just that . . ."

"It would be so good for my career. Olivier doesn't consider it a career."

"The money you make certainly classes it as a career."

"You talk to my husband."

"Look, I'm not going to try to persuade you to go to Australia. I promise. Let's have a nice lunch and put together a battle plan for the next book. When can you do it?"

"Can we put something in at the end of November? I know it's a long way off, but I'm reluctant to leave my desk while I'm on a roll." *Gives me more time to get something written.*

"That's fantastic. I don't want to interrupt your creative flow."

As Claudia was looking through her diary, Angelica heard the ping of a new message. There, highlighted in bold, was the name: Jack Meyer. "What about Thursday the twentieth?" Claudia suggested. "We can go to Sotheby's Café. I know you like it . . ." There was silence. "Angelica? Are you still there?"

She tore her eyes away from the screen. "Yes, yes, I'm here. Sorry, just got distracted by an e-mail." She flicked through her diary, eager to finish the call so she could read what he had written. "The twentieth of November. It's in."

"Great. I'll leave you to your writing and that e-mail!"

Angelica put down the telephone and turned back to her computer screen.

Dear beautiful Sage, In my case the desire to have what I can't have poses a tremendous challenge, which generates a great deal of happiness in the form of anticipation. Perhaps acceptance in its purest form is the key to *lasting* happiness. The trouble is that there is nothing pure in my form of acceptance, only frustration and rebellion as I fight against it. Surely if I accept my lot, I will never raise myself up to my true potential? What do you say to that? From Dog on Porch

With an increasing sense of guilt, she read it again. "Dear beautiful Sage . . ." He obviously wasn't worried that his wife was going to read his e-mails. She knew the rest of what he wrote referred to her and the challenge she posed. She was the object of his desire and quite unobtainable. Yet she didn't feel she was in danger. E-mail gave their letters a comfortable detachment. It wasn't like speaking on the telephone, or talking across the table at lunch. It enabled her to flirt in a way she would never have dared flirt in person.

She was aware that she was encouraging Jack for her own amusement, which wasn't really fair. She should stop it before it went too far. But she managed to convince herself that it was as much a game for him as it was for her. He probably had e-mail "friends" across the globe—what was one more?

So how should she respond to his thoughts on acceptance? She sat back and considered, chewing on a pen. The happiness of which he spoke was temporary, more of a high than a state of inner peace and harmony. She posed a challenge, and the desire to win her gave him the anticipation of happiness, but, having won her, the challenge would be gone and happiness would elude him once again.

Her fingers hovered over the keys. She knew she should wait a few days before replying. She didn't want to look keen. But the temptation was too great to resist, and besides, didn't she deserve a little innocent fun?

Dear Dog on Porch, The happiness you speak of is a temporary happiness. Imagine a dog on his porch. If he's straining at the lead and yearning for what is in the garden, he will only feel frustrated and unhappy. If he strays into the garden in chase of a rabbit, he might experience the pleasure of the chase, but then his happiness evaporates until the next rabbit. If he accepts that he must stay on the porch and lies there feeling the wind through his fur and the sun on his skin and doesn't yearn for that rabbit, surely then he will feel the deep inner contentment of just being. From a rather confused Sage

She was wrenched from her ponderings by Joe shouting up the stairs that he wanted to watch *Ben10* but that Isabel had stolen the control to watch *High School Musical.* "No television until you've done your homework," Angelica replied, skipping down the stairs. "Joe, you're first. Look, the sooner you do it, the sooner it's over, then you can watch *Ben10.*"

While Sunny made spaghetti bolognese for tea, Angelica sat with Joe at the dining room table. *Happiness is loving my children,* she thought as Joe read out loud. She watched her son's earnest face as he concentrated on the words and tried to imagine what he was going to be like as a man: handsome like his father, certainly, with her light eyes and fair skin. Outspoken like his grandfather. Unique in the way that every human being is a one-off.

Her mind drifted to Olivier, and she felt a twinge of guilt, though there was no fear of his reading her e-mails; he never set foot in her office. He wouldn't imagine her having a cyber friend like Jack. No one would. Olivier had a reputation for loving women. After all, he was French. In fact, if Olivier didn't chat up girls at every turn, people assumed he was ill or in a bad mood, and they were probably right. It didn't mean that Olivier didn't love her above all others, just that he needed the adrenaline rush of a flirtation and the confirmation that at forty-eight he was still attractive. But she, being English and less flamboyant, was reputedly a paragon of virtue.

Angelica drew Joe into her arms and gave him a bear hug. "You're brilliant," she exclaimed, savoring the smell of his hair and his soft skin against her cheek. Her children were still little, but it wouldn't be long before they were pushing her away, not wanting to be cuddled, and then she'd have no one to wrap her arms around, because Olivier was never here and when he was, his mind was still in the office.

"So, can I watch *Ben10* now?"

"Go on, then. Tell Isabel it's her turn." She watched him disappear into the hall. *My happiness depends on the health of my children,* she thought. *Not a lasting happiness because it is always clouded with fear. I fear things that might never happen. Wasted energy and yet, I can't stop myself. For every moment of bliss I fear the pain of loss. How would I cope without them? Happiness is like small islands in a sea of fear. Why can't fear be small islands in a sea of happiness? Why fear at all? Can't I just ac-*cept *things as they come and deal with them as they arrive?* She smiled wistfully as Isabel padded into the room.

When Olivier arrived home, the children were in bed and Angelica had cooked dinner. The table was laid in the kitchen with place mats and napkins, wineglasses and a single candle.

"This is romantic," he said, dropping his briefcase on the hall table.

"It's just the two of us." She noticed the silk and cashmere scarf around his neck.

"Good. I'm too tired to talk to anyone but you, and my head is still full of rampaging elephants."

"Have you taken anything for it other than aspirin?"

"Besides Nurofen, no. I think I'll have another inhalation before bed."

"Take Night Nurse."

"All right. I'll do that. Tomorrow, I'll stagger into work with a hangover."

"How's it been?"

"Terrible. Everything is down. This is serious, Angelica."

"I know, I've read the papers."

He sighed and sank into a chair. She poured him a glass of Bordeaux. He took a sip, and his shoulders relaxed.

"Take off your scarf and jacket, and I'll give your shoulders a rub."

"What's going on?" he asked, loosening his scarf. "Are you having an affair?"

"Silly! You just look so tense." She felt her cheeks redden.

"I *am* tense." She put his scarf and jacket on the back of his chair and proceeded to massage his neck. "That feels so good." Her fingers worked deep into the muscles, feeling them soften beneath her touch. She felt guilty about her secret e-mails, and her guilt made her a geisha to make up for it.

"I haven't given you a massage in years."

He laughed. "You never gave me massages even when we were courting. I was the one with the oil."

"And the magical hands." She was surprised to feel herself grow hot with desire.

"They still are magical, you know." He closed his eyes, and slowly his tension drained away, replaced by a physical yearning for a more primitive form of release.

He took her hands and pulled her round in front of him, pushing out his chair so she could sit astride him. "I want to make love to you," he murmured. "I have a beautiful wife. I should take more notice of her."

"With your sore throat!"

"It's feeling better."

Hypochondriac, she thought affectionately. "What about the children?"

"If we worry about the children walking in on us, we will never make love."

He pulled her head down and kissed her, letting her hair fall about his face. His lips were warm and tasted of wine. He was a good kisser; he always had been. He pulled her shirt out of her jeans and slipped his fingers inside. She felt his hands undo the clasp on her bra and then the sensual feeling of his thumbs on her nipples. It had been so long, they responded eagerly to his touch. She threw back her head and allowed his bristly chin to scratch the delicate skin on her neck as he kissed her. Aware of the danger of being caught by a sleepy child, Angelica wriggled out of her jeans and panties and sat astride him again, slipping him inside her with a well-practiced hand. They lost each other for a while, alone in their pleasure, until they reached the peak together. They remained entwined a moment longer, hearts racing, heads spinning with the sudden rush of adrenaline.

"That was spontaneous," she said, kissing his temple. It was damp and salty.

"It is like we are young and in love again." He stroked her hair. "We should make love more often."

"Life is busy," she said, climbing off and reaching for her clothes.

"We should make time for the important things. Now what's for dinner?"

• • •

Angelica watched him tuck into the lamb cutlets with relish. Sometimes it was as if food was his meaning for living. An unsatisfactory meal could ruin his whole week. She sipped her wine and ate slowly while he talked about himself. He didn't ask her about *her* day. There was nothing unusual about that: there wasn't a great deal to report, but suddenly it mattered that he wasn't curious. "Lehman's has crashed. Other banks are sure to follow. This is really going to affect everyone, even us."

"I know. I'm being careful."

"No unnecessary indulgences."

She stiffened. "I said, I'm being careful."

"I know you are."

"I've got money coming in."

"Sure, but the publishing world is going to be hit, too. People are going to cut out things they don't need, and books will suffer."

"Children still need to read."

"But you won't be paid such big advances in future. You watch: everyone is going to be pulling in their belts." She raised a reproachful eyebrow at the mention of the word "belt" and wanted to remind him that he didn't like her to wear one.

"The City will recover. It always does," she said instead.

"But it could take years."

"Well, until it does we'll just be careful."

"You'll see, even those big-time spenders like Kate and Candace will have to close their purses." She couldn't imagine their doing anything so rash.

"So how are the children? How was their first day back at school?"

"They had a fabulous day. Loved every minute."

"Who did you see?"

"Usual crowd. Scarlet, Letizia, Candace . . . Oh, I bumped into the dreadful Jenna Elrich."

"Now, she's a sexy woman."

Angelica's mouth fell open. "God, Olivier, have some taste!"

"She's very stylish. I like her look."

"You and Joe both," she muttered. "I suppose she looks glamorous to the uninitiated."

"She's well dressed."

"Overdone like a Christmas tree."

"Talking of which, I suppose we're going to spend Christmas with your family."

"I'm as unenthusiastic about them as you are."

"And then visit mine in France."

"I don't know whose is worse."

"Oh, yours win, hands down. No contest! But they redeem themselves by giving me lots of amusement!"

"I'm glad they amuse you. They depress *me*."

"So, cheap presents this Christmas." He wiped his mouth with his napkin. "This isn't the year for spending money, so don't go mad."

"I know, it's the thought that counts."

"If it were the thought that counted, they'd get nothing at all! If I remember rightly, you forgot to bring presents for my sisters last year, which just goes to show how little you think of them."

"They're charming, adorable women," she said, sucking in her cheeks. Olivier narrowed his eyes, but his lips curled up at one corner.

After dinner Olivier retreated to their bedroom with a mug of hot tea and honey. He switched on the news and ran a bath, taking his clothes off and hanging them neatly in the closet, scowling at his wife's clothes carelessly discarded on the floor along with Joe's Ben10 toys and damp bath towels.

Angelica went to check on the children. They were fast

asleep in their bedrooms, their faces innocent in the darkness. She pulled the duvet up over Isabel's exposed shoulders and stroked Joe's flushed cheek. Then she heard Olivier turn off the tap and climb into the water. Conquered by curiosity, she climbed the stairs to check her e-mails one last time before bed. If Olivier knew she was in her office, he would think it very strange. She never worked in the evening, let alone read her e-mails. But there, as she had hoped, was one from Jack.

Dear beautiful Sage, I think the dog would rather slit
his throat than face a life of no rabbits. I know I would!
Besides, doesn't it depend on the rabbit? Who's to say the
rabbit can't keep the dog interested? I think you should
consider the rabbit and not just dismiss her as a plaything
for the dog! As for yearning, it is part of the pleasure of
life. Without yearning there are no dreams—as a writer
you should know the importance of dreams—and without
dreams how can we reach our full potential?
Sleep well, lovely Sage. I am on my porch, but my dreams
are making me a happy dog. DOP

The City might be collapsing around her husband's ears; she might have to stop shopping; they were probably going to spend a miserable Christmas with her eccentric parents—but Jack made her feel desirable. He shone a light onto a part of her that no one else saw, and in the glow of that light she felt that hidden part awake and stir into life.

6

Being generous and loving spreads happiness that is then
returned to you tenfold. *In Search of the Perfect Happiness*

Olivier had gone to the spare room again, so Angelica lay in
bed alone, composing her next e-mail to Jack. She wished
Joe or Isabel would come to keep her company. She missed
the gentle sound of their breathing and the warmth of their
bodies beside her. She didn't miss Olivier; he smelled of
Vicks and snored.

By Saturday morning she had caught Olivier's sore throat.
She heaved a sigh and staggered into the bathroom, her eyes
heavy with sleep, and rummaged in the medicine cupboard
for some Day Nurse. Unlike Olivier, she wouldn't moan and
groan, but treat the symptoms with the right drug and push
through her day with typical British stoicism. She knocked
back a little cup of orange liquid and retched at the taste.

She returned to bed and squeezed in between the children,
who had come to join her, a pillow over her head to drown
out the sound of *Bug's Life* on the television. She thought of
Olivier asleep upstairs and felt her heart harden. He accused
her of running around Kate like a lady-in-waiting, but she
was expected to run around *him* like a devoted mother.

They had met at a summer wedding in Paris and spent all
night dancing in the cobbled courtyard beneath a canopy of
stars. Knowing how much she loved books, he always went

out of his way to find her things he thought she might like to read. He had been spontaneous then, always one step ahead of her desires, surprising her with his thoughtfulness. He had taken her to the opera and the ballet, out for dinner at the Ivy, for romantic weekends in the Georges V, holidays on the Riviera. He had bought her little presents whenever he had traveled abroad on business, and left notes on her pillow telling her how beautiful she was and how much he loved her. Occasionally, his notes had been more imaginative: *Claridge's, 3:30 p.m., room 305* and they had met like strangers and made love all afternoon, ordering dinner from room service. Then they had married and had children, and she had morphed into his mother. He no longer took her out for dinner or arranged treats, but complained about his throat or his stomach or whatever was troubling him, and asked her advice on which medicine to take. Yes, she had morphed into his mother. No wonder Jack made her feel attractive; it wasn't very hard to make her feel like a woman.

It was a bright, clear day, so she took the children into Kensington Gardens. The sun was warm and the park filled with children on scooters, people walking their dogs, joggers running along the paths, cyclists weaving down the Broad Walk. *If only the summer had been like this,* she thought, basking in the heat. Isabel and Joe made a beeline for the Diana Memorial Playground, scaling the mast of the pirate ship like monkeys. She sat on a bench and watched them, marveling at how much they had grown over the summer months. Then her mind sprang back to Jack and the e-mail she was going to send him. The anticipation of a reply was enough to cure her sore throat.

When she got home, Olivier had left a message on the kitchen table. "Gone for coffee. Be back at midday. What shall we do for lunch?" She imagined him sitting in Starbucks on

the High Street reading the papers and munching on a crois-
sant, wrapped in his scarf and jacket, and wished she had the
nerve to take the children off to Birdworld, leaving him to
organize his own lunch. Instead, she left them climbing the
magnolia tree in the garden and went up to her office.

Poised over the computer, she felt her irritation dissolve in
the excitement of this small, secret act of defiance.

Dear Dog on Porch, You see how difficult it is to put these
things into practice!

As a little aside and something else to get your teeth into,
isn't suffering part of this great school of life? Doesn't it
make us wiser, stronger, and more compassionate? If life
was a blast without pain or sorrow, would we die any better
for having lived?

It's a beautiful day here in London—I hope the sun is
shining on your porch and that all the rabbits are safely in
their burrows. From your ever more confused Sage

She turned off her computer and joined the children in the
sunshine, sitting at the table to watch them play. It wasn't long
before Olivier returned with the newspaper. As predicted, he
wore a scarf to emphasize his ailing throat.

"I had a bad night. It was agony this morning, I couldn't
lie in. I'm feeling much better now I'm up and have had my
coffee."

"I was thinking of taking the children to Birdworld."

"Good idea. I'll stay here and take it easy." She didn't
bother to mention that she, too, now had a sore throat. Olivier
never liked to share the limelight when he was unwell.

"I might take them off now. We can have lunch there."

"Is there anything for me to eat?"

"There's some soup in the fridge. That'll be good for your
throat."

"What time will you be back?"

"I don't know. Fourish."

"Okay." He looked disappointed.

"You can always come with us. It's not very strenuous walking around Birdworld."

He put his hand to his throat. "No, I'd better rest. You know what my sore throats are like." He hunched his shoulders, looking sorry for himself.

"Why don't you watch a DVD or something? You need to give your body a chance to recover. I'll make you a hot drink before I go." He seemed to swell beneath her apparent concern.

"Perhaps I will have a spoonful of that Manuka honey." He didn't make a move to get it.

"Good idea," she said getting up dutifully. "That's meant to be excellent for sore throats."

Angelica didn't really want to go out on her own. She would have liked Candace to go with her, but Candace spent every weekend at their house in Gloucestershire. Kate and Letizia were bound to be doing something more glamorous. Then she had a bright idea. She'd ask Scarlet. *She* was the sort of girl who relished a plan cooked up at the last minute, and William was notoriously easygoing.

As fortune would have it, Scarlet thought it a fabulous idea. She suggested all going together in her BMW, as it had ample room for two adults and four children. When she rang the bell, Olivier answered to find her in a denim miniskirt and pale brown suede boots. His mood lifted at the sight of her tanned thighs, and for a moment Angelica thought he might change his mind and come with them.

"I'm a little under the weather," he explained, torn between his desire to see more of her legs and his inclination to sulk in front of the television feeling sorry for himself.

In the end it was Scarlet who made the decision for him. "I don't want you infecting my children with whatever undesirable bug you happen to have," she said firmly. "I think you'd better go back to bed and sleep it off."

Olivier watched them drive away, wondering what he was going to do all afternoon without Angelica to look after him. He resented her for deserting him when he was ill. The least she could have done was rustle up something more interesting for lunch. As it was, he faced boring old soup. He brightened a little at the thought of dinner, certain that she would cook something more inspiring to make up for having abandoned him.

"I bet you're pleased to be out of the house," said Scarlet as they drove down Holland Park Road.

"He's like a bear with a sore head."

"More like a sheep!"

"I know, he's pathetic when he's sick. He brings out the worst in me. I'm irritated that he can't look after himself and guilty that I'm not nursing him as I should."

"All men are the same. It's Man-Flu. When William's sick, he starts talking like his old nanny. 'I think I need a *little* Vicks on my chest and a *little* lemon and honey.' Everything in the diminutive and delivered in his most wretched voice."

"Do we blame their mothers? Are our sons going to end up the same because of our overindulgence?"

"I hope not, but I fear so." Scarlet glanced at the four children in the back. The boys were playing Nintendo, the girls flicking through Isabel's owl book.

"I don't know whether Olivier's more annoyed that I'm abandoning him for the day, or that I haven't cooked him anything for lunch."

"Oh dear, what's he having?"

"Soup."

"Shame on you, Angelica!"

"I know. I haven't got round to filling the fridge. I'll find something more substantial for dinner, even if it means ordering out. You know what's annoying, though?"

"That he wouldn't cook for you if you were ill."

"Exactly. It's all one way. I'm the one who has to buy the food, put meals on the table, take his jacket to the dry cleaner—which reminds me, I still haven't picked up his Gucci jacket and trousers. Damn!" She sighed in frustration. "There's so much to do and so little time in the day! I have to think of all the domestic stuff, and yet I have a career, too."

"William's the same. I'm at the office all day, juggling my clients and my children, and yet he expects dinner on the table when he gets home—and not just soup and salad. That's men for you. Especially an old-fashioned man like Olivier."

"A *French*man like Olivier."

"At least you have that sexy French accent to listen to on the pillow."

When he's there, Angelica thought bitterly.

Once at Birdworld in Farnham, the children rushed into the shop, picking up furry toys of exotic birds and squeezing them to make them tweet. Scarlet's son Charlie made straight for the sweet stand. Scarlet strode in after them in her high-heeled suede boots and large sunglasses, turning every head.

Outside, Charlie munched from a bag of jelly beans while the others ran from cage to cage feeding the birds from the packets of seeds and dried worms their mothers had bought for them at the admissions desk. Scarlet and Angelica wandered after them, chatting, enjoying the sunshine and the sight of their happy children entertaining themselves.

"This was a fine idea, Angelica," said Scarlet, impervious to the stares she was getting, even from the birds.

"It's easy entertainment. I'd like to have a country place like Candace."

"We once rented a cottage near Tetbury, but now we've bought a place in Mustique there's no point. I can't cope with too many homes."

"I'd like to take the children somewhere hot for Christmas, but Olivier has decided to stay here and spend a long weekend in cold Provence with his ghastly family."

"He's wise: the depression's only going to get worse, and he's right in the thick of it. Glad we bought our house in Mustique before things went apeshit."

"I need sun at Christmas. I can't bear the short days. It's nighttime by three in the afternoon."

"You should come and stay with us in Mustique."

"If only. I had already looked into renting a house near Cape Town."

Scarlet's face lit up. "Oh, you could go and visit your friend Jack Meyer."

Angelica laughed casually. "He's not my friend."

"He'd like to be."

"I think he probably has enough 'friends.'"

"I'm sure he does."

"What's his wife like?"

"Lovely. She's South African, too. Very bright and clever, but really nice. They met at Harvard."

"Sounds rather terrifying."

"God no! She's so laid back she's practically horizontal— does a lot of yoga and meditating."

"Well, that's just up my street."

"She's a little too New Age for my taste. You know, crystals, incense, and angels! But she's a saint. Jack was very sick a few years back. He had cancer."

Angelica was shocked. "How awful. Is he okay now?"

"Oh yes, totally. He shrugged it off in that effortless way of his. You'd never have known there was anything wrong with him, except that he lost all his hair."

"My God, that must have been terrible. He has fabulous hair."

"A fine head as any I've seen. Now he's like a shaggy old lion again. He might be an incorrigible flirt, but he's devoted to Anna. He owes her a lot." Angelica didn't want to hear how much he loved his wife. "I think men just need to flex their muscles every now and then. They're not monogamous by nature. In fact, I think it's quite a struggle for most of them. So long as they feel attractive to other women, they're content to stay on the porch."

Angelica smiled at her friend's reference to the porch. "I'm sure Jack stays firmly on his."

Scarlet grinned at her mischievously. "I'm not so sure. Some dogs can't help themselves, however devoted they are to their wives. It's in their blood, like wolves or foxes. There's simply no taming them."

They had lunch at the café, then sat on little benches to watch a demonstration with owls. Scarlet hid behind a tree to make a phone call while the children watched the owls, enraptured. Angelica thought of Jack suffering from cancer and wondered whether his ordeal had inspired his reflections on life and its purpose. An illness like that could change a person profoundly. He hadn't mentioned it, so she decided she wouldn't, either. She wondered whether he had replied to her message.

They got home from Birdworld at six. Charlie and Joe fell asleep in the car. The girls listened to *High School Musical* and stared out of the window in silence. The day had exhausted them. Olivier appeared at the door, took in the delicious sight of Scarlet's smooth thighs, then asked Angelica what was for dinner.

"Steak," she replied, waving Scarlet off, a sleepy Joe leaning against her hip.

"Good, I'm ravenous!"

"How are you feeling?" she asked.

"So so." He shrugged in that French way of his. She noticed his scarf was still tied around his neck. "I think I'll have another hot drink." She knew she was expected to make it.

"The children loved Birdworld," she volunteered, irritated that he hadn't asked.

When she finally managed to get to her desk after putting the children to bed and making Olivier a Lemsip, there was no e-mail from Jack. She pressed Send and Receive again just to make sure, but no messages were displayed. She bit her bottom lip and frowned. Perhaps he had gone away for the weekend. No one checked their e-mails on a Saturday. She'd look again tomorrow, but realistically there was no point looking until Monday.

She went downstairs to run a bath to find the room filled with a cloud of eucalyptus. There, slouched in the armchair, a towel thrown over his head, sat Olivier inhaling a bowl of boiling water and Karvol. *My knight in shining armor,* she thought, rolling her eyes. *Sometimes I want to kick this dog right off the porch!*

7

People treat you according to how you allow yourself to be treated.   *In Search of the Perfect Happiness*

On Monday Angelica met Candace in the reception room at Ten Pilates in Notting Hill. Candace, immaculate in a beige tracksuit, smiled broadly and dropped her mobile telephone into her chocolate-brown Birkin.

"You look glamorous for the gym," said Angelica.

"This isn't just a gym, honey. This is the hottest ticket in town!"

Angelica looked around at the tall, willowy girls coming out of their classes, dabbing their necks and faces with towels. Among them she saw a face she recognized.

"Hey, doll," said Scarlet breathlessly. "It was hell today. David's on a roll." She turned to Candace. "Have you warned her about the Higgins Ten?"

"What's that?" Angelica asked nervously.

Candace enlightened her. "It's David's trademark. He counts ten and you think you're going to die, you've already done a minute or so and your ass is killing you. But just when you think it's over, he demands ten more. Does it every time. Don't be fooled by the countdown. There's *always* another ten."

"Hence Ten Pilates," said Angelica brightly.

"I'm not sure that's exactly what he had in mind," said

Scarlet. "More likely the ten torture beds you see before you." She registered Angelica's anxious face. "Don't panic, he'll be kind to you as you're a beginner. Have you had a pedicure?"

"No!"

"Keep your socks on then. Don't embarrass yourself!"

"She's joking," said Candace. "Trust me, he's not looking at your toes—that man's only interested in muscle!"

Angelica filled out the required health form, then followed Candace into the studio, where ten Reformer beds were lined in two rows in front of an enormous mirrored wall. Candace dropped her bag on the sofa and put her long hair into a ponytail. "Hey, David, I want you to meet my friend Angelica Lariviere." A lithe Australian with a thick mop of dark brown hair extended his hand.

"Good to meet you," he said with a smile. Angelica was not encouraged. *I'm going to have to sweat and heave and groan in front of that Adonis?* "Have you done this before?" he asked, and Angelica tried to look past his boyish good looks to the professional instructor who was going to turn her into a supermodel.

"No, it's my first time."

"Well, let me show you how these Reformers work." *Thank GOD he didn't say bed.* She followed him over to what looked like a rack of torture with ropes and springs, trying to take it all in so as not to make a fool of herself. "How fit are you?" he asked.

"Not fit at all. Two children, too much cake, sitting at a desk all day—you get the picture."

"No worries, we'll get you in shape." Angelica wished she'd had that pedicure.

"If you get confused, just watch me," said Candace, taking the Reformer beside her friend and lying on her back. "It'll soon become second nature." She put her legs in the air, threw a ring over her feet, and proceeded to stretch. "So, what's the news on the e-mail front?"

"Hot and heavy," Angelica replied, lying down and trying to stretch like Candace but barely managing to straighten her legs.

"You're crazy, Angelica. Where's it going?"

"It's not going anywhere. It's just fun."

"Perhaps, but be careful."

"Olivier's driving me insane at the moment. This is a distraction."

"It might get out of hand. Has he asked you out for lunch yet?"

"Of course not. He's in South Africa."

"Don't say I didn't warn you."

"Right, girls!" It was David, striding into the room, which was now full of stretching women. He turned the music up loud: Madonna singing "Hung Up" to the Abba sound track. "Let's get going. One foot on the foot bar and push it away."

"My leg's aching already," Angelica moaned.

Candace made it look easy. "Remember the Higgins Ten." Angelica began to sweat. "And by the way, this is just a warm-up."

"I'm in hell. Did you say it's an hour?"

"Just under. But think of the body you're going to have."

"It had better be worth it." *Think of Jack. I'm doing this for you, Jack. One, two, three, four* . . . By the end of the hour Angelica could barely stand, her legs were trembling, and the muscles in her stomach ached, even in repose. Her inner thighs had never worked so hard. "So how do you feel?" David asked. There was a mischievous curl in his smile.

"I think I'd rather give birth than go through that again."

"If you can just get through a couple of weeks, your body will adapt and you won't find it so hard."

"Or painful?"

"Or painful."

"He's born in the wrong century," said Candace. "He'd have found his niche in the Tower of London manning the rack—and probably enjoyed it!" She took a swig from her water bottle. "Look at him! He'd be so disappointed if we skipped out having not even broken into a sweat."

"No chance of that!"

"We keep coming back because you're the best, David," said Candace, raising her bottle in a toast.

"If I looked like you, Candace, I'd keep coming back, too," said Angelica.

"You will," David encouraged.

"No amount of lunges can give me those legs." She looked at her friend, beautiful in spite of the sweat that stained her T-shirt.

"Everyone's different," said David. "The point is to be the best you can be. So do you want to sign up for more classes?"

"I'll buy fifty," said Angelica. "God help me!"

"A woman on a mission." Candace gave Angelica a knowing look. "D'you think I can get you to Richard Ward as well?"

"Not if I come out looking like Jenna Elrich."

"Only Jenna can look like Jenna, and she's stuck with that for life, poor darling!"

When Angelica got home, she ran a hot bath and poured a whole sachet of Elemis Musclease under the tap. The water went brown and smelled as medicinal as Olivier's Karvol inhalations. She restrained herself from going upstairs to check her e-mails, not due to any lack of enthusiasm but because she didn't think she'd make it, her thighs hurt so much. She put on Dolly Parton and lit a couple of candles, dimming the lights because she loathed looking at her flesh in such an unforgiving glare. With a sigh, she slid into the water and rested her head, letting the warmth ease away the pain. In spite of her discomfort she was inspired by the Pilates class. David had a gift for motivating his clients, and she had left invigorated and determined to get back into shape. Candace had told her that it would take three weeks to see a real difference, but she could already feel it working. She closed her eyes, ashamed to find Jack's face bobbing to the top of her thoughts like a cork. The anticipation of another witty message from him sent a pleasurable ripple through her cramping stomach.

She climbed out of the bath and dried herself, taking her time. The wait would make his e-mail all the more satisfying. She rubbed cream into her body, adding a few drops of juniper essential oil for water retention, and sprayed herself with Jo Malone Red Roses. Feeling sensual, she delved into her Calvin Klein underwear drawer, choosing a bra and panties in dusty pink. It gave her a thrill to know that beneath her jeans and shirt she was wearing exquisite lingerie.

Angelica wore little makeup. She had naturally youthful skin and the pink cheeks of a girl raised in the fresh country air. With a touch of mascara and lip balm, she was ready to read her mail. Her excitement mounted as she climbed the stairs, her pace quickening in spite of her painful muscles. It took a while for her computer to start, but finally, the screen went blue and her icons appeared in neat rows. She clicked on Mail and the list appeared. She scanned the names in bold, but there was nothing from Jack. She pressed Send and Receive just to make doubly sure, but the words "No New Mail" appeared at the bottom of the page.

With a sinking heart she had no option but to face the blank page of her next novel. For a moment she considered writing to *him*. Did it matter that he hadn't responded to her last e-mail? Did their e-mails have to go back and forth like a tennis game? Even in tennis the opponent didn't always return the ball; often he missed, or hit the ball in the net. This was like a friendly tennis match—winning wasn't the aim. And she wasn't playing hard to get—she wasn't expecting to be got at all. This was an innocent friendship, and friends could write when they felt like it.

But then doubt set in. Perhaps he had got bored. Maybe his wife had found out and banned him. Or he might have gone away for a few days and forgotten to take his Black-Berry. What time of year was it in South Africa? He had said it was spring. He must be busy with the vines, surely. God, the list of possibilities was endless. The fact was, he hadn't replied and that was that. She was surprised by the depth of her disappointment.

She clicked onto *In Search of the Perfect Happiness* by Angelica Garner and sat staring at the pink letters and white page that followed. She sat there for half an hour without writing a single word. It began to rain. Light drizzle was blown about on the breeze like dust. Celine Dion sang "All by myself . . . don't wanna be all by myself . . ." and Angelica felt empty, like a well of dried-up ideas. As often as she lowered the bucket it came back as light as when it went down. Her agent was expecting another fantasy novel for children, laced with magic and monsters. She was never going to be Tolkien—she didn't have the patience or the genius to write such powerful allegories—but she usually enjoyed sinking into her imagination and spinning any reality she desired. But her imagination was as cloudy as cauliflower soup.

Her fingers hovered over the keys. The blank page stared back at her, goading her to spoil its perfection. Then an idea popped into her head from nowhere. An evil, unhappy sorceress falls in love with a good man and attempts to attract him with spells and potions. Nothing works because nothing ever does on good people. So she has to learn how to be good like him, because only a pure heart will win him. For every good deed she does she loses a little of her evil nature. Gradually her good deeds begin to make her happy and the less evil she becomes. She sets out on a quest and learns the secret of happiness.

Angelica was *quite* pleased with her idea. It was a mere husk—she'd have to fill it in and build it up—but at least it was a start. Forgetting her empty mailbox she began to develop her magical world, inventing names and language, customs and laws.

By three o'clock she had a better idea of her fantasy land, and, feeling happier for having started, she saved what she had written and closed down her computer. She clicked on her mailbox to find Jack still hadn't replied. She shrugged it off bravely; perhaps it was for the best.

It was raining, so she walked under an umbrella to pick up the children. It felt autumnal. The leaves in the park were beginning to turn yellow and brown. The skies were gray, the pavements shiny and wet. Only the pigeons seemed not to notice and hopped about cheerily as if every day was a picnic.

Outside the school, mothers gathered among nannies, huddling under umbrellas or sitting in their cars parked on yellow lines. As she approached she heard her name above the rumble of engines. It was Candace, waving exuberantly out of the window of her car. "Get in, Angelica." As she crossed the road Candace hissed at her. "She's told Pete she's pregnant!" Angelica peered through the window. Letizia and Kate sat in the backseat deep in conversation. The driver stared ahead, pretending not to listen. "Get in!"

"He doesn't suspect it's not his?" Angelica asked, squeezing in beside Kate.

"Why on earth would he? He's the philanderer in our marriage, not me—well, at least that's the way he sees it. He's over the moon. He says we've got to have marriage counseling, though, so we're strong for the new baby. A friend of his has recommended this woman called Betsy Pog."

"Great name," said Letizia with a giggle.

Candace laughed cynically. "You don't need marriage counseling, he just needs to keep his pooch in its pouch." They all laughed.

"No, really, Betsy Pog is my kind of woman. She's meant to be fantastic."

"She *better* be fantastic," Candace added.

"We're going tonight for our first session." Kate shivered with excitement. "What shall I wear?"

"A hair shirt?" asked Candace.

"Oh, I was thinking much more along the lines of a little Prada dress with my red Louboutins."

"Well, at least it'll look like you're trying," said Angelica.

"I *never* try," Kate retorted. "My style is effortless and effervescent."

"You might as well wear it while you can," said Letizia.

"God, don't remind me. The thought of maternity trousers and big shirts again! Hideous!"

"Darling, pregnancy is no excuse to dress badly," Letizia reproached her. "A woman is at her most beautiful when bearing a child."

"Sometimes you are so Italian!" Kate retorted, envisaging flat shoes with dismay.

"So is it public knowledge yet?" asked Candace.

"Have you told your mother?" Angelica added.

"Same question," said Candace.

"No, I haven't had my twelve-week scan. Don't breathe a word to anyone."

"Does your lover know?" Candace asked more keenly.

"He's not my lover."

"Whatever. Does he know?"

"No."

"You don't think he'll work it out when he hears you're pregnant?"

"I *know* he won't work it out."

Candace raised an eyebrow. "That's interesting, what is he? A priest?"

"Look, he's forgotten it even happened."

"But *we* haven't," said Candace with a grin.

"I'm not going to tell you," Kate retorted. "Not because I don't want to. You know I share everything with you three. But I promised him I wouldn't, and I must keep my word."

"What, because you always do?" said Candace. Kate was notoriously feckless.

"No, because I owe it to him and because the consequences of it getting out are too horrible to imagine."

Angelica narrowed her eyes. "So we know him."

"The plot thickens," said Letizia. "He's not one of our husbands, is he?"

Kate laughed. "You'd have to *pay* me to sleep with one of your husbands!"

"Me, too, honey," Candace joked, lifting her finger into the light. "I think I'm due another diamond."

The week passed without an e-mail from Jack. Angelica continued her Pilates classes and bore the consequent stiffness with fortitude. She buried herself in her writing and tried not to be too disappointed about Jack's sudden disappearance. It was inevitable that their correspondence would end at some stage. She had been naïve to imagine they could continue flirting indefinitely. He had probably moved on to someone else he had met at another dinner party—someone who was prepared to take the flirtation further, like his "friend" in Clapham. It had been fun. He had made her feel alive. She picked up the children from school, listened to Candace and Scarlet worrying about the credit crunch's effects on fund-raising and spending, and tried to shrug off the heavy feeling of anticlimax.

Then on the following Wednesday morning the world shifted back into place. She received a large royalty check from Holland and an e-mail from Jack:

> Dear beautiful Sage, I'm sorry I didn't reply earlier, I've been away. I think we need to discuss things in person. This dog is getting restless here on the porch and was wondering whether he might persuade you to allow him to take you out for lunch when he comes to London in October. You're no ordinary rabbit. DOP

Oh my God, oh my God, oh my God! What to do? Angelica wanted to have lunch with him more than anything in the world. But what would Olivier say? No, she knew exactly what he would say: *"Mais non, mon ange."* NO. *That* had to be avoided at all costs. But she couldn't lie, in case she was spotted. They couldn't go somewhere low-key in the back of beyond because if they were discovered they'd look even more suspicious. They'd have to go out in Chelsea and risk it. *What am I doing? I don't want an affair! I really,* really *don't. I just want a little fun. I just want to feel attractive. He doesn't want an affair either, for sure. Of course he doesn't.*

She reread the e-mail twenty times. Her mind was as clear as glass and whirring away like a new clock. *If I say no, I'll look churlish and presumptuous. And besides, I want to see him. I'm nearly forty years old. I think I'm entitled to do what I want. So Olivier can't be told. I'll say I'm having lunch with the director of my publishing house, then I'm covered if I'm spotted with a strange man. Olivier has never met my publisher, let alone my agent—actually, he's never met anyone from my working life. Schmuck! as Candace would say. Serves him right!*

Dear Dog on Porch, I think it's about time you used up that slack on that lead of yours. *Too flirty! What am I thinking? I've gone mad!*

Dear Dog on Porch, I'd love to have lunch. It will be fun to see you again. Where do you want to go? Let me know when you're over and I'll book . . . *No, that's far too keen! Typical woman wanting everything tied up neatly with a bow!*

Dear Dog on Porch, I'd love to have lunch. October is a good month for dogs. So many leaves to truffle through in the park! I think you'll find I'm actually a rather ordinary rabbit. On the subject of lunch—shall I put it down to research? From Curious Sage

As soon as she sent it she telephoned Candace. "Candace, it's me."

"Hi, honey, what's up?"

"Book me into Richard Ward at once."

8

Think, speak, and act for the Higher Good, and you will
be a lucky person.   *In Search of the Perfect Happiness*

So the e-mails began again. Jack was coming to London for
five days beginning the week of October 13, and Tuesday,
October 14, would be a fine day for lunch. He'd book somewhere and let her know nearer the time.

Angelica went into a spin, torn between her desire to see
him and her sense of loyalty as a wife and mother. Her moods
swung from ecstasy to panic. Her head throbbed with the
weight of her dilemma. As she lay awake at night unable to
sleep, her nails bitten down to the quick, her heart raced with
that elusive, mislaid magic.

She stopped eating cake and worked out four times a week
at Ten Pilates. David began adjusting the springs to make the
exercises more challenging, and soon she found that her body
no longer suffered such agonizing stiffness afterwards. Her
toenails shone fuchsia pink, and her figure began to change.
The waist that wasn't now was, and she belted her dresses
with pride. The Calvin Klein underwear drawer was opened
on a daily basis, but Olivier, so preoccupied with the FTSE
100, didn't notice. It didn't matter. The girls did, and even
Jenna Elrich found something nice to say.

"You look great!" she commented at the school gates one
afternoon as they waited in the autumn sunshine to pick

up their children. Jenna was taking advantage of the cooler weather to show off her new Burberry cape and boot-cut purple trousers. Her shiny Gucci loafers were so high she towered over Angelica. Around her neck she wore a silk Hermès scarf with just the right shade of purple flowers on it to tie in with the trousers, and hiding most of her face was a large pair of brown Chanel sunglasses. "What have you been doing? You've lost *so* much weight." *That* was classic Jenna, insinuating that Angelica had previously been the size of a hippo.

"Pilates."

Jenna looked her up and down. "You're unrecognizable."

"Hardly."

"No, really. I barely recognized you. You look fabulous. I'm surprised. Is it just Pilates, or is there something you're not telling me?"

"Sex," Angelica stated simply. "I'm just having an awful lot of sex."

Jenna's face crinkled with sympathy. "You *poor* darling. You need to go to the pharmacy and ask for some husband repellent."

Angelica laughed at the absurdity of the woman. "Does it work for you?"

"If only such a thing existed! I give my husband a minute. I'm like, 'Okay, darling, you've got sixty seconds. Go!' and I close my eyes and think of those Manolo shoes I want or that perfect little cashmere from Ballantyne. 'Right, minute over! Enough!'"

"Sounds like you're ready for an affair."

"Oh, there's no shortage of men who admire me." She laughed as if *that* idea was preposterous. "But John would divorce me, and right now, the way things are, I don't think I'll find anyone richer."

"Better hang on to him, then."

"Until he tells me to stop shopping. Really, if I was one of those wives, I would take a lover, for sure."

Angelica managed to extract herself and found Kate huddled in a group with Scarlet, Candace, and Letizia, telling them about her latest advice from Betsy Pog. "It's going really well. We have to tell each other three things we like about each other over breakfast and before we go to sleep at night."

"Can you find three things first thing in the morning?" Angelica asked.

"Can you find three things, period?" added Candace.

"It's a struggle, but I make them up if I can't."

"That's naughty, darling," said Letizia. "You have to give it a chance and do it properly."

"What does he say about *you*?" Scarlet asked.

"Oh, that's easy. The list is as long as the Mississippi." She giggled. "I think he's falling in love with me all over again. Then, we have to whisper a word, just a single word, into the other's ear when we're in public."

"Like what?" Candace asked.

"Sexy, horny, delicious, manly . . . that sort of thing."

"That's hilarious!" Scarlet laughed. "What does he whisper to *you*?"

"I can't say—I'm too embarrassed!" She bit her bottom lip, then relented. "It really turns me on. He'll sidle up and whisper 'Juicy' then wander off again, leaving me quivering with excitement."

"Oh *p-lease!*" wailed Candace.

"There are many roads to Rome. Besides, it must be working," said Letizia. "You're glowing like an oven."

"He can't get enough of me. I think being pregnant turns him on. It makes him feel virile."

"Little does he know," said Candace.

Kate shot her a look. "It's his. I'm sure it's his. I was just being overdramatic."

"Not you," Candace added with a grin. "You're *never* that."

The day before Angelica's lunch with Jack, she sat beside Candace at Richard Ward's Metro Spa in Duke of York's Square, sipping Earl Grey tea and waiting for Thomas to come and highlight her hair. The ruggedly handsome James was already adding lights to Candace's rich brown locks. Being a natural blonde, Angelica had never felt she needed dye, but Candace had convinced her that Thomas would lift her look while keeping it natural.

"Thomas will hide all your little flaws. He's a genius," she told her, extending one hand to the manicurist, who sat on a stool at her feet. "And he's a vault like me. He knows where all the elephants lie buried and will take that knowledge to his grave. Trust me, no code breaker can crack him."

The salon was vast—room upon shiny room of mirrors and sleek black chairs; legions of black-uniformed juniors washing hair and standing to attention behind the technicians, who were all frighteningly cool, suntanned, and good-looking; the air infused with the smell of Kérastase. "Ah, you must be Angelica," said Thomas, breezing in followed by a pretty junior with waist-length blond hair.

"This is she," said Candace. "You're to make her even more beautiful than she already is."

"Oh really!" Angelica protested, embarrassed.

Thomas scrutinized her hair. "I know just what you need. You have lovely hair, by the way—very thick and in good condition. You're lucky, it has a natural wave, but not frizzy— a cross between Farrah Fawcett circa 1974 and Meg Ryan of *When Harry Met Sally* fame. Leave it to me."

Angelica glanced at Candace, terrified. "Relax. Thomas knows what's good for you. Lie back and enjoy it." She grinned at James in the mirror. "She's a virgin, but she'll learn to be a hair whore like me."

James laughed. "The word 'whore' sounds strange coming from your pretty lips."

"You'd be surprised what I can come out with when pushed," she replied, giving the manicurist her other hand. "My angelic face fools people into thinking I'm a pushover, but my acerbic tongue gets me what I want."

"So, Angelica, you're determined to have lunch with Jack?"

"You think I'm mad."

"You know what? I do think you're crazy, but I also think you're entitled to have some fun. Just be careful."

"I will."

"You have a nice life. Don't go screw it up over a flirt. It's not worth it. Once you lose Olivier's trust, you'll never get it back."

"I won't lose it, Candace. I'm not intending to have an affair."

"Few women go out with the intention of having an affair. One thing leads to another, but it usually starts with lunch."

"He's a nice guy. I'm enjoying the attention. But that's all it is, I promise."

"I don't want to have to pick up the pieces."

"You won't have to. It'll just be lunch."

Candace caught James's eye in the mirror. He didn't look at all surprised. In his seven years at Richard Ward he had heard just about everything.

Thomas returned with bowls of dye and sheets of tin foil, and began pinning up her hair. Duffy's husky voice rang out from the sound system: "I'm begging you for mercy, why won't you release me." Candace flicked through *In Style* magazine with her free hand. "So where's he taking you?"

"Daphne's."

"That's a little dangerous, isn't it?"

"It's better to go somewhere normal than be seen in some obscure restaurant in Richmond."

"You have a point. What are you going to tell Olivier?"

"That I'm having lunch with my publisher."

"Whom he's never met."

"Correct."

"And if you see someone you know? How will you introduce him?"

"As Jack."

Candace raised an eyebrow. "You're really playing with fire."

"I know."

After Thomas had finished coloring her hair, a junior led Angelica into a room full of sinks and reclining chairs that looked more like beds. Vast flat-screen televisions playing CNN were set up on each wall. She lay back and let the girl wash her hair and give her a deep conditioning treatment and massage. She shut her eyes and emptied her mind of thoughts.

"Are you dead?" Candace leaned over her. "Oh, you can't be, you're snoring."

Angelica awoke with a start. "God, did I doze off?"

"You certainly did."

"Was I really snoring?"

"No, that was a joke. When you're finished, I want you to meet Robert. He usually does my hair. Today, he's going to do yours."

"I don't know how you find the time to do this every six weeks."

"Every six weeks? Honey, you've got to be kidding! I'm in here every week for a wash and blow-dry! Don't forget your bag," she added, dropping it into Angelica's lap. "You left it in the other room—with your brain!"

Angelica followed Candace through a couple of rooms full of clients reading magazines; having lunch in their chairs; getting pedicures, manicures, blow-dries, and haircuts. It was a glamorous world she was excited to be part of. Robert awaited her, a cherubic-looking man with gray hair and a bashful smile. "Over to you, Robert," said Candace, waving her manicured hand. Robert combed her hair into a middle parting. "You should have had a manicure," said Candace.

"That's one beauty treatment beyond me." Angelica looked at her short nails. "I can't do the Park Avenue princess look."

"You wouldn't want to, honey. That look is so over. The trick is to look polished without looking like you've had the sex appeal ironed out of you."

"You want to keep your curls?" Robert asked, scissors poised.

"I'd like to look like I've just got out of bed—looking perfect," Angelica replied.

Angelica buried herself in the October issue of *Vanity Fair,* trying to read an article on Marilyn Monroe and not sneak a look at her hair before it was finished. Her stomach was in a knot, and she wasn't sure whether it was at the thought of having lunch with Jack—or of having lunch with Jack with horrid hair. Their e-mails had heated up over the last few weeks. She hadn't gone too far, but she had certainly said things she might not have dared say to his face—with her husband sitting at the other end of the table. She was now worried that she would disappoint him. That she had looked better in candlelight. That in the bright glare of day she wouldn't look like the girl he had been flirting with by e-mail, and suddenly wish he hadn't.

"What if he doesn't fancy me?" she said to Candace, without taking her eyes off the page.

Candace shouted over the roar of the hair dryer. "It doesn't matter. You're not going to have an affair with him anyway."

"That's not the point. I want him to think I'm beautiful."

"If he doesn't fancy you, he'll stop e-mailing you and that'll be that—and a good thing, too." She looked across at her friend, and her face fell. "Oh dear."

"What?" Angelica nearly dropped her teacup. She was too afraid to look at her reflection. "Is it bad?"

"Bad, bad, bad."

"How bad?"

"Take a look."

Angelica's stomach swam on a wave of nausea. She raised her eyes. Then her fears evaporated at the sight of her ravishing bed head. "Oh my God. It's stunning."

"Go figure!"

"Robert. You really *are* a genius!"

"Thank you." He fluffed it up with his fingers. "The color's good, too."

"It really is." Angelica was thrilled. "Clever Thomas. I must thank him as well."

"There's no chance he won't fancy you. Unfortunately!" said Candace, staring at her with approval.

"I hope you're right. I just want to be adored."

"From afar."

"From afar."

Candace put down her magazine. "I think I should go with you."

"Well, think again," said Angelica, getting up with a new confidence. "I'm nearly forty years old. It's my time to have fun. The first step to happiness is good highlights and haircut." She delved into her wallet and pulled out a crumpled note. "This is for you, Robert, for putting down the foundation stone of my inner temple of happiness."

Angelica picked up the children at three-thirty. The only person not to compliment her hair was Jenna Elrich, who was too busy shouting into her mobile telephone like a sergeant major. But Angelica noticed her glance in her direction a couple of times, her face as green as granite. Letizia, Kate, and Scarlet were very impressed. "Anyone would think you were having an affair," said Scarlet.

"If they didn't know her better," Letizia added.

"She's married to a Frenchman. Looking good is what he expects," Kate said. "Betsy Pog told me to dress for Pete, so I went to Selfridges and bought a whole heap of lingerie. Pete is a real silk-and-lace man. Betsy says it's worth putting on just so that he can take it off."

"So what have you got on now?" asked Angelica.

Kate pulled down her jeans to reveal red lace knickers. "The bra is adorable."

"Divine," breathed Letizia.

"Nice," agreed Scarlet. "But I'm more fascinated by your stomach."

"*What* stomach?" Candace exclaimed.

Kate pulled up her sweater to show off her belly, still brown from her summer in the Caribbean, but as flat as a board. "Oh, it's growing," she said, patting it.

"Only you'd know," said Angelica.

"Has Betsy Pog told you to eat more?" asked Candace. Kate frowned at her. "She should. There's a starving baby in there!"

"It's early days," said Kate.

"Well, the poor creature can't survive without food."

"Speaking of which, don't forget my surprise dinner for Art next Thursday." Art was Kate's best friend, married the year before in a gay ceremony to Tod. "He hasn't the slightest idea, which is astonishing. I'm not known for my ability to keep secrets!"

"You're on your way," said Candace. "Which is a great shame."

• • •

When Angelica returned home, she set about doing the usual duties: homework, tea, bath, and bedtime stories. Every time she passed a mirror she glanced at herself with pleasure and a growing sense of unease. What on earth was she doing having lunch with Jack Meyer? And without telling her husband? She didn't dare consider the consequences were she to get caught. Candace was right, she was crazy. But she was confident that she would be able to keep it to a friendly flirt. That she'd be in control. That the last thing in the world she would do would be to risk the good life she had.

Olivier came home early to find her sitting on Joe's bed with Isabel on her knee, reading *Stone Soup,* her favorite children's book. Olivier stood in the doorway watching the trio in the soft light of the bedroom, noticing at once his wife's new hair and appreciating her changing figure. She caught his eye and smiled, registering the admiration in his gaze.

She finished the story and took Isabel to her room. As she walked past her husband, he took her arm and looked at her intensely. "You look really good, Angelica." She walked on, guilt clawing the inside of her stomach. She kissed her daughter and tucked her in, placing Splat the duck against her chest for her to cuddle. Then she put her son to bed, wrapping her arms around him for the Full Joe. He liked the routine and held her tightly. Olivier kissed their foreheads and chatted a little about their day and what they'd been doing. It was rare that he returned home in time to see them before bedtime.

They met in their bedroom. Angelica recognized the look on her husband's face from those long-ago trysts at Claridge's and the irony was not lost on her. He had taken off his jacket and tie and stood appraising her lasciviously.

"You look different tonight," he remarked, narrowing his eyes.

"I've had my hair colored."

"It's not just that. You're looking slimmer, too."

"I noticed you didn't like me wearing belts."

He looked surprised. "So you decided to make an effort for *me*?"

"Why not?"

"I'm flattered. Women don't often go to the gym for their husbands."

"What are you suggesting? That I have a lover?"

He dismissed such a ridiculous idea with a laugh. "Of course not. Women go to the gym to compete with their friends."

"I couldn't begin to. They're all taller and thinner than me."

"But you have sex appeal, Angelica. That's what I like about you. So you worked out for me, eh?"

"Yes." Her lie prevented her from looking him in the eye. She made to walk past him, but he pulled her into his arms.

"Just because I told you not to wear a belt?"

"You said my waist was the widest part of me."

"I did not!" He was genuinely apologetic. "Did I?"

"You did."

"I'm sorry. What a careless thing to say. If I hurt you, I apologize. So what do you do?"

"Pilates, Olivier. I realized I'd let myself go. I didn't want to be voluptuous anymore." She squeezed his firm shoulders. "Especially as *you* work out. I didn't want to end up looking ten years older than my buffed husband."

He laughed, and she remembered why she had fallen in love with him; he looked so handsome when his eyes were full of mirth.

"Take off your clothes," he demanded, turning to lock the door. "Let the children sleep." She began to unbutton her shirt. When he turned around, he noticed her pretty lingerie and frowned in bewilderment, his eyes tracing her body. "I've been sleepwalking for the last few months. That's what the

City has done to me. I'm a man who loves beautiful women, and yet I sleep beside one every night without realizing how fortunate I am!" He slipped his hands around her waist and she stood tall so he could feel how firm it was. "You look like the girl I met all those years ago, but with the maturity of a woman." She felt her spirits rise with satisfaction. He traced his fingertips across her stomach. "You've worked hard."

"I'm glad you can see the difference."

"*Ma chérie,* it's not the outside that's important but the inside. However, seeing as you've managed to get your figure back, permit me to appreciate it!"

He kissed her, raking his fingers through her hair—her *perfect* new hair. For a moment she feared he might ruin it and tossed it out of his reach. But what was she doing having lunch with Jack Meyer when she had finally managed to win her husband's approval? Her stomach churned with regret. It was too late to cancel. She'd enjoy a nice lunch, then scale down the e-mails. Jack had inspired her to get back in shape. Now she had her husband's attention, she no longer needed him.

9

Reach for the stars with your dreams and desires.
In Search of the Perfect Happiness

The following morning Angelica walked the children to school, bumping into Candace on the street on the way back. Effortlessly glamorous in a Ralph Lauren tweed jacket under a cashmere cape and tight blue jeans tucked into leather boots, Candace struggled to restrain her silver Great Dane as he tried to sniff the bottom of a passing Jack Russell. "He's obsessed with small dogs!" she wailed as Angelica approached her. "Enough, Ralph!" She took off her sunglasses and ruthlessly scrutinized her friend. "You're not going to wear *that* to lunch, are you?"

Angelica was scruffy in baggy jeans and trainers. "No."

"I'm pleased to hear it."

"I'm having second thoughts. What am I doing, Candace?"

"You tell me."

"Olivier came home last night and was so sweet. It suddenly dawned on me that it's *his* attention I'm craving—not some sexy stranger's."

"We all know that."

"So what do I do? Cancel?"

"No, it's too late."

"I feel awful. I've encouraged him. I'm a prick tease!"

"Yes, you are. But you still can't cancel."

"I'm such an idiot."

"Look, go have fun. Now that you know where your priorities lie, there's no danger of your getting into trouble."

"What if I get caught?"

"You won't. Olivier's hardly likely to walk into Daphne's in the middle of the day, is he?"

"I hope not—unless he's fired! I haven't told him I'm going."

"D'you fancy coffee?"

"Why don't you come home with me and help me select something to wear."

"Okay, let's go choose something cool and understated. But not trainers, please." Candace gave the lead a tug. "And you, Ralph, can sit in Angelica's garden and not chase squirrels."

At home, Sunny made them coffee and brought it up to Angelica's bedroom on a tray, while Ralph bounded about the small garden defying the instruction about squirrels. Candace took off her cape and began to go through Angelica's closet.

Angelica put on her favorite Dolly Parton CD and slipped out of her jeans and sweater.

"Wow, you really have slimmed down, Angelica. And I like your underwear, too. Where's it from?"

"Calvin Klein."

"Nice. What does Olivier think?"

She flashed her friend a bashful smile. "Let's just say he's rediscovered it."

"Well, that makes two of you." She pulled out a Vanessa Bruno floral blouse with an extended collar for tying in a bow. "This is cool. Just don't tie the bow, let it hang." Angelica put it on. "I think you should wear jeans. You don't want to look like you're trying too hard. This is just a friendly lunch: you're not interviewing for an affair. Wear these Rupert Sanderson shoes—they're fabulous and they'll give you height."

"That's the one thing Pilates can't do for me."

"But these can." She grabbed them off the shelf and threw them at her. "Where are those Stella McCartney jeans with cute little pockets at the front?"

Angelica studied herself in the mirror. "God, I don't recognize myself when I dress up. I still feel like I'm pretending to be someone else."

"Honey, you look fabulous."

"Only because of you, Candace."

"I'll happily take all the credit. I couldn't let you slip into that old cliché of the scruffy writer. Writers don't have to be badly dressed."

"I'm loving myself!" Angelica threw her arms up and laughed.

"And of course, you don't give a rat's ass about Jack anymore."

"I'm a little sad I'm already over him. What am I going to do now for entertainment?"

"Come shopping. It's safer."

"Now I know why you do it."

"There's method in my madness."

She looked at Candace steadily. "Have you ever been tempted?"

"I wouldn't be human if I wasn't tempted every now and then. But I love Harry, period. And you know what? If there's something positive I inherited from my mother, it's her backbone of steel. I've never found it hard to say no and walk away from trouble. You must learn to do the same." She tossed her her jacket. "Today is your first lesson."

Angelica parked her car in Draycott Place. It took a while to find a parking space, and when she did, she was so anxious she rolled into the Range Rover in front, knocking its bumper with hers. "Oh Lord!" she exclaimed, hastily reversing. She hurried out to assess the damage. To her relief, the Range

Rover was unscratched. Her own car was already grazed from past blunders; if she had just acquired one more scratch, she couldn't tell. She walked unsteadily up the road towards Daphne's, breathing deeply to calm her nerves.

She looked at her watch, not wanting to arrive before Jack. She was fashionably five minutes late. Inhaling a large gulp of air, she pushed open the door and strode in, holding her head high to convey a confidence she didn't feel. She lowered her voice at the desk and articulated his name with care as if it were a loaded gun. As she was led through the tables she glanced about her, relieved that she recognized no one.

Then she saw him sitting in the corner, reading the *Evening Standard,* and all her reservations evaporated at the sight of him, so broad he dwarfed the table. He sensed her approach, and his face opened into a wide smile. "The wise sage," he said, standing up to greet her. He dwarfed her, too, even in heels. She kissed him, breathing in the lime scent of his cologne and relishing for a fleeting moment the rough sensation of his cheek against hers. It was almost too intimate to bear, and she drew away, her face flushing crimson.

She sat down and laughed nervously. "So, the dog's been let off the porch."

"You can't expect a dog like me to stay at heel when there's the most delicious-looking rabbit in the garden!" The warmth of his expression brought him back to her in a sudden rush of desire. *What am I doing?* she thought anxiously. *When I'd lifted almost every paw out of the mud!*

"Oh really! You are funny!" she exclaimed, trying to brush off his comment with nonchalance.

He swept his eyes over her face. "You look different."

"Do I?"

"Yes. Your hair's lighter. I like it. You look great, Angelica."

"Now you're embarrassing me."

"Good." He grinned and leaned towards her, peering at her over his glasses. "You look even prettier when you blush."

In an attempt to keep the conversation under control, she said: "How long are you in the U.K.? I mean, are you here on business?"

"Kind of."

"Does your wife ever come with you?"

"Sometimes, but right now she's at home with the children. She doesn't like to leave them." He grinned at her mischievously. "Does Olivier know you're having lunch with me?"

"No, I never got around to telling him." He shot her a quizzical look, and she couldn't help grinning back at him. "Okay, so I lie. I knew he'd say no, and I wanted to have lunch with you. I mean, why not? There's nothing wrong with having lunch with a friend, is there?"

"Nothing wrong at all."

"It was just easier not to mention it. He's very jealous. But I won't have my wings clipped."

He gazed at her a moment longer than was comfortable, then laughed heartily. "Now *you're* funny!"

"Why?"

"Because you know as well as I do that there's *everything* wrong with having lunch with a man you've only just met. It's not wrong in itself, only wrong because your husband wouldn't like it. If it wasn't so, you would have told him and he would have told you to have a good time."

"Then the secret to happiness is not honesty," she rallied.

"I'd agree with you there, but that's a selfish kind of happiness, not the pure happiness you're searching for."

"Okay, so I'm selfishly taking my pleasure."

"Let's drink to that. What will you have?"

"A glass of white wine, please." She needed fortification.

"Then let me choose a bottle of good South African wine."

The waiter brought the wine, and Angelica took a swig, immediately feeling more confident. She began to relax as the conversation moved on to more mundane subjects and she no longer felt like a small prey in the shadow of a formidable predator. They discussed the menu, then he hailed the waiter and ordered for her. Olivier had done that, too, when they had first courted. Now he simply ordered for himself.

"So how's the book coming along?" he asked.

"Not well." She laughed. "It's amazing how much time can be wasted writing one's own name."

"I read your last book, by the way." He was clearly pleased by the surprise on her face.

"Which one?"

"The Caves of Cold Konard."

"And . . . ?"

"I really enjoyed it. In fact, I couldn't put it down. At first I thought I'd take a look just so I could say I'd read it. But I was hooked—on the second page, to be precise, when the cave isn't a cave at all. It's very clever. Then Mart carried me away. I identified with him even though he's just a boy. I suppose we're all children at heart, aren't we? Those Yarnies are dreadful, disguising themselves as Enrods to fool Mart into trusting them. They're the worst sort of enemy, and I know a few Yarnies back at home. It's all very magical, but at the same time very true to life. Really, I was impressed."

"Thank you."

"Olivier should read it. I think he'd be astonished by your talent."

"Oh, he's so busy."

"That's no excuse. You can always make time. He's probably jealous of your creativity."

"Oh, I don't think so."

"Trust me. He's working all hours in a bank churning figures. You're sitting at home, listening to music, surfing the waves of your imagination. How fantastic is that? I bet he's jealous you make money doing something that looks so easy and is so pleasurable."

"Except it's not easy at all, because I'm not sure that what I've written so far is any good. I can't seem to think of a single brilliant idea, just rather ordinary ones."

"Yet."

"I'm almost tempted to ask for time out to recharge."

"So you can work out the deep layers beneath the story?"

"Yes."

"Think of Tolkien. You almost do it with *The Caves of Cold Konard*. It wouldn't be difficult to add another layer. To make it more spiritual for those who want to read beneath the surface."

"I'm anxious about it. I've never done it before. It would be easy to continue on the same road."

"But good for you to challenge yourself. If you're bored of your books, your readers are going to be bored, too."

"I know. I've got to find something I'm passionate about."

"You're a woman of great passion, Sage. That comes across in *The Caves,* and it's contagious, which is why it's hard to put down. Even for an old book veteran like me!"

"You really think so? You're not just saying that?"

"Because I fancy you? No. I'll buy *The Silk Serpent* even if this is the last time we ever lay eyes on each other."

She stared at him a moment, a heavy sense of disappointment sinking to the bottom of her belly like a stone. The thought of never seeing him again caused her physical pain. She hadn't anticipated still being so attracted to him. She had hoped to have lunch and leave, drawing a line under a fun but innocuous flirt. But he drew her to him, like the hypnotic allure of a long-forgotten melody whose notes resonated deep within her soul.

He took a sip of wine. Neither spoke for what seemed like

a long while. The waiters brought their first courses and, as Angelica looked up to thank them, she noticed a familiar face at the other end of the restaurant. "Oh Lord," she exclaimed, shrinking back.

Jack followed her gaze. "Who have you seen?"

"Jenna Elrich. A Yarnie."

"The one with big hair and sunglasses?"

"That's the one. Don't be fooled: she's pure malice."

"She's either very insecure or her husband's given her one in the eye."

"Could be either, actually."

"She can't see you."

"Oh, she will. She's the sort of woman who can spot someone she knows a mile off. She'll be desperate to know who you are."

"I'm your publisher."

"Yes." She flushed at the flaws in the lie. "You don't look anything like a publisher!"

"I don't think you can generalize. My name is Leighton Jones and I'm your publisher from South Africa. If she comes over, leave me to do the talking."

She laughed into her glass. "That makes me tremble with fear. She's a wicked gossip."

"I'd like to give her something to gossip about."

"And ruin my marriage?"

He turned serious. "Do you want to go somewhere else? We can leave if you're worried?"

"No, we can't leave now, it'll look suspicious. Let's pretend we haven't seen her. If she comes over, you're my publisher in Johannesburg, simple as that. The more we make of it, the guiltier we'll look."

"You've got it all worked out."

"You don't know my husband. He's more jealous than you can imagine."

"You should be flattered."

"It doesn't work that way. Possessiveness is a ball and chain around our ankles. It curtails our freedom and makes us unhappy. The secret to happiness is to love without conditions."

"Which we know is impossible."

"We can at least try."

Jenna Elrich sat beside the window with a couple of women Angelica didn't know. The three of them were bad examples of too much Botox and not enough mirth. They picked at their food and sipped their water and lemon through tight, joyless mouths. Angelica turned her back, but she knew Jenna would recognize her. It was only a matter of time before she tottered over in her six-inch heels to find out who Jack was. If he wasn't so devilishly handsome, she wouldn't bother.

The wine Jack had chosen was very good. Angelica didn't like to drink at lunch, especially as she was driving, but Jack refilled her glass, and she felt pleasantly relaxed and soon forgot all about Jenna. They discussed love and the secret for happiness, and the more they talked the more Angelica entered his magnetic aura until she no longer saw or heard the other people in the restaurant. They were both stimulated by the arguments: she could see the enthusiasm in his eyes like a bright light behind them shining through. By coffee they had identified some of the most endemic obstructions to happiness.

"We should write a book together," Jack suggested. "It would be a big best seller."

"I think you're right. I'm feeling very inspired."

"Perhaps I can be your mentor. Whenever you need to discuss something, you can call me."

"I don't have your number," she replied with a shrug, knowing she was now cruising across another frontier.

"Then give me your phone." She rummaged through the

chaos in her handbag and pulled it out. Her heart raced at the obvious step she was now taking. Candace had been right. Lunch was not just lunch. He took her mobile and began to punch in his number. Then he held it up to her with a grin: *DOP.*

"Dog on Porch," she said, smiling back.

"Wrong! Dog *off* Porch," he corrected.

"You're very naughty."

He flicked open his phone. "Give me yours." She read out her number. He held it up. "Sage. Nothing naughty about that," he said, replacing it in his jacket pocket. "Now, when am I going to see you again?"

Angelica was flustered. "I don't know," she said. "Aren't you going back to Rosenbosch?"

"Not until Friday." He lowered his voice. "We haven't even touched on desire."

Angelica's cheeks flamed, and she dropped her gaze into her empty coffee cup. She thought of his secret lover in Clapham and reminded herself that flirting was just a game to him. "Desire is a basic animal instinct that should be avoided at all costs."

"Why?"

"Because it doesn't last."

"But it's a good place to start."

"If it's the appropriate journey to make."

"I'm already off the porch."

"But you're still on a lead."

"Sometimes desire is out of our control and the lead is broken."

"We shouldn't let it get out of control. We should raise ourselves up to higher thoughts, not succumb to our primal instincts."

He laughed affectionately. "Who are you kidding? You sound like a bad textbook."

"I know what's wrong, that's all."

"Don't try to analyze it. I know you feel attracted to me, too."

"I would never admit to it. I'm a married woman." But she felt the blood rush to her cheeks to give her away.

"It doesn't matter whether you admit it or not. I can sense it, like a dog. I know it's wrong, but I can't stop desiring you. It's not just your beauty—there are many beautiful women in the world—it's something else. Something unique to you that I won't even try to limit to a word. I felt it the first moment I met you. It hit me hard and left me reeling. I know I should walk away, but I don't want to."

"Well, hello, Angelica." It was Jenna, towering over the table in a blousy blue shirt with billowing sleeves, obviously the height of fashion. For Jack she took off her sunglasses, pushing them up into her hair.

"Leighton Jones," he said, coolly extending his hand.

"Nice to meet you," Jenna replied, smiling coyly. "You're from South Africa."

"Johannesburg."

"Beautiful city and such friendly people."

"Thank you."

"So, Angelica, how come you're having lunch with such a handsome stranger?"

"He's my publisher—aren't I lucky!"

"You certainly are. You know, I've always wanted to write a book."

"You should," said Jack. "Everyone has a book in them."

"Oh, I know I'd write a best seller. My life is full of incredible stories, and I've met the most amazing people."

"An autobiography, then?"

"*Un roman à clef,*" she replied in a flawless French accent.

"Well, when you do, let me know?"

"Do you have a card?"

Angelica was astonished by her forwardness. Jenna held out an expectant hand.

"You write the book first," said Jack with a smirk. "Then, once you've finished, get in touch. Everyone has good ideas; few manage to write them into anything resembling a book."

Jenna wasn't used to being rebuffed. She faltered a moment, then regained her composure. "Okay, I'll do that. Well, it's been nice meeting you. See you at the school gates, Angelica." Jack watched her walk away, which was what she intended, because she walked deliberately, swinging her hips.

"She's a good-looking Yarnie," he said as she disappeared round the corner.

Angelica rolled her eyes. "If that's what rocks your boat."

He chuckled. "It doesn't, as it happens. But I can appreciate good legs."

"How far off the porch would she tempt you?"

"Little more than a sleepy glance." He leaned back in his chair and sighed. "Anyway, I'm already off the porch. Remember, I know my Yarnies from my Enrods, and you, my darling Sage, are an Enrod through and through."

They remained at the table until after three o'clock. The restaurant was almost empty. Waiters bustled about clearing tables and laying up for dinner. Angelica reminded him that the children came out of school at half past. "Then I suppose I have to let you go," he said, waving for the bill.

"Thank you for lunch."

"The pleasure is all mine."

"I hope you have a good few days here."

"They will be good if you let me see you again."

"Jack . . . I don't know . . ." The effects of the wine had worn off, and she remembered who she was. "I have a family."

"I'm only asking for your friendship. I like you."

"And I like you, too. But it's not appropriate."

"Look, I've put my cards on the table, but I'm man enough to have you on your terms. As you observed, I'm still tied to the porch. Let me have a bark; I'm not asking for more than that."

She thought about it a moment. "All right, I'll see you again. You can call me."

He took her hand, and Angelica's spirits soared as his smile shone a light into the neglected recesses of her soul.

He paid the bill and accompanied her out into the street. It was still sunny, but long, damp shadows fell across the tarmac to remind them that it was autumn.

"So," she said, suddenly feeling awkward. "It's farewell."

"So long, Sage," he replied, putting his hand in the small of her back and bending down to kiss her. For a moment she felt unsteady as he pressed his lips to her cheek, taking his time. The lime of his cologne was subdued by the natural spice in his skin, and she breathed it in dreamily.

"Back to the porch," she said softly, pulling away.

She walked down the road towards her car, arms folded, head bowed, her thoughts still with him. She dared not turn around. When she reached her car, she unlocked the door and climbed in. Risking a look now that she was behind glass, she saw that he had gone. She remained a moment at the wheel, reflecting. If infidelity extended to thoughts, then she was guilty already.

10

It is only with darkness that one can appreciate light.

In Search of the Perfect Happiness

"So how did it go?" Candace was waiting for Angelica at the school gates. "Don't do that!" she snapped at Ralph, whose nose was buried once again in the bottom of a far smaller dog. "Really, I can't take him anywhere!"

Angelica was about to divulge the details when something snuffed out her intention, like a sudden pail of water thrown onto a bonfire. Her exuberance fizzled away beneath her friend's formidable gaze. Candace was her confidante—she could normally tell her anything—but this foolhardy leap over the marital border line was beyond her comprehension and approval. As much as Angelica longed to share, she knew what Candace would think—and she couldn't bear to incite her condemnation—or be persuaded to delete Jack's number from her telephone.

"It was really nice," she replied cagily.

"Nice?" Candace crinkled her nose. "Lunch with the vicar is nice!"

"Okay, it was fabulous. He's everything I remembered him to be. He's gorgeous, handsome, funny, clever, sensitive, witty, and thinks I'm delicious—which is almost the best thing about him . . ."

"But? I can hear a but . . ."

"He's married, and so am I. It's not going any further."

"I'm pleased to hear it."

"I don't know what I was thinking. I was a little embarrassed actually, sitting there as if I was about to embark on an affair."

"Look, you had a great lunch. You had a flirt. You feel good about yourself. Now go home and wrap yourself around Olivier. I'm not Catholic, but a few Hail Marys won't hurt."

Angelica laughed. "At least he propelled me into getting into shape."

"I thought it was Olivier's comment about the belt."

"I lied. It was Jack."

"Well, you can thank him for that, and Olivier will never know."

Angelica's mobile telephone bleeped in her handbag with a message. She thought of Jack's number hidden in there and felt a quiver of guilty excitement. Candace restrained Ralph, apologizing to another mother who picked up her terrier in disgust. Angelica delved into her handbag for the telephone while Candace summoned Kate, Letizia, and Scarlet with a wave. "Over here, girls!" she shouted into the throng of perfume and Prada. Angelica flushed as she read the text: **Loved our lunch, Sage. Fancy taking this dog for a walk in the park tomorrow morning? X DOP**

Candace looked at her quizzically. "Who's that from?"

"Sunny. She wants me to pick something up on the way home," Angelica lied, clicking the telephone shut and replacing it in her bag. It shocked her that she was able to fib with such ease.

The three girls came over to join them. "Hi, dolls. I'm just telling Kate and Letizia about this lad from Yorkshire I've hired for half term to teach the children football and tennis. If any of yours want to join them, they're most welcome," said Scarlet, who thought nothing of wearing tight black hot pants with boots to pick up her children from school.

"A manny?" said Candace. "I'm loving the sound of that!"

"Sort of—he'll keep them busy so I don't have to."

"Sounds perfect," Kate interjected. "We were going to go to St. Lucia, but Pete now has to go to Moscow, and I don't relish the idea of taking the children on my own, in my condition."

"It's an inspired idea, darling. How did you find him?" Letizia asked. "Might he be available for the Christmas holidays? Does he ski?"

"He's the son of a friend of mine. A fine young man who's nuts about Manchester United and sufficiently handsome that I won't tire of looking at him. I don't think he skis, Letizia, but I'll find out."

"Oh, will you, darling? I need someone to help over Christmas. Maria isn't legal, so she can't travel. Such a bore. A skiing manny would solve all my problems."

"Pete and I are thinking about renewing our marriage vows," said Kate, who knew just how to grab everyone's attention.

"Don't you think you should wait nine months?" Candace replied. "In case the baby looks like someone else."

"It won't," Kate retorted swiftly. "It's Pete's, I just know it. Mothers *know* these things," she added, as if she were the only one among them to have experienced motherhood.

"That's *so* romantic," Letizia sighed. "I love weddings."

"I thought it would be a good excuse for a beautiful new frock. Vera Wang sprang to mind, and I'd love all your children to be bridesmaids."

"So the credit crunch hasn't reached Thurloe Square," said Candace.

"If we're going to proclaim our love to each other, I want it to be monumental to reflect the size of our hearts."

"So are we talking St. Paul's?" said Candace.

"No, that place is jinxed. I thought something less royal and more glamorous. After all, our first wedding was in Cornwall—hardly the height of glamour."

"So where's this one going to be?"

"Mauritius!" She clapped her hands with excitement. "And I want all the children in floaty white dresses and breeches. Can you imagine how cute they're all going to look? And me in my Vera Wang dress."

"Sounds like an Estée Lauder advert," hissed Candace to Angelica, who rejoined the conversation after having drifted off into the park with Jack.

"It's just what we all need," she said. "A holiday in the sun."

"I thought June, just after the baby is born, then we return to London with suntans, ready for the summer."

"Has Pete agreed?" Scarlet asked.

"He'll do anything for me at the moment. He's feeling very macho and protective."

"It's a great idea. Not often that a girl gets married for the second time to the same man," said Angelica brightly.

"You know what I really, really want?" said Kate, biting her thumbnail. "You won't laugh?"

"We wouldn't dare!"

"To come up the aisle on a beautiful white horse."

They stared at her in disbelief. Even Candace was silenced. Kate looked from one to the other, waiting for someone to say something. Letizia made to speak but faltered.

"You're not serious," said Candace at last.

"I'm very serious."

Letizia recovered her enthusiasm. "I think it's a fabulous idea. Only *you* could get away with it, darling."

"And what? The kids come up behind in a cart?"

"No, they skip up in bare feet, scattering shells and flowers on the sand."

"You're joking," said Scarlet.

"No, I'm not." Kate looked hurt. "I thought it would be so romantic."

Candace dropped her shoulders and smiled. "You know what, honey? I'm with you all the way. If that's what you want, you go for it. It's your dream. Just don't put us in floaty white dresses with shells in our hair, please."

"Well, I had hoped . . ." Kate began, then giggled. "What do you take me for? You think I'd give you all the opportunity to outshine me at my own wedding?"

Isabel and Joe rushed out of the big doors, throwing themselves at their mother. Angelica wrapped her arms around both of them at once. "Good day at school?" she asked, as they competed to tell her about their day.

"You forgot my gym bag!" Isabel accused.

"Did I?"

"Silly Mummy. I had to sit out and read a book!"

"I'm so sorry, darling. But if I had the choice, I'd much prefer a book than the gym!"

She waved to the girls, then made her way up the street laden with the children's book bags and backpacks. They ran on ahead, hanging on lampposts and skipping over the lines in the pavement. Angelica strolled behind in a daze, reliving lunch with Jack and deliberating how to respond to his text.

She would love to go for a walk in the park, but the chances of bumping into someone she knew were high. She had got away with lunch, in spite of having been accosted by Jenna; she didn't dare risk it again. Her mind ached as she tried to devise ways of unpicking the Gordian knot: how to engineer a meeting without risking her marriage and reputation? How to see him without leading him on? How to enjoy the flirt while maintaining her distance? How to restrain herself? She couldn't deny that she was very attracted to him and was reminded of her teenage years and the crushes she had suffered at school. This was different; it was reciprocated. The feeling of being desired was intoxicating. She wanted to feel like that again. She couldn't fool herself; she was sliding down the slippery slope into adultery, and she knew it.

By the time she reached the house she was no nearer a solution. Sunny opened the door, and the children tumbled in, running into the kitchen to help themselves to the biscuit tin. The smell of fish fingers wafted out into the autumn air, and Angelica was reminded of where she belonged. She closed the door behind her and felt a sense of security within the four walls of her home. Her mobile burned in her handbag, but she ignored it, setting the dining room table for homework by way of a distraction.

Finally, bath time was over, and the children were in her bed watching an old DVD of *Robin Hood*. She stood alone in her bathroom in her pretty lingerie. The lights were dimmed, music playing softly, Dyptique candles burning. In the sensual atmosphere of her sanctuary, she decided that she would simply respond that she would love to see him again before he left for South Africa. What was the harm? He'd be gone in a week—this might be her last opportunity to see him, ever.

So she leaned against the sink and wrote a text: **Dear DOP, Park sounds good, weather permitting. X S**

She climbed into the bath, reluctant to get changed and go out. Olivier was going to meet her for drinks at Sotheby's, then they were joining friends at Harry's Bar for dinner. Another late night she didn't need. She'd have much preferred to stay at home, watching an old episode of *Frasier*.

Now that she was slimmer she could get into a favorite silver Ralph Lauren skirt and pale gray top. She admired her reflection, scrunching her hair between her fingers. She wished Jack could see her now, all dressed up, looking her best. What would she wear to the park? She couldn't ask Candace. A stab of guilt weakened her resolve for a moment. She hated to keep anything from her friend, but she didn't want anything to spoil her fun, not least her conscience.

She kissed the children, stroking their hair and soft faces. Engrossed in *Robin Hood,* they barely noticed her. "Be good for Sunny," she said, slipping on silver stilettos. "Hey, how do I look?"

Joe tore his eyes from the telly. He appraised her a moment while Angelica struck a pose. "Cool," he replied.

"As cool as Zeus's mum?"

He grinned. "Cooler."

"What good taste you have, sweetheart."

She waved at them. Joe turned his attention back to the television. Sunny was coming up the stairs to put them to bed. Angelica yearned for her own bed but picked up her clutch bag and left the room with a determined stride.

She sat in the taxi staring at her mobile telephone, willing Jack to send her another message. When it bleeped, her heart leapt with excitement, only to be disappointed when she read that it was from Olivier: he wasn't going to make Sotheby's but would meet her at Harry's Bar instead. She wasn't surprised and found that she didn't care, either. As the taxi turned into Bond Street she retrieved Jack's message and read it again.

Sotheby's turned out to be more fun than she had expected. William and Scarlet were there—Scarlet in the tightest pair of black leather trousers and transparent Chanel blouse—and a whole host of other friends. Everyone she talked to complimented her on her appearance, asking whether she had been away, or what she had had done, and she felt light-headed with all the attention.

At half-past eight she took a taxi to Harry's Bar. The club was already full of diners, sitting in the dim light at small round tables surrounded by paintings and mirrors and plants. Her friends were already there, but not Olivier. She weaved her way to the other end of the restaurant and greeted them all warmly.

"You look marvelous," said Joel de Claire, Olivier's oldest friend. "Why don't you sit there between Antoine and Roberto," he said, pointing at the empty chair at the far end of the table. "That way you can see into the club, and when Olivier arrives, you can scowl at him for being late."

"Angelica doesn't scowl!" protested Joel's wife, Chantal, flicking her wavy chestnut hair off her shoulder.

"Oh, you have no idea," Angelica quipped, edging around the back of the chairs. Antoine and Roberto stood up politely, and she kissed them both. They all sat down. Then Angelica felt her telephone vibrate with a message. While Antoine and Joel conversed across the table, Angelica sneaked a look at her text. To her astonishment it was from Jack: **Raise your beautiful eyes and look to ten o'clock.** A ripple of excitement washed over her. Suppressing a smile, she glanced through the gap beside Chantal, where Olivier was to sit. There, with his back against the wall, sat Jack, in an open-necked white shirt and jacket, his rugged face dark and handsome, his unruly hair swept off his face so that the blond streaks in it caught the light and glistened as if he had just returned from a day at sea. She was thankful for the dim light as her cheeks burned with pleasure. She turned her attention to the elderly couple at his table, a distinguished-looking pair, diligently reading the menu, and wondered who they were. When she looked back at Jack, he was grinning.

Her line of vision was suddenly blocked by Olivier, who stood before them in a navy Gucci suit and sensible tie, his face ashen in the candlelight.

"Bad day at the office?" Joel joked in French, patting him firmly on the back.

Angelica watched him unbutton his jacket and sit down. He blew her a weary kiss. The table all began to talk at once. Angelica's French wasn't very good, but she wasn't listening anyway. Her telephone vibrated with another message. **I'm bored stiff. Wish I could sit with you!** Without hesitation she typed back: **They're all speaking French! Mine is terrible. X** She was exhilarated when he replied instantly: **Meet me at ten by the restrooms.** She lifted her eyes and bit her bottom lip. **Yes.**

The remainder of the meal passed in a blur. Every time she looked at her husband she could see Jack sitting behind him. They caught eyes once or twice, but Angelica was quick to look away, afraid that Olivier would notice and turn to see whom she was flirting with. Antoine and Roberto were old friends of Olivier's, and, in spite of being charming and good-looking, they had the unattractive habit of speaking across her. She was weary of the financial crisis, but Antoine and Roberto both worked in the City and found the subject hard to resist. She rolled her eyes at Carla, Antoine's wife, who was being ignored by Joel for the same reason. She glanced at her watch to see that it was nine-thirty. *Half an hour to go,* she thought impatiently, picking up her wineglass and taking a sip. Her stomach churned with nerves. A dish of grilled sole was put in front of her, but she didn't feel hungry.

"Don't you think you should leave your work in the office?" said Chantal to her husband.

"I apologize," said Joel good-naturedly. "We're boring the girls."

"They might be bored to listen, but they are not too bored to spend," said Roberto without humor.

Veronica, his wife, rose to their defense. "There is nothing more boring than *not* spending."

"Darling," Roberto cut in, his Italian accent comic, "it is

worse than boring—it is a disaster. I predict that wives will take lovers when their husbands no longer make the money for them to whittle away."

"You must think us all very shallow," said Angelica stiffly.

"Most women are," Roberto continued. "I am afraid to say that a vast majority of women marry men for their money."

"I married Antoine for his genes," said Carla. "I needed to erase from the gene pool my father's family's famous nose. Antoine has the nose of a Greek god." They all looked at Antoine, and he dutifully lifted his chin.

"I married Olivier because he is a good lover," said Angelica, aware that she was about to deceive him.

Olivier preened. "What can I say, boys?" He laughed, the color now returning to his cheeks. "I might lose my money, but I'll always be a good lover."

Angelica glanced at her watch and placed her napkin on the table. "Excuse me," she said, getting up. "Won't be a minute." As she passed Olivier, he took her hand.

"Where are you off to?"

"The ladies'."

He pulled her down and whispered in her ear. "You're the best-looking girl in the room."

She glanced at Carla, Chantal, and Veronica, none of them famed for their beauty. "Not a great deal of competition," she replied, then walked off in the direction of the powder room, too frightened to glance at Jack, who watched her go and placed his own napkin on the table.

She walked downstairs, unsteady with nerves, and stood there waiting, heart pounding with anticipation and fear. It wasn't long before Jack appeared. Neither could contain their exhilaration at finding themselves in the same restaurant. "The Fates are on my side," he said, drawing her into his arms and kissing her cheek. Her head spun, but she didn't hurry to pull away.

"This is an incredible coincidence. Out of all the restaurants in London."

"I love Harry's. It reminds me of my misspent youth."

"How much of it did you misspend?"

"Not enough." He devoured her features from behind his glasses. "So are you going to meet me in the park tomorrow?"

"Don't you have any work to do?"

"Sure, but when there's a will there's a way. Actually, I don't have a meeting until the afternoon. Why don't we walk around the Serpentine? A morning stroll. I like to be near water; it is good for the soul."

Aware of the little time they had and reckless in his presence, she replied hastily. "Why not?"

"I'll bring some bread for the birds."

"I thought dogs ate birds."

"This one is a benign dog; you should know that by now." He looked at her in that intense way of his.

"And no chasing rabbits?"

"Why would I want to do that, when the most desirable rabbit is right here?" He raised his eyes to see Veronica, Chantal, and Carla coming down the stairs towards them. "You've got company. I'd better go. See you in the café on the Serpentine at ten." Before she could reply he had disappeared into the gents.

"We've decided to leave them to it," said Chantal.

"Men can be so boring," Veronica complained.

"Let's go outside. I need a cigarette," Carla suggested. "Besides, it's far too hot in here. Look at you, Angelica, you're burning up."

Angelica was indeed burning up, but not because of the heat in the club. She waited for them to come out of the ladies' room, then followed them back upstairs and outside, where the cool night air chilled her cheeks and the darkness hid her desire.

11

Have faith and you will succeed.

In Search of the Perfect Happiness

Angelica walked to the park, hands in pockets, her Moschino navy peacoat wrapped tightly around her. The sun shone golden in the autumn sky, setting the tops of the trees alight in a blaze of oranges and reds. The air was crisp and fresh, the roar of the morning traffic rising with the flight of pigeons. She put her head down, letting her hair fall about her face to hide her shame. It was useless denying her intention. She was on her way to meet the man with whom she was now falling in love.

Biting her bottom lip, she considered Olivier, her children, and her comfortable life. She hadn't done anything wrong—yet. Jack was merely a friend. Her life was still safely in her grasp, in one piece. She knew the consequences of having an affair; she had seen them in the shattered lives of friends who had been through the mangle of the divorce courts. She didn't want that. She didn't want to lose Olivier.

There was still time to walk away, but Jack's allure was too great. Surely it was possible to enjoy his company without sex? To look from afar and dream of another life without having to taste it? He lived in South Africa. As painful as it was to think of his leaving, it was also a relief; the distance would save her from herself.

She reached the café by the Serpentine a little early, so she sat on a bench and watched the ducks. She smiled as she thought of his promise to bring bread. She still derived pleasure from feeding them with her children, and he clearly did, too. It was an attractive quality to enjoy the natural world. Olivier only ever noticed birds when he had a gun in his hands. A jogger ran by, his breath misty in the morning air, his face red with exertion. A group of young mothers with toddlers in strollers sat drinking coffee at a round table in the sun, their eyes red-rimmed with exhaustion. Angelica remembered interrupted nights and was grateful that her children were now old enough not to disturb her sleep.

Then Jack came striding purposefully through the trees, and she stood up to meet him. He waved when he saw her, his face creasing into a joyous smile. She felt at once uplifted, her heart filled with light. She waved back, glancing around furtively to see if she was being watched.

"I feel like a schoolgirl playing truant," she said when he reached her. But he pulled her into his arms without a care for secrecy and kissed her cheek. The electricity of his touch was so powerful that she caught her breath. In that brief moment she forgot all about Olivier.

"You *look* like a schoolgirl playing truant." He laughed. "Relax."

"Did you bring bread for the ducks?"

"Of course." He delved into his coat pocket and passed her a plastic bag of bread crumbs. He watched her dip her fingers in and come out with a handful. "So how was last night?"

"Dull. All anyone wanted to talk about was the financial crisis."

"I nearly fell off my chair when I saw you walk into the club. You looked like a silver angel floating through the darkness."

"I didn't see you when I came in."

"I saw *you*. God bless mobile telephones, and God bless you for breaking the rules and leaving it on."

"I always leave it on vibrate in case the children need me. It was an extraordinary coincidence." She threw crumbs onto the water and watched the ducks swim swiftly over to eat them.

"I couldn't take my eyes off you. I can't take my eyes off you now, either."

"Really, you are funny."

"You always say that when you're embarrassed. It's an endearing defense mechanism."

"It's just that I'm not used to being complimented."

"I don't believe that for a second."

"Really, I'm not."

"Look, I'm holding back here. If I could, I'd shower you in compliments."

Her heart accelerated like a trapped bird's. "I thought we were just going to be friends."

"We are. I never said I wouldn't say what's on my mind." He took her hand, sending a shiver all the way up her arm. "You know how I feel."

"I'm still surprised that you can talk so openly about your feelings. Men usually don't. They're usually muzzled." She slipped her hand out of his grasp.

"Englishmen perhaps, not South Africans. But I've learned to say what's on my mind because I might never get another chance." He poured the last crumbs to the pavement, where a gaggle of fat pigeons waited eagerly to peck them up. "Let's walk."

They set off around the pond. The water shone like a gilded mirror as the sun rose higher in the sky, and Angelica felt the warmth on her face. "It's beautiful, isn't it?" she said, reluctantly putting her hands in her pockets so that he couldn't hold one, wishing that they were in some distant city so he could.

He took a deep breath. "Very beautiful." They walked on in silence, taking in the glory of such a magnificent morning.

"I'm mad, you know," she said after a while.

"I know. You're married. I'm married. What we're doing is crazy. But I can't help myself. If I can't be your lover, I'm content to be your friend." He laughed and shook his head at his own dishonesty. "No, I'm not content to be your friend. I'm smitten with you, and all I can think about is making love to you. Don't say I'm funny and brush me off with a laugh. I'm not at all funny. I'm a very sad man."

"Jack . . . don't . . ." She remembered his lover in Clapham. Perhaps Scarlet had got it wrong.

"Listen, I'm a terrible flirt. I'm the first to admit it. But this is beyond a flirt and a first for me, if you can believe that. I'm walking into unknown territory with a great big FORBIDDEN sign hanging across the pathway. But I know that if I don't seize the moment, it might never present itself again. Life is short.

"You have a wife, Jack, and children. Let's just be friends. Isn't that what a really wise sage would advise?"

"If that's all you're prepared to give me, then I have no choice but to accept. I'd rather see you as friends than not at all." He bent down and picked up a small stone, throwing it into the water so that it bounced three times before sinking. "It's wrong of me to try to persuade you to give me anything more. I'm going back to South Africa on Friday. I wish you could come with me."

"You know that's impossible."

"I'd say come out with Olivier and your children, but I don't think I could stand to see you both together."

"I'd never get away with coming out on my own."

"So it's walks around the Serpentine." He looked away. "Why do I have to meet you at this time in my life?"

"If we had met fifteen years ago, we might not have liked each other."

He looked back at her, his eyes dark and sad. "Oh, I'd always have liked you."

They changed the subject and discussed the previous evening. Angelica made him laugh as she imitated her friends. He told her of the people he would introduce her to in South Africa—fun, bohemian people who didn't talk about finance, but discussed books and films and art. "As ironic as it is, you'd get on very well with my wife."

"I don't think I'd want to meet her. Not now."

"We haven't done anything wrong except declare a mutual attraction."

"That would be reason enough for Olivier to explode into a jealous rage!"

"Anna would shrug it off with a smile."

"Broken on the wheel, I suppose."

"Indulgent, actually." She didn't like the sound of Anna, or the look on his face when he spoke about her. "Take me out of the equation, and you two would find you had a lot in common."

"I'll never know," she replied tightly.

He grinned as if he could see her jealousy as colors swirling around her head. "I'm flattered you mind."

"I don't mind, actually. You can tell me all about Anna if you wish." Her voice sounded tense even to her.

"She's not a beauty like you, but she's beautiful on the inside. There are many different ways of loving, and I'd be lying if I told you I didn't love her. I don't know you well enough to love you, but I'm *in* love with you, and right now I think about you more than I think about anyone."

"Am I meant to take that as a compliment?"

"Yes, the fact that I'm being honest with you sets you apart from any other woman I've ever fancied. It's easy to tell someone you love them to get what you want, but that's not love. That's desire, lust, attraction, or fascination. You only start to truly love someone when you fall *out* of love with them, when you love them in spite of their faults, most often *because* of them."

"Well, that is honest, I suppose." She felt her spirits sink.

"It's the greatest compliment I can give you."

"Then it's true to say that I love Olivier. I'm not sure that I'm *in* love with him anymore. Wouldn't it be nice to experience both at the same time? The constant comfort of love and the exciting thrill of in love. Are you in love with Anna?"

"No."

"But you love her. So surely you don't want to hurt her?"

"No. I don't want to hurt her."

"Wouldn't she be hurt if she knew you were, as you put it, falling in love with me?"

"I think she would." He stopped walking and rubbed the back of his neck, looking up at the sky as if he'd find an answer there. Finally, he shook his head and stared at her thoughtfully. He suddenly looked old. "It's complicated, Angelica. I wish I could explain, but if I did, I'd ruin the magic of our meeting. Right now, all I really care about is being with you. I'm aware that I'm leaving soon, and I want to feast my eyes on you for as long as I can before I go. I wish we had met twenty years ago."

"I was a very unattractive twenty-year-old," she replied with a laugh, relieved that they weren't going to talk about their spouses anymore.

"I don't believe that for a second."

"You'd have tossed me a glance and moved on to someone prettier. I know your type."

"Then if you believe in karma, what goes around comes around. You are my penance for all the irresponsible flirting I've done over the years."

"I'd hate to think of myself as a penance."

"I've met someone I really want but can't have. That's the most bittersweet penance there is."

"I imagine a man like you has women tucked away in every corner of the globe."

"I don't tuck people away, and I don't intend to. If you think this is a game to me, you're wrong. It might have started out as an entertainment, but it's got a hell of a lot more serious." He thrust his hands into his pockets. "I didn't plan to fall in love, Sage. Not at this stage in my life."

They sat on a bench beneath a chestnut tree, watching the world move around them. People met and parted, and Angelica wondered how many were illicit meetings like theirs. By lunchtime neither could believe that three hours had gone by. In an effort to prolong the morning, they found a small café in Knightsbridge and ate a simple lunch of smoked salmon and salad. Angelica no longer worried about being caught. Having lunch with Jack felt like the most natural thing in the world. She didn't glance around like a fugitive but focused on his gentle brown eyes and listened intently to everything he said. If anyone had bothered to look at them, they would have thought them lovers by the way they gazed at each other, oblivious to the rest of the city, and by the natural way he occasionally took her hand or played with her fingers, and by the way they laughed with such abandon.

In a short time they'd both return to their separate lives. It seemed incomprehensible sitting there together that they had lives beyond each other. But that time eventually came. Jack had an appointment, and Angelica had to pick up the children from school. Their conversation dwindled as they felt the heavy anticipation of their parting. He took her hand across the small table and leaned towards her. "I want to see you again before I go."

"Is that wise?"

"That's irrelevant. If we were always wise we'd never enjoy making mistakes."

"I don't know, Jack."

"I'm only asking for one more morning. Don't pretend you're doing any writing at the moment." His grin was persuasive—and she did want to be persuaded. "Aren't you feeling inspired?"

"Yes, you're very inspiring—for a different genre altogether."

"Then write something different. Follow your instincts."

"I don't dare."

"Why?"

"Because Olivier will know."

"No, he won't. He'll think it's your imagination—if he reads it."

"Sod's law, this will be the first book of mine he reads."

"It'll be the best book you've ever written."

"So I suppose you want a dedication?"

He chuckled, but she thought she saw sorrow in his eyes. "No, I just want to see you again before I leave."

"You'll be coming back, won't you?"

He shrugged. "Who knows where life will take us? I don't want to take any chances. Please, Angelica. I won't pounce, I swear it."

"Maybe."

He grinned in that roguish way of his, and Angelica wondered whether she had imagined the sorrow.

They parted in the street. He hailed a cab, and she watched him wave through the back window until he was swallowed by traffic. She turned and set off towards Kensington, the scent of his cologne still fresh on her skin.

Gray clouds now moved across the sky, driven by a chilly wind that whipped through the trees, causing the orange leaves to fall to the pavement like rain. Their morning together seemed nothing now but a sunny dream. It must have drizzled while they were in the café, for the tarmac glistened and the air was damp. Autumn had snatched the magic that had been theirs so briefly. Now that they had parted, she longed for him with every fiber in her body. She regretted her reluctance to see him one last time before he left for South Africa and wanted to text him to reassure him that she wanted him as much as he wanted her. But as she approached the school, she remembered once again who she was and where she belonged.

She met her friends with a heavy heart, knowing that she was unable to share her predicament. Candace noticed it at once. "Are you all right, Angelica?"

"I'm fine," she replied, shrugging it off. "I went out last night, so I'm a bit tired."

"You don't look tired."

"Makeup."

She wasn't convinced. "I didn't see you at Pilates this morning."

"God, I totally forgot!"

"You were missed."

"I'm going mad."

Candace looked at her friend suspiciously. "So what were you doing?"

"Trying to write my book."

"How's it going?"

"I've begun at least. A meager plot that seemed good at the time, but now, on reflection, is rather old hat."

"Well, at least you've started. It's more important to write than work out."

"I know."

Candace raised her eyes to see Jenna striding towards them. "Oh Lord, it's a gaucho. Doesn't that girl ever take off her sunglasses?"

"Hi!" Jenna gave a little wave. "Isn't it cold all of a sudden?" She didn't look in the slightest bit cold in her cowboy hat, cashmere poncho, and riding boots.

"It was lovely this morning," said Angelica.

"I've already begun," said Jenna with a triumphant smile.

"Begun what?" asked Candace.

"My novel. Didn't Angelica tell you? I'm writing a novel based on my life."

"Wow! Best seller," said Candace flatly.

"I didn't realize how easy it is to write a book. I always thought of you toiling away, Angelica, fighting to get it done before your deadline. It's a piece of cake." She gave a little sniff. "At least for me."

"Well, you're not quite Tolstoy," said Candace, her jaw tensing with irritation.

"No, it's more like a modern Edith Wharton."

"I can't wait to read it," said Angelica, trying to keep a straight face.

"You will read it, then you can put me in touch with that delicious publisher of yours . . . what was he called? Leighton something."

"Leighton," said Angelica with a blush. She couldn't remember what he had said his last name was. "Jenna met him when we were having lunch at Daphne's," she said to Candace, whose bewildered expression was replaced by a knowing smile.

"Oh, *him*," she said. "He *is* delicious. Such a shame he's gay."

"Gay?" Jenna was appalled.

"Yes. He breaks hearts all over the world. Only a man can win him."

"God, I would never have guessed!" Jenna had gone pale.

"Good luck with the book," said Candace, tapping her arm. "We could all do with a little Edith Wharton."

The big doors opened and one by one the children were handed over to their mothers or nannies. Jenna pushed her way to the front of the queue.

"I don't think we'll ever see that book of hers," said Candace. "Shame!"

"I forgot to tell you I'd bumped into her!"

"What else did you forget to tell me, Angelica?" Candace looked at her sternly. "Are you seeing him?"

"No!"

"It was just lunch?"

"Yes. I told you, it was just lunch. I'm sad, that's all. Life is a little less bright without his e-mails to keep me going—and I really liked him."

"It's for the best, though, Angelica. You have a nice life." Candace was now satisfied. "You'll get over him."

"Of course. But I can't tell you how much I'd like to see him again." That, at least, was true.

12

You can't control what happens to you in your life but you can control how you react.

In Search of the Perfect Happiness

Angelica took the children for a playdate at Letizia's house. She sat in the airy green sitting room drinking tea with her friend while the children played upstairs. Letizia looked glamorous in a pair of gray flannel trousers and a dove-gray cashmere top, a few inches taller thanks to Tod's pumps.

"I love the idea of the manny," she told Angelica, playing with the array of Van Cleef gold necklaces that hung down to her navel. "I mean, Maria is a nightmare! She's got to go. I cannot cope with that sour face at the breakfast table every morning, and I know she thinks I'm a tyrant."

"You *are* a tyrant, Letizia," said Angelica with a grin. "But it's not her place to judge you. You pay her to do a job; she should at least do it with a smile."

"I've spoiled her, darling; that's the trouble. At the beginning I gave her every goodie bag from every party I went to, and I bought her a really generous birthday present from Links. Now she thinks I owe her a living."

"They all have a sell-by date."

"Well, she's well past hers; she's beginning to smell!" She waved a hand under her nose. "*Schifosa!* I feel unwelcome in my own home."

"See what this manny of Scarlet's is like. If you like him and Scarlet's not employing him over Christmas, take him skiing with you."

"It's such a great idea, especially for Alessandro. He's too old to have a nanny now, but a boy who can teach him football sounds ideal."

Angelica's mobile rang with a message. She knew instinctively that it was from Jack. While Letizia continued talking, she pulled it out and read: I'm pining for you, Sage. When can I call you? DWOP She bit her bottom lip, wondering what DWOP stood for. Letizia didn't notice the color in her cheeks. "And what about Kate's wedding?" Letizia continued. "I'm so excited. It's wonderful that they're patching it up. Although I wouldn't trust Pete as far as I could throw him. I mean, it's shocking. He's married to one of the loveliest girls in London, and he has to skulk around having affairs. It's disgusting and disrespectful."

Angelica wanted to repeat what Olivier had said: that in spite of Kate's beauty, she was neurotic and flaky and probably very hard to live with. But she held her tongue. Letizia was fiercely loyal about her friends. The only one with whom Angelica could really speak her mind was Candace.

"Let's hope that's all over," she said instead.

"Do leopards change their spots?"

"Some do."

"I'm not sure Pete's one of those. Still, it will be a great wedding. We're all going to stay in the Saint Géran . . ."

". . . and waft about in white linen."

"Yes." She laughed. "With shells in our hair! *Madonna!*"

When she got home, Angelica perched on the loo seat while the children played in the bath. She read his text again, ignoring Joe, who threw one of his big dinosaurs to the bath mat with a loud clunk. She tapped in her reply: **Don't pine. I hate to think of you sad. Call me at 8, if you like. X Sage.** Another dinosaur landed on the mat, covered in foam. "Do you want to watch TV before bed?" she snapped.

"Yes, but . . ."

"No buts, Joe. Stop throwing things out of the bath, or you'll go straight to bed." She knelt down to wash their hair, now on a mission to get them both into bed by eight.

Joe got to watch *Scooby-Doo.* Isabel sat at her pink dressing table while Angelica dried her long brown hair. She opened her drawer and played with the tray of makeup she had collected from her mother's old lipsticks and eye shadows. Angelica watched her daughter's reflection fondly, determined that she would never do anything to jeopardize her secure little world.

At last they were in bed. She had read them a couple of chapters of *Despereaux,* which she had enjoyed almost more than they did, then lovingly kissed their foreheads. A Full Joe from her son had completed the bedtime ritual before she had turned off their lights. With a sigh of relief she walked back into her bedroom and lay on the bed, her mobile in hand, awaiting his call.

At five minutes past eight it rang. She could see from the DOP in the display screen that it was Jack. Her belly lurched with guilty pleasure. "Hello," she said in a soft voice.

"I miss you," he replied with a sigh.

"I miss you, too."

"That makes me feel a lot better."

"What does DWOP stand for?"

He chuckled. "Dog Well off Porch."

"Dog Soon to Be Back on Porch," she replied wryly.

"I don't like to think of going home without you."

"I'm a little big for your suitcase."

"I'd buy one big enough if you said you'd come."

"It's not going to happen, Jack."

"I'd love to show you Rosenbosch. It's so beautiful at this time of year. It's spring. Everything's so fresh and new. I'd take you riding across the veld, into the mist on the hills, and we'd sit at the top, and, once the mist had lifted, I'd show you the whole valley. It would take your breath away."

"It already has."

"Do you ride?"

"I grew up in the country and was obsessed with ponies."

"Good. Then I have just the horse for you. A chestnut so sweet natured you could gallop at full speed and never fear falling off or being run away with."

"I'd love that. I haven't felt the wind in my hair for years."

"Then let me. Make up an excuse. I'll organize your ticket."

"How would you explain that to your wife?"

"You're my friend."

"She'd be a fool if she believed that, and I don't think she is a fool."

"She's not, but she's tolerant."

"She really wouldn't mind if I pitched up to stay?"

He hesitated a moment. "I really don't think she would. Look, I would behave myself. I respect her a great deal. I just want you *near*."

"There would have to be a very good reason for Olivier to let me go. There are practicalities you haven't even considered. I don't have a nanny. Who'd pick up the children every day? It's not as easy for me to leave as it is for you. My children have homework every evening, and, unless Olivier gets sacked, which I hope he doesn't, I'd have to hire someone to cover for me, and Olivier hates having strangers in the house."

"Then it's really impossible." His voice sounded so low she felt a stab of pity.

"I'm sorry."

"Me, too." There was a pause. She could hear his breathing down the line. Then his tone lifted. "What are you doing tomorrow night?"

"Kate's giving her friend Art a birthday party."

"You have to go?"

"Yes, I do."

"You can't cancel?"

"Absolutely not."

"Tell them you're sick and come and have dinner with me."

"I couldn't."

"Which part couldn't you do?"

"Both, Jack. I couldn't lie to my friends, and I couldn't have dinner with you. It would be folly."

There was a pause while he devised a plan. "Then let's meet after the party."

"I don't know . . ."

"Look, I leave on Friday."

"It's too dangerous."

"What about Friday morning? We can walk around the park again."

"We got away with it once. I can't do it again."

"I have to see you, Sage. What's the harm in two friends meeting for the last time?"

At that moment she heard the front door slam. She sat up with a start. "Oh Lord, I think Olivier's home."

"Text me. I'll meet you tomorrow night. You can leave the party early. We can go someplace, a bar . . ."

"It's risky."

"I know."

"If I get caught . . ."

"London's a big city."

"You'd be surprised." She heard Olivier's footsteps on the stairs. "Got to go," she hissed urgently. She heard him hang up without saying good-bye, and said loudly for Olivier's benefit, "Better go, Mum, Olivier's home."

He came in looking moody, tossed his jacket onto a chair, and loosened his tie. She got off the bed.

"What's for supper?" he asked.

"I thought we could order in something. What would you like?"

"A Chinese. Ring Mr. Wing now, I'm ravenous."

"Fancy a glass of wine? I do."

"Yes, be an angel and bring it up here, will you? I've had one hell of a day. It's very tough." He sighed heavily. "I hope you're writing your book, Angelica. We might need your earnings if I'm laid off."

"You think you might be?"

"Nothing is certain."

"God, Olivier. That's terrible."

"I know. Things are really bad."

"But you're going to be okay, surely?"

"Didn't you hear what I just said?" he snapped impatiently.

"Yes, I'm just being optimistic."

"Well, now isn't the time to be optimistic. If I'm laid off, we'll be in trouble. Your earnings will be important."

"My new book comes out in the spring."

"Good. Let's hope it sells well."

Angelica went downstairs to order the food and pour the wine, seething with resentment. She didn't imagine Jack would come home in such a foul mood and demand that she order the food and pour the wine. He admired her books, he had even read one, which was more than Olivier had ever done. Now he had the cheek to tell her that what *he* considered a small home industry might actually be important. Well, she knew it was important. Her fans all over the world knew it was important. Jack knew it was important. If Olivier bothered to read her royalty statements, he'd realize just how important it was. But compared with his vast banker's salary, her earnings were as raindrops in a lake—inconsequential.

Furiously, she ordered the dinner then sat in silence as they ate it at the kitchen table.

"Thank God we're not going out tonight. I'm shattered."

He didn't notice that she hadn't laid the table or lit a candle. She no longer felt guilty about fancying Jack. In fact, she felt she deserved a flirtation. If her husband wasn't going to cherish her, Jack would—and if he really pushed her, she'd find a way to get to South Africa. In the gloom of Olivier's bad mood the thought of riding across the veld was extremely enticing.

"Are you going to talk to me, or are you just going to sit there sulking?" Olivier asked.

"You don't need to get at me just because you've had a bad day."

"Haven't you read the papers? It's not just a bad day. Things are really going sour. We're careering headlong into a recession. Probably the worst we've had in one hundred years. I need your support, not your condemnation."

"I'm not condemning you, Olivier. I just don't like your implying that my books are some kind of last resort if we hit bad times."

"I'm grateful for them. We might need them." He spread plum sauce onto his pancake, then piled it up with duck and onion slices.

"But your implication is that they can be brushed aside. I might as well be knitting bootees for the local children's shop by the tone of your voice."

He put his hand on hers and sighed resignedly. "I would never imply that what you do has no value. It has tremendous value not only to you spiritually but to us financially. All I'm saying is that they might become our only source of income."

She withdrew her hand. "You've never read one."

"No, it's true. I haven't." He took a large bite and began to chew. As he did so, his hostility lifted and he smiled. "I will."

"Don't bother. You're busy." She no longer cared whether or not he read one. In fact, she rather wished he wouldn't so that she could continue to hold the grudge, justifying her seeking consolation from Jack.

"I'm sorry I'm hard to live with at the moment. Ask any of your friends who is married to a banker. It's not fun anymore. I can't even tell you to go and spend a few grand in Gucci." He shrugged helplessly.

"I'm far too busy writing anyway."

"This is very good." He rolled another pancake. "We should have this more often. I had forgotten how much I like Mr. Wing."

Before she went to bed she sent Jack a text: **I'll meet you at eleven tomorrow night. X Sage.** No sooner had she sent it than a message came winging back: **I'll wait at the end of the street in a taxi. What's the address? DOP.**

Olivier slept beside Angelica, but the gap between them was as big as Siberia. Angelica lay on her side facing away from him, dreaming of Jack and riding across the South African veld on a beautiful chestnut mare. Everything about him was romantic. The way he was so happy to discuss life. The way he spoke about his feelings. The way he loved nature. The way he noticed *her*. With him she felt attractive, feminine, mysterious, and cherished. With Jack she was someone totally different, someone Olivier had forgotten. And she liked that someone very much.

The following morning felt unlike any other. Olivier had gone to work. The children were getting ready for school, Sunny was preparing breakfast downstairs, she was dressing . . . but the air around her had changed; it was now charged with possibility. She walked the children to school and kissed them at the door. She had coffee with Candace, Letizia, Scarlet, and Kate. She listened to Kate's arrangements for Art's party: she had filled the house with silver helium balloons so that you couldn't see the ceiling; she had ordered a cake from Jane Asher that was "to die for"; she had Mustard doing the catering; and she had hired a karaoke machine for all those aspiring singers to show off their talents—and yet Angelica moved through her day knowing that, whatever happened, at eleven o'clock her world would change. She sensed it like a bird sensing an earthquake.

She had lunch with Scarlet at Le Caprice, then picked up the children at three-thirty. They walked through the park, feeding the geese on the Round Pond. She sat on a bench while the children played with the birds, considering her life and the fork in the road that lay ahead of her. She didn't want to leave Olivier; in spite of his moodiness she loved him. But Jack had injected her life with excitement and given her a high from which she was reluctant to come down.

The children grew tired and hungry. They walked back past Kensington Palace, Joe bending down to pat every dog, Isabel hanging off the railings like a parrot. Sunny gave them tea. Angelica supervised their homework at the dining room table. Everything was the same as always, except in her head, where everything was different.

She dressed for dinner, choosing a vintage midnight-blue dress Olivier had bought her in Paris the first year of their marriage. She had always loved that dress, but it was only since losing weight that she was able to wear it. Olivier threw a shadow across the room. He stood in the doorway, watching her. Without asking he turned up the lights and wandered in, taking off his jacket. "So you're going out."

"Yes, to Kate's party for Art."

"Oh yes, I forgot." He ran his eyes up and down her body. "You look *très jolie*." He pulled a face. "Shame you're going out. I'd like to take that dress off."

"No time, I'm afraid," she said, slipping past him.

"You smell nice, too."

"Oranges."

"Nice." He looked at her longingly and a little lost.

"Thank you."

"Don't be too long."

"Why, are you going to miss me?" She hadn't meant to sound so sharp.

"Of course. I like your company." He narrowed his eyes. "You're not still angry with me for last night?"

"Of course not."

"I haven't seen you for ages."

"You saw me last night."

"That doesn't count. We should spend more time together."

"Sure." She grabbed her evening bag and tossed her hair.

"I'm sad that you look so ravishing, but not for me."

"It's not my fault you're not coming. You still can."

He dithered, and for a terrible moment she thought he might change his mind and go with her. "No, I'm tired. Just don't be too long."

"It'll go on all night, Olivier. You know what Kate's karaoke evenings are like."

"Karaoke! I'm definitely not coming to hear a bunch of Hoorays singing out of tune to YMCA!" He laughed unhappily. "Let's go out for dinner tomorrow night, just the two of us."

"No, let's stay in. I'll be tired."

"I thought you might like a night out, just us."

"I would, but not tomorrow."

He threw himself onto the bed, crossing his feet. "What's for supper?"

• • •

Angelica arrived at Kate's just as Scarlet and William were ringing the doorbell.

"Where's Olivier?" William asked.

"Not coming. Hates karaoke."

"Well, that makes two of us. That's the point where I think I'll leave you all to it," he added.

"And when the party will really get going." Scarlet giggled as William nudged her playfully.

Inside, the guests waited in the sitting room for Art and Tod to arrive. The effect of all those silver balloons was magical. Candles covered every surface and were reflected in the big ornate mirrors that hung above the mantelpieces. Waiters weaved through the throng with trays of champagne and cocktails. Angelica took a glass of champagne and found Candace talking to Letizia and Kate. All the husbands were there except Olivier, but Angelica wasn't in the least bit upset. All she could think about was eleven o'clock.

At last the couple arrived. Tod flung open the door and Art's face was a picture of astonishment and pleasure. He swept his eyes over the faces of his friends and settled finally onto Kate's. "You naughty girl!" he said, throwing his arms around her small frame and lifting her off the ground. "I love you, I love you, I love you!" he breathed into her ear.

"Happy birthday!" she exclaimed, raising her glass, and everyone in the room raised theirs.

"Let the party begin!" Tod shouted, and, as if by magic, the lights were turned up and music resounded through the rooms.

13

Live in the present because it's all there is.

In Search of the Perfect Happiness

"Angelica, darling, you look peachy," said Art, towering over her. At six feet four he was handsome in an aristocratic, chiseled way, with intelligent gray eyes and glossy brown hair that flopped over his face.

"Happy birthday, Art," she said, smelling his spicy perfume as he bent down to kiss her.

"What is that scent? It's delicious," said Candace. "Though kind of overpowering!"

"State secret," he replied. "I don't want you all smelling like me."

"You don't look anything like fifty," said Angelica.

"Don't mention the five, please, it hurts. You're as old as you feel."

"Or as old as the woman you feel," said Angelica with a giggle. "That's what my father always says."

"Not in my case. Tod is nearer the six, but don't tell him I said so."

"Kate has really pushed the boat out on this one," said Candace, gazing around the room.

"She loves me," he said casually.

"Don't we all?" It was impossible not to think the world of Art.

"You two are enough to turn a gay man straight. I'd better circulate, or I'll get into trouble. There's no such thing as a free dinner."

"Isn't he adorable?" Candace asked as he made his way through the throng.

"Adorable!"

"You don't think . . . ?" She scrunched up her face as if trying to conjure an impossible mental picture.

"What?"

"That he's the mystery man?"

"You mean, Art and Kate?"

"Yes."

"Absolutely not. He's devoted to Tod, and he's gay. Anyway, she's convinced herself that Pete's the father."

"Well, she might be right. But we'll know when he's born and doesn't look anything like Pete!"

"I wager he looks nothing like Art."

"Come on, let's take a look around. He's sure to be in here somewhere."

They worked their way through the room. Candace sized up every man with eyes as sharp as an eagle's. Angelica watched the clock. Minutes passed slowly, and sometimes, when she looked, they seemed not to pass at all. She felt dizzy with nerves, unable to concentrate on what anyone said. She forgot people's names and blundered into more than the odd faux pas. Raising her glass cheerfully, she blamed the champagne. Due to her somewhat daffy charm, she got away with it.

Dinner was buffet style, and Angelica helped herself to a small portion of salad, which she picked at on the sofa with Candace and Letizia, too anxious to eat. Kate flitted about in a short cashmere dress that barely covered her bottom.

Her belly was still as flat as a biscuit, which prompted the girls to question whether she really was pregnant.

"It wouldn't surprise me if she's making up the whole thing," said Candace. "Then we'll all be swept into the drama of the miscarriage."

"She's just skinny. I showed even before I was pregnant," said Angelica.

"She should be showing by now, especially as it's her third child. But that stomach is as tight as a trampoline." Candace watched her take Art's cigarette and sneak a quick drag. "Would she be smoking if she was pregnant?"

"I don't think she's making it up. She was in a real state, remember? And we all saw the lines go blue on the tests," said Letizia.

"True, you can't manufacture that," Angelica agreed.

"She's not holding back on the alcohol, either. Actually, I'd go further and say I think she's tipsy."

"If the child is like his mother, he'll have the constitution of an Irish navvy." Angelica laughed.

"She's a mystery. Where's Pete, by the way?"

"Probably with Olivier—they both hate this sort of party."

"He's in Russia," Letizia interjected. "But you're right: he hates karaoke, and he's not fond of Art, though I can't think why. Everyone loves Art."

"Look, Art's a ladies' man," said Candace. "Heterosexual men don't get him. He makes them feel nervous because he's such a beautiful creature. It's a crying shame for women that the best-looking men are gay." *Not all*, Angelica thought, and glanced at her watch.

It wasn't long before the karaoke started. William left with a few other husbands who found the sound of tuneless shrieking too much to bear. Kate kicked off with "It's a Heartache," followed by Scarlet and Tod singing a harmonious rendition of "I Got You Babe." Nothing could persuade Angelica to take to the floor, even fortified with champagne and the anticipation of disappearing into the night to meet Jack. She sat back on the sofa and laughed at the sight of her friends blithely making fools of themselves.

The next time Angelica looked at her watch it was eleven o'clock. The world stood still as her stomach plummeted. She had waited so long for this moment, but now that it was here she shied away, like a pony at too high a jump. She paled and drained her champagne glass, driven by the sense of inevitability that had propelled her through her day. Without a word to anyone she got up and slipped out into the hall. A waitress retrieved her coat, and she wrapped it tightly around her as she stepped out into the cold. It was crisp and clear outside, the sky studded with stars; at the end of the street a taxi waited beneath a bright lamp.

Angelica walked towards it, her steps accelerating, tap-tapping over the pavement. She could see him through the back window, silhouetted against the light of the lamp, and her heart inflated like one of Kate's silver balloons. She reached the cab, and the door flung open. Glancing back to make sure she wasn't being watched, she climbed in. Jack didn't wait to ask permission. He pulled her into his arms and pressed his lips to hers hungrily. Angelica wasn't surprised or horrified that he had broken his word; his kiss felt like home.

The old cabbie looked in his rearview mirror and grinned. If he wrote about everything he'd seen going on in the back of his taxi, he'd have a best seller to boast of. The trouble was, he could barely manage to write a shopping list, let alone an entire book. He shook his head regretfully and pulled out into the street.

Jack's mouth was warm and soft, his chin rough against hers, his embrace the firm hold of a man reluctant to let her go. He slipped his hand beneath her coat, and she felt the heat in it up and down her dress. She yearned for him to touch her skin, to feel his fingers caress her dark and secret places, and her desire made her forget herself. He kissed her neck and throat, sending an exquisite tremor through her body, and she let out a deep moan, pressing herself against him.

As the taxi swung around corners and stopped at traffic lights, Jack and Angelica clung to each other, savoring the magic, aware that tomorrow a plane would take him away to the other side of the world.

The taxi drew up outside Number 11 Cadogan Gardens, and Jack climbed out. The sight of the hotel and the rush of cold air as he opened the door brought her to her senses. She shrank back into the seat in terror. "I can't . . ." she faltered. He leaned in and reached for her hand. But she shook her head and looked away, embarrassed. "You know I can't."

He said something to the cabbie, but Angelica couldn't hear for the ringing in her ears. For a dreadful moment she thought he was telling the man to take her home, that he was going to walk away in displeasure, but he climbed in beside her, closed the door, and drew her back into his arms, kissing her temple and nuzzling her cheek.

"It's okay," he said gently. "I shouldn't have presumed. I couldn't help myself. Forgive me." She lay against him, relieved that he didn't think less of her. "I have all these good intentions when I'm not with you, then the minute I see you I just want to carry you upstairs and make love to you."

She lifted her face. "I can't go home to Olivier smelling of you. What will he think if I turn up in the early hours of the morning? I'm the kind of girl who's in bed by eleven."

"You don't have to explain. I'll take you home. But not before I've kissed you again. Just drive, cabbie. Anywhere you like."

• • •

The taxi drove around Bayswater and Notting Hill, while Jack and Angelica sat entwined in the backseat, nuzzling and kissing each other like young lovers. It was past midnight when it rattled up Kensington Church Street and into Brunswick Gardens.

"So, it's good-bye, Sage." He took her face in his hand, and she pressed her cheek against it. It had all happened so quickly. A few meetings, a dozen e-mails, and now a brief taxi ride, and yet they felt there had never been a time when they hadn't known each other. His eyes were sad as they swept over her features, as if this was the last opportunity he'd ever have to feast on them. His sentimentality moved her, and she turned her head to kiss his palm. "I'm already missing you," he murmured. "Let me memorize every feature so I know you by heart."

"Come back soon," she whispered, fighting back tears.

"You come to South Africa. I'll take you up to Lowry's Pass, and we'll drink wine and watch the sunset. There's no place more romantic. I'll hold you until the last flicker of light disappears behind the hills."

"Oh, Jack. If only . . ." She felt her throat constrict.

"Promise me you'll come."

"I can't."

"Then just pretend. I want to hear you say it."

She stared into his pleading eyes. "All right. I'll come. I promise."

The tension in his face melted. "Then I'll wait for you there."

He cupped her face and kissed her for the final time, then watched her open the door and step into the street. She took a moment to compose herself, standing beneath the streetlamp, smoothing down her coat. He would have walked her to her door, but it was too risky. Instead, he watched her walk quickly up the pavement, arms folded, shoulders hunched against the cold, her figure growing smaller as she was swallowed into the darkness. At last, she arrived at her house. She turned and stood there a moment, staring back at him. Then she gave a small, cautious wave. Reluctantly, he told the driver to take him back to the hotel.

Angelica watched until the taxi was out of sight. She remained on her doorstep for a few minutes, wiping her face and scrunching her hair between her fingers. Then she took a deep breath and unlocked the door. Stepping into the light of her home, she should have felt guilty, but she just felt sad. The dream dissolved in the glare of reality, and once more she was reminded of where she belonged.

She took off her coat and kicked off her stilettos, then padded up the stairs in her stockinged feet. Olivier was lying in bed watching television. It was midnight: he had waited up. He glanced at her and registered at once her stricken face. "Are you all right, Angelica?" He sat up in alarm.

"I'm fine. Just desperately tired."

"You look like you've been crying."

She forced a laugh. "Crying with laughter probably, at all those terrible karaoke singers!"

She walked into the bathroom and closed the door behind her. She undressed, watching her reflection with grim satisfaction, as if it didn't belong to her but to a deceitful, conniving stranger. She didn't care that Olivier would think it odd that she showered in the middle of the night: she felt compelled to soap away her guilt. It hurt to think of Jack flying off the following day, but she knew it was for the best. She had played with fire and nearly burned her whole family. Standing under the water, her hair squashed into a shower cap, she closed her eyes and emptied her mind. The burden of so much emotion was too much to carry. She listened to the water fall about her like rain and felt the comforting warmth wash over her skin.

Olivier slept pressed up against her, his arm resting protectively over her stomach. She could feel his breath on her shoulder and was reminded of those early days when she had treasured each second of their closeness. Now she wished he were Jack. She sank into her imagination, visualizing riding across the South African veld with him beside her, grinning in that raffish way of his that made her heart swell with happiness. Eventually, she slipped into sleep—a seamless transition into Jack's world, where it was just the two of them.

In the morning Olivier was gone. He hadn't woken her up by turning on the light as was his usual habit, but had crept into the bathroom and dressed quietly. The children alerted her to the time by climbing into her bed and turning on the television. She opened one eye to see the clock on her bedside table. It was a quarter to eight. She sat up in panic, switched off the television, and sent the children downstairs to Sunny. Then she dragged herself into her closet, pulled on a pair of jeans and sweater, and sat over a cup of coffee while the children wolfed down their breakfast as fast as their small teeth would allow.

She was late getting them to school. The front door was closed, and she was forced to ring the bell and apologize for her tardiness. It was clear from her pale face and bloodshot eyes that she had overslept. She kissed them hastily and watched them run down the corridor, hoping that she had remembered Joe's games kit and Isabel's ballet bag. No sooner had she set off back up the road than her mobile rang. Her heart stalled when she saw that it wasn't Jack but Candace.

"Good morning," her friend said chirpily.

"Hi, Candace."

"You sound flat."

"Hangover," she lied. "I could barely get up this morning."

"I didn't see you leave. What time did you go?"

"About eleven-thirty. I didn't want to break up the party."

"It got rather debauched, actually. We got an ass shot from Art."

"What, he mooned?"

"I kid you not. Totally hilarious. He pulled down his trousers and flashed his backside."

"Why?"

"He sang the finale, totally pissed. There were only a few of us left. But you know what?"

"What?"

"He has a birthmark on his butt cheek that looks like a strawberry."

"Really?"

"Huge, you can't miss it. He said his father has one, too, in exactly the same place. How weird is that?"

"Weird." She tried to lift her voice, but she felt leaden.

"You sound like you should go back to bed."

"I think I might."

"Don't even bother trying to write today. You know what you need?"

"Tell me."

"Lunch with the girls. Kate's already called, suffering from anticlimax. Alessandro was up being sick in the night, so poor Letizia barely got a wink. Scarlet has declared that she is spending all day in bed, but the rest of us could do with a Bellini and a gossip."

"And an early night."

"You're sounding like me."

Angelica walked slowly up the road, eyes on the pavement, hands in pockets. There was a cold wind, and heavy clouds threatened rain. She wondered what Jack was doing, whether he was at the airport. Perhaps he was already in the air. Their snatched moments the night before had only made things worse. Instead of fizzing with excitement, she felt flat and abandoned. Life without Jack lay ahead, bleak and long, like the dead of winter. Before she had known him she had been content with her lot. Now she found it lacking; she had tasted the forbidden fruit and found her regular diet bland by comparison.

She reached the house and put her key in the lock. Sunny stood in the hallway all wound up like a clockwork doll. "Is everything all right?" Angelica asked, bewildered. The air smelled of summer.

"A man came round," Sunny explained.

"What man?"

"A man with a van." She pointed into the dining room. "He brought these." Angelica peered into the room and her jaw dropped in amazement. The entire room was filled with red roses. She could barely discern where the table was for the vases of flowers. "Was there a note?"

Sunny shook her head. "Nothing. He just brought them in and left."

She felt her telephone vibrate in her handbag. "It's okay, Sunny. I think I know who they're from."

I will never forget last night. Your loving Dog. I'm afraid the porch is no longer in my vision.

Angelica blushed. "Oh, Sunny. What am I to do with all these flowers?"

"We'll place them through the house."

What will Olivier think? "I'll take three with me to lunch. Put the rest wherever there's a space. My godfather is full of surprises." *Why would my godfather give me flowers? And so many? Think!* Sunny began to take vases of blooms upstairs while Angelica called Jack.

The sound of his voice renewed the intimacy between them, and she was transported back to the night before. She could hear the metallic noise of the airport in the background; he was already on his way.

"You're very naughty, filling my house with roses," she said tenderly.

"I'm glad you got them."

"The dining room is filled with them!"

"I won't get you into trouble, I hope."

"He won't even notice. He's rather distracted by work at the moment. How did you get them to me so fast?"

"I bribed a friend to go to the flower market and buy as many as he could carry in his van."

"That's very resourceful."

"He owed me one."

"Must have been something big to get up that early in the morning."

"It was." He paused. "I wanted to show you how much you mean to me."

"I'm convinced." Love was like a game of snakes and ladders: one moment you're sliding down a snake, only to find a ladder to carry you back up to great heights.

"I'll never forget our night in the taxi."

"It wasn't what I had in mind."

"Nor me. I was going to be good."

"I'm glad you weren't."

"So am I. I'll take that memory back home with me, so on lonely nights I can replay it over and over and remember the beautiful English girl I've left in London."

"I wish you didn't have to go."

"I wish you could come with me."

"Impossible."

"I know. Fools' dreams. You get writing your book now."

"I don't know what to write about."

"Of course you do. Write about us."

"I don't write adult fiction."

"Now is the perfect time to start. You said you wanted to do something different."

"I don't like unhappy endings."

"Then give us a happy ending."

"I don't know how to do that."

"You work it out. You're the novelist."

"Things don't always work out in fiction. Look at all the great love stories, *Gone with the Wind, Anna Karenina, Romeo and Juliet*—they don't end happily." There was a long pause. For a moment she thought she had lost the signal. "Are you still there?"

"Still here," he said at last, but his voice had changed. He sounded as miserable as she had felt that morning. "Give us a happy ending, Angelica. I don't know how you can do it, but do it for me. I'm afraid, in reality, there *is* no happy ending for us."

She felt a lump at the back of her throat. "As long as we're friends, I think I can live with that."

"I'll e-mail you. You let me know when I can call you."

"Mornings," she replied hastily. "After I've dropped the children at school. I'll be at my desk, trying to think of a happy ending."

When she hung up, she retreated to her bedroom and closed the door behind her. With a groan she flopped onto the bed and cried into the pillow. She knew it was ridiculous to cry over a man she barely knew, but it was as if his departure had sucked the air out of the city. There was nothing left to breathe.

14

It is only with darkness that one can appreciate light.
In Search of the Perfect Happiness

Angelica drove to the West End with three vases of roses in the back of her car. She parked in Albemarle Street and made her way down to the Wolseley, situated in the magnificent old motorcar showroom on Piccadilly. With its high ceilings, chiseled arches, and elegant stairway, the restaurant echoed the grandeur of Renaissance Italy.

It was already buzzing with London's most fashionable. Their chatter echoed off the pretty yellow walls and black-and-white checkerboard floor. Angelica looked around for the girls, recognizing a few friends in the sea of faces. Jason at the front desk put down the telephone and greeted her by name, but Angelica had already spotted Candace waving her bejeweled fingers from a round table in the center of the room.

"There you are!" she said as Angelica joined them.

"You look like I feel," said Kate, taking in her drawn features and shadowy eyes.

"You'd better feel fabulous, or I'm walking straight out of here," Angelica joked.

"Let's face it, we all feel pretty rough," Candace conceded.

"But don't *ever* say I look it!" Kate drained her Bellini. "Hair of the dog." She raised her empty glass to the waiter. "Another one for me and one for my friend."

"That baby's going to be break-dancing by dessert!" said Candace.

"It's mostly peach juice," Kate defended herself. "Besides, I read somewhere that champagne is actually really good for a baby."

"Like, what, a Jordan interview in *Hello!* magazine?"

"No, something far more highbrow, like *Vogue.*"

Letizia applauded her. "It's amazing what little gems one picks up in that magazine. Most of them mine, of course. Not *that* one, I hasten to add!"

"Oh, give me a break," said Candace, rolling her eyes. "If champagne is good for your baby I'll eat my Birkin."

"The lizard one that's particularly chewy?" asked Kate.

"I'd even go as far as to suggest the croc—not only outrageously expensive, but totally indigestible."

"Imagine that coming out during a colonic?" Kate suggested.

"I'm sure they've seen a lot worse," said Angelica.

"Like the salami you ate at your twenty-first birthday party," Letizia cut in.

"Oh, please. I'm looking at the menu!" exclaimed Candace, fanning her face.

"Darling, last night was amazing," said Letizia. "I never thought I'd get into karaoke, but actually, I got quite competitive."

"You were the dark horse, Letizia. Your rendition of 'Stand by Your Man' with that husky Italian accent made me want to cry," said Kate.

"Tears of pain?" interjected Candace.

"No, I thought, *That's me.* I could have kicked Pete out, but I chose to win him back. I stood by him. I *am* that song."

"And you deserve a medal after that emotional battle!" Candace smirked cynically.

"I think we all deserve medals," said Angelica. "As much as I love my husband, he can be very demanding."

"There's no one more demanding than Olivier," Candace agreed.

"But he's so handsome," Kate gushed. "I wouldn't mind waking up to him every morning."

"Be my guest." Angelica laughed. Candace raised a thoughtful eyebrow.

"There's more to a man than his looks," said Letizia. "At our age, we get the faces we deserve."

"Which is why I still retain my beauty," said Kate with a giggle. "I'm a thoroughly splendid human being."

"And you have a splendid face, darling," Letizia agreed.

"When it moves," Candace hissed under her breath for only Angelica to hear.

"What are you going to do for Olivier's birthday?" Kate asked. "It's next week, isn't it?"

Of course, she was absolutely right. "How on earth do you know when his birthday is?"

"I have a funny memory when it comes to the names of people's children and birthdays. I never forget."

"So when's mine?" Candace asked, quick as a flash.

"I'm not at my best after a glass of champagne, but if I remember rightly, you're a Virgo."

Candace was surprised. "You're spot-on, but that's not difficult: I'm a typical Virgo."

"Letizia's June twenty-eighth—home-loving Cancer; Angelica's March sixth—typical, idealistic Pisces; Scarlet's August twenty-first—very Leo; and you, Candace, are somewhere in late September."

"The twentieth, actually. I'm more than impressed, I'm astonished you remember anything about anyone else!" said Candace.

"I have a few gifts."

"Well, I'd completely forgotten Olivier's birthday," said Angelica "I don't even have a gift."

"Book a table at the Ivy and say it's been booked for ages," Letizia suggested. "A surprise. We can all emerge from under the table, if it would help."

"Oh, I think he'll be too stressed out to even remember. If it wasn't for his adoring mother, who will ring at dawn, it would be just another day."

"For Pete's, which is at the beginning of December, I'm going to whisk him off to Rome for the weekend. He loves opera."

"Which bores you to tears," said Candace.

"That's not the point. It's *his* birthday."

"That's surprisingly selfless of you, Kate."

"I can be generous." She grinned wickedly. "After all, he's being very generous to me."

"So? Out with it? What did he get you?"

The waiter brought the Bellinis. Kate took a sip, enjoying making them wait. "He's giving me a lot of his *time*," she said with emphasis.

"Not his wallet?" Letizia asked.

"Oh, anyone can buy a girl presents, but not all men are good lovers."

"Now you've got me," said Candace, leaning forward. "Go on."

"Twice he's woken me up in the middle of night. *Down there!*" The girls looked from one to the other in astonishment.

"You're kidding!"

"Wouldn't you rather sleep?" asked Letizia, who needed at least eight hours a night.

"I don't really wake up. I just ride a beautiful wave without ever opening my eyes." She looked dreamy—and more than a little tipsy.

"So what's in it for him?" Candace demanded.

"The pleasure of giving," said Kate sanctimoniously.

"I think *he* deserves the medal!"

In the wake of that revelation, they all buried their faces in the menus and ordered. Angelica felt flat in spite of being with her best friends in the glamour of the Wolseley, having left the dining room back at home filled with flowers. While Jack's visit to London had been in the future, she'd had something to look forward to; while he'd been in the city there had been the possibility of meeting him. Now that he had left the country, all chance and anticipation were gone. Nothing in the future except an enticing mirage made up of their impossible desires.

"Angelica, you're very quiet," said Letizia, smiling at her sympathetically.

"Hard to get a word in when Kate's on form," said Candace.

"I'm feeling a little down, actually," Kate retorted. "Though one would never know, of course. Have another Bellini, Angelica. I'm suffering a terrible anticlimax after my party, too."

"Art's party," Candace corrected.

"Whatever," said Kate. "All that preparation, one blissful night, and blink—it's gone."

"I'm just tired, but I can't complain. It was a tremendously good party." Angelica smiled weakly. She felt as if the slightest comment would make her cry. "I have three big vases of roses for you all," Angelica continued in order to change the subject. "My godfather filled the dining room with them."

"Nice godfather," said Letizia.

Candace was unconvinced. "What's your godfather doing sending you flowers?"

"He's a bit eccentric. He hasn't remembered my birthday in ten years. The flowers, he said, were to make up for it."

"Well, I'll happily take them home. Might tell Pete they're from a secret admirer," said Kate.

"Isn't that a bit close to the bone?" said Candace, but she was looking at Angelica.

"Oh, that's all in the past, and besides, he's not an admirer. Never was and never will be."

"Well, that narrows the field."

"It was a silly mistake, and I'd really appreciate it, Candace, if you'd drop the subject now that I'm preparing to renew my vows with Pete. I have my first meeting with Vera Wang next week, and Christian Louboutin is going to make me a pair of shoes especially."

"Do you need shoes on a beach?" Candace asked.

"All girls need shoes, wherever they are," Kate replied tartly.

"Sandals, then," said Angelica, trying to get into the spirit of things.

"Flats? God, no!" Kate exclaimed. "I won't have Candace towering over me on my wedding day."

"Imagine having everyone towering over you all year round," said Angelica, taking a gulp of her Bellini and feeling a little better.

"Good things come in small packages," Letizia reassured her kindly. "I don't even think Gaitano knows my real height. Mind you, I'm not that familiar with it, either. My heels are almost stuck onto my feet."

"Well, I like to tower over everyone, especially you, Candace. That way I always feel at a slight advantage," said Kate with a grin.

"It's not Candace's height you need to worry about, darling," said Letizia. "It's her tongue."

"Someone has to keep all your pretty little feet on the

ground," Candace replied. "Roses, eh, Angelica? Nice godfather." She gave Angelica a knowing look, and Angelica knew she had been discovered.

After lunch Angelica led the girls back to her car and handed them each a large bunch of roses.

"*Madonna!* These are amazing!" Letizia exclaimed, burying her face in the petals.

"The whole house smells of them," said Angelica. "I'll keep one for Scarlet."

"What's Olivier going to say?" Candace asked gently.

"He won't even notice now I've given some of them to you." But Angelica couldn't look at Candace. Her friend was far too clever not to work out what had really gone on. Candace took her roses, kissed Angelica good-bye, and hailed a taxi with Letizia and Kate, whose long bare legs shivered in the cold. Angelica watched them go, consumed with guilt.

She didn't see Candace at the school gates. The four-by-fours double-parked and jostled for the few free parking places, packed high with luggage for the weekend in the country. Isabel and Joe ran out excitedly, throwing her their book bags and backpacks, waving good-bye to their friends. Jenna Elrich swept up the pavement in a fur-lined cape and cap, her hair falling down her expensive back in a glossy ponytail. "I'm so stressed out," she complained to Angelica. "I've got to go to Paris this evening for a concert in honor of the Sarkozys tomorrow night, and the dress I wanted to wear is lost somewhere over the Channel."

"How do you mean, lost?"

"I sent the luggage ahead, but it hasn't arrived."

"Where did you send it?"

"To the Georges Cinq, of course. Lord knows what I'm going to wear."

Angelica didn't have the patience for this ludicrous woman.

"Oh, I'm sure you can find some old frock in those cupboards of yours."

"That's just it. They're all so last season!"

"Oh, God forbid!"

"Exactly. Carla will be in Chanel couture, for sure. I'm going to have to leave the kids with my mother and go shopping."

"What hell!"

"I hate shopping."

"You disguise it well."

"Just because I always look elegant doesn't mean I enjoy the process. In fact, I positively loathe running around department stores. I've called Selfridges Personal Shopping. They should be able to find me something, don't you think?"

"Have a glass of champagne and let them do all the running?"

"Quite."

Angelica edged away. "I hope you find something to wear and enjoy the concert. Sounds very glamorous."

"No, it's a bore. I so hate traveling."

"The train is rather convenient, I think."

"Train! Dear God, no. NetJet, but even so . . ."

"A plane's a plane," said Angelica, fully aware that a NetJet plane *wasn't* simply a plane but a luxurious penthouse with wings.

"Better hurry. Have a good weekend." She rushed off in her five-inch-heeled boots, leaving a whiff of Dior in her wake.

Angelica called her children. "We're going to have a great weekend," she said, taking Joe's hand.

"What are we going to do?"

"Nothing," she said with a smile. "Absolutely nothing."

As Angelica had predicted, Olivier didn't question the flowers. He was used to her filling the house with white roses and assumed that she had gone a little over the top with red ones for a change. The City was a sterile place to work; it was heartening to come home to warmth, color, and music. He usually hated her scented candles and blew them out the minute he walked into the room, but now he viewed them with a fondness that surprised them both. The financial crisis was changing the world so fast he found himself clinging to the one place that didn't change at all: his home—complete with flowers, scented candles, and Dolly Parton.

That night, while Olivier sat in the study watching the news and chatting to friends on the telephone, Angelica reflected on her marriage. Olivier loved her. Naturally, after so many years of marriage, they took each other for granted, but she didn't doubt that he loved her. Jack didn't love her in the same way. His love was fueled by lust and the allure of the forbidden. She loved Olivier in that deep, familiar way that is no longer aware of itself. Her feelings for Jack fed off the way he made her feel as a woman. She was two people. The woman Olivier knew and the woman Jack knew. Were they to meet, neither would recognize the other.

PART TWO

Experience

15

Darkness serves the light; it is our greatest teacher.

In Search of the Perfect Happiness

It snowed over half term. A thick layer of sparkling white sugar covered the countryside like icing on a Christmas cake. Angelica took Joe and Isabel to stay with Candace in Gloucestershire for a couple of days while Olivier remained in London trying to keep his head above water as the City sank with the share prices. The children built snowmen and swam in the indoor pool while Angelica and Candace curled up by the log fire, drank tea, and gossiped. Candace didn't mention the roses, nor did she refer to Jack, although the handsome South African stood between them like a neon elephant in the room. Angelica knew she had been discovered—Candace had the instincts of a panther—but she didn't want to hear advice; she knew what it would be and would ignore it. She read her texts in the privacy of her bedroom and spoke to him late at night after everyone had gone to bed, sharing the minutiae of their day, their thoughts, and their dreams, but mostly they whispered the sweet nothings of lovers. The deeper Angelica became embroiled in her secret, the further she drifted from her friend, for honest intimacy was the glue that bonded them.

She spent Halloween with Scarlet and Ben Cannings, her manny, the exuberant lad from Yorkshire whom Scarlet had employed to teach her children football. Tall and hand-some, with a thick mop of dark hair and soft brown eyes, he was mature for his age and chivalrous in the tradition of well-educated northern men. He whisked the children into Battersea Park and entertained them while Scarlet and Angelica went to Hamleys to buy them costumes for the trick-or-treating street party they were to join after dark. Isabel wanted to go as an owl, which was the only costume Hamleys didn't have, while Joe was content to dress up as one of the skeletons displayed in every shop window in town. Scarlet's children wanted to go as Harry Potter and Hermione Granger and kill all the witches.

As they left the toy shop laden with shiny red bags they bumped into Jenna Elrich climbing out of her chauffeur-driven car in a flurry of leather and fur. "Great minds think alike," she said, mobile telephone clamped to her ear. "Zeus now wants to go as a bat, and Cassandra has demanded another princess dress. Pink is the only color she'll wear. Thank God the twins are too small to demand anything except chocolate! I hope you haven't bought the last bat!"

"They're all yours," said Scarlet, looking her up and down disdainfully.

"I'm taking them to the Louis Vuitton party. Are you going?"

"Trick or treating for us," said Angelica.

"Oh, I hate all that ringing bells and running around. One bumps into so many dubious people coming into Chelsea to check out the big houses. I'd be very careful if I were you . . . Hello!" she barked into the telephone. "Yes, it's Mrs. Elrich. Am I speaking to the manager? Must go," she mouthed at the girls and flounced off into the shop, leaving her chauffeur in the cold, standing to attention beside the shiny blue Range Rover.

"Well, *she* won't have to dress up. She already looks like a witch with those poor animal tails hanging off her cape," said Angelica, linking her arm through Scarlet's.

"The perfect target for Charlie and Jessica! Perhaps we'd better pop into Louis Vuitton for some target practice before we hit the streets. Let's go and find your owl."

"But where?"

"The Disney Store." She waved at an approaching cab. "If we don't get lucky there, you can always buy her a pretty brown cape from Marie Chantal."

At the beginning of November Barack Obama became the first black president of the United States, and Kate hired a healer to cleanse her house of all the negative energy emitted during the acrimonious years of her marriage. Candace rolled her eyes at Kate's latest fad and ordered another Birkin for Christmas. Having worked for seven years before her marriage in the Ralph Lauren press office in New York, she was well plugged into all the stores and was immediately placed at the very top of the waiting list. Scarlet bribed Ben to move in over Christmas as her children's official coach and tutor, in spite of Letizia's pleas to loan him to her for her skiing holiday over New Year's. And just when Angelica was resigned to never seeing Jack again, her agent made an unexpected proposal over lunch at Sotheby's Café on Bond Street.

Claudia ordered champagne and raised her glass to Angelica. "This is to you," she said, her eyes twinkling with excitement. "And to the successful optioning of *The Caves of Cold Konard*."

Angelica was stunned. "You're not serious?"

"Totally serious."

"Who?"

"The Cohen-Rosh brothers—Stephen and Marcus. They're

the hot new producers in Hollywood. Very now, very happening, *very* cool." She liked to emphasize the important words in a breathy whisper. "Toby will be calling you to discuss the details. I think he wants to tell you himself, so act ignorant. We have *not* had this conversation."

"Fine by me." Angelica's head swam, already visualizing the red carpet at the Oscars and panicking about what to wear.

"On another note, I know you won't go to Australia, but what about South Africa? They really want you, and the book is doing so well out there. It'll give *The Silk Serpent* such a boost." Angelica blanched, which Claudia mistook for refusal. "Before you say no, it would be a week, not a minute more—a few days in Jo'burg and a few in Cape Town. Back-to-back interviews, radio, and a few talks to literary groups. They love you out there. They're a big market for you. Think about it."

"I'll go," Angelica replied steadily.

Claudia nearly choked on her champagne. She dabbed her mouth, leaving red lipstick on the napkin. "You what?"

"I'll go."

"Right, okay, great."

"I didn't want to go to Australia because it's too far. I can't be two days away from my children. But South Africa is nearer and the same time zone, almost."

"You'll love it. The South Africans are so friendly and warm. They'll put you up in the nicest hotels and treat you like a queen."

"I'd like a couple of days at the end to visit a friend." She could barely control the tremor in her voice.

"Sure." Claudia was surprised. "I mean, if that's not too long for you to be away. We can arrange anything you want."

"Research."

"For the next book?"

"Yes. I'm feeling inspired."

"Good."

"I'm going to do something different, Claudia."

"Not too different, I hope. Your readers will expect more of the same, and you don't want to disappoint them."

"I'm writing this one for me."

"Okay." Claudia looked a little anxious, but she couldn't complain: she'd got Angelica to agree to South Africa. "Can't wait to read it."

After lunch, Angelica kissed her agent good-bye and walked down Bond Street towards Piccadilly. Her legs felt unsteady, as if she were walking on jelly, and her head spun. She had agreed to go on a book tour to South Africa. What would Olivier say? How would she manage to tell him without giving herself away? She wasn't a very good actress. This was going to be the lie of her life. Anticipation rising with each step, she found a bench in Green Park and sat down.

The gardens were littered with crispy brown leaves, the sky was a dull pigeon-gray, but she felt as happy as if her heart were flooded with sunshine. She pulled out her telephone and pressed Jack's number. It rang a few times before he answered.

"Hello there, you." His voice was full of affection.

"I'm coming to South Africa."

"My God, when?" His excitement rippled down the line, and she smiled into the telephone.

"Next year."

"I have to wait that long?"

"Only a few months."

"How have you managed to pull that off?"

"Book tour. My agent just told me. I'm going to promote the new book."

"So what are we looking at? February?"

"Maybe."

"February is beautiful. You must come and stay."

"I'd love to." She thought of his wife and her exuberance deflated.

"Come for a long weekend."

"I've requested a couple of days at the end of the trip."

"A couple of days? That's too short. Come for a long weekend. Four days."

"I don't know . . . What will your wife think?"

"It doesn't matter. I want to spend time with you. Where will you be before?"

"Jo'burg and Cape Town."

"I'll come and see you."

"I'd love that."

"I couldn't bear to think of you in the same country as me without being able to see you. I'll pick you up at the airport."

"I'm going to have to work." She laughed at his enthusiasm.

"All work and no play . . ."

"I'll make time to play."

"I can think of a few games."

"Will you be allowed off the porch?"

"I'm already off the porch, darling. I was off the porch the moment I laid eyes on you at Scarlet's."

"Then we'll meet in Johannesburg."

"I can't believe it."

"Neither can I. I haven't told Olivier yet."

"He won't ban you from a book tour, surely?"

"I hope not. But I'll have to convince him that it's really necessary."

"Darling, it is more necessary than you know."

"Not sure he'll agree with you."

"When are you going to tell him?"

"Tonight."

"Let me know what he says."

"I'll text you."

"I love your texts." He paused, then lowered his voice to barely a whisper. "I think I'm falling out of love with you, Sage."

She remembered their conversation by the Serpentine: that you truly start to love someone only when you fall *out* of love with them. "You don't know me well enough to fall out of love with me," she replied softly.

"I feel I've known you forever."

"But you haven't, Jack."

"True, and we don't have forever. But I'm living for now. And at this very moment, you're here with me, and that's more than I could wish for."

She put the mobile in her handbag and smiled to herself, the warmth of their conversation wrapping her in a pair of invisible arms. An old tramp in a ragged black coat was sitting on the next bench. He stared at her, his arms folded against the cold, a bottle of something toxic in a brown paper bag beside him. At his feet a skinny greyhound shivered in a dirty little coat of its own. Her heart buckled with compassion. Aware of her own good fortune and fueled by happiness, she delved into her handbag for a five-pound note. When she gave it to him, he blinked at her in surprise. "You're a pretty lady," he said, shoving the money into his pocket.

"Thank you," she replied.

"I'd like to fuck you." He grinned at her toothlessly, and Angelica's stomach churned in disgust. She hurried away, wishing she hadn't parted with that five-pound note. *No good deed goes unpunished,* she thought as she hailed a taxi outside the Ritz Hotel.

That night she went to see the new James Bond film in Leicester Square with Olivier, Joel, and Chantal. At dinner afterwards at the Ivy, Angelica decided to tell Olivier about her book tour in front of his friends. That way he'd be less likely to refuse her. "Darling," she said after he had eaten a healthy portion of lobster and drunk almost a whole glass of Sancerre, "my publisher wants me to go to South Africa on a book tour in February."

"That sounds fabulous," Chantal enthused.

"It's not all that fabulous. Book tours are really hard work," Angelica replied, watching Olivier nervously. She took a sip of wine and hoped he couldn't see her heart jumping through her sweater.

"I didn't think you wanted to go on book tours." Olivier's face clouded.

"Well, I have to go sometime, and I've said no to Australia."

"I agree: that's too far for a mother to travel," said Chantal. "But South Africa is so pretty."

"Pretty and dangerous," interjected Joel.

"Oh, I'll be perfectly safe."

"I had a friend who was nearly murdered in Johannesburg." Chantal rolled her eyes. "*Mon cher,* everyone has a friend who was nearly murdered in Johannesburg. Being held up with a gun is as common as being accosted by those *Big Issue* people over here. They are on every street corner. But don't worry, Angelica, I'm sure you will be well looked after."

"I don't like the sound of it," said Olivier, having considered it. "Who's going to look after the children?"

"I'll get someone. Chrissie, for example, or Denise—the children trust them." She hoped those nannies who had worked for her in the past would be available.

"Do you want to go?" Olivier asked.

"I'd like to. It'll be good for my career, although I'll miss the children dreadfully."

"And your husband," Chantal reminded her. "Husbands need their wives more than children. Especially French husbands." She gave Joel a playful nudge.

Joel laughed. "I don't like to let Chantal out of my sight.

But what can I do?" He shrugged. "I'd do anything to avoid her sulking."

"I don't sulk!"

He let his jaw drop. "Chantal, you were *born* sulking! If you didn't get your seasonal shopping trip to New York, your face would be in a permanent scowl that no Botox or collagen could cure."

"You're so silly!" She laughed. "Well, Olivier. This is a dilemma. What are you going to do? A girl needs a bit of freedom from time to time. It's good for the marriage."

He thought about it a moment. "I agree. It is good to be apart every now and then. How long will you be gone?"

"I don't know. Just over a week."

He pulled a face. "More than a week?"

"It's a one-off," said Angelica hopefully. Joel refilled Olivier's glass.

"I don't think you've ever been away for so long."

"Which is why she deserves to go. You men are always traveling," said Chantal. "We, on the other hand, stay at home, look after the children—"

"And spend our money," interrupted Joel.

"There has to be some compensation, surely!" Chantal protested. "I gave up a good job to be a mother. Angelica has a good job as well as being a good wife and mother. For that she deserves a break."

"It's not fun, I promise you. But apparently these tours really boost sales, and my next book is out in February."

"It's not the money I care about," said Olivier, whose pride prohibited him from admitting that he might be struggling financially. "As long as the children are taken care of. You can't expect me to come home early to help with their homework. And as long as you are safe. I want you back in one piece, Angelica." He took her hand. She noticed how tired he looked around the eyes.

"It'll be fine. I'm hardly going to be roaming the streets at night, or lurking in dangerous places."

"Perhaps you should go with her!" said Joel.

Angelica was horrified. "And leave the children without either parent?" she exclaimed. "In which case I'd rather not go. Forget it, Olivier. It doesn't matter. Besides, I haven't said I'll go."

It was a gamble, and she held her breath. He took a gulp of wine. The waiter came with their main courses and placed them on the table. Olivier's mood lifted at the sight of his steak.

"Go," he said, picking up his knife and fork. "I'll survive without you for a week or so. At least I won't have to contend with all your makeup littered around the bathroom."

"No dimmed lights and scented candles, Leona Lewis and Neil Diamond."

He raised his eyebrows. "I might even surprise myself and miss them."

Angelica knew she would have to tell Candace that she was going to South Africa. There was no point lying about it. Candace would find out one way or another. But instead of telling her immediately, as she normally would, she decided to wait until nearer the time. She confirmed the dates with her agent: February 7–15, just before half term, and agreed to stay at Jack's vineyard for the last three days.

At the beginning of December, the girls gathered at Scarlet's house for a Christmas lunch. Scarlet had decorated her home with a large fir tree in the hall, its branches heavy with gold tinsel and big glass balls that shone like glittering bubbles amid the fairy lights. On the top sat the silver star Charlie had made at school out of tin foil. The bannisters were interwoven with garlands of holly and berries, and mistletoe laced the door frames. Choirs singing carols resounded from invisible speakers, and a fire raged in the grate beneath a row of cards draped decoratively on ribbon. On the hall table a tray of tall purple flutes fizzed with the finest champagne.

Candace arrived bearing a big scented candle from Jo Malone, which Scarlet placed in the middle of the coffee table and lit. Letizia bought faux-diamond collars for the cats, while Kate had gone to SpaceNK and filled a bag with her favorite beauty products. Angelica bought *The Shopaholic's Guide to Buying Online* and some cookies from Ladurée.

"Well, dolls, isn't this a fine way to spend a rainy afternoon?" asked Scarlet, sinking into the sofa, a glass of champagne in hand. "I love all the presents. Must make a point of throwing lunches more often!" Outside, the wind swept through the plane trees, whipping away the last remains of autumn.

"It's been an exhausting few months," said Kate, who now looked like she'd swallowed a football. She patted her belly that strained against her little Ralph Lauren cashmere dress. "Amelia wants me to call it Jordan. Phoebs says that if it's a boy, he can go back. She absolutely doesn't want a brother."

"Just call the stork," said Candace.

"If only one could put in an order and have it delivered like a pizza." Kate laughed. "I'm bored of being the oven!"

"What does Pete think?" Letizia asked, pulling Taz onto her knee to attach her new collar.

"Naturally he wants a Russian name."

"Very romantic," said Angelica, envisaging Lara from *Dr. Zhivago.*

"Vladimir," Candace suggested in her best Russian accent.

"Please, no," said Kate. "For this one I want a name that no one else has."

"You'll have to make it up, then," said Candace.

"Angelica, you're good at names. Your novels are full of weird words."

"How do you know? You've never read one!" said Candace.

"I read the back-of-the-hovel one in Waterstone's," Kate retorted.

"Caves, not hovels," Letizia corrected.

"Whatever, I saw a whole lot of extraordinary names."

"On your way to the magazine section," added Candace.

"I have ADHD—I can't possibly get through a whole book. Anyway, the point is that Angelica is good at names. She has a wild and wonderful imagination." She turned to Angelica. "Will you think of a name for my baby?"

Angelica laughed. "That's too much responsibility."

"You don't want to get it wrong," Candace warned, drawing a line across her neck with her fingernail.

"Don't be ridiculous," said Kate. "I only want suggestions."

"Which you'll disregard," said Candace.

"Just flick through *Grazia* for inspiration," Scarlet interjected. "I don't think there's a celebrity who hasn't chosen a mad name for her child."

"Like Apple, Suri, and Bluebell." Kate knew them all.

"If you want a name that no one else will give their child, try Jane or Mary," said Candace. "Trust me, she'll be the only one of her generation."

Lunch was in the dining room. They gossiped about the people they had in common, dragging up the same old names to peck at like vultures. Scarlet thought Jenna Elrich's husband was having an affair with Caterina Tintello, having seen them together at Annabel's. Letizia was sure Hester Berridge had had a face-lift, although Scarlet disagreed, claiming that she'd never put that sort of money into anything other than her horses. However, they weren't the only group of women to gossip: London was visibly vibrating with rumor. "I hear that you're going to South Africa," Kate said to Angelica. Angelica was caught off guard.

"South Africa? When?" Letizia asked.

"Book tour," Angelica replied casually, unable to look at Candace. "The dates haven't been finalized yet."

"I was in Michaeljohn yesterday, having my hair cut by the fabulous Enzo, and found myself sitting next to Chantal de Claire."

"Karma," said Candace. "What goes around, comes around."

"Sounds very glamorous," said Scarlet. "There's a fabulous spa near Cape Town—now, what's it called?"

"It's not at all glamorous. It's really hard work, giving talks and interviews. It's relentless. No fun at all. I'm literally spending a few days in Jo'burg and a few in Cape Town."

"Wedgeview," said Letizia. "It's in Franschhoek. My mother went there last year and said it was fabulous. Maybe we should all go with you!"

"A fine idea," said Scarlet. Then to Angelica: "You can pop in and visit your old flame Jack Meyer." Angelica felt her cheeks flush and took a big gulp of wine. "They have the most beautiful vineyard called Rosenbosch."

"I don't think I'll have time for that, sadly. Olivier will only let me go for a week, and it'll be packed with work." She caught Candace's eye.

Candace put down her knife and fork and placed her hands in her lap. "You know what, Angelica, if you want to go to that vineyard, you'll make time. No one ever turned down an opportunity like that because they didn't have the time."

By that, Angelica knew she meant an affair. And as always, she was right.

16

Count your blessings and watch them multiply.

In Search of the Perfect Happiness

Angelica dreaded Candace's confronting her about Jack. But it was inevitable. Candace was not the sort of girl who swept things under the carpet and dissembled when she was furious or upset. Angelica knew she'd always tell her the truth, even though the truth hurt. The only consolation was that her friend had a big heart, and her advice was never for her own selfish ends. Candace was immune to jealousy, secure in her own skin and solid in her beliefs.

The moment came over coffee in Starbucks on Kensington High Street an hour before picking up the children for the Christmas holidays.

"Look, Angelica," Candace began, stirring her cappuccino. "I know you're still communicating with Jack. I've known it for months. I don't mind that you haven't told me. I shouldn't expect you to tell me everything." Angelica made to speak, but Candace stopped her. "No, let me finish. I also know that you're going to see him in South Africa. I have strong instincts, so don't deny it. And I know you saw him the night of Kate's party for Art, and I know you've been texting—and probably calling, for all I care. The point is, I'm your friend, and I'm concerned about you. I can't let you walk into something that has the potential to tear your family apart. I have to warn you because you don't seem capable of seeing the pitfalls yourself."

"I know the pitfalls."

"No, you don't. You *think* you know the pitfalls. If you really knew them, you'd make damn sure you avoided them at all costs. Right now, you're in love. You can't see beyond your desire, which is totally understandable. Desire clouds a person's judgment. But I beg you, cancel your trip and stop communicating with him. This is way more dangerous than you can imagine, in your state of mind."

"Firstly, I'm not having an affair."

"An affair is not simply sex, Angelica. You're having an affair of the mind, and that's almost worse. If it was just sex, I'd say, do it, finish it, and leave it alone. An affair of the mind is an addiction and therefore far harder to quit."

"We're friends."

"No, you're not. Friends want the best for each other. If he's pursuing you, then he's not your friend: he's only thinking of himself and his desires. If he really cared about you, he'd leave you to your husband and your children."

Angelica began to bite her nail. "I probably won't see him in South Africa."

"Bullshit. You've already arranged to see him. Don't tell me that you haven't already told him you're going and that he hasn't already invited you to his farm. What on earth does his wife think? Will she be there? Have you asked? Will his children be there? What will Olivier say when he finds out? Which he will, because they *always* find out, one way or another. Are you the only one he's chasing? From what Scarlet says he has a girl in every town."

"No, he doesn't," Angelica replied quickly.

Candace raised an eyebrow. "Oh dear, you have got it bad. Look, you have to ask yourself the questions: What does he want from you? Where's it going to go? Do you want to leave

Olivier and the children and run off with him? Are you going to break up two families to be together? Is that what you want?"

"Of course not!"

"Then drop it, Angelica."

They drank their coffee in silence while both digested what had been said. Finally, Candace drained her cup. "Are you and Olivier having problems?"

"No."

"Things are really bad in the City at the moment. Olivier is probably terrified of losing his job. He must be beyond stressed out."

"He is very stressed and completely self-absorbed," Angelica replied bitterly.

"So he's not listening to you. You're not listening to him. He's not giving you attention. Look, it happens. Romance gives way to domestic life. That's what marriage is. But you have to work at keeping the romance burning. Maybe you should both go away without the children. Be a man and woman together rather than a mother and father. Remember what attracted you to him in the first place. If your lives are running parallel but not touching, then you have to rebuild the tracks. Olivier's a really great guy, and he loves you. Isabel and Joe depend on you. Their entire world rests on you and Olivier. You break up, the foundations crack beneath them. The simple truth is that you can't have everything you want in life. Duty has to come first when you've brought two little people into the world. It's your responsibility to give them a solid base camp for life. Don't think it isn't."

Angelica sighed heavily. "I hear you."

"You know, we live in a disposable culture. We run a hole in a sweater, we don't mend it like our mothers used to do, we trash it and buy a new one. We want something we can't afford, we buy it anyway, on credit, and pay later, because you know what? We think we deserve everything we want. We think our happiness is a right, like our right to live on this planet. We're the 'me' generation, and it's all about how to make 'me' happy. So we desire another woman's husband, we feel we have a right to him, because our happiness is paramount, and God forbid anyone stand in the way of that. There's no sense of duty or responsibility anymore, and I know I'm sounding like my grandmother, but she lived a more moral life, where she made her vows before God and kept them, whether she was happy or not. It wasn't all about 'me'—but about taking responsibility for one's choices and putting duty before personal gratification. I don't want to preach, but you're happy with Olivier. Sure, he's not an easy man, but he makes you laugh when he's on form, and you love him. Do you really feel you deserve another woman's husband? Do you really feel Olivier deserves to be a cuckold? Do you really feel your happiness is more valuable than Joe's and Isabel's, that you have a right to have an affair whatever the cost?" She sighed and took a sip of coffee while Angelica stared forlornly into her cup. "Selfishness is all part of the sickness of our world. The crazy idea that we have a God-given right to be happy all the time and if we're not, something's not right—but hell, it's not our fault!"

"Wow, you should run for president!"

"I'm good at rhetoric."

"You sure say it like it is."

"I just don't want to be the person who says I told you so. By then it's too late and all the eggs in the basket are broken—and they're such fine eggs!"

"You won't be that person, I promise." *You're the sage, not me,* Angelica thought bleakly. "You should write a book."

"Of course I should write a goddamn book, but I can't write like you. I don't have that gift, unfortunately. Besides, why share my wisdom with the rest of the world?" She shrugged on her cape and hooked her caramel Birkin over her arm. "It's not ready for me yet!"

Candace gave Angelica a lift to school. The pavement heaved with leggy mothers with sheepskin jackets and Anya Hindmarch handbags, and pale-faced children in immaculate green coats and hats, waving good-bye to their friends and teachers. The street was blocked with shiny Mercedeses and BMW Jeeps, solemn-looking chauffeurs in navy suits idling beside their vehicles. Joe and Isabel bounded out like excited puppies and flung their arms around their mother.

Candace kissed Angelica affectionately. "You have a good Christmas," she said, giving her a sympathetic look.

"I'll be fine. Christmas with my ghastly parents. New Year's in Provence with Olivier's ghastly mother and sisters. No texts to get me through it all. No warm Caribbean sea to lose myself in. But I'll be fine. I'm made of strong British stock!"

"There you go," said Candace, smiling. "You hold on to that great sense of humor."

"If I can't cry, I might as well laugh."

"Call me if you need me."

"I will." She looked at her steadily. "Thank you."

"Don't mention it. What are friends for?"

Angelica had no intention of giving up Jack. As far as she was concerned, she hadn't done anything wrong. He made her laugh, and he made her feel attractive, and she didn't see anything wrong with that. So they were falling in love with each other, but they were wise enough to know when to stop, weren't they? And a little flirt with danger was not a crime; it made her happy.

She was relieved the holidays had arrived at last. She never wrote when her children were home, so she had the perfect excuse to abandon her desk. Claudia was in for a shock. She had barely started her new book and what she had written wasn't satisfactory. Meanwhile, sales of her paperback were good and she had received proof copies of *The Silk Serpent*, which had a fabulous shiny snake on the front with bright red eyes and a green forked tongue. She immediately sent one to Jack.

The children were very excited to be home. They played in the garden, climbing the magnolia tree and feeding the birds. She took them to Kew Gardens, where they walked along the celebrated treetop walk, holding hands to reassure Angelica, who was afraid of heights. They made daily trips to Kensington Gardens to give bread to the swans and scale the pirate ship in the Diana playground. Angelica took them for a walk around the Serpentine, remembering the morning she had spent there with Jack and allowing her heart to flood with nostalgia. It was now bitterly cold, and frost hardened the ground and froze the trees into bent and twisted shapes like crippled old men. The skies were gray, darkness came early, and crows cawed into the icy air as they pecked the grass for worms.

Angelica turned her thoughts to South Africa. She googled images of vineyards and dreamed about riding across the veld with Jack, the sun on their faces, the wind in their hair, their cares boxed up and left behind. They spoke often.

On Christmas Eve Angelica and Olivier drove up to Norfolk to spend a couple of days with Angelica's parents and sister. Angelica always dreaded going home but returned yearly out of duty and a misplaced sense of pity. She began to feel anxious the moment they left the city. Her stomach contracted into a tight ball, and she had to wind the seat down and lie flat to stop it from hurting. Isabel and Joe sat in the back quietly playing Nintendo while Olivier listened to Radio Four.

Angie and Denny Garner lived in a bleak gray house on the edge of an equally bleak estuary. They had bought the house in the 1960s when Denny, who would have preferred a big house in Gloucestershire, could only afford a big house in an unfashionable corner of Norfolk. Angie longed to be part of the glamorous set who danced the night away at the Café de Paris. But she settled for her husband's swinging parties at Fenton Hall, where she wore little dresses from Biba and faux-fur coats from Carnaby Street, hopping from lap to lap like a bunny, glass of cheap champagne in one hand, joint in the other. Her hair had been piled into a blond beehive then, her lips pale, eyes heavy with kohl and fake lashes. She had once been chocolate-box pretty. Now her face was swollen with the excesses of alcohol and cannabis, her beehive badly dyed an unsavory orange to match her skin. While his wife had expanded like a soufflé, Denny was as slim as he had been in his youth, though his long hair was now gray and tied into a thin ponytail. For Denny and Angie the world had stopped turning in about 1975. Angie staggered through their tasteless home in silk kaftans and bell bottoms, Denny in high-waisted tight trousers and big-collared flowery shirts from Deborah&Clare, always unbuttoned to expose his narrow chest and gold chains. They still held parties where cannabis cake put everyone in the mood for sex. There was nothing less redolent of the glory days than Angie and Denny's impoverished and meager swinging scene, where the main subject of conversation was ill health and death.

Angelica was embarrassed by her parents. She'd rather die than introduce them to her friends in London, keeping them secret like a stain on the carpet hidden beneath a rug. As a teenager she had longed for them to be like other people's parents—sensibly dressed in Barbour jackets and green wellies, with sleek dogs misting the glass of their Volvo estates. Olivier, on the other hand, found them entertaining and couldn't understand why his wife was so appalled.

"You didn't grow up with them," she explained. "I'd hide

in my room and play music really loudly so I didn't have to listen to them all downstairs. What was acceptable when they were teenagers became grotesque as they grew older. I didn't want to think of my mother having sex with other men. I just wanted them to be normal like everyone else."

"No one's normal," Olivier reassured her. "People present as normal, but really everyone hides some sort of weirdness behind closed doors."

"There's weird and weird—my parents' weirdness is a unique brand."

"Which is why they're such fun. They're originals."

"Thank God He broke the mold after He made them; otherwise, I'd be just the same. Mercifully, I was spared that life sentence."

"At least they were loving parents."

"I suppose. But all children need boundaries. We never had any. I longed for proper family meals at the table and regular bedtime. We just did what we wanted and saw too much. They thought it was natural for children to see their parents having sex."

"It explains why you were so prim when I met you."

"They almost put me off for life."

Olivier grinned mischievously. "I gave you a taste for it."

"I needed an older, continental man with experience." She took his hand and smiled back. "Otherwise, I might have remained a virgin all my life."

"You're too sexy for that. Someone would have snapped you up." He glanced at her. "You're looking very good these days, you know."

"Thank you."

"I'm glad I married you."

"And I'm glad I married you." She pushed thoughts of Jack and Candace to the back of her mind. "We're lucky, you know. What we have is very special."

"I might be a bad-tempered devil sometimes, but I do love you, Angelica. Things haven't been easy these past months, and I know I've been neglecting you. But I've never regretted marrying you."

"I know. And together we have made the two sweetest children on the planet."

She turned to find them fast asleep. She squeezed his hand, and he squeezed it back. In that fleeting moment she saw her life with clarity, as if she were above her body, looking down. Jack didn't belong there. But the moment didn't last. Soon they were motoring up the drive of Fenton Hall and the children were waking from their nap. Olivier slipped his hand away and replaced it on the wheel. Angelica wound up her seat and prepared for the worst.

The car pulled up on the gravel, setting off security lights that lit them up like actors on a stage. Denny appeared in the porch with a cigar between his lips, hands in the pockets of his jerkin. A flurry of fluffy dogs scurried out like big rats, sending the children into squeals of panic. Angelica coaxed them out of the car, bending down to stroke the dogs to prove that they weren't going to bite. Olivier waved at his father-in-law and went round to the boot to see to the bags. Angelica took Joe and Isabel by the hand and led them inside.

"Hi, Dad," she said.

He put his arm around her and planted a smoky kiss on her cheek. "You look smashing, darling. Go and see your mother—she's in the kitchen with Daisy." Angelica took the children through the hall, where a grand piano stood in front of a sweeping staircase and pale green sofas clashed with the blue patterned carpet. She recalled the times she had sat at the top of those stairs watching the parties below. Her father at the piano, a girl on his knee, her mother in a miniskirt and platform boots singing Marianne Faithfull songs, the hall smoky enough to hide where people put their hands.

On the walls were large black-and-white photos of Angelica and her sister Daisy as children in white hippie dresses with buttercups in their hair, big Andy Warhol prints in psyche-delic colors.

She heard her mother's voice before she reached the kitchen. "Well, he's not going to be worth a great deal now, love. You should have squeezed him for as much as you could get out of him a year ago at least." Angelica sighed and stepped into the room.

"Ah, Angelica." Angie left the Aga and sailed across the room like a galleon to press the children to her spongy bosom. Both Isabel and Joe recoiled as they were smothered in red lipstick and Yves Saint Laurent's Opium. "You've grown so big. Look at you! You're adorable. Both of you."

Daisy was sitting at the kitchen table looking pale. "My lot are upstairs in the attic, if yours want to join them. They're playing with Dad's trains." Joe's eyes lit up, remembering the gigantic model railway from the year before.

"Come on, Isabel," he hissed, taking her by the hand. Angelica watched them go, hoping they wouldn't bump into the dogs on their way through the hall. As there was no scream-ing, she deduced that her father and Olivier were still outside chatting.

"Hi, Daisy," she said, kissing her sister. Daisy looked her over in surprise.

"You've lost weight," she said.

"Have I?"

"Yes, you have, love." Her mother appraised her admir-ingly, taking a drag of her cigarette. "It suits you. After all, you have to be careful: you have my genes. Daisy's lucky she's skinny like her father."

"So how are you, Daisy?" Angelica asked, pouring herself a glass of Chablis.

"Well, since I last saw you, which was, what? Oh, a year ago!" She laughed, trying to make light of it.

"I know, it's crazy, but life has been so busy."

"Streatham isn't the other side of the world."

"I know. We should make more of an effort to see each other."

"Ted and I are now officially divorced, but he won't settle."

"I told her, she's missed the boat now. I can't imagine he has much money to give you," interjected Angie.

"He's been made redundant," Daisy informed her.

"I'm sorry to hear that," Angelica replied truthfully. She knew Daisy didn't get paid much as a piano teacher.

"Life's a bummer."

Angelica took a gulp of wine and braced herself for her sister's defensiveness. Ever since she had married Olivier and made a better life for herself, Daisy had resented her. "I know how hard it is, Daisy," she said sympathetically.

Daisy sniffed. "I don't think you have the slightest idea, Angelica."

"I've made a delicious fish pie," said their mother cheerfully, opening the Aga door to look at it. "Denny loves fish pie. I've asked a few friends over for drinks tonight. Just locals. Jennifer and Alan Hancock, Marge and Tony Pilcher. I've always had a bit of a thing about Tony. He's a dreadful old roué!" She laughed throatily.

Angelica caught Daisy's eye and knew they were both thinking the same thing—remembering their parents' parties with horror.

"You look good," said Daisy, defeated by the onslaught of memories that only Angelica shared. "I love your blouse. Where's it from?"

"Oh, Harvey Nichols, I suspect," she replied vaguely.

"I bet it was expensive. I mean, too expensive for me." Daisy fiddled with the buttons on her Gap shirt.

"You can borrow it anytime, Daisy."

"I don't know how that's possible, seeing as we never see each other."

"I gather your books are doing very well, love."

"They are. Actually, I'm going on a book tour in February." Angelica brightened at the thought.

"Really, how wonderfully glamorous. Where are they sending you?"

"South Africa."

"Goodness me! Denny and I went to Cape Town one year when you were little. We stayed in a charming little boutique hotel—it was a delight. I lay beside the pool all day while Denny showed off on the diving board. He had a very sexy pair of red swimming shorts in those days. I wonder whatever became of them."

"Who's going to look after the children?" Daisy asked.

"I have Sunny, of course, but I'll need someone to come and supervise the children's homework. I'll find someone."

"It's easy if you have money. I could never go away like that, being a single mother and having to do it all on my own."

"I don't know how you do it, Daisy. You're brilliant: cooking, cleaning, looking after the children, and working as well. You're a domestic goddess as well as a talented musician. You're amazing, really."

"It's what I do. I don't know any other way. You know, I couldn't have your life. I couldn't get up every morning and . . . do my hair." She shrugged and gave another little sniff.

Angelica stared at her. Once she might have been quietly offended by such an aggressive comment. But now she just laughed. "Well, of course. I mean, my books write themselves. I have all the time in the world to do my hair."

17

Laughter is the greatest healer.

In Search of the Perfect Happiness

The following morning, Joe and Isabel ran into their parents' bedroom at dawn carrying stockings full of presents. Angelica had taken enormous pleasure filling a pair of Olivier's shooting stockings for each child, and the wool was stretched to capacity. Angelica wondered what Daisy had bought her three children and felt a wave of pity at the thought of them opening their meager stockings on Angie and Denny's bed, without their father to enjoy it with them.

She remembered opening her own stocking with Daisy: her mother fighting a hangover with a bottle of pills, chain-smoking in bed in a silk nightie that barely contained her bosom, her naked father on the floor doing press-ups. There were always lots of dogs, and the room smelled of damp fur and Opium. Their presents had been generous. Her mother was extravagant. Denny wasn't rich, but he couldn't deny her anything, and he liked her to look good. And she did, in those days. Her nails were always manicured, her hair in an updo. Her clothes had been cheap, but somehow she had pulled it off. Not a lot had changed. Her father still did press-ups, her mother still wore Opium, the dogs still slept on their bed. Only now Angie's nails were false, her hair badly dyed, the fake tan too orange for her skin, and of course her once voluptuous figure had ballooned so that her clothes had to hang around her like drapes over an ugly table. Angelica didn't want to imagine the sight on the bed and thanked God it wasn't her own children having to witness the pill-popping and chain-smoking and her mother's breasts, sagging like old udders.

The night before had been a trial for Daisy and Angelica. Angie had appeared in a blue silk kaftan that fell over her bosom like a waterfall. Her turquoise eye shadow shimmered from her false black lashes to her overplucked eyebrows, and her lips were pale beige, clashing against the copper tones of her skin. Denny's trousers were tight, emphasizing the un-seemly bulge that clearly excited his wife, for she grabbed it with a pudgy hand and gave a dirty laugh. "Hey, handsome!" she breathed, pressing against him.

"I think I've pulled!" he said to Olivier, raising his eyebrows suggestively.

Olivier caught Angelica's eye and grinned. Angelica smiled back, grateful for his support. For the first time she realized what a unique man he was for not thinking less of her because of her appalling parents.

Jennifer and Alan Hancock arrived first, a mousy couple clearly in awe of their hosts and very nervous. Jennifer sat on the club fender, unable to take her eyes off Denny's crotch, and Alan agreed with everything Angie said, however ridicu-lous. When Marge and Tony Pilcher arrived, Angie was trans-formed into a coy little girl. Her voice went soft and babyish, she pouted and giggled, she even blushed through her tan. Denny stood with one foot on the club fender right in front of Jennifer so that she had a clear view of what he obviously believed were his most significant assets. He smoked a cigar, showing off the gaudy signet ring that sat on his little finger like a Quality Street toffee. His nails were too long to be masculine. Olivier filled glasses with pink champagne and passed around the nuts, observing the party with amused detachment.

Angelica talked to Marge, a sturdy woman who liked gardening. She tried not to look at her father, whose crotch was now so close to Jennifer it was indecent.

"Did you know Trudy Trowbridge died last week?" asked Tony, dragging on a joint and handing it to Angie.

"Oh goodness," she breathed. "How old was she?"

"Seventy-three," said Tony.

"Too young," said Marge. "I'll be seventy-eight in March."

"You're as young as you feel," said Alan, looking at Angie for approval.

"As young as the *woman* you feel," added Denny.

Angelica rolled her eyes, then gasped as Tony gave her a squeeze.

"Then I'm very young indeed," he chortled.

"I'm not even seventy," Angie lied. "You can feel me anytime, darling."

Tony released Angelica and tossed a glance down the ravine of Angie's cleavage. In spite of her cheap hair and copper tan, her plumpness made her skin relatively wrinkle free. She could easily have passed for a sixty-year-old.

Daisy found them all intolerable and went to play the piano. Angelica remained on the sofa a while, listening. She admired her sister. Angelica hadn't picked up her flute since leaving school. She wasn't even sure where she'd put it and, were she to find it, if she'd remember how to play. She exchanged a glance with Daisy and smiled encouragingly. Her sister smiled back; the same complicit smile they had shared as children. But after a few pieces Angelica excused herself to check on the children, not that anybody cared, and Olivier followed her upstairs.

"Bloody hell, I can't believe they still behave like this!

They're in their seventies!" Angelica exclaimed as they walked down the corridor towards the children's bedroom.

"They don't think they're dinosaurs," said Olivier with a grin. "They've all grown old together. To each other, they are the same as they've always been, and I know you won't agree, but your mother was obviously very pretty in her youth."

"I thought I was going to be swept into an orgy when Tony grabbed me."

"I'd never let that happen."

"The old lech."

"I'm a young lech." Olivier swung her around and kissed her.

"How can you feel horny when *that's* going on downstairs?"

"I only have to look at you to feel horny."

"I feel nauseous."

"Thank you!"

"Not because of you, silly."

"Let them get on with it. They are not you. They just brought you into the world. And I toast them for that."

Angelica laughed. "That's all you can toast them for. They're an embarrassment. Thank God I'll never have to introduce them to my friends. Can you imagine what Candace would think?"

"Her commentary would be priceless. But she's your friend, so she would sympathize. No one who loves you would condemn you for having wacky parents."

"I'm very grateful *you* don't," she said seriously.

He kissed her forehead. "Are you crazy? There's nothing of your parents in you that I can see."

"Wait until I'm seventy!"

Now she lay in bed as the children opened their stockings, taking pleasure from being just the family, away from London and all the stress Olivier seemed to bring home with him every evening. She cast a thought to Jack and wondered whether he was trying to contact her. Her mobile telephone had no reception in Fenton, unless she went down to the estuary, where, for some reason, it worked on a small and desolate bit of beach. She had warned him she might not be able to communicate, and right now she didn't mind. Olivier had made love to her after dinner, and she had relished his attention. He had always been a sensitive lover. Afterwards, they had lain entwined, laughing about her parents and their atrocious friends. Then they had imagined how things might have gone had they not been there. Laughter had enabled her to talk about it without the usual stab of embarrassment. Once she detached, there *was* something very funny about Denny and Angie's swinging scene; it was tragic only if she identified with it.

Joe and Isabel were delighted with their presents. Joe's had been wrapped in red; Isabel's in pale blue. Neither could understand how Father Christmas had known exactly what they wanted, but accepted that it was due to the letters they had written over half term and sent up the chimney at Candace's house in Gloucestershire. Olivier lay half asleep in spite of the racket around him. He grunted every once in a while to prove he was awake and slipped his hand over his wife's leg to give it a squeeze. Angelica couldn't remember the last time they had lain in bed like that, all together. On weekends he usually slept in the spare room to get a lie-in. She smiled to herself and remembered Candace's advice. She was absolutely right, of course. What she had was indeed precious—a fragile flame she should do everything in her power to nurture.

Joe and Isabel ran off to get dressed. Angelica lay in her husband's arms, savoring the warmth of his body and the comfort of that familiar place on his shoulder. There was no place for Jack there in the marital bed. At that moment she seriously considered canceling her trip to South Africa and deleting his number from her telephone. It had been fun, but not fun enough to risk destroying her marriage.

After a while she got up and opened the curtains. The countryside was covered in a crisp coating of frost. The sky was a pale, watery blue, the rising sun shining weakly down on the frozen earth. Seagulls wheeled over the estuary beyond the gardens, their cries haunting the wide stretch of dirty sand where smaller birds pecked on debris left by the retreating tide. It was a lonely scene, but beautiful in its desolation, and Angelica stood a while watching it, longing to be able to describe it in her writing. She imagined small creatures emerging from the rocks, long slimy legs striding over the little rivers that ran down to the sea, round bellies as green as the weeds that lay carelessly over the sand, bulbous eyes scanning the expanse for trespassers. Troilers, she thought: greedy, nasty Troilers, and suddenly she had the beginnings of a story. The story she had been trying to write.

With a rush of excitement she rummaged in her handbag to find a pen. While Olivier showered, she sat on the bed, scribbling furiously as the ideas came in quick succession. It was as if a dam had broken, allowing inspiration to flow freely once again.

At breakfast, in a pair of J Brand jeans and a Phillip Lim blouse, she sipped coffee while the children played with their new toys, too excited to eat. Daisy watched her enviously. The lost weight gave her cheekbones definition and her eyes seemed bigger and brighter. Her clothes looked expensive, especially the Yves Saint Laurent coin necklace Olivier had bought her for her last birthday. Daisy scowled into her bowl of cereal. Denny and Angie were still in bed, having practically slept through five grandchildren opening stockings on top of them. "I bought most of their presents in the sales," said Daisy. "There were great bargains because of the credit crunch."

"Clever you. Olivier would love me to be a little more economical," Angelica replied.

"I was rather extravagant before the divorce, but now that Ted is refusing to give me any money, I have to be really careful."

"He'll have to settle in the end."

"If he has any money left."

"He can't squirrel it all away."

"You'd be surprised. I always thought I'd make millions as a concert pianist. I thought you'd be the penniless writer. Funny how wrong one can be."

Angelica didn't attempt to contain her impatience, even though it was Christmas. "You know, Daisy, if you stopped looking at your glass as half empty all the time, you'd find that you are incredibly blessed. You have three beautiful children and a roof over your head. A smile might attract a nice man, and who knows, if you're fun to be with, he might even marry you." She got up. "I'm going for a walk. I'm not going to apologize for being who I am. If you have a problem with me, it's *your* problem. Don't try to make it mine. I've only ever been kind to you. Olivier can look after the children for a change."

"I'll look after them," Daisy volunteered, not knowing how to react to her sister's melodramatic outburst. Joe and Isabel were too busy playing with their cousins and their new toys to notice.

Angelica marched down to the estuary in a state of outrage, to that little bit of beach where her telephone would work. She wanted to call Candace and let off steam. She buttoned up her navy peacoat, buried her face in her cashmere scarf, and thrust her hands into a pair of gloves. A woolly hat kept her head warm, leaving her curly hair to bounce over her shoulders and down her back as she walked. The wind whipped against her cheeks, but it felt good. She inhaled the icy air and felt it burn the bottom of her lungs. The sun was a little stronger now, and she could feel it when the wind relented.

Her booted feet crunched the frost as she strode down to the beach. Besides a few birds, the landscape was dead. It was hard to believe that bulbs slept beneath the frost and buds would later emerge from those lifeless branches. She loved winter. It was bleak and forlorn and somehow extremely beautiful.

Daisy infuriated her. The way she made sneering little comments designed to cut her down to *her* size. The way she only ever saw the negative—what she *didn't* have, *couldn't* do, *wouldn't* enjoy, instead of celebrating her good fortune.

It was cold and damp in the enclave. She sat on a rock and pulled out her phone. At least she was out of the wind. An intrepid seagull approached in the hope of stealing something to eat, but Angelica had nothing to offer. She watched the gull with its long yellow beak and black eyes and thought of Jack. He'd know the name of every bird on the estuary. She found herself smiling as she scanned the sand and sky for others, envisaging Jack with his pair of binoculars and pockets full of crumbs.

She could see her breath on the air as she scrolled to find Candace's number, but before she could finish, the phone bleeped with a message. She knew it was from Jack. Happy Christmas, Beautiful. I miss you. Try to call me if you can. If I don't answer, it's because I can't. My thoughts are with you all the time these days—can you feel them? I'm sending them straight into your heart. Yours always, DOP

Moved by the lonely beauty of the beach and the longing that loneliness induced, she canceled Candace's number and pressed the speed dial for Jack's.

With a thumping heart, knowing she was more than foolish, she listened to the ringing tone. A small part of her just wanted to hear his voice and leave a short message. That small part knew it would be wiser to call Candace instead. But the larger part wanted to speak to Jack and feel cherished on that dull, colorless day. *I'm only going to wish him a Happy Christmas,* she thought.

At last he answered, and his voice, now as familiar as her favorite cashmere sweater, resonated with sunshine. "I was hoping you'd call."

"Happy Christmas, Dog on Porch," she said, feeling warm all over.

"Where are you? It sounds windy."

"Down on the bleakest beach in Norfolk. The only place my mobile works."

"I'm in the garden. It's really hot. I'm glad you called. I miss you."

"I miss you, too." And she meant it, the fire in her heart now rekindled. "You sound so close, like you're right here with me."

"I *am,* in thought."

"If I close my eyes, I can feel you."

"I wish you were here. February is so far away."

"It'll come quickly."

"It had better. I can't wait too long."

"Why is it that time goes fast when you're having fun and slow when you're miserable?"

"Because there is no such thing as time. It's simply a way of measuring one moment to the next. It's all in our minds."

"You're turning into a philosopher."

"I'm morose these days, my darling. I need you here to make me laugh." His voice sounded so flat, she felt her heart flood with compassion.

"Don't be morose. You're in a beautiful place, with your lovely daughters. It's Christmas."

"That's why I'm morose. Beauty often makes one melancholy. It's all transient. Nothing lasts."

"There's always the promise of something better around the corner." He didn't reply, so she continued, determined to make him happy. "Your daughters are growing up, but think of the pleasure in watching them blossom."

"Right now I'm dwelling on the past, not the future. The past is solid. It's happened. No one can take it away from me."

"Focus on the present, Jack. The present is the only reality. Yesterday is gone, tomorrow doesn't exist but in your imagination. Now is really here."

"No, I'm focusing on February and what I'm going to do to you when I see you."

"You are funny."

"I've embarrassed you," he said brightly, and she smiled, knowing she had cheered him up.

"Yes, you have."

"I've never made a secret of wanting to make love to you."

"Perhaps you should have."

"And miss out on your embarrassment? I'd love to see you right now. I bet you're blushing."

"I'm not telling."

"You're lovely to kiss."

"Thank you."

"I bet you're lovely to kiss all over."

"Really, Jack, stop!"

"This is working. I'm feeling better already."

"So it's true, the secret of happiness comes from one's state of mind."

"I suppose it does. Before you called I felt so depressed. But now, with the simple thought of taking your clothes off, my misery has lifted and I'm in a better mood than I have been in in days."

"Don't get too excited. You might get into trouble."

"Anna and the children have gone to church."

"Why aren't you with them?"

"I'm not feeling like snuggling up to God today."

"Okay. I've never heard that excuse before."

"Let's just say He's not in my good books at the moment."

"Now, why's that?"

"For a number of reasons. But I don't want to ruin my mood by discussing His shortcomings. Let's talk about making love again. Where was I? Oh yes, I was unwrapping you like a Christmas present . . ."

After she had hung up, Angelica sat gazing out over the estuary. Her spirits had soared up there with the gulls, and she felt as if her heart would burst with happiness. Right now she loved who she was. She felt deliciously wicked, a femme fatale, capable of doing anything she wanted, as if the world turned for her and her alone. She took off her woolly hat and ran along the sand, arms outstretched like a bird. She relished the sensation of letting herself go. The wind swept in from the sea, cold against her skin, raking rough fingers through her hair. Laughter bubbled up from her belly, and she released it into the air with the furious squawking of seagulls, their breakfast interrupted. She didn't feel guilty and she didn't sense danger. She rode the wind without a care for those on the ground.

18

Move with the current, it is resisting the flow that causes
problems.   *In Search of the Perfect Happiness*

Angelica and Olivier accompanied the family to church. Joe
and Isabel mucked about with their cousins, giggling at the
vicar's booming voice, whispering loudly about the dandruff
on the collar of the old man in front, until they had to be
split up. Daisy smiled apologetically, aware that she was in
God's house, where resentment had no place, and Angelica
smiled back, relieved that her outburst had caused her sister
to be contrite.

She dreaded lunch and present giving. Daisy would apologize for not being generous, then make Angelica feel guilty for
spending so much. Her nephews and nieces would wait impatiently for her gifts, which were always more exciting than
their mother's: another gripe Daisy would add to her long
list of resentments. Joe and Isabel were always given things
they didn't want and had to thank their aunt through gritted
teeth, whining later to their mother, who always left hers and
Olivier's gifts until last, for that very reason.

Later Olivier and Angelica would take the children for a
walk with Daisy and her three. Once out of the house things
would improve. The sea air would sweep away their irritation,
the sight of the horizon draw them out of themselves, and at
last they'd manage to discuss their parents, the shared hor-

ror being the only thing they really had in common. Sometimes Daisy and Angelica could laugh together at Angie
and Denny's expense, but more often they couldn't. Daisy
hadn't escaped like Angelica had; like it or not, Daisy needed
them.

By the time Olivier packed up the car, the suitcases having been in the hall since breakfast, Angelica was desperate
to leave. She was even looking forward to staying in Provence
with Olivier's ghastly mother and sisters. At least with them she
could detach—they weren't *her* family. Unlike Daisy, Marie-
Louise and Marie-Celeste were extravagant and spoiled and
grumpy in the way only the French can be. Olivier's mother,
Marie-Amalie, worshipped her son, treating him like a prodi-
gal prince, elbowing Angelica out of the way as if she were
an unwelcome appendage and not his wife. Olivier adored
his mother, which blinded him to her faults, leaving Angelica alone with her gruff but delightful father-in-law, Leonard,
which was where she was entirely happy to be.

During that week Angelica called Jack more frequently than
ever. The texts flew back and forth, giving her a vital lifeline
to hold on to while Olivier sat chatting to his mother, and his
sisters bitched about their friends beside the fire in the coldly
elegant drawing room. Sharing her stories with Jack enabled
her to see the funny side of her situation. She enjoyed hearing
him laugh down the line as she imitated Marie-Louise snorting disapproval and Marie-Amalie chastising her for writing
books when she should be seeing to her husband's needs. "It
is not right for a woman to work when she has a husband to
look after," she said. "And anyway, who reads them?"

Jack's laugh was satisfyingly loud. "I do," he said. "I've just
finished *The Silk Serpent* and loved it. Even better than *The
Caves of Cold Konard*. Tell her that!"

"I think you're my biggest fan."

"You *know* I'm your biggest fan! I think you need rescuing, darling."

"It'll be over soon, and life will go back to normal."

"I think you should take a stand. No more in-laws. You didn't marry them when you married Olivier."

"You want to bet?"

"Don't be afraid to speak your mind. At worst you'll just offend them; at best you'll offend them so much you won't ever have to see them again."

"I love my father-in-law—he makes it bearable."

"Don't let them walk all over you, Angelica. You're far too nice."

"I'm learning to be nasty."

"Just keep your boundaries strong. Don't let them break through. And smile as if you know something they don't. It always works. A little secretive smile always does the trick!"

"How do you know that?"

"Because my mother has that look on her face all the time, and it drives me mad!"

It was a relief when the children went back to school for the Easter term and Angelica found herself once again reunited with her four friends, at the center table in Le Caprice. Jesus, the charming Bolivian manager, sent them a round of Bellinis on the house, and Angelica savored the sensation of being back in civilization after what had been an extremely uncivilized Christmas.

"Thank God that's over for another year," she said, raising her glass to Candace, Scarlet, Kate, and Letizia.

"You think yours was bad? Do you want to know what Pete gave me?"

"No, let me guess," said Candace, narrowing her pale eyes. "An ironing board."

"No, he gave me a boob job."

"What?"

"He said I might need one after having the baby. Either that or a tummy tuck."

"Did you give him a penis extension?" said Candace scornfully.

"Or a good clip around the ear," Scarlet added for good measure.

"I hope you told him where he can stick his vows?" said Angelica.

Kate grinned mischievously "No, the ceremony is still on. You think I'm going to let him worm his way out of my big day by starting a fight?"

"I'm curious, darling. What *did* you say?" Letizia asked.

"That my body is a temple carrying his precious child."

"Or someone else's precious child..." Candace added wryly.

"No, it's definitely Pete's. No question. Don't know why I ever doubted it."

"A teeny weeny insignificant thing like a date?"

"I'm not a total idiot. So, it could possibly be Mr. X's baby. Possibly. But right now I'm not prepared to go there. I want to have a serene pregnancy. Look what happened when I had Phoebe? Pete and I fought all the time, and she came out in a right state, poor thing. She's still very temperamental. So I meditate daily and take deep breaths through the nose, like this." She placed a hand on her belly, closed her eyes, and inhaled through flared nostrils.

"Oh God, it's the Virgin Mary." Scarlet laughed.

"Nothing immaculate about *this* conception," Candace interjected.

"You're not going to tell us, are you?" asked Angelica.

"No," Kate replied firmly. "Look, I'd happily tell you, but

I have to think of *his* feelings. My New Year's resolution is to put others before myself."

Candace arched an eyebrow. "It's going to be a tough year."

"You'd be surprised how altruistic I've become."

"Go on, surprise us," said Candace.

"I've already turned a blind eye to a text Pete received from The Haggis."

"You cannot be serious!" gasped Letizia.

"She's still hanging around?" Candace was astonished. "I thought she was well past her sell-by date."

"So did I!"

"How did you manage to see it?" Angelica asked.

"Did you sneak a peek?" Candace added.

"*I* wouldn't dare!" Letizia interrupted. "My marriage exists on trust. If I mistrusted Gaitano for a second, the whole thing would unravel."

"Honey, Kate's marriage exists on *mis*trust. As soon as they start *trusting* each other, the whole thing unravels!"

"I think you have a point, Candace," Kate conceded, draining her Bellini.

"I'd love William to get a few sexy texts," said Scarlet. "Then I wouldn't feel so guilty when I get mine."

"*You* get sexy texts?" Kate rounded on her jealously. "Why don't I get any?"

"Really? Who from?" Angelica asked.

Scarlet shrugged nonchalantly. "Oh, loads of people. You'd be surprised. In my line of work I meet men all the time."

"Gay men," said Candace. "I didn't think the fashion world was in the business of straight men."

"I'm talking about the men behind the scenes. They're very naughty! They have my number. It's very easy to flirt that way. I'd never take it any further, but it makes me feel good." Candace caught Angelica's eye. Angelica dropped her gaze into the menu as the waiter came to take their orders. "It's got nothing to do with what I feel about *them,* but how they make me feel about *myself.* Complete, unadulterated vanity," she continued breezily.

"You dark horse, Scarlet!" Letizia was impressed.

"Not called Scarlet for nothing," Candace added. "I'll have crispy duck salad to start, then the chicken," she told the waiter. "No mashed potato."

"So do you want to know what The Haggis said, or not? Soup to start, duck salad as a main course and make it big. I'm hungry."

"Ah, I see eating is a New Year's resolution as well as altruism," said Candace. "*Now* I'm surprised."

"Well, go on. We're listening," said Letizia. "Did you sneak a peek?"

"Not exactly. I mistook Pete's telephone for mine. They're identical."

"Sure they are," Candace commented under her breath.

"Well, mine has a sticker on it, actually. But the ring tone's the same, and he was in the shower, so I opened it and read it."

"And?" said Scarlet.

"What did it say?" Letizia and Angelica asked in unison.

"Hey sexy, you haven't been in touch . . ."

"In touch. That's a good one," said Candace. Kate didn't understand. "Well, surely she meant that he hadn't touched her for a while."

"Goodness no! She's far too stupid to think up something witty like that."

"It doesn't necessarily mean that Pete's been cheating on you since he agreed to stay on the porch," said Scarlet.

Angelica thought of Jack on his porch and brightened at the prospect of seeing him again in only a few weeks. She glanced at Scarlet and knew that *she* could enlighten them a bit on the advantages of texting. In comparison to her, Scarlet was an amateur.

"She's stalking him," said Kate.

"I hope she's not a bunny boiler," Letizia added.

"No bunnies to boil." Kate laughed coolly.

Candace looked at her through narrowed eyes. "You don't seem upset?"

"Valium," said Kate simply, taking a calm breath and smiling serenely. "It's a wonder what a teeny weeny little pill can do for one's stress levels. Really, I've never felt better. Highly recommended." They all stared at her. "Got you!" She laughed, but no one joined her. "Just a joke. You think I'd be so irresponsible?"

"Honestly? Yes," said Candace a little nervously. "At this rate your baby will come out laughing."

"Well, he'll have a good sense of humor if he's anything like his father," Kate replied.

"Which one?" asked Candace, then she added with a chuckle: "Or are they both comedians?"

Angelica picked up the children from school in a good mood. She felt light-headed after three Bellinis, and happy to be back in her comfort zone. She was even pleased to see Jenna Elrich, whose suntan and sea-bleached hair were usually enough to deflate her joy. But her spirit was flooded with generosity, and she listened sympathetically as Jenna moaned about the beach house in Mustique and the chalet in Switzerland, the inefficiency of builders and decorators, and she didn't mind a bit when Jenna told her how pale she looked. She had put Norfolk and Provence behind her and was looking forwards, to South Africa.

When she got home, there was a man sitting on her doorstep in a pair of khaki trousers and a blue shirt. Around his waist was a tool belt. As she approached, he lifted his eyes and smiled sheepishly. "Hi, love, I hope you don't mind me hanging out on your doorstep for a moment?" His accent was East End, as was his affability. He didn't look dangerous. In fact, his face was boyishly good-looking, with big blue eyes brimming with honesty.

"Of course not," she replied, smiling back politely.

She unlocked the door and let the children run inside. She closed it behind her and threw the children's backpacks onto the dining room table. The children ran off to the playroom. Just as she put the kettle on to make a cup of tea, the doorbell rang. She knew it was the man on her doorstep before she opened the door.

"I'm really sorry to bother you, but I'm in a bit of a pickle. I'm a carpenter. I'm working on that building opposite." He moved so she could see the house covered in scaffolding. "Big job, that is."

"I bet it is," she replied.

"Anyway, Steve has run off with my jacket by mistake. It's got my wallet and phone inside. I've been waiting for him to come back, but it's been an hour. He must have gone home without realizing."

"Oh, that's awful. Do you want to borrow our telephone? My husband's upstairs, I'm sure he won't mind," she lied, thinking that was the sort of thing Candace would do, if she was ever foolish enough to let a strange man into her house—which she most certainly wasn't. But this man didn't look dangerous.

"That's really good of you. Look, my name is John Stoke." He put his hand in his breast pocket. "Here's my card." She looked at it. John Stoke, carpenter. *Might be useful,* she thought, *if ever I need one. Which I most certainly will at some stage.* She noticed his hands were big and rough and splattered with paint. "If you don't mind, I'll just call my mobile and see if he picks up."

Angelica showed him into the kitchen, where he pushed in the number. She made two mugs of tea. "Damn! He's not picking up." He sounded desperate. "I live in Northampton. I don't even have money for the train. Would you mind if I call my wife?"

"Go ahead. Milk or sugar?"

He looked embarrassed. "You don't have to make me a cup of tea."

"You're freezing."

"Well, it *is* cold out there without a coat! Milk, two sugars. Thank you." He rang his wife. "Hello, love, it's me . . . I've been bloody stupid, Steve's run off with my coat . . . Good question, he left his on-site, but it's all locked up now. I thought he'd come back once he'd discovered his mistake . . . Yes, I'll get home . . . I'm not sure, I'll think of something . . . Yes, I know it's Robbie's birthday, I'll make it, don't worry . . . I'll call you when I've worked out what to do . . . This nice lady has let me use her phone . . . She lives opposite the site . . . Yeah, I know, I'll tell her . . . Okay, 'bye . . . She says thanks for looking after her old bloke!"

"Not at all. Why don't you call your boss?" She handed him his mug of tea.

"I don't have his number. It's in my phone." He shrugged. "I'm self-employed. I have a different boss every week."

"Look, how much do you need? I can lend you some money to get you home, and you can pay me back tomorrow. You're working opposite, after all."

"I can't ask you to do that! You don't know me. For all you know I might run off and never come back."

"The small amount I have in my wallet won't get you very far, I'm afraid."

"Well, it's very kind of you. I feel bad, but I won't refuse your offer, because I don't know how I'm going to get home otherwise. It's our Robbie's birthday. He's going to be six."

"Same as our daughter."

"You know how much it means to be there."

"I certainly do." She opened her handbag and delved inside for her wallet. "I have fifty quid. Will that get you home?"

"That's more than enough. I'll pay you back tomorrow, I promise."

"I trust you."

"Thanks for the tea. Just what I needed. I feel much better now. It's cold out there."

"You can't go out in just a shirt."

"Oh, I'm strong. I'll survive."

"But it's freezing. I was wearing gloves and a hat, and I was still cold."

"But you're a lady. I'll bet you're not used to laboring outside like I am."

"Why don't you borrow a coat?" She marched into the hall and opened the cupboard where Olivier's coats hung in a neat row. She pulled out a navy one. "I won't tell him if you don't," she said with a grin. "Give it back tomorrow, and he'll never know."

"I couldn't."

"Go on. It's subzero, and it's only going to get colder." She looked outside. It was already dark.

"Well, all right. You're really kind. Not many people like you around these days. People are so guarded. The world is a less friendly place than it used to be." He shrugged it on. "Nice."

"Cashmere."

"Very nice."

She handed him the money. "You go carefully now, and I'll see you tomorrow."

"I look like a real gent in this." He laughed, and she opened the door. "I start at seven in the morning."

"I'll be up. You know what children are like, and I have to get them ready for school. Just ring the bell. If I'm not here, give it to Sunny, my housekeeper."

"God bless you." He smiled at her gratefully and thrust his hands into the pockets. "'Bye now."

Angelica felt virtuous helping out a stranger in need, and still a little tipsy. She called the children into the dining room to do their homework and forgot all about him in the pile of Kipper and Biff books and math. When Olivier returned, she didn't bother to tell him. She certainly didn't want to admit that she'd lent a total stranger one of his favorite coats. In the morning she was so busy getting the children dressed and down to breakfast that she didn't give the carpenter a thought. They were late for school, distracted by the snow that had fallen in the night. It was only when she returned home that she remembered him.

She expected Sunny to mention that he had dropped in with the coat and money. But Sunny said, "No one has rung the bell."

"How strange."

Sunny shrugged. "Perhaps he is over there," she said, pointing to the building, teeming like a hive with builders.

"I'll go and ask them," she replied, already feeling a little sick, expecting the worst, envisaging Olivier's rage. She wrapped her coat around her and hurried across the street. The snow had melted on the road, but the pavement and gutters were still white—as white as her anxious face. She approached a builder standing in the doorway in grubby overalls. "Excuse me," she said. The man looked her up and down appreciatively. "Is there anyone who works here called John Stoke?"

The man frowned. "No John Stoke. John Desmond, but no John Stoke."

"Carpenter. Young, blue eyes. Charming?" She faltered a

moment, before continuing optimistically. "Is there, by any small chance, anyone called Steve?" The blank look on his face made her stomach swim. "No Steve," she murmured helplessly.

"No Steve." He smiled at her sympathetically. "Madam, have you been had?"

19

The outer world is a reflection of your inner, so focus on
the beauty within you.   *In Search of the Perfect Happiness*

When Angelica called Candace and told her what had
happened, her friend erupted into peals of laughter. "Oh my
God, Angelica!" she exclaimed, catching her breath. "What
on earth possessed you to let a strange man into your home?
With your children in the house? Are you crazy?"

"The builder opposite says he's notorious. The clever thing
is he never asks for money. He didn't ask me once."

"But you offered anyway."

"I was being kind."

"I do love you, Angelica!"

"I'm not loving myself a great deal this morning. And
Olivier's going to love me a lot less."

"You're not to tell him!"

"I have to . . . It's his favorite navy Ralph Lauren coat. I am
in such deep shit."

"You know what? I wouldn't tell him. I know I don't often
advocate lying, but in this case, when his reaction is so predictable, I'd make something up. You lost it at the dry cleaner's."

"That *is* believable."

"I'm not sure telling him the truth will do your marriage
any good. Especially when you're about to go off to South
Africa."

Angelica ignored her insinuation. "How could I be so gull-ible?"

"It's not in your nature to be cynical."

"I even pretended Olivier was upstairs."

"So you didn't totally trust him."

"I tried to think what you would do in the same situation."

"You know exactly what I would do. I'd send him down to the nearest pub to ask the publican to borrow his phone. A woman alone in the house with children? You've *got* to be kidding me!"

"If he'd just run off with my money, I wouldn't have minded. Whatever possessed me to give him Olivier's coat? Why didn't I give him one of mine?"

"At least you were sane enough not to do that."

"I'm such an idiot."

"Don't torment yourself! It could have been so much worse. He could have taken the children."

"Now you're really frightening me."

"Good. Now you won't be so naïve again. You can't go around trusting people, just because they have nice faces and seemingly honest blue eyes."

"Do you think he'd been watching me?"

"Of course he'd been watching you. He chose you because he knew you were a sucker."

"I hope he won't come back."

"He's too smart to make *that* mistake. But you have to go to the police and tell them exactly what happened. He's prob-ably working his way through Kensington and Chelsea. They have to catch him before he gets to Kate's!"

Angelica spent an hour at the police station on the Earls Court Road, telling a nice young officer exactly what had happened. It was of little consolation that the man was a notorious thief, preying on the kindness of women like her, who felt sorry for him. The fact that she had lost Olivier's coat remained. However, she resolved not to tell him. She'd make something up when he discovered that it was missing. His wrath over her vagueness was a lot better than the alternative.

She did, however, tell Jack. His reaction was unexpected. He didn't laugh like Candace. His first thoughts were for her safety. "It could have been really nasty, Angelica. You mustn't ever let anyone you don't know into your home." He sounded really anxious. "Promise me you won't do that again!"

"You can be sure of that. I can't afford to lose another coat!"

"Who cares about the coat! I care about you."

"You're very sweet."

"You've got to take better care of yourself. Have you got good locks on your door?"

"I think so."

"Don't be vague and British about this. The world is a dangerous place."

"We live in a very safe area."

"Don't kid yourself. Nowhere is safe. You have to put good locks on the doors, a camera outside so you can see who's there, and don't ever open the door without asking for ID if it's a deliveryman. Don't trust a van and a uniform. They can be copied as easily as a child's fancy-dress outfit. Keep your wits about you."

"This isn't Johannesburg." She laughed, feeling a surge of tenderness towards him.

"I thank God for that."

Inevitably, Olivier discovered the coat was missing a couple of days later. She said she'd ring the dry cleaner's and find out whether they could locate it. "They can pay for a new one if they've lost it," he said, then forgot all about it. Angelica was relieved.

A couple of weeks went by. Now she was able to laugh about it, sharing the story with the girls, who teased her affectionately until Kate told a story about giving two hundred pounds to an Indian fortune-teller on Sloane Street who told her not to wear black on Tuesdays, and knew her mother's maiden name and the name of her favorite flower. Who would have guessed red peonies, after all? He showed her photographs of his orphanage in Delhi, and when she said she had only twenty pounds in her wallet, he informed her politely that there was an ATM machine around the corner. Angelica's story was forgotten, and Kate was back where she was happiest, at the center of everyone's attention.

Angelica began to pack for South Africa. She was so excited, laying everything out on the bed before folding her clothes carefully into her suitcase. It would be sunny and hot, so she packed pretty Melissa Odabash kaftans and white palazzo pants and sandals, and booked into Richard Ward for highlights and a pedicure.

The children weren't happy that she was leaving them, but she had managed to bribe Denise, their old nanny, to work the week with strict instructions to spoil them rotten. She felt a painful wrench at the thought of separation.

The evening before she was due to leave, a policeman arrived at the door. Olivier was home. She was in the kitchen with Joe, listening to him read *Harry Potter*. Olivier happened to be in the hall looking through the post, so it was he who answered the bell. She strained to hear their conversation. Although she couldn't make out every word, she picked up enough to know that Olivier was being told about the carpenter and the coat. She felt the earth give way beneath her and cursed herself for going to the police station. Why hadn't she kept her mouth shut? Joe pressed her to listen. She swallowed her anxiety and managed a smile of encouragement. "I'm listening," she said. Joe read on, but Angelica wasn't listening.

She was frantically planning her excuse. She knew Olivier would be furious.

She heard the door close, and a gust of cold wind blew into the kitchen. She shivered. Olivier stood in the doorway. His face was gray. "Joe, go and play with your sister, I want to talk to your mother." Joe knew something was wrong. He glanced at his mother anxiously.

"We'll read later," she said, wanting to save her son from any disquiet. She closed the book and watched Joe reluctantly leave the room. With a heavy sigh she raised her eyes to her husband. Unlike Jack, his first thought was not for her safety but for his coat.

"It was my favorite. I'd had it for twenty years. Why didn't you tell me?"

"I was too ashamed," she replied truthfully. No point in pretending otherwise.

"You lied. You said it was at the dry cleaner's."

"Yes, I'm sorry for that. I wanted to avoid your fury."

"Well, you only delayed it."

"So I see."

"Why didn't you show him the safe and offer him your jewelry? Why did you stop at the coat?"

"Don't be sarcastic."

He frowned and leaned against the sideboard. "Sometimes you baffle me, Angelica. Your dippiness is sometimes charming. But now it's just worrying. I'm not sure that I can trust you."

The insult struck her. "This isn't about trust. Or rather, it's not about your trusting me, but my trusting a stranger. It happens to people all the time. I'm sure Kate would have done exactly the same."

"Kate would have given the keys to her house. That is not a good comparison."

"Look, I made a mistake. It's only a coat."

"You let a total stranger into our house. He could have hurt the children!" He sighed melodramatically. "Well, I suppose I should be thankful that you didn't hand them over so guilelessly."

"Now you're being ridiculous."

"I don't know that I can trust you where they are concerned. You put them in danger."

Angelica stood up, fists clenched at her hips as if she were about to strike him. "How dare you question my ability to look after the children! You don't know the half of it. You're in the office all day, returning late in the evening in a bad mood. Who looks after them on a daily basis? Who's there to make sure they are picked up from school and fed? Who does their homework with them lovingly, every day, so that they understand their lessons? Who picks them up when they fall? Who kisses them better? Who tucks them in at night?" Then she fired her most lethal weapon. "Who do they run to when they need reassurance or when they hurt themselves? Don't *ever* call me a bad mother. I'm a bad wife, sure, I'll accept that. And you know what? Right now I don't care. I gave your coat away . . . I wish I'd given *you* away!"

Olivier watched her stride out of the room and into the hall. She grabbed her coat and handbag and marched into the cold street. Olivier heard the door slam and remained rooted to the floor in astonishment. When he had calmed down, he realized that he had gone too far.

Angelica ran down Kensington Church Street, turning right at the church to sit on one of the wooden benches in the garden behind. It was dark, and she was alone. The old York flagstones glistened with damp. Not even pigeons ventured out on such a cold night. She wrapped her coat tightly around her shoulders and sobbed uncontrollably. The injustice of his accusation had wounded her deeply, as if he had taken a blade and sliced through the roots of her identity and pride. Joe and Isabel meant everything to her.

When she had stopped crying, she pulled out her mobile telephone and dialed Jack's number. The rings seemed to go on forever, but when he finally answered, the sound of his voice assuaged her anger, replacing the hate in her heart with love. A mental picture formed of Jack on a mountain flooded with light, while Olivier dwelt in a valley of shadow. Her spirit longed to join Jack up there where it was warm and radiant.

"Olivier is the sort of man who says things he doesn't mean in the heat of the moment. Don't begrudge him for feeling frightened, Angelica," he advised after she had told him what had happened.

"He's hurt me," she said, her eyes again welling with tears.

"My darling, don't cry. You'll be out here the day after tomorrow and in my arms as soon as you get to the hotel."

"If it wasn't for my children, I'd never want to come back."

"When you told me the story, you frightened me, too."

"But you were kind."

"That's my nature. I'm not hotheaded. I'm philosophical, and besides, I don't imagine you'll ever let a stranger into your home again, or give away one of Olivier's precious coats."

"He's very proud of his clothes."

"There's no point getting angry with someone when they know very well how foolish they have been. There is no better teacher than experience."

"I wish Olivier felt like that."

"Experience is *his* best teacher, too. I bet he regrets saying that to you. He'll learn to think before he speaks."

"I don't want to go home."

"You have to face him and make up before you fly out tomorrow."

"I don't have the heart to."

"Then take a walk, let the wind blow your anger away. Think about positive things."

"Like you."

"If that helps." He chuckled, and she felt the gloom lift a little.

"Life is too short to waste even a moment being angry. Every second is precious. Go home, wrap your arms around your children—that'll make you feel better. Then wrap your arms around Olivier and make up."

"I'll do no such thing. He should apologize first."

"Perhaps you have to be the bigger person this time."

"I'm not feeling big at all. I'm feeling hurt and furious and very small."

"Not the Sage I know, debating the secret of happiness, talking so fluently about the need to love unconditionally and detach from our egos. If you detach now, your pain will disappear because it is attached to your ego. No ego, no pain."

"How simple that sounds. But I have a very long way to go."

"Perhaps, but you could take a great big leap forward right now and make that distance shorter."

"Why have you suddenly become so wise?"

"I'm only telling you what you would tell me in the same situation. I am the voice of your Higher Self."

"If my Higher Self sounded like you, I'd listen to it all the time." She laughed and took a deep breath, no longer angry.

In comparison to Olivier, Jack shone like a knight in shining armor. While Olivier had exploded with fury and accusation, Jack had cared only for her safety. For the first time she allowed herself to wonder what it would be like to be married to Jack. She didn't attempt to work out how such a thing could be achieved, but she fantasized about it. She remained on the bench a while, arms folded, gaze lost in the dark, imagining what life would be like with Jack. Her visualization infused her spirit with joy. Did she love Olivier? Or was she so used to being married to him that she mistook familiarity for love? Right now, she felt no love at all, just resentment and the desire to wound him back.

She looked at her watch. She had been gone an hour. There was no avoiding going home. Slowly she walked back up the road, head bent against the wind and drizzle. She saw the lights on and thought of the children wondering where she was. Their need pulled her home, as if she were attached to them by an invisible cord, rooted in her heart.

Olivier heard the door close and appeared in the hall looking anxious. His face was white, and his eyes had lost their shine. "Where have you been?" He sounded defeated.

"For a walk. I had to get out." He watched her take off her coat and hang it in the cupboard.

"I'm sorry I overreacted." She shrugged, unable to dislodge her resentment. "I should not have accused you of being a bad mother."

"No, you shouldn't have."

"I didn't mean it. I was just angry. I can buy another coat."

"Whatever."

"I can't buy another wife and children." He grinned sheepishly, hoping for a sign that she had forgiven him, but she remained stiff and unyielding. "Do you want to know what the policeman said?"

"Not really."

"They've arrested the man. You have to go down tomorrow morning to identify him."

"I'll ask him for your coat."

"I don't care about the coat!" he growled impatiently. "Besides, he won't see you."

"That's a blessing."

"I care about you. I'm sorry, *ma chérie*."

She let him draw her into his arms but remained detached, as if she were above, watching him hold someone else. "Aren't you going to forgive me?" he asked gently, pulling away to look into her eyes.

"I'm hurt, Olivier. I can't simply snap out of it like you can."

"What more can I do?"

"You said the most awful thing. I can't pretend I didn't hear it."

His face reddened with frustration. "I wish I hadn't said it. Let's throw that moment away. It never happened."

"You should think more carefully before you accuse."

"I know. I'm an idiot! But you can't fly off to South Africa feeling angry. What if something happens? The last words we will have said to each other are in anger. I would never forgive myself."

She stared at him a moment, as if seeing him anew. "It's always about *you*," she said boldly, empowered by the apprehension on his face. "Everything is always about you."

"What do you mean?"

"I'm going upstairs to bathe the children. I don't want to talk about this anymore. I think a week in South Africa is just what I need—what *we* need. I'm tired of running around you, Olivier."

Angelica climbed the stairs without glancing back. When she had disappeared, he walked into the kitchen and poured himself a large whiskey, leaned back against the sideboard, and hung his head.

Angelica bit her lip, suppressing her guilt. She had allowed herself to drift past another frontier, down the river towards the inevitable waterfall—and she hadn't even tried to grab the hand outstretched to stop her.

20

One often finds one's destiny on the road one takes to avoid it.   *In Search of the Perfect Happiness*

The following evening Angelica was in the plane, on her way to South Africa. She sat in her business-class seat, drinking a second glass of Sauvignon Blanc, trying to dull the ache in her heart as she replayed the parting scene with masochistic fervor. Joe had cried, burying his face in her neck, asking her over and over why she had to leave him. His stricken face and unyielding grip had weakened her resolve, and it had taken all her strength to pull away. If the book tour hadn't been so meticulously planned, she would have canceled, but so many people depended on her now, it simply wasn't possible. And it was only a week. She had pressed her lips to his wet cheek and whispered, "I'll be back for the Full Joe." Isabel had cried, too, but only because Joe cried and she didn't want to be left out. Although only six, Isabel was made of stronger stuff. She was content with her bribes and the fact that she'd have her father to herself. He had promised to come home early every evening in time to read them a bedtime story. Isabel was happy to be left with her father; for Joe, only his mother would do.

Angelica felt light-headed. It was a welcome feeling, masking the bruising caused by her row with Olivier and her parting from the children. She had kissed her husband coolly. He had held on to her for longer than was necessary, hoping for a softening in her demeanor. But her resentment was such that even though she willed herself to be loving, her heart refused to give in, remaining as tight as a clenched fist. Now that she was suitably tipsy, she could convince herself that she didn't regret her behavior, that she had every reason still to begrudge him. The balance of power had never tipped so far in her favor before, but it was a hollow victory. Candace would have said that she had prolonged their row to give her the perfect excuse for adultery. She took another swig of wine and tried not to think of Candace, or to question her motives for prolonging her sulk. She drained her glass, almost convinced that given the way Olivier had treated her, she deserved someone to cherish her.

She ate dinner, watched *Vicky Cristina Barcelona,* then lay flat beneath her blanket and fell asleep. She didn't dream of Jack or Olivier, but of Joe and Isabel, their anxious faces pulling her heartstrings so hard they tore the flesh and bled.

When they landed in Johannesburg, it was early morning, but already the light was dazzling. Used to the gray, cloudy skies of England, she squinted in the glare of the royal blue sky and let the sunshine lift her battered spirits.

Sweeping her family to the back of her mind, she turned her thoughts to Jack. She had told him not to meet her at the airport as the publisher's rep was going to pick her up and take her to her hotel. She'd have time only to shower before having to go downstairs for a lunch event. Although she had an afternoon talk with a ladies' reading group in Pretoria, she had made sure that dinner was left free, explaining to her agent that she'd be tired after her flight and would go straight to bed. Jack was meeting her for dinner, somewhere quiet, but they had arranged to speak beforehand as she wasn't sure what time she'd make it back from Pretoria.

The thought of being on the same continent as Jack filled her with nervous excitement. She was moving inexorably towards an affair, and, even if she had second thoughts, it was too late to stop now; she hadn't the will to turn the tide. It was that sense of inevitability that turned her stomach to jelly. But Candace was safely tucked away on the other side of the world, her voice of reason lost in the great distance that separated them, and she didn't think of her family. She was in South Africa, far from anyone she knew, far from the *Angelica* she knew. Here, she could be anyone she wanted to be and somehow it wouldn't count—she'd step back into her own skin on her return.

As she walked into Arrivals, a pretty, brown-faced girl stood holding a handwritten sign with her name on it. Angelica waved, and the girl smiled in recognition, weaving nimbly through the crowd to greet her. "Hi, I'm Anita," she said, laughing bashfully at her crude sign. "Sorry about this. I wasn't sure I'd recognize you. Welcome to Jozi." They shook hands.

Angelica delighted in her accent. It reminded her of Jack. "It's good to be here," she said truthfully, inhaling the foreign air and tasting in the atmosphere the anticipated sweetness of forbidden fruit.

"You look radiant, considering the long flight. Was it okay?"

"I slept most of the way."

"Good, so you're not too tired for your lunch event?"

"Not at all."

"We're fully booked, which is great. We even had to turn a few people away. It's going to be fun."

They walked through the airport and out into the car park, where the midsummer heat was luxurious. Frothy trees shimmered in the breeze as birds flew in and out of the branches. Anita was cool in a black sundress with red pumps, and Angelica couldn't wait to change out of her jeans into something lighter. They climbed into the hot car, and Anita turned on the air-conditioning. Piles of papers and files lay across the backseat, and at her feet was a bag containing bottles of water and shiny red apples. "In case you get thirsty," she said, handing her a bottle. "Now, we're going straight to the Grace. It's really pretty. I think you'll like it. It has a lovely garden behind with a swimming pool, so if you want to lie out this afternoon for an hour, be my guest. We'll be leaving for Pretoria at four."

"Busy schedule!"

"Claudia made it very clear that you wanted to squeeze as much as possible into these five days. I gather you have children to get back to."

"And an irate husband."

"Oh, he doesn't like you to go away?"

"No. He likes the domestic routine to stay the same. He's very persnickety. He likes things neat and tidy, from the way he folds his shirts to the way I slot into the home, looking after the children."

"Then it's good for you to get away."

"Absolutely." She breathed heavily, savoring the novelty of being unencumbered. "I'm going to enjoy having 'me' time."

"Spaces are good for relationships. You realize how much you miss each other."

Angelica laughed and put on her sunglasses. "I'm not missing him yet!"

She turned her gaze onto the leafy streets of Johannesburg, devouring the exotic sights with fascination. Anita gave her a tour of the city as they drove into the center. What struck her immediately was the lack of people on the pavements. There were no mothers pushing prams, no joggers on the way to the park, no dog walkers. Houses hid behind tall, forbidding walls fitted with spikes and alarms; security guards stood at the gates, suspicious and watchful. No one seemed very keen to get out and enjoy the frothy plane trees and rampant bougainvillea.

"There's a terrible problem with crime. Everyone has a story to tell. It's very sad, and it's not getting any better. The only thing you can do is fortify your house so it's as safe as a castle. If you're a woman on your own, you don't drive at night, and if you do, you don't stop. Not even at robots."

"Robots?"

"Traffic lights." She laughed. "I know, foreigners always find that funny."

"So life goes on in people's houses?"

"Behind those walls you will find some of the most beautiful homes you have ever seen. Luscious gardens with palm trees and swimming pools, bright flowers and exotic birds. They live well. But for all that, they sacrifice their freedom."

"Is it worth it? Why don't the rich move somewhere safer?"

"Because their friends are here. Their lives are here. The climate is perfect. But don't forget, we can't take much money out, and Europe is very expensive. If you're wealthy, what can you do? Leave it all behind and start again?"

"Is Cape Town as bad?"

"No, Cape Town has less crime. It has a more European feel, being on the sea. I'd prefer to live there, but my work is here, so I have no choice."

"But there's still a problem with crime?"

"Wherever you get a vast divide between rich and poor, you're going to get crime."

"And in the countryside?"

"It's everywhere. You have to be constantly vigilant. For us, it's second nature. Talking of which, don't wear those rings."

Angelica glanced at her diamond engagement ring and diamond eternity ring. "Really?"

"Unless you want your finger sliced off." Anita watched her blanch. "Don't panic, you can wait until you get to the hotel. But then I'd put them away somewhere safe."

"I've never taken them off."

"No time for sentimentality. Better to be safe than sorry." Angelica toyed with them. *I'll put them back on with my skin.* But somehow, removing her wedding ring felt worse than removing her skin.

They arrived at the Grace Hotel through a shopping mall. "Safer than walking outside," Anita said, and after their conversation about crime, Angelica was grateful. The mall was busy with shoppers, like an ant colony where all the action takes place underground. Sweeping her eyes over the shop fronts, she thought she'd rather spend the afternoon there than lying by the pool, burning. "There's a really good African market around the corner. If you like, I'll take you there this afternoon. Full of jewelry and fabrics. It's quite touristy, but you can haggle and get the prices down. There are some really nice things, once you get your eye in."

The Grace was an elegant, old-fashioned hotel with comfy red sofas, gilt mirrors, mahogany furniture, and brass fittings. Angelica was reminded of London. They checked in swiftly, and Anita left her with the porter. "You have an hour or so to relax. I'll call you from here when it's time to come down." Angelica was happy to be left on her own in her room. She tipped the young man, who smiled appreciatively, left her suitcase on the luggage rack, and departed. The room was tasteful and airy, with tall windows, pale green walls, a king-size bed, and a mahogany desk. They obviously valued her highly to put her in such a grand hotel. She went to the telephone to call Olivier. She longed for news of the children. But as she picked up the receiver she felt her resentment resurface. In spite of wanting to hear news of Joe and

Isabel, she didn't feel ready to speak to her husband. She put the receiver down and went into the marble bathroom for a shower. She'd leave Olivier to stew and call Jack instead.

Any doubts about her intentions were carried away with the soap. She closed her eyes and let Jack's broad face surface in her mind. She found herself smiling with guilty anticipation at the prospect of kissing him again. She could almost feel his bristles on her skin, his breath on her neck, and his big arms around her body. After showering, she sat in her towel and took off her rings. They were not easily removed, and she had to twist and turn and pull. With a sigh of resignation she slipped them into the pocket of her wash bag. Her hand looked naked without them, but she felt free.

She switched on her mobile and reluctantly sent a text to Olivier with the hotel telephone number, adding that he wasn't to call her as she was busy at an event. Jack had called three times. She pressed redial. It rang only once before he answered. "There you are!" His voice was so cheerful she forgot all about Olivier.

"At last."

"At the Grace?"

"Right here."

"I can't believe you're in the same city as me."

"Neither can I."

"So you've got this lunch event."

"Here at the hotel."

"Then what?"

"Nothing until four, when I have to go to Pretoria for a teatime event."

"Then dinner with me." She sensed his grinning into the telephone.

"Dinner with you."

"I don't think I can wait that long."

"Well, you have to."

"My God, you're here in Johannesburg. It feels so surreal."

"It's beautiful."

"It is now, because you're in it."

She laughed, embarrassed. "You are funny!"

"What's your room number?"

"Two-o-seven."

"I'll call you this afternoon."

"I can't wait."

"Neither can I." He seemed in a hurry to go. Reluctantly, she hung up.

Her spirits high with excitement, she rummaged in her case for something to wear, pulling the contents onto the carpet, where they remained in an untidy heap. She chose a duck-egg-blue sundress from Heidi Klein and wedge espadrilles. Her skin glistened with body oil and an abundance of Stella McCartney rose and amber eau de toilette, and she scrunched her hair dry so that it fell over her shoulders in thick curls. In spite of the creases on her dress she was pleased with her appearance. She waited for Anita to ring from downstairs. Looking at her watch, she had twenty minutes to kill. She went and stood at the window, looking out onto the sunny gardens below, smiling at the small birds that played merrily among the trees and gardenia bushes.

The sound of the doorbell made her jump. Expecting Anita, she strode over to open it. To her astonishment, Jack stood in the corridor like a shaggy brown bear, his mouth curled into a triumphant smile.

"I couldn't wait," he said, taking her in with one greedy sweep of his eyes. Before she could reply, he pulled her into his arms, shuffled into the room, and closed the door behind him. "My God, you smell delicious." He buried his face in the crook of her neck and inhaled hungrily. Angelica laughed with delight, then gave in to the sensual feeling wash-ing over her like a tide of warm honey. Her legs weakened and she felt her stomach lurch, as if plummeting from a great height.

He placed his lips on hers, and she felt his bristles scratch her chin, then the warm, wet sensation as he parted her lips with his tongue. She forgot about Anita and the lunch event as he unzipped her dress and ran his hands up her back and around to her breasts, caressing her nipples with his thumbs. She let out a low moan and threw her head back. Her dress floated down to her feet, where it remained like a blue pool around her ankles. Before her legs gave way, he lifted her in his arms and carried her to the bed. For once her mind was lost for words, neither condemning nor justifying her infidelity. It remained empty and detached, allowing a sensual wave to wash her into a transient paradise where it was just her and Jack, at liberty to love each other.

He took off his glasses and placed them on the bedside table. She laughed. "Can you see me?"

His eyes looked bigger without them, the color richer, with a shade of sage green making them almost gray. "My sense of touch is more than enough to satisfy my need to savor you." Gently, he brushed her hair off her face, tenderly kissing her forehead, her temples, her cheeks, and her chin, tracing her jawline with his tongue. While he played with her ear his hand stroked her belly and hips, moving down to her thighs and over her silky Calvin Klein panties. She closed her eyes, parted her legs, and invited him in with a wantonness that surprised her. With an ecstatic sigh she was swept over the final frontier.

A little later, the telephone brought them back to reality with a jolt. They lay entwined, their naked limbs thrown over each other casually, hearts slowly decelerating with their breathing. "That's my call for lunch," she whispered with a laugh. "How do I look?"

"Glowing." He pressed his lips to hers with a smile. "Shame you have to go. I could do that all over again."

"We have an hour this afternoon." She sat up and picked up the telephone. "I'll be down in a minute," she told Anita.

"I can think of a lot of mischief we can get up to in one hour."

"That was pretty good for twenty minutes."

"Tonight, I'll take my time."

She got up and hurried into the bathroom, picking up her dress on the way. When she saw her reflection, she laughed throatily. Her hair was wild, her cheeks raw, her mascara smudged beneath her eyes. She washed herself with a flannel, repaired her makeup, and sprayed another cloud of scent across her chest. When she emerged, Jack was already dressed in a biscuit-colored suit with an open-necked blue shirt. "You look smart," she said, walking over to kiss him again. "I was so shocked to see you, I didn't notice."

"I've got a grand lunch to go to."

"Oh?"

"There's a really hot speaker who's come all the way over from London just to talk to us."

She narrowed her eyes. "You're not coming to *my* talk, are you?"

"Believe me, there's only one hot speaker in the whole of Johannesburg."

"You can't!"

"Why not?"

"There isn't room for you. It's fully booked."

"I know. I must have been the last person to get a ticket."

"How?"

He shrugged. "I'm your cousin."

"My cousin?" She looked incredulous.

"They have to make space for family."

"You're going to distract me."

"I hope so. I'd be very put out if I'd gone to all that trouble not to have any effect at all."

"Now I'm really nervous."

"Don't be. I'm your biggest fan, and besides, I've read *The Silk Serpent,* which is more than can be said for the rest of the guests downstairs."

"They can buy their copies today."

"And they will, when I tell them what a work of genius it is." He pulled her into his arms and kissed her again.

Anita was waiting in the lobby downstairs. They walked out of the lift together as if it was the most natural thing in the world. "This is Jack Meyer, my cousin," said Angelica. Anita shook his hand, but she was more concerned with getting her author to the event on time.

"Everyone's here waiting. Let's go." Angelica caught Jack's eye and grinned.

"Good luck," he said. "I'll put up my hand and ask the first question."

"That would be really helpful," said Anita. "People are often a little shy."

"Not in Johannesburg," said Jack.

"Well, that's true. We're a pretty outspoken lot. But still, it'll be good to get the ball rolling."

The dining room was full of eager-looking children with their parents and grandparents. Jack and Angelica were immediately separated. Anita led Angelica into the crowd to meet her fans, while Jack wandered over to the other side of the room, where he stood by the window, watching her. She felt his eyes upon her like the sun, and once or twice raised hers to lock comfortably into his gaze like a sunflower that automatically finds the light. *This is what it would be like if I had another life,* she thought, staring at the handsome man who, only moments ago, had been making love to her. She pulled away and turned her smile on the children, thanking them for coming out to meet her on a Sunday, shaking hands with their parents, who told her how they had read *The Caves of Cold Konard,* too, and couldn't put it down. All the while she was fizzing inside because Jack was there, in the same room, breathing the same air.

21

Joy is not in things; it is in us.

In Search of the Perfect Happiness

Later that afternoon, Angelica lay in Jack's arms on the hotel bed, her naked body pressed against him, her leg wedged comfortably between his. They molded together perfectly, like intertwining branches of a gum tree. She didn't feel guilty. It felt so natural, and they were so far from her London life and the risk of getting caught. It wasn't hard to pretend she was single again.

Her talk had been a success. Jack had been true to his word and asked the first question. She had struggled to maintain her composure as the room had grown quiet and everyone had turned their attention to her. She was barely aware of what he asked, so distracted by his charisma that lit him up like some supernatural being—or perhaps it had been the sunlight streaming through the French doors behind him that had made it almost impossible to see him but in silhouette: his shaggy, unkempt hair framing his darkened face, his imposing stature that dwarfed the two women sitting on either side of him, the granular tone of his voice that resonated with the intimacy of their lovemaking. She was filled with gratitude that, for the moment at least, this leonine man belonged to her.

Marjory Millhaven, who had organized the event, clapped

her hands exuberantly, announcing to everyone that Jack was the speaker's cousin. A shadow of anxiety had passed across his face as the entire room had strained to get a better look at him. A few young mothers had tittered appreciatively, and Angelica had hastily answered his question, moving swiftly on to the next. So pleased was she with her lunch that Marjory was reluctant to let Angelica go, insisting at every attempted departure that she stay another ten minutes. Aware that the clock was gnawing through her afternoon with Jack, she hastily signed more books, talked to each child who approached her, and finally extricated herself by promising to come back another year.

"You were a real pro today," Jack said, running his fingers through her hair. "As your cousin, I was very proud."

"You were brave to come."

"I know. South Africa is a small place. There was a chance I might have known someone, but I didn't."

"What would you have done?"

"Pretended you were my cousin," he replied nonchalantly, as if it really wasn't such a big deal.

"Does your wife know you're here?"

"Yes, and she knows I'm taking you out for dinner."

Angelica was astonished. "She doesn't mind?"

"You're my friend."

"Do you sleep with all your friends?"

"Only you." He kissed her forehead. "I can't lie to her."

"So you've told her how you feel about me?"

"No, she hasn't asked."

"But if she did ask, what would you tell her?"

"She won't. She respects my boundaries."

"Isn't she at all possessive?"

"We've been married twenty years. She knows me well enough to give me my freedom."

"She sounds extraordinary. Do you offer her the same freedom?"

"She doesn't require it." He sounded like Olivier. Were all men such hypocrites?

She sat up to challenge him. "So it's all right for you to have an affair, but not for her?"

"She doesn't want one."

"How do you know?"

"I know."

"You have a very peculiar relationship."

"You'll understand when you meet her. She's unique."

Angelica had no desire to meet her. "Are you sure it's a good idea?" she asked, seeking reassurance.

He pulled her back into his embrace and squeezed her. "Are you crazy? You're coming to Rosenbosch whether you want to or not. Don't think about Anna." Sensing her unease, he added: "Live in the moment, Angelica. Leave my marriage to me."

Angelica tried not to think about Anna as she sat in the car with Anita on the way to Pretoria. The traffic was heavy on the highway, shantytowns quivering in the heat and close enough for her to get a stirring sense of their poverty. Anita told her about the history of her country, what it was like living under apartheid, and the positive future she so passionately believed in. Angelica made all the right noises, half listening, half replaying the stolen hour she had enjoyed with Jack. She knew she should telephone Olivier, if only to put him out of his misery. Perhaps she had been unfair to treat him so coolly. But Joe would want to talk to her, and she dreaded hearing his voice, knowing it would drag her back to the reality she had so deliberately left behind. While she was removed from her family, she felt disconnected, as if she were living another woman's life.

Anita parked the car in the parking lot, bribing the attendant to watch it, as was the custom.

"What would happen if you didn't pay him?" Angelica asked, following her towards the restaurant.

"He'd probably steal it himself!" She laughed.

The restaurant was a log cabin. Angelica took a deep breath, bracing herself for another talk. But as she stepped into the foyer she was transported into the world of Cold Konard. The lights were dimmed and the walls decorated to look like the inside of a cave, hung with extravagant garlands of fake green weeds and purple and red crystals the size of footballs. She peered into the dining room, which had been cleared for what was obviously a children's tea party. About fifty children were running around in fancy dress—as Mart and Wort, Yarnies, Elrods, Mearkins, and Greasy Grouchoes.

She laughed with delight. "This is how it must feel to be J. K. Rowling," she said to Anita as an oversize Wort strode over to welcome her.

"I'm Heather Somerfield, or Wort," she said, snorting in amusement at her effort to dress in character.

"You look terrific!" said Angelica, though the Wort she had invented was a five-foot elf, not a monumental egg. "I'm so flattered by all the trouble you've gone to."

"The children love you. They're so excited you're coming. And so are we. I wanted to dress up as a Mearkin, but they don't make green leotards in my size."

"You look great as Wort."

"Come and meet the children. There are some more convincing Worts in there." She marched into the dining room and clapped her hands like a headmistress. "Girls and boys, it gives me great pleasure to introduce Angelica Garner, the author of *The Caves of Cold Konard*." The squeals petered out as the children stopped their games and stared at her shyly. Angelica wished she had come in costume. It was clear that the talk she had planned for a ladies' reading group would not be appropriate here. She'd lose their attention in the first sentence, and it would be horribly embarrassing. "So, Angelica, what would you like to do?" Heather looked at her expectantly.

Good question . . . what indeed? Angelica thought anxiously. She gazed back at the fifty pairs of painted eyes and hesitated momentarily. They all looked so keen and expectant, waiting for her to speak. But she couldn't talk about inspiration to a group of small children who had all made the effort to dress up. They required enchantment. She peered through the fog in her mind, trying to find something to grasp. Then, as if by magic, the fog lifted, and her mind was clear.

"I want them all to sit around me," she said excitedly. "I have a story to tell."

"A chair, Megan, now now," instructed Heather to a celery-thin Mearkin. Megan hurried over with a chair and placed it in the middle of the room. Both women gently pushed the children forwards. They shuffled towards her and sat down in a semicircle, nudging one another and whispering behind hands.

Angelica leaned forwards and lowered her voice dramatically. "Have any of you heard of Troilers?" The children shook their heads. The whispering ceased. "Fat, slimy, ugly, greasy Troilers, who inhabit the estuary where an oily black river meets the sea. These Troilers, who live in holes in the banks of the river, eat creatures of light called Dazzlings. Beautiful, ethereal, weightless creatures, without whom the world would descend into the hands of these evil Troilers. The more Dazzlings they eat, the stronger and more powerful they become and the darker the sky grows as, little by little, all the light in the world is consumed. So the Dazzlings need help, and who better than Conner and Tory Threadfellow of London. Why them? you might ask. Especially as they are humans and the only way to get to this plane of existence, which is here, around us all the time, is in dreams. Well, let me enlighten you on how it is done and why two children—oh yes, they have to be children—are the only people in the whole world who have it in their power to restore the Dazzlings and their light . . ."

The children stared unblinking as Angelica wove the tale she had conceived in Norfolk. She was astonished at how fluidly her ideas came to her and how clearly she saw them, like gazing through a limpid pond into a magical world below. It was as if it had always been there, only before the water had been cloudy.

Heather and Megan sat drinking tea at a round table, as enraptured as the children. Anita caught her eye and shook her head, incredulous that she was capable of weaving such a tale off the cuff. Angelica felt her imagination released at last and propelled into vibrant color. Her spirits soared. The more the children responded, the more ideas came. She had her story. It was simple and so obvious, and yet her own apathy had prevented her from seeing it.

At the end the children remained seated, hoping for more. The celery Mearking and egg-shaped Wort thanked Angelica, and the whole room erupted into applause. She glanced around to find the doorway filled with restaurant staff and parents.

"What a wonderful story you have shared with us today," said Heather, her cheeks rosy beneath the face paint. "I hope that's a little taster for the next book?" She raised an eyebrow, and Angelica nodded. "Oh good!" She clapped her hands again. "We're very fortunate to have lots of copies of Angelica's new book, *The Silk Serpent,* which she has agreed to sign. And I'm glad to see some parents over there who have money to pay for them!" She snorted again and showed Angelica to a table and chair in the corner that had been set up for her to sign books. "Would you like a cup of tea?"

"I'd love one," said Angelica, sitting down. She rummaged unsuccessfully in her bag for a pen.

"Megan? A cup of tea for Angelica, now now."

Megan returned with a cup of tea and a pen, and Angelica signed books and chatted with the children. They had all lost their shyness and found a great deal to say. The party continued, and trays of sandwiches and pretty pastel cupcakes were brought in. Angelica sipped her tea, light-headed with all the compliments. She felt the warm glow of success and basked in it. The prospect of spending the night with Jack just added to the surreal charm of the day.

"So what are you going to do tonight?" Anita asked as they drove back towards the city. The evening light had mellowed into a soft, amber glow, settling over the buildings like a diaphanous veil.

"My cousin is taking me out for dinner."

"Jack? He's very handsome. Is he married?"

"Yes. He has three children. They live on a vineyard in Franschhoek. I'm going to stay the weekend at the end of my tour."

"Oh, that's where you're going. I knew you were off somewhere. You'll love Franschhoek; it's really beautiful."

"I'm looking forward to it." Once again she nudged Anna to the back of her mind.

"Do you ride?"

"It's been a while. But hopefully it's like riding a bicycle—you never forget."

"I'm glad you're having time to see a bit of our countryside while you're here."

"Oh, I couldn't just dip in and out, and family's family. I couldn't leave without spending time with Jack."

Anita dropped her off outside the hotel, and she hurried up the steps, two at a time. A pair of uniformed doormen opened the doors, and she burst into the foyer, where Jack stood up to meet her. He dropped his newspaper on the coffee table and grinned broadly, striding towards her. She ran into his embrace without a care for who might be in the room. He kissed her ardently, enchanted by her enthusiasm.

"How did it go?"

"It was amazing. All the children had dressed up as my characters, and they had decorated the restaurant like a big, slimy cave. They had gone to so much trouble."

"Wow! You've hit the big time."

"I'm a big fish in a teacup."

"Better than no fish."

"I'm a *hungry* fish." She noticed he had changed out of his suit into a pair of jeans and a green polo shirt. "Where are you staying?"

"Here."

"No, I mean, where have you put your things?"

"Here." He shrugged casually. "I've taken a room here, too."

"You've got it all planned, haven't you!"

"A dog needs to know where he's going to lay his head at night."

"But you know you're laying it next to mine."

"I wasn't sure you'd want me to."

"After London?"

"Well, I wasn't going to take you for granted."

"That's very gallant of you."

"Of course. I've managed to entice you here—the last thing I want to do is scare you away."

He led her into the street, where a taxi awaited them. The sun had dipped behind the buildings, leaving a gentle heat. The African driver got out to open the door, and they climbed in. Jack took her hand. The way he looked at her was almost bashful.

"I'm very happy you're here, Angelica Garner."

"I'm happy to be here, Jack."

"I never believed you'd come."

"It was a fluke."

"Or destiny."

"Perhaps."

"I can't really believe you've pulled it off. I dreamed of this, but never expected it to come true."

"Dreams so often don't."

"Have you made up with Olivier?"

"No, I'm still angry with him." She shuffled closer. "Let's not talk about Olivier, or Anna, or our children. Let's enjoy this short time we have together. I want to enjoy being this fabulous woman I am when I'm with you."

"Do I make you feel fabulous?"

"Yes, I feel sensual, liberated, witty, sexy, *alive*. I feel bigger and better than I do when I'm me."

"You're still *you*, my darling," he said, laughing at her exuberance. "You are all of those things. They have always been part of you. If you focus on your right arm hard enough, you forget that your left arm exists. That's all it is. You're focusing so hard on being Angelica that you've failed to notice the Sage beneath."

"You've brought her out. Imagine how many people go through life without discovering all that they can be."

"We all have the potential to be many things. But life might not necessarily give us the opportunity to play those parts."

"I'm glad it's given me the opportunity to play *this* part, even if it's just for a week."

"The secret to happiness is living in the moment."

"I know," she teased, rolling her eyes. "It's all there is."

Jack took her to a cozy little restaurant in the center of town. It didn't matter if he bumped into someone he knew for he had already told his wife he was going to take her out for dinner. Angelica didn't understand their marriage. Surely, no self-respecting wife would allow her husband to fly to another city to take a woman out for dinner. She wondered what story he had concocted and how easily she had swallowed it.

They sat at a table in the corner. The restaurant was full of color. In London women wore so much black; in Johannesburg they were like fine birds of paradise, in turquoises, oranges, and reds. She sipped her wine and gazed at him across the candlelight.

He smiled at her from behind his glasses, his eyes full of affection. "Are you happy?"

She sighed with pleasure. "Very."

"Because you're living in the moment, at last."

"I don't want it to end."

"That's very female."

"What? Wanting a moment to last forever? Don't you?"

"Yes. I love life. I want to live forever. I have a very strong feminine side."

"Yes. I remember now. *A life without love is like a desert without flowers.*"

"You have a good memory."

"For things I consider important."

"I'm flattered."

"My happiness is always marred with sorrow. I anticipate the end of it, or the loss of it. I wish I could really enjoy the moment without that fear."

"How about if you just let go of that fear? After all, what will happen will happen, and your negative thoughts won't change that. You have a choice to enjoy dinner with me, or sit here worrying about leaving. The fact remains: you *will* have dinner with me. It *will* end. We *will* go home. The choice is yours as to whether you enjoy it or not."

"But it's very human to crave continuity and reassurance.

If someone could tell me that my children will reach old age in good health, I could enjoy them without this terrible fear of losing them or of their getting sick."

"Look, life deals you a set of cards. You don't know what they are, but they determine what happens in your life: whether you get sick, knocked over by a car, face bereavement of some kind. Those things are here to teach us about ourselves, about love and compassion, and to test us so we grow into better human beings. So how do you maintain any control? By the way you *choose* to react. Think about it: a postman comes with a letter containing news. The fact is that the letter contains news. Whether it's good or bad depends on how you look at it."

"But if it says my mother is dead?"

"Then your reaction would be one of sorrow . . ."

"Depends on how I view my mother."

"You've answered your own question. It depends on how you feel about your mother. The news isn't inherently good or bad, it just *is*. It's your attachment to your mother that makes you happy or sad. The point is that the happiness of our lives depends on the happiness of our thoughts. Think positively, and life will be positive."

"You should write a book on this. You're much more of a philosopher than me. I am totally in the dark." She drained her glass. "I thought I had life taped. But then I realized that life's trappings, life's luxuries, although they make living easier—and no one likes luxury more than me—they don't create happiness in themselves. It's the sunshine, the trees and flowers, beautiful scenes, music, the embrace of loved ones, that create happiness. They fill us up inside with something magical and intangible."

"It's loving *yourself*, Sage, and giving love." He reached across the table and took her hand. "You ask a man who's survived a brush with death, and he will tell you that happiness is just in loving life and appreciating living. But most people take life for granted and crave more and more material things in the hope that a smarter house or a better car will fulfill them. You ask a woman who has lost a child and she will tell you that the only thing in the world that will make her happy is to hug her child again. Of course, we can't all live like that, but there are lessons to be learned from those people. Love is the only thing that can make us happy. Love is like a bright light that burns away resentment, fear, hate, and loneliness. Life is so precious. The tragedy is that people only realize that when they are on the point of losing it."

He stared at her for a long moment, his face suddenly sad. She stared back, her stomach cramping with dread. He looked as if he was on the point of telling her something important but hesitated.

"Your fish, madam," said the waiter, and the moment passed. Jack sat back to allow the waiter to place the dish in front of him, and to compose himself.

"That looks good," he said, smiling. The sorrow had passed, like a rain cloud, leaving him sunny again. Angelica felt a sense of foreboding but couldn't detect from where it came.

22

The bend in the road is not the end of the road, unless you fail to make the turn.

In Search of the Perfect Happiness

That night they made love again. A warm breeze slid in through the open window like a silk ribbon caressing her skin, bringing with it the scent of gardenia from the garden below. In the pale moonlight she was able to lose herself and her fear as she and Jack feasted upon each other. She could focus on the sensual pleasure of his touch and forget the look that had passed across his face. She could dwell in the present because that was all they had. But daylight soon flooded the room with the eagerness of a new day crammed with possibilities, and there was nothing they could do to hold it back. Her fears returned with the sunshine, and her sense of loss engulfed her.

"I don't want you to go," she whispered, pressing her sleepy body against his. "I've just found you."

"I don't want to go, either. But you have to work. I can't hang around all day." He swept her hair away from her face and kissed her temple. "And I have work to do, too."

"I can't live in the present, Jack. I can't do it. I think about the future, and my fears overwhelm me."

"You have to try. None of us knows the future. We might think we do, but Fate holds the cards and we can't see them."

"I know what's on the cards. I will return to London on Sunday and leave you here. I can't bear it."

"But we will have a wonderful few days at Rosenbosch."

"I want a lifetime of wonderful days."

"We all want that."

"Why do you have to live so far away?"

"Don't analyze everything, Sage. Let it go."

He got up and opened the curtains, filling the untidy room with daylight. Her clothes lay strewn across the floor and over the chair, spilling out of her case like entrails. Since arriving in South Africa, she hadn't had time to catch her breath, let alone unpack. She watched him gaze at the gardens below and take a deep breath, as if he were inhaling the trees and bushes and flowers and birdsong. He stood with his back to her, his magnificent physique broad and tanned, except for the paler marks left by his swimming shorts. She wanted him to take her again and stretched out on the bed expectantly. He turned around and grinned.

"You're coming to Rosenbosch, and that's all I'm thinking about. One step at a time. If you look too far ahead, you lose the Now. I've been looking forward to Now for a very long time. Let's just live it."

"Show me how." She reached out and laughed as he climbed onto the end of the bed like a shaggy lion, burying his head in her stomach.

Then he was gone and she was alone in the shower, wondering how she was going to get through the next few days of events without Jack there to come back to. The room looked bigger without him filling it. The emptiness was as loud as the silence. She was happy to leave it and get on with her day. The sooner she began, the sooner she would finish and the sooner they'd be together again. Rosenbosch stood at the end of the week in a magical aura of light, like the Disney fairy-tale castle at the end of a dark tunnel. Without losing her focus, she'd slowly make her way towards it.

Anita waited for her in the foyer. They had a brunch at eleven, a literary lunch at one, and a book club tea at four. Angelica's heart sank at the prospect of having to be enthusiastic and gracious when all she wanted to do was curl up beneath the duvet and wait for the few Jackless days to be over. If she could just get through Monday and Tuesday in Johannesburg, Cape Town on Wednesday would be one giant step towards Thursday evening, when Jack would pick her up from the Mount Nelson Hotel and drive her to Franschhoek. She had done what she had promised herself she would never do: fallen in love.

She climbed into Anita's car and opened a bottle of water, staring blankly into the car park. At that moment her telephone buzzed with a message. While Anita organized her files in the backseat, Angelica stole a quick read. **I love everything about you, Sage. I'll call you tonight at eleven. X Dog Happily on *Your* Porch.** She smiled with gratitude that Jack had found his way into her life and injected it with such enchantment. His texts and telephone calls would carry her through to Thursday. Beyond that was just unthinkable.

However, there was one telephone call that she was unable to avoid. At midday, when they were en route to the literary lunch in Pretoria, Olivier called. "Hi," she said coolly.

He sounded nervous. "Are you okay? You didn't call. I've been worried."

"I'm fine. Just on my way to an event. All gone well so far."

"*Bon.* Are you still angry with me?"

"I've just been run off my feet."

"No, you're still angry. I understand. Will you accept my apology now you're on the other side of the world?"

"I'm not angry with you, and of course I accept your apol-

Santa Montefiore

ogy. We all say things we don't mean. Let's forget it ever happened. How are the children?"

He answered in detail, which was uncharacteristic for Olivier. "They're on great form. Joe got mentioned in dispatches for hard work. He was very pleased and showed me the newsletter himself. He's missing you. We all are. But he's not unhappy, so you don't need to worry. He's just counting the days for you to come home. Isabel has fallen out with Delfine, but there's nothing unusual about that. They seem to break up and make up ten times a day as far as I can see. She's made a paper caterpillar with Joe for the days you are away, and each day they tear off a segment. Every day I give them a treat. Yesterday I took them for tea at Patisserie Valerie. They loved it and ate those raspberry tarts. They made a terrible mess, but what the hell. They had a good time."

"You must have left work early."

"I'm happy to leave work early at the moment. There's not much to do except damage control, and there's no pleasure in that. I'm enjoying spending time with the children, actually. They are highly entertaining. Candace has asked us for the weekend, which is very kind of her and a great help to me, as I'm not very competent on my own, as you know." Angelica felt a wave of compassion. He was making an effort to be a committed father.

"Give Candace my love. I'm very grateful to her for rescuing you. The children will have a great time in the country."

"I'm going to take the morning off on Monday so I can pick you up from the airport."

"You don't have to do that."

"I know. I want to. I've had time to think and reflect. I'm not too proud to see the error of my ways and make a change. Sometimes it takes a little distance for us to realize how much we care."

"Let's just forget the whole incident."

"Yes, please." He sounded relieved. "So tell me, how have your events gone so far?"

While Angelica talked, Anita drove, trying to look like she wasn't listening. But once she hung up, Angelica felt she had to explain.

"We had a row before I left. My husband's very temperamental. I'm glad that he's apologized."

"Ag, shame," said Anita, her face crumpling with sympathy.

"No, it's not a shame at all. It's really quite an achievement. He's French and very proud."

"Here we say 'shame' when something is very sweet."

Angelica laughed. "Shame and robots. I should start putting together a little dictionary."

"And your children?"

"They've made a paper caterpillar with segments for every day I'm away. Each day they tear a segment off."

Anita grinned at her. "Shame!"

"If you saw my husband in a temper, you wouldn't be so quick to say shame."

"Sounds like he's missing you."

"He is."

"They're always the same. As soon as you're away and they have to run the household and look after the children, they stop taking you for granted."

"He's full of appreciation."

"At least you had your cousin here to look after you."

Angelica contained her amusement by opening her telephone to text Candace. "I know, if it wasn't for Jack, I wouldn't have been allowed to come at all." She hesitated over the letters. Perhaps it would be a good idea to mention Jack and Anna and their invitation to Rosenbosch to Olivier the next time he called, just to cover herself. The way the grape-vine worked in London there was no chance she'd manage a weekend there without its getting back somehow.

Dear Candace, thanx for having my lot for the weekend. You're a star. Olivier is so grateful! Missing you. All well out here. Beauti-ful weather—glorious! Catch up on my return. XX Angelica. A few minutes later, Candace replied. **Glad it's going so well. Can't wait to hear all about it. We're missing you here. Kate's latest crisis will have you in hysterics! Love, Candace X** She clearly couldn't resist adding a word of warning: **Be careful!**

Although Angelica was curious to know about Kate's latest drama, she didn't want to think about next Monday. She didn't want it all to be over. She wasn't ready for her old skin, and she certainly wasn't ready to see Candace and the mirror she held up to reflect her guilty conscience.

Sustained by Jack's texts and his late-night telephone calls, the week went faster than she had anticipated. She said good-bye to Anita in Johannesburg and flew to Cape Town, where she was met by a rep called Joanna. As they drove towards the city, Angelica was horrified by the endless sea of shanty town-ships that seemed to lay siege to it. The heat shimmered off the corrugated iron roofs that gave pathetic shelter to the mul-ticolored boxes that people called home, and telephone poles rose into the air like masts of beleaguered ships after a terrible battle. She wasn't sure she could live in a country where such poverty was so visible and so overwhelming. Surely it would be impossible to find happiness in the shadow of such misery.

Angelica was relieved to leave the shantytowns behind for the immaculate, gleaming prettiness of the city. It was almost possible to forget that such ugliness existed as they drove up the palm tree–lined avenue to the Mount Nelson Hotel, set-tled in the shadow of the magnificent Table Mountain.

Angelica loved Cape Town on sight. The city smelled of freedom after the claustrophobic sense of fear in Johannesburg. Azure skies stretched out above the ocean, where gleaming white yachts and brightly colored fishing boats bobbed about on the water, disturbed occasionally by sleek cruise liners and vast containerships bringing produce from all around the world. The rocky coastline reminded her of the French Riviera, and yet the differences were unmistakable. The sun blazed down upon the mixture of gabled Dutch architecture, noisy African markets, and cobbled streets resounding with the sound of the muezzins calling the faithful to worship. The delightful concoction of European, African, and Islamic influences gave the city a unique exuberance. It was hard to imagine an angry underbelly of poor Africans seething on its outskirts, as menacing as any outside Johannesburg.

She sat on the terrace of the Mount Nelson in the sunshine, inhaling the sweet scents of freshly cut grass and neat borders of bright flowers where fat bees buzzed contentedly among the lavender and roses. She drank Coca-Cola and sat comfortably back in her chair, her spirits buoyant now that she was on the final leg of her tour, with only a day and a half of back-to-back interviews before she would be released at last to spend time with Jack.

They lunched with a journalist from the *Mail & Guardian* newspaper, an eccentric woman with the steady, forbidding gaze of an exotic bird of prey. Angelica chatted happily about her impressions of South Africa and her desire to come back. The bird of prey tucked into her lunch, enchanted by Angelica's ebullience and charm. While Angelica felt her heart swell with love for Jack, she radiated love to all around her, and it was hard to finish the interviews, so happy were the journalists to bask in her luminosity. She felt love for everything and everyone, and, with her heart so charged, there was no room for fear.

They had a window of free time in the afternoon, and

Joanna drove her to the graceful white beaches of Camps Bay. They motored up the long, palm-lined avenue that ran parallel to the sea and bought grenadilla ice cream from an exuberant African seller, shouting, "Grenadilla lolly, make your life jolly." The sea was freezing, and Angelica pulled her foot out with a surprised yelp.

In the evening, after an interview in town, Joanna took her up Table Mountain, where she stood in humble silence at the splendor of the view before her. All humanity lay below in miniature, from the myriad of ships in the bay to the elegant mansions in the wealthy suburbs. Wide sandy beaches, rocky slopes, towering skyscrapers, and the grim shantytowns shimmered beneath a cloud of dust. She stood in awe, feeling the wind on her face and the diminishing heat as the sun descended slowly below the horizon. Up there she felt small and insignificant, and yet she felt part of everything—as if she were made of air. She wished she were a bird so she could open her wings and fly on the breeze, high above her cares.

The following day she sat at the hotel giving interviews. After lunch they had a couple of hours to go shopping. Joanna drove her to a vast African market, where she wandered contentedly among the richly colored fabrics, wooden carvings, and beaded jewelry. She chatted to the sellers, bought embroidered white pajamas for her children and a beautiful game of Solitaire, whose base was carved out of dark wood and whose balls were made of many different types of crystal. She envisaged it sitting proudly in her sitting room and laughed at the thought of Joe and Isabel playing with the pieces and losing them under the sofas. The image of her children caused her heart to twist with longing.

Her last interview finished at four. She packed her suitcase, struggling to fit everything in and having to sit on top in order to zip it up. Finally, she waited in the lobby for Jack. Having put off telling Olivier about her weekend plans she realized that if she didn't do it now, it would be too late. So she called him on his mobile. It rang a few times. She mentally rehearsed what she was going to say, concentrating on making light of it. When he didn't answer, she was relieved to leave a message. "Hi, darling. It's me. Just to say that I bumped into Jack Meyer and his wife Anna here in Cape Town. You remember him from Scarlet's dinner? Probably not. Anyhow, they've asked me for the weekend, which is really nice of them considering my Saturday afternoon event has been canceled and I would have had to hang around here on my own. So I'll be on my mobile if you need me. Give my love to the children. Have a great time at Candace's and give her my love. My plane gets in at seven-thirty on Monday morning if you're still keen to come and pick me up. Totally understand if you're not. It's a schlep. Big kiss. 'Bye." She hung up and winced. Had she gone on too much? Would he believe her? She ran over what she had just said, trying to remember it word for word, searching for any slipups. *Tant pis,* she thought. *What's said is said.* She hoped he wouldn't detect that she was lying.

While she waited, her thoughts turned to Anna. She had no desire to meet Jack's wife. She wished they could spend the weekend together alone, without the jealous glances of another woman who had more claim on him than she did. It would be easier, she thought, if Jack moaned about her, but he hadn't made even the smallest derogatory remark. He had made it clear that he loved his wife. He had also suggested that the two of them would get on very well. But Angelica had no intention of liking her. She was anxious about having to hide her feelings, having to skulk about, stealing moments while Anna was in another part of the house or perhaps in the garden. She hoped that Jack had made plans so that she didn't have to spend time with his wife.

When Jack finally strode into the lobby, her fears melted in the glow of his cheerful smile. Aware that she was in his town, she was careful not to throw herself at him like she had in Johannesburg, although her heart was ready to burst with joy. He bent down and embraced her affectionately, raising his eyes over his glasses to case the room for anyone who might know him.

"You all right, Sage?" he asked, his gaze softening. "You look radiant."

"I love Cape Town."

"I knew you would."

"Everyone is so friendly."

"The sunshine makes everyone smile."

"Do you think Londoners would smile more if we had sunshine all the time?"

"You don't need sunshine, Sage. It's already inside you." She laughed and watched him pick up her case and walk outside. "What have you got in here? The entire contents of the African market?"

"I bought some lovely things."

"So I see." He glanced at the necklace dangling over her breasts.

"Pretty, isn't it?" She grinned. "How long to Rosenbosch?"

"Just over an hour."

"So I have you all to myself for an hour?"

He smiled at her mischievously. "We might have to stop en route. I don't think I can sit all the way to Franschhoek and not touch you."

Jack put the suitcase in the back of the car and climbed in. Before driving off, he pulled her into his arms and kissed her.

"You're more beautiful than you were in Jo'burg," he said, caressing her face with his eyes. "Just the sight of you is enough to restore my spirits."

"Did they need restoring?"

"They did," he replied, nuzzling her. "I can't wait to show you my home. And we'll be just in time for a sundowner at Sir Lowry's Pass."

"That sounds enticing."

"Oh, it is. I've brought a picnic. Tonight, the sunset will be more spectacular than ever."

23

Keep your face to the sunshine and you cannot see the shadows.   *In Search of the Perfect Happiness*

They drove out of Cape Town, past the monumental panorama of rocks known as the Twelve Apostles, jutting sharply towards heaven. The dual carriageway cut through the vast, flat plain beneath a cornflower-blue sky. In the distance, velvety green hills rose to meet the horizon, where feathery clouds caressed their voluptuous curves as they moved swiftly on down the valley. They passed rich farmland, where the soil was red and the crops tall and golden, and vineyards with vines planted in neat rows giving the impression of thick fields of corduroy. Jack held Angelica's hand, glancing at her occasionally and smiling. The scenery was so dramatic and so vast that Angelica yearned to be part of it. How romantic to live surrounded by such beauty, all the time.

Finally, they arrived in Franschhoek. The name was written up on the hill ahead in big gray stones. Angelica felt her belly cramp with anxiety at the thought of meeting Anna. By now the sun was setting, turning the hills flamingo pink. Sensing her nervousness, Jack squeezed her hand.

"I want to take you up to watch the sunset before I show you Rosenbosch."

She smiled at him gratefully. "I'd love that."

With the window down, she could smell the fertile soil

and camphor trees. The air was warm on her face, the light soft and wistful on her skin. She gazed at the gleaming white houses and picket fences adorned with pink and white roses, the neatly mown lawns and pretty verandas, and loved Jack all the more because he was part of it.

He took a left turn and drove up a dusty track, leaving the town behind. The valley darkened around them, but the horizon blazed with liquid gold, setting the sky aflame. After a while he pulled over and they climbed out. He opened the boot and extracted a small green hamper. "We can't watch the sunset without a drink. Follow me, I have the perfect spot for our sundowner." Angelica hurried after him. "We don't want to miss it."

Up there on the hillside they were alone with the sound of roosting birds and crickets chirruping in the grass. They sat down, and Jack took out the bottle.

"One of ours," he said proudly, showing her the label. "A particularly good 1984 Chardonnay."

Angelica laid out the glasses and Jack uncorked the bottle and poured. They sat in silence a moment, savoring the taste. Angelica felt the chill all the way down into her belly, followed by the pleasant lightness in her head. She felt the cramp slacken in her stomach and took a deep, satisfied breath.

"So what do you think, Sage?"

"Just as I expected: delicious," she replied truthfully.

He was pleased, holding up his glass triumphantly. "It's not bad. Not bad at all."

She took another sip. In the distance the gold had darkened to a deep red, as if a giant furnace blazed just beyond the hills. Gray clouds hung heavy in the white sky; the valley was swathed in a shadow of dusky pink.

"I love it here, Sage. It fills me up inside in a way that nothing else can. I suppose I feel close to nature. Close to heaven."

She took his hand, feeling a sense of melancholy wash over her. "Why is it that beauty makes us think of heaven?"

"Perhaps it reminds us that the beauty of nature far exceeds anything that human beings are capable of creating. It makes us feel small and insignificant and in awe of a Higher Power."

"Or perhaps it connects with the divine inside us, so on some deeper, unconscious level we feel part of it all. Maybe it simply triggers a long forgotten memory of where we all come from and for a moment we are gripped by a yearning to return home."

"Whatever the reason, it makes us sad."

"Because it's so fleeting."

"Like life."

She frowned, reminded suddenly of the cancer that had brought him so close to death. "Which is why we have to live in the moment," she said, smiling at him gently. "I'm living in the moment right now, Jack. I'm not thinking of yesterday or dreaming of tomorrow. Right now I'm here on the hillside with you, among the birds and crickets, and I couldn't be happier."

Jack took her wineglass and placed it on the grass with his, then drew her into his arms to kiss her. She lay against him and closed her eyes, relishing the sensation of his rough chin and warm lips. The spicy scent of his skin blended with the lime of his cologne—a smell that was becoming familiar to her. She fantasized that they were married, living in this stunning country, drinking their own wine, watching the sunset every evening and never growing tired of each other.

Finally, the furnace died away, leaving the gray clouds to hang snugly over the hills like blankets. It was twilight when they walked back down the hill. The magic was over, and Angelica was left with the unsettling prospect of meeting Anna.

They climbed back into the car and drove down the hill into Franschhoek.

"So what am I to expect?" she asked, staring ahead at the little flies caught in the headlights.

"She'll love you. You're just her type."

"I'm sure you're wrong." She glanced at him, but he didn't reply. "So are your children going to be there, too?"

"No, only Lucy, our youngest. Sophie and Elizabeth are staying with friends in Cape Town."

Angelica began to bite the skin around her thumbnail. "I feel guilty, coming into your family like a cuckoo."

He took her hand and squeezed it. "Don't feel guilty, Sage."

"I do. I mean, I'm going to meet your fifteen-year-old daughter. She'll shake hands and smile, not knowing that I've been sleeping with her father. It's so deceitful. It's not what I wanted."

"It's not what I would choose, either. There's a lot about my life that I wouldn't choose. But there it is."

She glanced at him and noticed his jaw tense. His anxiety made her feel a lot better. That was the first time he had implied that things weren't all well with Anna. *But how could they be?* she reflected. For if he were blissfully married, would he have room in his heart to fall in love with her? If she were blissfully married, would she have fallen in love with him? She gazed out the open window and tried tossing her fears into the darkness.

"Here we are."

He turned the car into the driveway, a long, straight dust track overhung with an avenue of towering camphor trees. Ahead, the lights of the house blazed into the semidarkness.

"Home sweet home," she said, bracing herself.

The house was a pretty whitewashed building constructed in the mid eighteenth century in the Dutch style, with dark green shutters and gables sealing the pitched roof at both ends. In the middle, above the front door, an elaborate gable framing the upper-story window was the house's main feature. Big terra-cotta pots stood against the wall planted with what looked like fruit trees. Dogs began to bark as the car drew up in front.

"You have a lot of dogs," said Angelica, her stomach as tight as a ball of elastic bands.

"We love dogs. Some are rescue animals, others we've bought, one or two have just joined us for a while because they like the food." He turned off the engine. "So what do you think?"

"It's really lovely, Jack. I can't wait to see it in daylight."

"Tomorrow I'll give you a guided tour of the whole estate. We'll take the horses out and have a picnic lunch on the hill. You're going to love it so much, you won't want to go home."

Angelica inhaled the exotic scent of camphor. "I think I already do."

Her attention was diverted by the front door opening to reveal a slight woman in floppy white trousers and a man's shirt, her brown hair tied casually in a loose ponytail. What struck her, though, was not her elegance but the warmth of her smile. It was the smile of a woman who knew nothing of her husband's infidelities and had swallowed his explanations without a single, questioning chew.

"Welcome!" she cried, almost bouncing down the steps to greet her. She was the same height as Angelica but half the size. A delicate woman with fine, chiseled features; a long aquiline nose; strong chin and jaw; and bright, twinkling eyes the color of the gray clouds that Angelica had just seen from Sir Lowry's Pass. "Jack has told me so much about you. I feel I know you already."

Angelica was caught off guard. She allowed Anna to embrace her and couldn't help but smile back, albeit apologetically. "It's so nice to be here, finally," she replied. "I've been looking forward to it all week."

"Well, come on inside."

Jack remained outside with the dogs, hauling her suitcase out of the car. Anna disappeared into the house. Angelica followed her over the polished wooden floorboards, past a round table adorned with a heavy brass pan of gardenia that filled the air with its sweet, sultry scent. The walls were off-white and quite bare but for a couple of large paintings of fruit set in heavy wooden frames. "How was the sunset?" Anna asked.

Angelica tried to answer casually, but her mind was whirring with all sorts of questions. "The most beautiful I have ever seen."

"Sir Lowry's Pass is one of my favorite places in the world. I told Jack to take you, if you arrived in time. It's never the same. Sometimes the sky is pink, other times orange, gold, even purple. What was it tonight?"

"Molten gold."

Her smile was almost triumphant. "Good. So you saw it in all its glory. I'm so pleased." Angelica searched for some hint of bitterness, however small or well disguised, but found none.

Anna led her upstairs, across the landing decorated with bookcases and into a large bedroom with tall old-fashioned windows such as one might see in English Tudor houses, divided into many smaller square panes. In the center of the room stood a high four-poster bed, made of the same rich reddish-brown timber as the floorboards.

"This is a stunning room," Angelica enthused, inhaling the smells typical of a house cooling down at the end of a hot day.

"I'm glad you like it. That bed's very comfortable. I've had guests who have failed to get up for breakfast because they don't want to get out of it. If you'd like breakfast in bed, just let me know."

There were attractive lines around her mouth and eyes. She wasn't beautiful, but her face was arresting as her vibrant personality shone through. Angelica couldn't help but like her. She doubted there was a single person on the planet who didn't like her.

The sound of Jack's heaving her suitcase up the stairs made them both turn around. "Here come the whole contents of the African market." He laughed and lifted it onto the antique wooden chest at the end of the bed.

"I hope you came with an empty suitcase," said Anna.

"I should have. I didn't expect to shop. I was meant to be worked like a donkey. I didn't think I'd have time."

"Well, at least you brought a big case."

"And there's a man in the house strong enough to carry it."

"Only just," said Jack. "How about a drink on the terrace?"

He strode past them and descended the stairs. Anna followed lightly behind, and Angelica felt a wrench in her heart. They both belonged here; she didn't. She cursed herself for having the audacity to feel envious when it was she, not Anna, who was the impostor.

Outside, they sat on green gingham cushions at a table overlooking the gardens. The moon lit up a pagoda in the middle of a small, ornamental lake. White roses wound their way up the poles, and lilies floated on the water like pretty little boats. Beyond, the range of rocky mountains was silhouetted against the sky. The croaking of frogs and clamor of crickets were carried on a warm breeze, and jasmine scented the air beneath the awning. Anna had already laid the table for dinner and placed a vase of freshly cut roses in the center. Angelica couldn't fail to notice her sense of style. Everything—from the black-and-white-tiled terrace to the chunky crockery decorated with painted green elephants—was touched by her self-assured good taste. She was one of those rare women blessed with flair: whatever she touched was rendered attractive, whether it was the way she decorated her house, the way she dressed, or a simple gift she might wrap for a friend, slipping a pretty butterfly under the ribbon. Angelica knew her type and admired her.

"I love your pagoda," she said.

"That's my little space. It's where I meditate. My family know not to disturb me when I'm there."

"You meditate?"

"Every morning and every evening. At sunrise and sunset, for an hour."

"You have amazing self-discipline. I only manage once a week. I never find the time."

"You have a busy London life. You write books, you have small children, you have a husband and a house to run. I didn't meditate for two hours a day when our children were little, more like twenty minutes, snatched at the end of the day and then with half an ear on the children in case they woke up and needed me. Try to find ten minutes at the beginning of your day, before you start working. Just a little time to go within yourself and find that quiet place. It's very restorative, and keeps you looking young."

"Well, that's an incentive."

"You wouldn't think I was nearly fifty, would you?"

"You're joking!" Anna didn't look older than forty.

"No, it's true. I can only put it down to meditation and trying to find serenity in my day-to-day life."

Angelica looked across the table at Jack, who was pouring the wine. "Anna should write the book on the quest for happiness."

She laughed, and there was a sweet charm in the way her nose crinkled. "So many books have been dedicated to that elusive subject. If I knew the secret to happiness, I'd have levitated into nirvana by now. But I'm here, very human and full of flaws."

At that moment Lucy appeared from the sitting room with a scruffy dog in her arms. She was tall and pretty, with curly light brown hair and big brown eyes, like her father. "Ah, Lucy," said Jack. "I want you to meet Angelica Garner, a friend of mine from London."

The girl's eyes lit up. "I love your books," she said, extending her free hand.

"Who's that?" Angelica asked, nodding at the dog.

"This is Domino. He found his way into our garden—"

"And into Lucy's heart," continued Anna.

"Come and join us," said Jack.

"Do you mind if I don't? I've already eaten, and I want to do some more on my project."

"What project is that?" Angelica asked.

"I'm doing a project on the Russian tsars for school."

"That sounds interesting."

"A lot of work."

"Do you have to cover all of them?"

"Just the important ones."

"Cherry-picking."

"Yes." Lucy laughed. "I'd rather be reading your new book. I gather Daddy's already read it." She raised her eyes to her father and grinned. "When will you give it to me?"

"If I give it to you now, you'll never finish your project." Jack's eyes were full of affection as he watched his daughter. "*The Silk Serpent* is your reward."

She shrugged. "Better get back to my laptop. Are you staying all weekend?"

"Leaving on Sunday."

"Good, I'll see you tomorrow, then." She kissed her parents and retreated inside.

"You have a beautiful daughter," Angelica said to Anna.

"There's not a lot of me in her," Anna replied. "She's her father's daughter."

"Lucky girl to be so tall."

"She is lucky. They're all tall like Jack. It cannot be said that my husband hasn't improved my family gene pool." Angelica noticed the way she gazed at her husband. There was something sad in it, wistful perhaps. His eyes slid away as if not wanting to see.

They drank wine, ate from a spread of salads, chicken, and bread, and talked about life. Angelica forgot to be jealous of Anna. It was as if she were a mythical enchantress blinding Angelica to her own fears and resentments. There she sat in her white linen shirt, her skin radiant and brown, her compassionate eyes glittering in the light of the hurricane lamps, smiling with a gentle peacefulness as if nothing bad or unpleasant in the world could touch her. When she looked at Angelica, she did so with affection, as if she were looking at her own daughter. Angelica wanted to feel antipathy. Anna stood between her and the man she loved, but she could find nothing but gratitude for the warm welcome, and the desire to hear her talk more.

When Anna disappeared into the house with the dishes, Angelica was left at the table with Jack. She lowered her voice and leaned towards him. "Anna's a very special woman," she said. She wasn't sure whether she was asking a provocative question or making a genuine statement.

But Jack smiled triumphantly. "I told you you'd like her."

"She's very wise."

"Like you."

"I'm not wise, Jack. If I was wise, I'd walk away from here right now and return to my husband and children." She dared touch his hand across the table. "Why do you want me, when you're married to such an amazing woman?"

"Don't compare yourself to Anna. I don't."

"What does she think I'm doing here? Doesn't she suspect anything?"

"She doesn't have a possessive bone in her body."

"So she knows."

He shrugged. "I don't know what she knows. But she likes you."

"I can't imagine her disliking anyone."

"Oh, she does, believe me. She can turn very frosty."

"I think she sees the good in everyone."

"I've seen her turn frosty if she feels her children are threatened, for example. She's not all sweetness and light."

"You know, the most ridiculous thing is that I want her to like me. Yet here I am sleeping with her husband. It's awful. I'm a really bad person." *Candace is right: I'm thinking only of myself and my right to happiness.*

"Don't let me hear you talk like that. I told you, leave my marriage to me. It's not your problem. If you want to feel guilty, then feel guilty about Olivier. Anna is *my* wife and *my* responsibility. Does she look unhappy to you?"

"No."

"Then don't worry about her."

"I didn't go into this considering your wife. I was only thinking about us. If I'd met Anna before, I'd never have entertained an affair. Never."

He let go of her hand, sensing Anna returning from the kitchen with dessert. "Then it's my good fortune that you are only meeting her now." He grinned mischievously. "When it's too late to back out."

After dinner Jack played the piano in the sitting room. A cool breeze slipped in through the French doors, bringing with it the sweet scent of jasmine and damp grass. Anna and Angelica sat on the sofa drinking coffee, listening to the music, the dogs sleeping on the carpet at their feet. Jack played sad tunes that made Angelica's hair stand on end. His face was anguished, as if the music was coming directly from a tormented soul. He didn't play from a score but from memory, and he closed his eyes to allow the melody to transport him. Angelica was so enthralled she didn't notice Anna, wiping away tears, until he had finished. "Now I'll play something happy," he said, as if making a conscious effort not to look at his wife.

"Anything," Angelica replied, feigning cheerfulness. "Just don't ask me to sing."

Later, when Angelica was in bed trying to sleep, she heard the doleful sound of the piano again. She didn't dare get up in case Anna was with him. She lay listening, carried on the notes to a dark and melancholy place where dreams were unfulfilled and wishes hung suspended in the air, never to be granted. She felt a heavy sense of loss and the wetness of tears on her pillow. She could fantasize as much as she liked, but she and Jack would never ride off into the sunset and live happily ever after. Her thoughts sprang back to her children and made her feel suddenly quite desolate. What was moving Jack to such sorrow? When she finally drifted off to sleep, she dreamed of him, a distant, misty face in the sky. The faster she ran, the farther away he drifted, until she cried out in her sleep and woke herself up in panic.

24

Expand your view beyond the ego's range.

In Search of the Perfect Happiness

The following morning Angelica was awoken by the excited clamor of birds in the plane trees outside her window. A dog barked in the distance, and guinea fowl exploded into a round of indignant complaint. She lay a while, relishing the foreign sounds, barely daring to believe that she was there at Rosenbosch. She climbed out of bed and crept across the squeaking floorboards to open the curtains. The sunshine tumbled into the room, and she squinted and threw an arm across her eyes. Blinded for a moment, she held on to the wall for balance. Then she tentatively opened her eyes.

The beauty of the view was breathtaking. The gardens glistened in the dawn light, beneath the bluest of skies. Towering pine trees and extravagant red flowering gum trees threw shadows onto the immaculately mown lawn, where white and blue hydrangeas grew in the borders, intermingled with forget-me-nots. Beyond, the vineyard stretched out to the hills beneath an eerie layer of mist that lingered like smoke. She noticed a lone bird of prey circling high in the sky, silently watchful for signs of breakfast below. The pagoda stood in the tranquility of the morning, in the middle of the ornamental lake. The surface of the water shimmered like a mirror, reflecting the perfection of the heavens above, and small, energetic birds fussed about the roses. She wondered whether Anna was in there meditating. She didn't think there was any place on earth as peaceful as that little pagoda.

Not wanting to miss a moment, or give herself time to dwell on her children, she dressed in a pair of white trousers and light plimsolls, throwing on a diaphanous floral shirt. She left her hair to fall about her shoulders and sprayed herself with scent. She had noticed that Anna wore no makeup. Her style was effortlessly glamorous, though she doubted Anna would ever use that word to describe herself. So she didn't bother with her usual morning ritual and skipped downstairs, bare-faced.

She went into the kitchen to find a jovial-looking African woman in a bright yellow headdress, piling up a tray with coffee and bread. "Good morning." Her smile was dazzling against the rich brown of her skin.

"Good morning. I'm Angelica."

"Very nice to meet you, Miss Angelica. My name is Anxious. Master is out on the terrace if you want to join him."

"Thank you. I will."

"Would you like some coffee?"

"I'd love tea . . ."

"I have a pot of tea ready. Madam likes jasmine tea in the morning, but I have Earl Grey if you would prefer." The tray looked heavy, but Anxious lifted it off the table with ease and bustled efficiently towards the terrace. Angelica followed her.

Jack was at the table reading a newspaper, surrounded by his dogs. When he saw her, he jumped to his feet.

"Good morning, Sage," he said, taking her around the waist and kissing her cheek.

He smelled of shaving foam and lime cologne. His hair was damp and pushed off his forehead into a thick froth of unruly curls. Behind his glasses his eyes shone with enthusiasm, the crow's-feet searing through his temples like deep scars. He looked more handsome than ever.

She withdrew, afraid that his wife or daughter would notice their intimacy, and took a seat beside him. "Where's Anna?"

"Gone off with Lucy to help with the harvest."

"I thought she might be meditating in her pagoda."

"She's done with that by six."

"Don't you have to help, too?"

"Technically, yes. But as you're here I'm going to entertain you."

"I'd be more than happy to pick grapes."

"I know, but I want you to myself. Besides, they started hours ago and will be finished by half ten. If the grapes come in too warm, they're useless for good wine. You shall survey the harvest from the comfort of a pretty chestnut mare. Faezel and Nazaar are bringing them around at nine-thirty."

"That sounds like heaven. I've dreamed of riding over the hills with you."

"Anxious is making us a picnic, aren't you, Anxious?"

Anxious lifted her eyes over the teapot and grinned at him affectionately: "Yes, Master." She poured into Angelica's cup.

"I'm going to show Angelica the estate."

"Tell her to wear cream: the sun is very hot, and she is very pale."

"You'd better do as Anxious says," he teased, watching her big body vibrate with a chuckle. "I've done as Anxious says for the past thirty-five years, haven't I, Anxious?"

She shrugged. "Some of the time. Most of the time, no."

"When will the picnic be ready?"

"Just now, Master." She put the teapot down and went to fetch it.

"She's a real character. I love her like my own mother."

Angelica sipped her tea and helped herself to toast. Across

the garden she could see a couple of dark-skinned men working in the borders, their heads protected by white hats. The sound of their chatter floated across the lawn with the twittering of birds.

"It's so beautiful here, Jack. I don't ever want to leave. I hate to think of returning to our winter: the short, bleak days; the cold, damp air; the bare trees and borders of dead flowers. Here it's so lush and fragrant. The light is so bright, the sky so blue, the green greener than I have ever seen it. Everything is an extravagance of color and scent. Even you look browner and glossier out here."

He took her hand. "I'm so happy it's touched you like it touches me. I love this place more than any other. When I die, my ashes will be scattered beneath those hills."

"A fine resting place."

"I'll never leave."

She looked alarmed. "You'll come back to London soon, I hope."

"If you're there, then I'll devise a good excuse." He looked at her fondly, but his smile faltered.

"I'm looking forward to riding out. I haven't ridden a horse in years."

"Don't worry, Fennella is very placid. She'll look after you. And so will I!"

At nine-thirty two men appeared with the horses. Jack's was a fit-looking gray mare, with the legs of a racehorse, while Angelica's was smaller and sturdier, with a gentle face and soft brown eyes. She approached Fennella and stroked the white blaze down the center of her nose; the mare nodded with pleasure, snorting through dilated nostrils.

"She likes me," said Angelica, patting her thick neck.

"She's a good girl," said Faezel.

"Just the sort of horse I need."

Jack took her foot and lifted her into the saddle. "How does it feel up there?"

"Oh yes, it's all coming back to me now."

"All right?"

"Yes. Lovely view."

She took the reins and tried to remember what to do with them. Jack swung into the saddle with the artlessness of a man who has spent most of his life on a horse. He thanked the boys, then trotted up to the terrace, where Anxious stood with the picnic basket. He heaved it behind the saddle, then tied it securely in a specially tailored harness. "Thanks, Anxious. We're all set. See you later."

"I'm glad your friend is wearing a hat. That skin is like an orchid."

"Anxious wants to be reassured that you put on sun cream."

"Of course," Angelica shouted back.

"Does she know how to ride?"

"If she doesn't, she will by sunset." He chuckled as Anxious shook her head disapprovingly, and cantered back to Angelica, who hadn't yet dared move. "Let's go."

Tentatively, she gave the horse a squeeze. She needn't have bothered. Fennella knew to walk alongside Jack's horse, Artemis.

"You know Franschhoek was once known as Olifantshoek, Elephant's Corner, because, being bordered on three sides by mountains, the valley was ideal for elephants to raise their young. They liked the isolation."

"Are there any elephants here now?"

"No, but we have loads of other wildlife. We might see some steenbok, and of course there are plenty of birds where we're going."

They made their way up a dusty track, alongside a thicket of pine trees. The vineyard stretched out lush and luxuriant, and in the distance they could see the grape pickers among the vines like giant bees, the buzz of their chatter rising into the still air.

"All this is yours?"

"All mine," he replied proudly. "Before me it belonged to my father and before him to my grandfather, who bought it as a young man."

"Is your father still alive?"

"No, he died when I was a teenager."

"It can't be easy growing up without your father."

"I still miss him. He was a wonderful man."

"And your mother?"

"She lives in Denmark. She tried to make us all leave with her, but I don't hold the same fear of the place as she does."

"She fears it? Why?"

"South Africa is very troubled. You know that. Crime is rife. It's not a safe country to live in anymore. But we've been lucky."

"Your mother went far."

"She's Danish, so she went home. She lives in the country-side, in a crumbling old farmhouse, with my brother and his wife and their children. They come out every year, and I've made the detour to see them on the way back from London. Wild horses wouldn't drag her here. E-mail has reduced the gap between us, and we speak a lot on the telephone."

"So you have no family here anymore, besides Anna and your daughters."

"That's right. It's just us now."

"How sad that so beautiful a place is marred by crime."

"When you see the differences between the haves and the have-nots, it's really not at all surprising. But it's the price you have to pay to live in such glory."

"It's a hive of activity over there," she said as they approached.

"We're two weeks late in starting this year due to the un-usually long winter rains."

At the end of each row was a red or white rosebush, planted to reveal the first signs of disease before it hit the vines. A flurry of butterflies fluttered in the air, dropping onto the flowers to sip the nectar.

"Look, there's Lucy."

Lucy looked up over the vine and waved vigorously. Beyond her, Anna was busy picking and chatting to the African women who came from nearby towns to help. The sound of singing drifted down the narrow avenues between the vines with the chuckling of black guinea fowl.

"What happens once the grapes are picked?"

"You're really interested?"

"Of course. I've never thought beyond my glass of Sauvignon."

"Then I'll give you a tour before we head off into the hills."

Angelica was enchanted by everything at Rosenbosch, from the beauty of the countryside to the functional charm of the winery. They tied the horses in the courtyard outside the farm buildings, designed in the same Dutch style as the main house, and Jack took her inside to show her the winemaker, stopping to chat with workers on the way. Finally, down in the dank darkness of the barrel cellar, they were alone.

Jack pulled her into his arms and kissed her hungrily, as if he had been waiting all morning for an opportunity, holding her close and inhaling her scent.

"You smell so good," he breathed into her neck, and the warmth on her skin made her shiver. "I really love you, Sage."

He swept her hair off her face and gazed at her features as if committing them to memory. She allowed herself to be enveloped by his giant frame and nestled happily there, his words echoing in her ears and in her heart.

• • •

They rode up into the hills, where low shrubs and bushes, known as fynbos, grew in abundance, pollinated by birds. Jack pointed out the orange-breasted sunbird and the yellow-fronted bee-eater with its yellow wings and bright red throat. The mist had lifted, leaving the way open for the sun to blaze down ferociously. Angelica could feel it on her forearms and through her shirt. The horses walked at a steady pace, and she began to feel confident in the saddle. As they climbed higher a light breeze swept across her face, and she was grateful for its cooling fingers. After a while, they arrived at a small plateau, where a copse of tall pines gave shelter from the sun. They dismounted and led the horses into the shade.

"We'll set up our picnic here," he said, lifting down the basket. "Let's see what old Anxious has prepared for us."

He laid out a green tartan rug and put the basket in the middle. Angelica sat down and fanned her face with her hat, pushing her sticky hair off her forehead. Jack opened the basket and took out a bottle of wine in a cooler. Anxious had packed a small bucket of ice, smoked salmon, lemon, bread, pâté, and salad. Everything was neatly wrapped and insulated with ice packs.

Hungrily, they tucked into their picnic. The wine was refreshing, mixed with ice, and there was grenadilla juice to quench their thirst.

"So how's your book going?"

"I've come up with a brilliant idea."

"About the secret of happiness?"

"No. About greasy green Troilers." She pulled a face. "I don't think I'm qualified to write about happiness."

"Sure you are."

"I love exploring ideas, but I can't put them into any coherent order. They're scattered thoughts and arguments, like we've been having over the Internet. I'm still searching."

"Keep a diary. Perhaps you could turn that into a book one day."

She laughed. "And risk someone's reading it?"

"Would Olivier really read your diary?"

"No, I don't think so. But things haven't been good between us recently, so he might be tempted were he to see it lying around." She bit into her pâté sandwich. "This is really good."

"Homemade duck liver pâté."

"You should sell it."

"We do, only locally."

"Quite industrious, aren't you?"

"We have to be resourceful. It's not easy at the moment."

"Maybe *you* should write the book. You're much wiser than me."

"I think we should write it together."

"Now you're talking. You can do the serious stuff, and I'll do the fluffy stuff."

"You're not fluffy, Sage."

"You know what I mean. You're more intellectual than me."

"I wouldn't say that. But we would make a good team, bouncing ideas off each other all the time."

"Okay, what if we did write a book together, what would we call ourselves?"

He thought about it a moment, chewing on smoked salmon. "D. O. Porch."

She laughed. "That's hilarious! What about Fido Porch?"

"Doesn't quite have the right ring to it."

"No, you're right, it doesn't."

"Let's think laterally."

"I'm rather light-headed, I'm not sure I can think at all."

"Go on. Wine loosens up the imagination."

"You think?" She looked doubtful. "Just makes me silly."

"The sillier the better. We want something that's eye-catching."

"Like Marmaduke Picnic?"

"Now you're on the right lines."

"Marmalade Pickthistle. Migglethwaite Harp. Humpfink Danwit."

"Now I see how you get all those crazy names for your characters. A few glasses of wine and you're at your most creative." He helped himself to another slice of bread and spread it with pâté. "Tomorrow we've asked some friends over from a neighboring vineyard for a braai."

"What's a braai?"

"A barbecue."

Her face lit up. "That's it! Something Braai."

He nodded thoughtfully. "I like Braai. It has an eccentric ring to it, doesn't it?"

"Braais are symbolic of happiness, because we all love our food."

"What about the Something?"

"*I've* thought of Braai. *You* have to think of the Something."

"All right. Leave it with me. I'll come up with something for Something."

They finished lunch and drained the bottle. Lying on their backs, holding hands, they gazed up into the kaleidoscope of pine needles to the glimpses of bright blue sky above. The wind picked up. Known as the southeaster or Cape Doctor, it took the edge off the searing heat. Down in the valley Anna, Lucy, and the grape pickers would be enjoying lunch. Angelica was pleased to be alone in the quiet with Jack, where time seemed to stand still. Nothing else seemed to matter but Jack and her and this precious afternoon without commitments or cares. They could lie in the shade, talk about life and love, and pretend they had forever.

At five, they sat up and watched the sunset. Angelica thought of Anna and how much she loved the changes of light and color at the end of the day. It perplexed her to think that she had suggested Jack take her up to Sir Lowry's Pass the night before. It was as if she was pushing them together. She didn't seem to be watching out for stolen glances, hoping to catch them in a romantic tryst, willing them to trip up so that she could throw accusations as she had every right to do. She left them to their own devices, as if she didn't care what he did.

As the sun turned the sky pink and gold, Angelica hugged her knees, the bubbly feeling in her belly souring with melancholy.

"Have you had many lovers?"

He frowned at her. "What kind of question is that?"

"Does Anna tolerate them?"

"My darling, what's inspired this line of thought?"

"I don't know. The sunset makes me think of her."

"She'll be enjoying it down there with the workers."

"You should be with her."

"We have enjoyed thousands of sundowners together. I only have one more with you."

She inhaled the fragrant air, filling her lungs before letting it out in a rush. "Anna knows we're lovers, doesn't she?"

"If she does, she hasn't said anything."

"But she suggested we watch the sunset last night. Isn't that behavior a little odd for a wife?"

"Anna's not like other wives. We make our own rules."

"Are there others like me?"

He put his arm around her and pulled her towards him. "Don't be silly. There's no one else like you."

"Really? Scarlet suggested you had a lover in Clapham."

He stared at her. "She said what?"

"She saw you with a woman in Clapham."

The horror evaporated. "Ah, the lovely Mrs. Homer."

"Who's Mrs. Homer?"

"An old lady of eighty. Scarlet needs her eyes tested. You don't need to be jealous of Mrs. Homer." He placed his lips on her temple and left them there for a long while. "You don't need to be jealous of anybody."

"Not even of Anna."

He sighed. She sensed he was deliberating how to respond. Finally, he pulled away and gazed at the hills on the other side of the valley.

"Look, she's her own person. She's a free spirit. She doesn't own me, and I don't own her. We love each other, which is a choice we make, not conditions imposed on us by an institution, and how we choose to love each other is our own business and no one else's. We conduct ourselves in a manner that respects the other. She doesn't judge me, and I don't judge her. We're friends and soul mates. But the way I feel about you is different from the way I feel about anybody in the world. You have to trust me."

She leaned her head against his shoulder and let the amber light warm her face. "I do trust you, Jack," she said. But still something wasn't quite right. There was something he wasn't telling her.

25

When you love unconditionally, there is nothing to forgive.
In Search of the Perfect Happiness

That evening, they had dinner on the terrace with Lucy, Anna, and a friend of Lucy's called Fiona. Anna was lively, despite having toiled all morning in the fields with the grape pickers. Her eyes were bright, her smile uninhibited. Angelica watched her closely, trying to decipher her. But she seemed to have no side, and she certainly didn't seem to be hiding anything.

In the middle of dinner the telephone rang, and Anxious came onto the terrace to tell Angelica that her husband was on the line from London. Angelica was brought back to reality with a jolt. Her first thoughts were for her children, and her chest compressed with fear. Why on earth would Olivier be calling her at Rosenbosch? How had he got the number? It must surely be an emergency. She hurried after Anxious into the sitting room.

"Hello, Olivier?" She could barely restrain her impatience.

"Hi, darling? How are you?" His casual voice dispelled her anxiety.

"Is everything all right?"

"Everything's fine. I tried to call you on your mobile, but it's always switched off. As you didn't call me back, I got the Meyers' number from Scarlet."

"You had me so worried. I thought something terrible had happened to the children."

He laughed. "They're here. They want to say hello." Angelica's eyes brimmed with tears. She felt the familiar pull in her chest and swallowed hard. "I'll pass you over. They're really missing you."

Angelica waited tensely as Olivier passed the telephone to Isabel. "Hello, Mummy."

"Hello, my darling. Are you having a nice time with Daddy?"

"I miss you." Her voice was small, and Angelica felt the tears spill onto her cheeks.

"I miss you, too, darling. But I'm coming home on Monday. We can have tea together. Shall we buy a cake at Patisserie Valerie on the way home from school?"

"The raspberry ones with cream?" The thought of cake cheered her up as Angelica knew it would.

"Any cake you like."

"I've painted you a picture."

"I can't wait to see it."

"Have you seen any animals?"

"Lots."

"Elephants and lions?"

"Lots of birds."

"Will you bring me back a bird?"

"There's a really pretty one called the orange-breasted sunbird. Sometimes they fly in a flock of thousands."

"Can I have one for my birthday?"

"I'm not allowed to take them out of South Africa. But I've bought you some pretty things."

"Do you want to speak to Joe?"

"Pass him on. I love you, darling."

"Love you, too, Mummy."

She wiped her cheeks with the back of her hand and waited while Isabel dropped the telephone, picked it up, and handed it to Joe.

"Come home, Mummy." Joe's voice was even more pathetic than Isabel's had been.

"I'm coming home on Monday."

"Why can't you come home now?"

"Because I have to take a plane, darling."

"Will you sleep on the plane?"

"Yes, for a whole night. Has Daddy been looking after you well?"

"He takes us to Patisserie Valerie."

"That's nice."

"But I want you to come home, because you're my best friend in the whole world."

"I miss the Full Joe."

"I'm empty."

"I'll be home on Monday to give you a great big cuddle and fill you up. You only have three more segments on your caterpillar, don't you?"

"We tear one off tonight before we go to bed."

"Then you'll only have two left."

"Yes. One more, then you come home."

"And give you the Full Mummy."

"Yes."

"I love you, darling. Will you pass me back to Daddy now?"

Joe kissed the telephone. His breathing was so close to the receiver that Angelica could almost touch him. "I love you in my heart," he said, before passing her back to Olivier.

Angelica could barely speak for the ball of emotion lodged in her throat. The longing to hold her children was visceral. For a moment she came to her senses. What was she doing out there with Jack, when her children were in London, needing her?

"So how's it going out there?" Olivier's voice reminded her of the old life she wasn't sure she wanted anymore.

"It's been a whirlwind," she croaked.

"I bet the Meyers' vineyard is really beautiful."

"It is. It's the most beautiful place I think I've ever been to. The sunsets are just magical."

"We miss you, Angelica. *I* miss you."

Something inside her cramped with fear. The echo of the children in the background made her want to hurry home with her guilty tail tucked between her legs in remorse, like a disgraced dog.

"I miss you, too," she replied automatically. But she didn't miss him at all; she was envisaging her children in South Africa where they could run wild like the steenboks of the veld.

She hung up and sat a while on the sofa, the image of Joe and Isabel playing among the vines burning a hole in her imagination. It was there that Jack found her.

"Is everything all right?" he asked, sitting beside her. She looked up, and a shadow of concern darkened his face as he registered her drying tears. "What's happened, Angelica?"

"Nothing. He just had me worried, that's all."

"The children are fine?"

"Yes. Everything's fine. I didn't expect him to call me here. He got your number from Scarlet. I truly thought something dreadful had happened. He frightened the life out of me." She placed a hand across her pounding heart.

"Do you want a drink?"

"Or two?"

He put his arm around her and pulled her close. "You'll see them on Monday."

"I know." She lowered her voice. "That's what terrifies me, Jack. I want to see my children, but I don't want Monday to come. I want to stay here with you."

"Don't think about Monday, my darling. It's still a long way off, and we still have many hours together." He stood up and offered her his hand.

She took it, rising to her feet. "I want you *and* my children, Jack."

"I know." He squeezed her hand reassuringly. "Come on, let's finish dinner, then we can sit in the pagoda and look at the stars."

Angelica felt she had to explain her tearstained face, so she repeated what she had told Jack about Joe and Isabel and how much she missed them.

"I hope I'll worry about them less when they're older."

Anna smiled serenely. "You worry about them more as they get older because the dangers get worse the more independent they become."

"Oh, Mum!" Lucy complained. "Come on, Fiona. I think it's a good time to leave." The girls excused themselves and disappeared into the house.

Anna laughed. "The trick is to worry about things where you have a certain degree of control, not about things over which you have no control at all."

"I worry about *everything*," said Angelica hopelessly.

"Worry is a negative emotion. It does nothing but eat away at you. If worry changes nothing except your state of mind, then it is better cast aside. Do you pray?"

"Yes. Mostly when things are bad."

"That's okay. But you pray for your children?"

"Of course."

"Then worry is like *negative* prayer. You're simply wrapping them in your dark thoughts. If you send them love, your thoughts reach them as light. Don't send them your fears, send them your love. Be constructive."

"Do you really believe in the power of prayer?"

Angelica looked at Anna and Jack, who were holding each

other's gaze for a long moment; she felt the chill of an outcast. They shared an understanding with which she could never hope to compete.

"I believe in miracles," Anna continued. "But I also believe there are things in our lives that are set in stone, things we cannot change, even with the power of prayer."

"Such as?"

"Death. When we have served our purpose, it is simply time to go home, whether we are young or old."

"I fear losing my children, all the time," Angelica confessed.

"So do I. But everything life throws at us is to teach us important lessons. We can't control what happens to us, but we can control how we react. The greatest freedom man has is choice." Angelica looked at Jack. Now she knew where he got his ideas. "Nietzsche said, 'He who has a *why* to live can bear with almost any *how*.'"

"Do you have a why?" Angelica asked.

"Yes. My life has purpose. There is purpose in everything life throws at me, good or bad. But no one can tell anyone else what their purpose is. Everyone must find it out for himself."

Angelica wondered what Scarlet would make of this conversation and smiled inwardly at the thought of her cynical face and rolling eyes.

"Let's go and look at the stars," said Jack, draining his glass.

"You go. I'm tired from picking all those grapes this morning. Tomorrow will be the same, so I think I'll go to bed early. I hope you don't mind."

Angelica felt guilty that her spirits lifted at the thought of being left alone with Jack. "Can I pick with you tomorrow?" she asked, getting up.

Anna looked pleased. "Of course. More hands the better."

"Then that is settled," said Jack, pushing out his chair. "We'll be up at dawn to pick. We'll have a braai here for lunch. Then I want to take Angelica into Stellenbosch."

"Good idea," Anna agreed.

"We can stop at Warwick on the way back for a sundowner."

"What's Warwick?"

"A beautiful vineyard about half an hour's drive from here."

"Don't forget I'm taking Lucy into Cape Town tomorrow afternoon. We won't be back until late." Anna embraced Angelica affectionately. "No more worrying, okay?"

"I'll try."

"Think positively. You won't help them by worrying about them. But you can help them by sending them positive thoughts of light and love."

"Then that is what I'll try to do."

"Good night. It's an early rise tomorrow, with the sun. You don't mind if I knock on your door to wake you?"

"Not at all. I want to join in. I've never picked grapes before."

"Sleep well, then—and enjoy the stars from my little pagoda." She smiled at her husband, a smile so loving that Angelica was left more confused than ever.

She walked down the garden with Jack and his dogs, cradling the cup of peppermint tea that Anxious had brought her. A bright moon threw long shadows across the lawn from behind the pine trees. Frogs croaked loudly from the lily pads, and crickets chirruped in the grass. The air was infused with the aromatic scent of damp soil and the heady perfume of gardenia and rose. They walked across the stepping-stones to the pretty white pagoda. In the center was Anna's meditation mat. Around the edge was a sofa and four big, comfortable armchairs in navy and white ticking. They sat together on the sofa, and Angelica slipped off her shoes and curled her legs beneath her. Jack lay back, stretched out his long legs, and threw an arm behind Angelica, pulling her close.

"You get all your ideas from Anna, don't you?"

He feigned ignorance. "What ideas?"

"Existential ones. Don't pretend not to know what I'm talking about. Either that or she's got her ideas from you."

"Okay, so she's taught me a lot about life."

"I thought it was something special that we shared."

"It is."

"Well, not exclusively."

"Does it matter?"

"I suppose not."

"I'm just as wise."

She sighed. "None of us is as wise as Anna."

"You're ten years younger than her. When you're her age, you'll be just as wise."

"I don't know. She was born wise, I suspect. Some people are. I'm just on a search."

"We're searching together. Don't forget Somebody Braai— *In Search of the Perfect Happiness*. Our groundbreaking work in progress."

"So what shall our first chapter be about?"

"The happiness of your life depends on the quality of your thoughts." He kissed her hairline. "When I think about you, I'm happy."

She took his hand and wrapped it around hers. "When I think about you, I'm happy, too."

They watched the stars twinkling above the shadowy silhouette of the mountains, discussing their book with zeal. The dogs lay on Anna's mat, lulled to sleep by the low monotone of their voices and the warm night air. When they retreated inside to go to bed, they crept up the stairs like schoolchildren returning from a midnight adventure. Jack followed her into her bedroom and pressed her against the back of the door to kiss her. He didn't attempt to do anything more than that.

"You need to sleep. We have a big day tomorrow."

"I wish we could curl up in bed together," she whispered.

"So do I. But you wouldn't get much sleep."

"I want you to make love to me again."

"I will." He kissed her nose. "But not tonight."

"It should be enough just to be near you. But it isn't."

His smile was so tender, her stomach seemed to flip over. "Just one more kiss, then I have to release you."

Once Jack had gone, she undressed and brushed her teeth, humming contentedly. She resolved not to think about Monday. After all, it wasn't the end of the affair, just the end of the weekend. There would be many more. Their love would grow, and they'd cross the world to be together.

She slipped on her nightdress, feeling the sensual pleasure of the silk against her skin, and wished Jack was waiting for her in her bed, his arms outstretched. She went over to the window, where a sugary breeze swept gently through the gap between the curtains. She pulled them aside and leaned on the sill. The valley had a romantic allure, set in shadow beneath a luminous navy sky, glittering with stars. She listened to the crickets, the distant croaking of frogs, the secret scurrying of nocturnal creatures hiding in the undergrowth. Then she saw a figure lit up in the moonlight, walking across the lawn. It was Jack. She caught her breath. Where on earth was he going at this time of night, and why hadn't he asked her to go with him? He was alone, but for one of his dogs, who trotted along beside him. It was a strange time to walk the dog. She went to bed feeling uneasy.

It seemed like the middle of the night when Anna knocked on her door to wake her. She mumbled something incoherent and opened her heavy eyes. It was still dark. Reluctantly, she got up and staggered over to open the curtains. The lawn was haunted by the memory of Jack walking across it during the night, and she felt her insides twist with anxiety. Now a light mist hung in the valley, replacing the luminous night. The air was cool, dogs barked in the distance, the chatter of guinea fowl added to the dawn chorus. She sensed the vineyard stirring to life with the smoke wafting up from the laborers' cottages. She dressed hastily and made her way downstairs, where Anxious had prepared a light breakfast on the terrace. She found Jack at the table. He didn't mention his nocturnal adventure, so she didn't, either, but she was relieved to find him in a happy mood. She dismissed her fears; there was nothing wrong with a man walking across his own lawn in the middle of the night if he felt so inspired. Perhaps he couldn't sleep. They ate quickly and headed out to the farm buildings as the first rays of dawn bled into the sky.

The air was charged with anticipation. The burly Afrikaans farm manager was barking instructions to the farmworkers as they prepared to head into the Sauvignon Blanc vineyards to pick the fruit. A bakkie drew up with a truckload of women and children from town to help with the picking, their singing rising merrily out of the mist. Jack strode about, talking to the workers, taking the manager aside for a quick word, deriving pleasure from being busy. Angelica stood with Anna, Lucy, and Fiona, thrilled to be part of the scene.

The tractors started up, and they were all carted off into the fields as the sun began to rise. Angelica was given gloves, a pair of cutters, and a crate. Anna explained how to use them. Then they set to work side by side, chatting as the guinea fowl waddled up and down the aisles, pecking at the soil. It was strenuous work, but invigorating, and Angelica's spirit swelled with pleasure as the light expanded and flooded the valley.

When the crates were full, they carried them to the tractor, which rattled back down the track to the winery. By ten o'clock the mist had lifted and the sun blazed down unobstructed. Half an hour later they were called to a halt, the sun now too hot to carry on. Finished for the day, they returned to the farm for refreshments. A table was spread out in the shade with traditional Cape food: bobotie, breyani, ghema curry, and koeksisters, washed down with wine. Angelica mingled with the workers, chatting and laughing, asking questions about their lives and listening with interest to their answers.

Angelica and the girls swam in the swimming pool to cool off before lunch. The pool was concealed behind a hedge with a pretty white hut to change in. Sun loungers were set in a row on the paving stones, and Anxious appeared with grenadilla juice on ice. Angelica wallowed in the cool water, taking in the fruit trees and climbing roses, listening to the girls' light chatter and the twittering of birds. She felt stiff from riding the day before, and her arms ached in a pleasurable way from her morning's work.

Just before lunch, Kat and Dan Scott arrived from the neighboring vineyard. Kat was athletic and blond, with pale blue eyes and full pink lips that curled into an infectious smile. Her long legs stretched out slim and brown beneath a miniskirt, and her toenails were painted bubblegum pink. Her handsome husband was unable to take his eyes off her and grinned indulgently at everything she said. Jack cooked the braai beneath a shady plane tree, the dogs circling like greedy wolves in the hope of scraps. Anna held court in the pagoda as Kat and Dan told them about their honeymoon in Brazil, and Dan, never one to miss an opportunity to amuse, told stories against himself that had everyone holding their stomachs from laughing. Angelica remembered when she and Olivier had been so happy. She glanced at Jack and knew that *they* could be happy like that, were they ever given the chance. Was it beyond probability that one day they might end up together, holding hands and flaunting their love like Kat and Dan?

Kat turned to Angelica. "Jack tells us you're going to War-wick this afternoon."

"Yes, I hear it's beautiful."

"Oh, it really is. It has a stunning view of Table Mountain. You must go for a sundowner."

"It produces the most delicious wine," said Dan knowl-edgeably. "The Sauvignon Blanc is unique because of a spe-cial hybrid of peach tree planted by a horticulturist called Professor Black. They were the first variety to withstand the southeaster. After the professor's peaches were removed they planted the first Sauvignon Blanc. You can definitely taste peach in it. It has a unique bouquet."

"Oh, and they have that gold cup that two people can drink out of at the same time."

"Tell her the story," Dan encouraged his wife.

Kat took Dan's hand and smiled at him fondly, stirred by a happy memory they shared. "It's a lovely story. Once there was a beautiful maiden called Kunigunde, who fell in love with a young, ambitious goldsmith. She refused the hand of many rich suitors and finally confessed her secret love to her father, a powerful nobleman. He was so angry that he threw the young goldsmith into the dungeon. Kunigunde's heart was broken. She pined for him and began to fade away with grief. Finally, her father relented and told the goldsmith that if he could make a chalice from which two people could drink at the same time without spilling a single drop, he would be free to marry his daughter. Of course, he never believed such an invention was possible. But the goldsmith was inspired by love, and with love anything is possible. So he set about making this special cup. His fingers formed an exquisite skirt-shaped chalice, the like of which no one had ever seen before. At the top stood a model of his virtuous and beautiful Kuni-gunde, who, with upraised arms, held a small, movable cup. It was simple, yet ingenious. Two people could easily drink from it at the same time without spilling a single drop. The king was astonished but stood by his promise. No one was happier than the young couple, who earned his blessing to marry and lived happily ever after." She gazed languidly at Dan. "We've drunk from it, haven't we, Danny?"

"And not a drop was spilled," he replied.

"Thank God! I imagine it's very bad luck if it does!"

"I can't wait to see it." Angelica felt inspired by the story that showed how with love anything was possible.

"Shame your husband isn't here with you."

Anna laughed lightly. "Don't worry. I'll lend her mine."

They all laughed with her, except for Angelica, who didn't know how to respond. She sipped her grenadilla and tried to hide her blushes behind her hair.

"And don't forget to toast good old Professor Black!" Dan added merrily.

26

The best way to predict the future is to invent it.

In Search of the Perfect Happiness

That afternoon Jack and Angelica drove to Stellenbosch. Jack parked the car, and they wandered up the harmonious streets of Cape Dutch houses, beneath avenues of leafy plane trees. The white buildings gleamed in the dazzling sunshine, beneath an uninterrupted cerulean sky. They stopped at a café, sitting at a small round table on the pavement in the shade of a green-and-white umbrella.

Their mood was buoyant after their morning in the fields. They chatted about their book, and Angelica bought a few more presents for Joe and Isabel. It hadn't occurred to her to buy anything for Olivier. At four they drove to Warwick Wine Estate for tea. Nestled beneath the shadow of Simonsberg Mountain, Warwick was a charming old vineyard in the Cape Dutch tradition.

They were met by James Dare, a laid-back Englishman with a hearty laugh and irrepressible sense of humor. They drank the famous Professor Black Sauvignon Blanc on the veranda as Jack and James discussed the quality of the grape. The sun threw a vibrant palette of reds and golds across Table Mountain, and fish eagles circled the dam in search of supper.

Before they departed, Angelica requested a drink out of the famous marriage cup.

"So you know the story?" said James.

"Kat Scott told me at lunch. It's a lovely tale."

"I'll ask Belle to go and get it." He called to his wife.

"Is it bad luck to drink with a man who is not my husband?"

"Not at all. It's not just a symbol of love and faithfulness, but of good luck, too."

"Wonderful! We all need good luck," she said.

"How long are you staying?"

"I leave tomorrow evening." She pulled a face. "Don't! I can't bear it. I've had such a magical time. South Africa is the most beautiful country I've ever been to. The countryside is spectacular. I've never seen such magnificent sunsets. If it wasn't for my children, I think I'd stay forever." She avoided Jack's eye, although she felt his gaze as surely as if it were sunshine.

Belle brought out the marriage cup, a shiny chalice just as Kat had described.

"How very clever!" Angelica exclaimed, taking it so she could get a closer look.

The metal was intricately engraved and highly polished. She gave it to James, who turned the skirt upwards. "Professor Black Sauvignon Blanc 2008 vintage," he said, pouring. "Right, Jack, you hold it towards you at an angle. Angelica, this is for you." He poured a little into the movable cup. Angelica, dizzy from the wine she had already consumed, began to giggle nervously. She looked into Jack's brown eyes and put her lips to the cup. Without taking their eyes off each other, they both drank. She didn't know whether it was nerves or the alcohol, or the silent words she read behind his glasses, but she began to laugh, snorting through her nostrils so that her cup tipped and wine dribbled down her chin. This made her laugh all the more. Infected by her amusement, Jack and

James joined in as Belle put her hands on her hips and shook her head.

"I hope you're not superstitious," she said with a grin.

"What will be, will be," said Jack when he managed to control his mirth. "Spilled wine won't make the slightest bit of difference."

"Oh dear! I'm so sorry," Angelica apologized, wiping her chin. "Has that ever happened before?"

"No," James replied, chuckling. "Most people take it very seriously."

"Luckily, you're not married," said Belle. That made Angelica laugh all the more. *If only they knew,* she thought. *If I wasn't laughing so much, I'd cry.*

Jack and Angelica were still laughing in the car on the road back to Rosenbosch. It was now dark. The sky was almost purple, the valley lit by a round, pregnant moon. Stars shone bright as cut glass. They held hands, aware that this was their last night together.

"Anna won't be back until late."

"What are you suggesting?"

"That we make love in the pagoda."

"Anna's pagoda?"

"It's not hers. It's *ours.*"

"I'm not sure it's the place to commit adultery."

He glanced at her, frowning. "You leave tomorrow. I don't know when I'll see you again. I want to have you tonight."

She smiled and squeezed his hand. "We'll think of something."

They drove down the avenue of camphor trees. The lights were on in the house. Jack looked at his watch. It was seven-thirty.

"I had hoped Anxious would have gone home by now," he said.

"You can send her home, can't you?"

"Of course. I just want to be alone with you."

They drew up and climbed out. He stood a moment, staring at the door, a frown lining his forehead.

"What's wrong?"

"I don't know. Nothing." He shrugged off his doubts and opened the front door. "Anxious!" The house was silent. He glanced at Angelica, his face suddenly pale.

"Are you all right?"

"I don't know. Get back into the car."

"I'm not leaving you alone."

"Do as I say."

But she followed him through the house to the terrace. As he opened the kitchen door Angelica saw blood on the tiles and caught her breath in horror.

Before she could scream at the sight of the dead dogs, a gang of Africans swept onto them like birds of prey. They seemed to materialize from nowhere, wrapping grubby hands over their mouths and pointing guns to their temples. Jack didn't struggle, knowing they would have no compunction about shooting them, too. The men whispered urgently to one another in a language she didn't understand and marched them through the hall into the dining room. Angelica was so paralyzed with fear they had to drag her. There, in the corner, sat Anxious, her bright smile reduced to an unhappy line of fear. She raised her bloodshot eyes to Jack.

"I'm sorry, Master." She began to cry.

"It's not your fault, Anxious. Angelica, don't struggle, and do everything they tell you to do. For God's sake, don't look at their faces."

He proceeded to speak to them in their own language. Pleading for their lives, she assumed. Telling them to take everything but their futures. Even in that moment of deepest terror, Angelica couldn't help but be impressed.

They bound their hands behind their backs and their feet together with ties they must have found in Jack's bedroom, then ordered them to sit on the floor beside the dining room table, back to back.

"Those are my favorite ties," he hissed at Angelica.

"God, Jack. How can you joke at a time like this?"

"Fear."

"The dogs . . ."

"Don't."

"Are they going to kill us?"

"Not if we do as they say and remain calm."

"I'm so frightened."

"We're in this together, Angelica, and we'll come out of this together. I won't let them hurt you." His voice was so full of conviction, she believed him.

A gang member with bulging black eyes knelt beside Jack. "Where are your mobile phones?" he demanded in English. His breath smelled of spirits.

"In my shirt pocket," Jack replied calmly. He delved into Jack's shirt and removed his phone.

"Where's the safe?"

"We don't have a safe."

"You're lying."

"There's cash in the study, top right drawer. We have nothing to hide."

"Everyone has a safe."

"We were robbed ten years ago. After that, we decided not to have a safe. Take what you want and go."

Bulging Eyes hissed at another gang member standing by the door and ordered him to go to the study to find the money. Angelica was petrified. She thought of her children and how much they still needed her. *Remain calm, don't cry, hold it together for Joe and Isabel. They won't kill us. They'll take everything valuable and leave.*

Bulging Eyes leaned over Jack. "We're going to tear your house apart, and if we find a safe, I will personally cut your throat like an animal."

Angelica was too shocked to cry. She felt as weak and vulnerable as a little bird. Was it naïve to pray for help? Was it possible that someone might have seen them enter and called the police? She closed her eyes and prayed.

"There's no safe," Jack repeated.

Angelica opened her eyes and looked over at Anxious, the personification of her extraordinary name. She was somehow smaller than before, as if the air had been punched out of her. Her right cheek was beginning to bruise. Angelica sent a hasty prayer to God, requesting only that their lives be preserved. *I'm not ready to leave my children,* she pleaded. *Or Olivier. Oh, Olivier, what have I done? Please God, forgive me. I promise from now on I'll be good. Don't let them separate me from my children, I beg of you. Let us live. Please God, let us live.*

A moment later the man appeared with a cash box and spoke to Bulging Eyes, who grew red with fury. "Is that all you have?" he spat. "A few thousand dollars?"

"The rest is in a bank. We don't keep much cash in the house. There's silver in the pantry."

Another man rushed in with Anna's jewelry box.

"There must be more than this!"

"My wife doesn't wear jewelry."

Bulging Eyes turned his attention to Angelica and her bound hands hidden from view. He grabbed her arm, yanking it out from behind her back with such force she thought it would dislocate. "All women like jewelry." He clearly thought she was Jack's wife. He grabbed her fingers and noticed they were bare. She silently thanked Anita for making her hide her diamond rings in her wash bag, although, in the circumstances, she would happily give them up in exchange for their lives.

"I'm going to ask your wife where the safe is. If she doesn't tell me, I'm going to enjoy her." He ran the barrel of his gun up her naked leg, hovering on her thigh. His grin was so lascivious she knew he meant it.

Her heart stalled, but she felt Jack's hot back against hers and was encouraged. "There is no safe," she repeated bravely.

Overcome with impatience, Bulging Eyes called out, "Somebody!" Somebody appeared at once—a tall, lanky African with cheekbones as sharp as polished granite. Bulging Eyes ordered him to watch the prisoners while he disappeared into the hall. Somebody jiggled from one foot to another, pointing the gun at Jack.

"He's not going to find a safe that isn't there," said Jack impatiently. "Help will arrive at any minute. Why don't you take what you have and go before it's too late?"

"Sorry about the dogs," Somebody replied. "I like dogs."

"Listen, Somebody. I don't care about money or possessions. They are replaceable. I only care about my family. If I had a safe, I'd open it for you and give you everything inside. You have to believe me."

"The boss heard that you have a safe."

"Then it's misinformation."

Somebody shrugged. "He'll kill you. He's killed before, many times. He enjoys it."

Angelica closed her eyes, drowning in a sense of helplessness.

Bulging Eyes returned looking more livid than ever. In his hand he held a kettle. Kneeling down, he hissed into Jack's ear. "If you don't tell me where you hide your money, I'm going to boil your penis." He plugged the kettle into the wall and turned his bloodshot eyes to Angelica. "Then I'm going to kill your wife like a pig."

Angelica's head swam as she gazed into the abyss. "Oh God!"

"Be calm!" Jack hissed. "You are a sensible man. Why would I risk my life and that of my wife and servant for something as unimportant as money and jewelry? I've told you, there is no safe."

He then began to talk in their language once again. A heated discussion followed as the kettle began to steam. Suddenly another man appeared in the door. A shout resounded from the front of the house like a bullet. Bulging Eyes stood up in alarm. He hurried into the hall a moment, then returned, his face taut with panic.

"Where are the keys to your car?"

"On the table in the hall. By the front door." There was hope in Jack's voice. Angelica clung to it like a rock climber to a rope.

"I know you're a liar!" he accused. His face looked like a swollen bladder about to burst. Pointing the gun at Jack, he fired.

Angelica wasn't aware of the gang leaving the house, piling into Jack's car, and speeding down the drive. She heard Jack cry out, then saw the stream of blood making a pool around them. She froze in terror, her mind flooding with fear.

"Jack!" she cried, desperately trying to wriggle her hands out of the tie. "Jack! Speak to me." Jack began to laugh. "Oh, Jack! Please don't die!" She shuffled around so that she could see him, all the while working on her hands.

"They shot me in the shoulder."

"Are you in pain?"

"Not really." He looked at the puddle. "I'm ruining the rug."

"You're going to be okay."

Anxious whimpered in the corner.

"They cut the phone lines. No one will find us now," she wailed.

Finally, Angelica's hands slipped through the tie. She didn't feel the pain as they were forced through the material. She released her legs and set about doing the same for Jack.

"Hold on, Jack. You're going to be fine. I'm right here." From somewhere she found a strength she didn't know she had. "We're going to get out of this, my darling. You're going to be fine." She pulled off her shirt and wrapped it around the wound, pulling it tightly to stave the blood flow. "I'm not going to let those bastards take you from me. I've just found you, and I intend to keep you."

She got up, staggered over to Anxious, and untied her hands and feet.

"Go and get help, as quickly as you can!"

Angelica's voice was commanding, and Anxious gathered herself, grateful to be of use once more. She hurried out of the room, determined to raise the alarm.

Angelica ran into the kitchen, past the pile of slaughtered dogs, to the telephone. As Anxious had informed her, the line was dead. For a moment she slumped over the sideboard, defeated. The dead dogs lay like sodden coats, reminding her of the gravity of their predicament, and she gave in to a wave of helplessness. *This is not happening,* she thought, closing her eyes. But it *was* happening, and she had to be strong for Jack. Pulling herself together, she grabbed some tea towels and returned to the dining room. As she pressed the towels into Jack's shoulder, she noticed he had gone very pale.

"Hang on, Jack. You're going to be all right. Help is on its way."

"I have something to tell you, Sage."

"Nothing matters, darling. Don't waste your energy."

"I'm dying."

"You're not. You're going to be okay."

"Listen to me, Angelica." His tone was firm. She stopped talking. He held her naked arm with a blood-soaked hand and stared into her eyes. "I've been dying for years."

Her stomach lurched with his constant reference to his own mortality. "What are you talking about?"

"I have lung cancer, Angelica."

Her hands began to tremble as she mopped his shoulder with a tea towel. "I know. Scarlet told me. But you're better now."

"No, I'm not." He winced with pain as she put pressure on his torn flesh. "It came back. There was nothing more the doctors could do for me. I'm dying, Angelica, whether I die of a bullet to my shoulder or from the cancer in my lungs. The truth of the matter is, I have very little time to live. That is why I wanted to live it fully."

"It's not true!" She began to shake with frustration. "I'm not going to listen to this! We need to get help! I'm not going to let you die."

"It doesn't really matter one way or another. We've had fun, haven't we?"

"And we'll have more fun. More sundowners. More rides across the veld. Our lives are just beginning."

But Jack shook his head forlornly. "No, my darling Sage. My life is ending."

"I won't believe you! I've dreamed of growing old with you. I've fantasized about leaving Olivier for you, bringing the children out here, starting afresh with the man I love. I've dreamed of sacrificing everything for you. Don't tell me you're dying. I won't believe you!"

"You must. I didn't want to tell you and spoil everything. But there's a very good chance, by the size of this pool of blood, that I might die at any minute. So I want you to know the truth: that you have kept me going these last few months. That without your love and laughter I would have sunk into depression as my life slowly ebbed away."

She stopped attending his wound and slumped beside him.

"Are you telling me that all the while we've been together, you've known that you're dying?"

"Yes. I should have told you, but for my own selfish reasons, I couldn't. At first you were just another beautiful woman who captured my attention. But you are different from every other woman in the world." He rested his head against hers. "I love the way you make fun of yourself and the way you laugh. I love your vagueness and your vulnerability, and yet your intelligence shines out in spite of your lack of confidence. I love the way you challenge yourself and the way you write, allowing your heart to spill onto the page. I love the way you blush when I compliment you and the way you make love with such abandon. There's no one else like you, Sage. Before I knew what I was doing, you crawled beneath my skin and I realized I couldn't live without you. I thought I knew what love was, but I hadn't a clue until I loved you. You gave me the will to live. You made me feel strong enough to beat anything life threw at me, including my cancer. But not even your indomitable spirit could beat that." He winced again as the pain seared through his body. "I wasn't in London on business, but seeing a healer I hoped might save me."

"Mrs. Homer."

"Scarlet's scarlet woman!" He chuckled weakly.

"Oh, Jack."

"I was clutching at straws. I so want to live. I haven't done half the things I want to do."

"You'll do all those things and more."

"No, I won't. I won't live to take my daughters down the aisle. I won't watch them become mothers. I won't be there to support them when they fail, to knock the lights out of boyfriends who treat them badly. I won't ride with you across the veld and picnic at Sir Lowry's Pass and make love to you. I just won't be here anymore, and that is impossible to comprehend or accept."

"And Anna?"

"My darling Anna . . . Every time I look into her eyes I see my own death reflected in them. I see her pity and her sorrow. When I look into yours, I see the man I always was. I see myself as you see me. If I had told you the truth, you would have looked at me in the same way that Anna looks at me. I couldn't bear that."

"So, it *is* true."

"I wish it wasn't."

She fought back tears, determined not to let Jack see her cry. "I don't want you to leave me, Jack. I've only just found you."

"It is better to have loved and lost than never to have loved at all." He smiled, knowing they would usually laugh at such a cliché.

"Better for whom?"

"I'm sorry, Sage."

"Did you ever think about *me*?"

"I thought about you all the time. I wanted to tell you."

"But what? You couldn't find the words?"

"The only words that matter are that I love you."

"I'm not sure, Jack. The truth matters if we are to trust each other." She waited for him to reply. When he didn't, she turned to look at him. His eyes were closed. "Jack?"

Suddenly, the house was swarming with people: farmworkers, police, ambulance men, and Anna, ashen with terror, bending over her husband as he was carried out on a stretcher. Lucy was crying over her dead dog, being comforted by Anxious, now restored and keen to be of use. The farmworkers' wives handed around mugs of tea and biscuits. Angelica sat on the sofa in the sitting room with the chief of police, recounting what had happened, while he made his way through a large plateful of shortbread. Now that it was all over, she began to tremble with the aftershock, as cold as if it were the middle of winter in spite of the blanket that had been placed around her to protect her modesty. She suddenly wanted more than anything to call Olivier. She longed for home with a yearning so powerful it overwhelmed her.

Anna left Jack in the capable hands of the ambulance staff and came back to the house. She looked small and frail, but her face remained composed.

"Is he going to be okay?" Angelica asked apprehensively. The chief of police went in search of another biscuit.

"He's lost a lot of blood, but he's going to live."

Angelica bit her lip and began to cry. Anna sat beside her and put her arms around her. "But he's still going to die?" she whispered into Anna's ear, clinging to her like a shipwrecked sailor to a piece of driftwood.

"Yes. He's going to die."

A vise tightened its grip on her sinking heart. "I didn't know."

"I'm sorry."

"How long has he got?"

"Not long. A few months. No one knows."

"I feel such a fool."

Anna pulled away and looked at Angelica with compassion. "If you're a fool to love Jack, then so am I."

"No, you're a good person, Anna. *I'm* bad."

"My dear Angelica, you've made him so happy. There's nothing bad in that, at least, not from my perspective."

"It doesn't make you unhappy that I love him?"

"Why would it? There are many different ways to love, and the human heart has an unlimited capacity. If that wasn't so, you wouldn't have the space to love both your children, *and* your husband, *and* Jack. But you do. You love them all. I don't begrudge Jack for loving you, either. Even if he wasn't sick I wouldn't hold him back. We don't own each other, Angelica. We just choose to be together while we live this life here on earth. I don't possess his heart. I have no right to. But since he is dying, he knows he has my blessing to live his last months, weeks, days, hours, as he chooses."

"You are a truly exceptional woman, Anna."

"I don't feel at all exceptional, but I do know that my love for Jack has made me a better human being. It's a good feeling to know that I love him enough to take pleasure from his happiness."

"Olivier isn't anything like as generous spirited as you. If he knew about . . . well, he'd be furious."

"The greatest measure for good and bad is not a book of laws. They differ from culture to culture. What is bad in one country is considered good in another. No, the best gauge is whether or not you are hurting someone else. Adultery is not a sin in my marriage, but it is in yours because Olivier would be deeply hurt by it. Therefore, it is not right."

"I should call him." Angelica felt contrite.

"Yes, you should."

"I'll go upstairs and see if those bastards have taken my passport. I hid it in my wash bag with my rings."

Angelica got up. Her legs felt unsteady. Anna accompanied her into the hall. Now that they were being honest with each other, she felt she could ask her anything. "I saw Jack walking across the lawn in the middle of the night. Where was he going?"

"Jack doesn't like to sleep, Angelica. He fears that there is always a chance he might not wake up. So he walks. It makes him feel better."

"I sensed something wasn't right. I just couldn't put my finger on what it was."

"I see it in his eyes every time I look into them." Angelica frowned at her. "Fear, Angelica. I see his fear of dying, and it breaks my heart."

"I didn't set out to fall in love with him, Anna."

"I know. But you have a family who need you. You must go back to them." Angelica nodded and made to leave, but Anna stopped her.

"One other thing," she said, taking Angelica's hand.

"Yes?"

"Jack has had many lovers during our marriage, as I'm sure you know. But he's never lost his heart before. They've always come and gone with the seasons. But you?" She smiled kindly. "You're beyond the seasons, Angelica, like the sun."

PART THREE

Wisdom

27

Life is a celebration.

In Search of the Perfect Happiness

Angelica sat at the kitchen table in her house in Brunswick Gardens, hugging a mug of tea. It was raining, the clouds thick and gray like gruel. The trees were bare, twisted and gnarled in the cold. One or two people hurried past beneath umbrellas, their footsteps disappearing as they strode down the pavement towards the High Street. Olivier poured himself a cup of coffee.

Sunny went upstairs tactfully to tidy the children's bedrooms. Olivier had told her the terrible news about the robbery the night before, and she had taken the children to school that morning while Olivier had driven to the airport to meet his wife. He had never seen Angelica look so pale and thin. It was as if she hadn't eaten for the entire week—and Olivier, usually so imperturbable, had stayed up all night watching television, unable to sleep for worry.

Angelica had dreaded going home to the bleak winter weather, but now she embraced it. Those low hanging clouds and the light, persistent drizzle were as familiar to her as family. Heathrow had felt like home, the friendly English passport controllers like relatives. She had run into Olivier's arms and clung to him, hoping that if she pressed herself close enough there'd be no space for her adultery. He need never find out. Nothing would come between them to prize them apart.

He had asked about Jack on the way back in the car. "He's going to live," she had replied, then collapsed into violent sobs. How could she explain that while one wound healed, the other in his lungs would surely kill him? How could she explain the depth of her love and the degree of his betrayal? Would she have chosen to love him had she known he had only months to live? Would she have allowed herself to get so close only to lose him in the end? Had he really loved her at all?

She sipped her tea and felt better now that she was home. She had climbed back into her skin with haste and remorse, only to find that it no longer fit so snugly. It didn't matter. It felt familiar, and she was pleased to put it on again with her rings. She longed to hold her children, but knowing they were in the same city was good enough. Her old life was where she had left it, and nothing had changed but her heart, which no one could see.

She watched Olivier pour hot milk into his coffee. While she had focused on Jack, she had ignored the fact that Olivier wasn't only her husband, but her best friend, too. She had chosen not to see his good qualities and concentrated solely on the qualities that irritated her in order to justify her affair. He had apologized for their row about the coat, but she hadn't forgiven him: while she was still angry she felt entitled to Jack. The truth was that Olivier, in spite of his impatience, was funny and charming and affectionate. He was suffering at work, in the very center of the crisis that was shaking the financial world, trying to hold it all together for her and the children, and she hadn't been there for him. She had shirked her responsibility to her family for a fleeting, dead-end affair. She stared into her tea, plagued with guilt.

"I think you need to talk to Candace," said Olivier, sitting down at the table. She looked into his clear blue eyes and realized that she had forgotten how beautiful they were.

"Not yet, Olivier. I want to talk to *you*."

He looked surprised, but she knew he was pleased. "Do you know what I was thinking when I was tied up there in the dining room not knowing if I was going to live?"

"Joe and Isabel."

"And you, Olivier." Her eyes glittered. "I felt remorse. I wished I had never said a hurtful word to you in our entire marriage. I wished I'd appreciated you, not grumbled about your imperfections. After all, I married you for those."

"Did you?" He grinned, and she was reminded of the first time that smile had captivated her all those years ago in Paris. It hadn't changed; she had just grown used to it.

"Yes, because it's your imperfections that make you different from everyone else. Without them you wouldn't be you."

"That's very sweet of you, but I'm not sure that's true."

He took her hand across the table. It was smaller and smoother than Jack's. For a moment she longed for the rough, calloused hand of the rugged South African, but she had to put him behind her now. She belonged with Olivier. If she concentrated on him hard enough, would she forget Jack had ever existed?

"I have had time to think while you have been away, and certainly, last night, I did more thinking than ever. When you went to South Africa and we had had that fight, I worried I was losing you. But last night, I felt close to losing you in a different way. I just wanted you home, where you are safe. I love you, Angelica, but I also need you. I am nothing without you. I'm half a man. I know I am difficult, selfish, and demanding, but I am going to make a conscious effort to be a better husband and a better friend."

"We'll both make an effort."

Angelica lowered her eyes in shame. She hadn't even bothered to remember his birthday back in October. It would have passed like any other day had his mother not called at seven in the morning. Angelica had rushed to Gucci and bought him a jacket and a pair of brown lace-ups, and Kate had managed to book her a table for two at the Ivy.

He lifted her hand to his lips and kissed it. "Before you call Candace, you'd better call your mother."

Angelica looked at her husband in horror. "You told her?"

"Of course. She's your mother. You could have been killed, Angelica. She has a right to know. Besides, I didn't know what state you'd be in once I got you home. Don't be angry. At least I fended her off. She threatened to drive down this morning. She's worried sick."

"Sure she is." Angelica chuckled cynically.

"Just call her."

Angelica dialed Fenton Hall with a sinking heart. The last thing she needed was her mother fussing over her. It rang only twice before Angie picked it up and breathed down the line in a little-girl-lost tone of voice. "Is that you, love?"

"Yes, it's me."

"Thank the Lord you're safely home. My God, we've been worried about you. I'm coming down right away."

"You don't need to."

"I'm your mother, and I want to!"

"I'm fine. It was horrid, but it's over."

"I'm coming. There's nothing you can do to stop me. Your father and I have been beside ourselves with worry. This is a wake-up call, as loud as any I've ever heard."

"I promise you, I'm fine," Angelica protested.

"But I'm not. I need to see you, love. Surely *you* understand a mother's need?"

Angelica did, indeed, understand a mother's need. Grudgingly, she relented. "All right, I'll see you later, then."

• • •

News traveled fast along the buzzing network of grapevines that crossed oceans. Anna had called Scarlet, who had called Kate, who had called Letizia, who had called Candace, who had waited tactfully for Angelica to call her.

"Oh my God, Angelica, are you all right!" she exclaimed down the telephone. "You don't know how happy I am to hear your voice!"

"Oh, Candace, you're going to say I told you so."

"I promise I won't. I'm coming over right now. Oh, and the girls are coming over for lunch, but don't panic, we're bringing our own food."

"Now, why doesn't that surprise me!"

She put down the telephone and hurried upstairs to take a quick shower. There was no point moping about. The sooner life got back to normal, the better. The thought of her friends brought on a strange craving, like homesickness—a longing for what was routine and familiar.

Olivier went to the office. Angelica cried in the shower. She thought of Jack in his hospital bed, and she cried for the cancer in his lungs and for the inevitability of his demise. She recalled the last thing he had said to her, that the only important words were that he loved her. So why did she doubt him? Then she cried with fury at his concealing the truth and taking his pleasure without any regard for her tender heart. Did he not once consider what impact his death might have on *her*? Was he just going to satisfy his own need for validation and then leave her adrift? Or didn't it matter, seeing that he'd be gone and no longer responsible for the lives destroyed?

Angelica was still in her bathrobe when Candace rang the bell. Sunny let her in, and Angelica called to her from the landing. The moment she saw Candace's concerned face she began to cry all over again.

"Honey, it's going to be all right," said Candace, opening her arms. "Hearts get broken, but they mend." Candace was so tall, she hugged Angelica as if she were a child, then walked with her into the bedroom.

Angelica curled up against the pillows. Candace took off her Ralph Lauren tweed jacket and laid it carefully on the upholstered armchair in the corner. The room smelled of figs from the Dyptique candle Angelica had lit in the bathroom. The television was switched on to the Top 40 music videos. Candace took the control and turned it down, then kicked off her shoes and joined Angelica on the bed.

"Okay, so what happened out there?"

"I lied to you, Candace. I went out to South Africa with the intention of having an affair. I encouraged the row with Olivier to justify it. We met the moment I set foot in my hotel." Angelica picked up the cord of her dressing gown and began to play with it like a cat's tail.

"Well, I know all that." She laughed gently. "I know *you*, silly. But you know what? You can teach a person knowledge, but you can't teach her wisdom. That can only come from experience."

"Now I have the wisdom of an old woman."

"You look like an old woman with all that crying."

"I daren't look!"

"It doesn't matter. We'll sort you out before the girls get here."

"I'm glad they're coming."

"I thought you would be."

She sighed. "I just want things to go back to the way they were."

"They can never do that, but you can learn to live with the experience."

"I was so frightened."

"Wait, you're getting ahead of yourself. So you met him in Johannesburg?"

"He was staying in the same hotel. We made love. It was perfect and heavenly, and I forgot about Olivier and the children . . ." She raised her eyes, ashamed. "You'd be surprised how easy it is to forget yourself."

"Go on."

"He went back to his farm; I continued my events. We met again in Cape Town when he drove me to Rosenbosch."

"His farm?"

"Yes, the most beautiful vineyard you have ever seen. Oh my God, Candace, it's like paradise."

"I can imagine."

"But first he took me up to this pass to watch the sunset. He'd brought wine, and we drank and laughed and watched the sky turn red and gold. It was amazing. Then we went to his house, and I met Anna, his wife, and she asked me about the sunset. She had told Jack to take me up there."

"A little odd, didn't you think?"

"It gets even stranger. I got the feeling that she was purposely leaving Jack and me on our own, as if she knew we were having an affair and condoned it."

"What's she like?"

"She's incredible. I liked her the moment I saw her. I didn't want to, but I couldn't help myself. She has an extraordinary charisma, as if she's a glowing lightbulb and I'm a fly."

"Honey, you'd *never* be a fly!"

"A moth."

"A butterfly."

Angelica smiled and sniffed. "A very small creature. There's no side to her. She is wholly good and kind and generous, and there's nothing she doesn't know about."

"Where's the catch?"

"There *is* a catch." Angelica tried to control her tears by blinking. "But wait. We spent two magical days together, and Anna left us alone all the time. Then, on Saturday evening, we drove back from a neighboring vineyard. Jack sensed something was wrong. But we were so determined to spend our last evening alone together that we marched in. Anxious wasn't there . . ."

"Anxious?"

"The maid."

"She's really called that?"

"She really is."

"I *love* it!"

"Poor Anxious. She was tied up and dumped in the dining room. They had slaughtered all the dogs. They were piled up there in the kitchen like skins. It was horrible. This gang of blacks descended on us. I thought we were dead. I was so scared. But Jack was very calm. They wanted to know where the safe was, and Jack kept telling them there wasn't one, but they didn't believe him. You know, one of them was called Somebody."

"Wow! That's a cool name, too! Shame I've finished breeding."

"He didn't really want to be there, you could tell. Anyway, the leader shot Jack on his way out, for no reason. Jack was bound and helpless, and he just shot him."

"Is he going to be okay?"

"Yes. He bled a lot. Oh my God, the amount of blood. You wouldn't believe a person could bleed so much and live. But he is stable. Now for the catch."

"Here, let me get you a tissue."

"I don't have any."

"Then loo roll will have to do." Candace padded into the bathroom and came back with a whole roll. Angelica dabbed her eyes gratefully. "So what's the catch?"

"Jack is dying of lung cancer."

Candace's jaw swung open in astonishment. Even she couldn't have foreseen that. "He's dying of cancer?"

"Yes. He told me as he bled onto the rug. He said it didn't matter one way or the other because he was going to die anyway."

"Holy shit!" Candace shook her head. "This is *really* heavy duty."

"I know. I didn't believe him at first, but he insisted. He said he was sorry that he hadn't told me earlier, but he hadn't wanted to spoil things."

"Hold on. He encouraged an affair *knowing* that he only had a limited time to live?" Now Candace was cross.

"Yes. He said I made him feel like the man he used to be, whereas his wife looked at him with pity."

"Oh great! So he uses you to forget his illness?"

"I suppose so."

"How *selfish* is that? I *told* you he was selfish. You know, if he had *once* considered you and your family, he would *never* have pursued you. I *knew* he was selfish right from the start." When Candace got angry, her nostrils flared and she emphasized her words with verve, as if punching them out with her anger.

"I believe he loves me."

"Of *course* he loves you! What isn't there to love? But he shouldn't have made you fall in love with *him*."

"If I had listened to you that day in Starbucks, none of this would have happened."

"And the girls would have nothing to talk about!" Candace laughed.

"That's not true. I imagine Kate has kept you all busy this past week."

"And some!"

"Oh dear."

"I'll let her fill you in. The last thing I want to do is steal her thunder, and besides, I'm not done yet."

"Okay, so the last thing he said to me before he passed out was that the only important thing was that he loved me."

"And you haven't spoken to him since?"

"No. But get this? Anna told me that she loves him enough to take pleasure from his happiness."

"From his screwing around?"

"I wouldn't put it quite like that. She isn't possessive. She really isn't."

"She's clearly not from this world."

"I think you're right. She told me that he has had many affairs but that he's never lost his heart to anyone like he lost it to me."

"Generous of her to share that with you." Candace raised an eyebrow cynically.

"I'm not sure that he does though. I feel wretched and betrayed. I left yesterday evening on my scheduled flight without a word to him. I'd hidden my passport and rings in my wash bag." She fingered her diamonds fondly.

"Clever you."

"Only because the rep in Jo'burg told me to. Thank God for her."

"I'd hate to think of those brutes running off with your beautiful diamonds."

"So would I. I don't know what they ran off with. Not much, I suspect. South Africans don't keep large quantities of money and jewelry in the house for that very reason."

"I don't know whether to admire Anna or mistrust her."

"If you met her, you certainly wouldn't mistrust her. She's the real thing, I tell you."

"So what are you going to do?"

"I'm hoping you're going to tell me."

"You really want my advice?" She chuckled. "I'm rather wary of giving it to you, after all you've been through."

"No, I want you to tell me what is right. I'm ready to listen now."

"Okay, if you're sure."

"I am. I should have listened to you months ago."

"You love him, that's obvious."

"Yes, I do. But I feel hurt, and I don't want to risk losing Olivier or the children. I know I've been foolish and selfish, too. I'm definitely part of the 'me' generation. I want to call him now . . . more than anything in the world. I want to make him better. But I know it's got to end."

"Well, here's the deal. You write him a letter, and you tell him it's over. I don't think it would be wise to speak to him, considering he's in the hospital recovering from a bullet wound, and it'll be harder on you if you hear his voice. Then you go upstairs to your office and block his e-mails and delete his address from your system and his number from your telephone, and you make a conscious effort to send back any letters he writes to you and any e-mails that he manages to send you. Trust me, he'll try to find you."

"This isn't going to be easy."

"Of course it isn't. But it could be a whole lot worse. Think about the mess if Olivier found out."

"Right, I'll do it."

"You've got away with it, which I never thought you would."

"My fingers have been burned."

"Honey, your whole life could have gone up in flames! Now, we'd better tidy you up. If the girls see you looking like this, they'll think you've given up on life!"

Angelica put on a pair of skinny flare jeans from Gap and a cashmere sweater from Paul & Joe. She dried her hair and applied some makeup. Candace sat on the loo seat watching her.

"Phew, it *is* you after all. I wasn't quite sure." They both laughed.

"You're a great friend, Candace."

"Well, I hope so."

"Joking apart. You've made me feel so much better about the whole thing."

"You just needed to make sense of it . . . then deal with it."

"I was so confused. I love him, and yet I feel so hurt."

"And angry."

"A little."

"If it were me . . ." She sighed heavily and flared her nostrils. "Well, it just *wouldn't* be."

At one o'clock the girls arrived on her doorstep en masse. Even Kate was on time for once. Loaded with presents and bags of lunch, they marched into the house, embracing Angelica with such fervor one might have been forgiven for thinking she'd just risen from the dead.

"You're so pale!" Kate cried, studying her face to check her features were still in place. "I want to hear every detail. Then I want to fill you in on *my* life, which couldn't get any stranger."

"We've brought sushi," said Scarlet, dumping her bag on the dining room table.

"I'm ravenous," said Letizia. "Let's spread it out and tuck in."

"Not before a glass of wine. I don't know about anyone else, but the sight of Angelica's white face has scared the life out of me." Kate opened the fridge and pulled out a bottle of Chardonnay.

"I think Angelica needs a shot more than any of us," said Scarlet, going to the cupboard and grabbing the glasses by their stems. Her jeans were so tight they could have been painted on. She stood on tiptoe in spite of her high-heeled black PVC boots, which gave her at least another three inches.

"Thank you all for coming," said Angelica, laying the table.

"Are you crazy? They've been dying to come all morning," Candace exclaimed.

"We've been so worried, darling," said Letizia kindly. "When Kate called me, having heard from Scarlet, I had to sit down. I mean, to have all those horrible men on top of you!"

"On top of me?"

Kate pulled a face. "So I exaggerated a little," she admitted sheepishly.

"They weren't on top of me. They tied me up and dumped me in the dining room. Besides that, they didn't touch me."

"Oh! I'd have been offended," Kate quipped. "Just joking! Had any of them come anywhere near me, I would have died!"

"No, you wouldn't. The prospect of telling all your friends afterwards would have sustained you," said Candace.

"It must have been a real nightmare," said Scarlet, placing the maki rolls in neat lines on the serving dish.

Letizia had found a vase for the purple tulips she had brought and placed it in the center of the table, taking a step back to admire her creation. "Now, isn't this divine. Spring is just around the corner." She tossed her glorious mane off her shoulder. "But an early spring is in your dining room, darling." Angelica thanked her.

"I bet it was stunning in Franschhoek," said Scarlet.

"It was."

"It's a crying shame there's all that poverty and homelessness," mused Letizia. "I mean, if it wasn't for the crime, which is beyond anything we have here, it would be the perfect place to live."

"It's so easy to forget when you're there, in someone's

home. I drove past shantytowns of such squalor, but the minute I was at the vineyard it was as if that squalor belonged to another country. Then it invaded their home, and I realized why people leave and start again on other continents."

"I'd like to live in Italy," said Kate brightly. "In a magnificent palazzo."

"Well, of course you would." Letizia laughed.

Candace rolled her eyes. "You'll have your moment, Kate. But right now the spotlight's on Angelica, and you know what? I think she deserves it."

28

Vulnerability is your strength.

In Search of the Perfect Happiness

They all sat around the dining room table, listening to Angelica recounting her adventure. She didn't get emotional this time, having processed the experience with Candace. Besides, none of the others knew about her affair. They finished the bottle of wine. It was only the prospect of having to pick up their children from school that prevented them from opening another. Kate insisted her baby enjoyed alcohol in spite of Candace trying to convince her otherwise. Finally, after they had devoured all the sushi and the gory details of dead dogs and bullet wounds, Kate's moment arrived.

"Go on, tell her," said Candace.

"You mean, you haven't already?"

"Of course not. It's not my story to tell."

"That never stopped anyone," said Scarlet.

"What's happened?" Angelica asked, glancing at Kate's belly. At least the baby was still in the right place.

Kate said melodramatically, "I've walked out on Pete once and for all."

"You haven't!"

"I have. It took a lot of courage—"

"And a few drinks," interrupted Candace.

"But I couldn't take his philandering anymore."

"The Haggis is still in the picture?"

"Honey, she *is* the picture."

"What about the baby?"

"It might not be his," Kate conceded.

Candace shrugged and raised her eyebrows at Angelica. "Still no name."

"It's irrelevant. Pete is the father of all my children."

"Unless you have any more," Scarlet added.

"You never know," said Kate with a smirk.

"So where are you living?"

"When I said I walked out on Pete, I didn't mean I *literally* walked out of the house. God forbid! I walked out of our *marriage. He* walked out of the house. He's camping at a friend's."

"What about Betsy Pog?"

"That old harridan!" quipped Candace.

"At least we can say we both tried."

"To be fair," said Scarlet, "you tried more than him."

"Darling, he didn't try at all," agreed Letizia.

"He's trying to win me back, but I've already moved on." The secretive smile indicated that she literally had.

"Go on, Angelica, ask!" Candace demanded.

"Who is he?" she complied.

Kate's grin swallowed her entire face. "He's, now wait for it . . . Count Edmondo Augustino Silviano di Napoli. And he comes with a beautiful palazzo overlooking the sea."

"Are you sure he's not making it up?" Angelica asked.

"Sounds like he owns the whole of Naples." Scarlet laughed.

"Counts are two a penny in Italy," said Candace.

"He's the real thing," Letizia insisted. "I promise you."

"It really doesn't matter," Kate replied. "He's gorgeous."

"So what are you going to do about the Vera Wang wedding dress?"

"Maybe she'll make use of it in her palazzo," said Candace.

Kate was appalled. "If you think I'm going to hurry down the aisle with another man after all I've been through, you don't know me at all."

"Such a waste of a beautiful dress!" Letizia sighed.

"I'll give a wedding dress party. Everyone has to come in their wedding dresses."

"Honey, half the guests won't be able to get into their wedding dresses!" said Candace.

"They can have them let out," said Kate.

"Why don't you put it in a box? You're young. I can't believe you're going to go through the rest of your life as a single woman."

"Single no, unmarried yes. I'll never trust men again."

"They all say that," said Candace.

"I'm having fun. Pete is trying to woo me back. Edmondo is whisking me off to Rome and whispering sweet nothings to me in Italian, not to mention the flowers and jewelry. I'm enjoying the attention."

"That, I can imagine," said Candace.

"I'm dying for you to meet him."

"So what have you done with your tickets to Mauritius?" Angelica asked.

"Given them to Art and Tod. They're so excited. Two weeks at the Saint Géran hotel, business-class flights on Virgin, all paid for by Pete."

"They struck it lucky!"

"I think Art deserves it. He's seen me through the rough times."

"And Tod deserves it for having put up with him sitting on the telephone with you night after night," Candace added.

"Well, exactly," Kate agreed. "After all, it's my New Year's resolution to be generous. This is the new generous me." She smiled angelically.

"It's so easy to be generous on other people's money!"

Kate turned to Candace and pulled a face. "I've got to begin somewhere. Small steps for me, giant steps for mankind!"

When Angelica picked the children up from school at half-past three, she forgot about the robbery at Rosenbosch in the comforting familiarity of her old life. Joe and Isabel flung themselves at her, clinging to her coat like monkeys, competing to be heard. The three of them held hands and walked up the street and into Kensington Gardens, where the pale, winter sunshine had managed to find a break in the clouds and stream through. They walked up the path towards the palace, and Angelica listened to their news. They had so much to tell her, and she gave them all her attention, soaking up their love and letting it revive her.

Once they got home the children rushed upstairs to see what presents their mother had brought them. They bounced on the bed as she unpacked her suitcase, delving through her memories to pull them out. Joe and Isabel tore at the paper excitedly. But nothing delighted Isabel as much as the little bottles of shampoo and body lotion that Angelica had taken from the hotels. She ran to her bedroom, her arms full of loot, to try on her pajamas and to put the bottles in her dressing table drawer in tidy rows. Joe was happy with his gifts, but it wasn't until he had given his mother the Full Joe that he was able to put the week behind him. He lay against her, nuzzling into her neck, and Angelica held him tightly, thanking God that she was alive to enjoy her children.

While they played in their bedrooms, Angelica went upstairs to her office. She switched on her computer and began to sort through her post. It was surreal how quickly life returned to normal. Rosenbosch began to feel like a dream. With a suspended heart she clicked on her e-mails. She barely dared breathe as the list came through. She scanned it, wishing for an e-mail from Jack, knowing that he hadn't sent one.

There was only one thing to do: write her letter and send it off. Delete his details from her e-mail and telephone. She should have done it months ago, before she had fallen so far, before her vanity had overpowered her. She pulled out a sheet of monogrammed writing paper and turned on her iPod, choosing Ennio Morricone's sound track to *Once upon a Time in the West*. She wrote in turquoise ink to match the printed address at the top of the page, and she wrote with care, choosing her words judiciously.

My darling DOP, this is the hardest letter I will ever have to write, but for my own sanity and the good of my husband and children, I feel there is no other ending for us—with all the will in the world I am unable to find a happy *one. As you said when you lay bleeding beside me, "We've had fun, haven't we?" We've had more than fun, Jack, we've shared something rare and magical. You've shown me my wings and taught me how to use them.*

I am trying to understand why you chose not to be honest with me and to forgive you, but I'm not like Anna; I'm full of human frailties while she has surely been touched by the angels. My heart bleeds for you and for us as I leave you in the loving arms of your wife and daughters. But it's just not meant to be. We were given a glimpse of paradise, but now the clouds have closed and that glimpse has gone forever. I know I will never see you again but in my dreams.

Rest well, my love. There's no one more qualified to accompany you along your final path than Anna, although I will be with you in my thoughts. Please don't try to contact me; it will only make it harder for both of us. I will always love you. Sage

She wept as she wrote it, wiping her eyes on her sleeve so that she didn't smudge the ink. So it really was good-bye. She wrote the envelope and sealed it, staring at the address and remembering those camphor trees, the pavilion on the lake, the mountain range, the sunsets, and Jack with his wavy hair swept off his broad face, his gentle brown eyes, and his roguish grin. Then she cried all over again because it hurt so much to think of his dying.

She deleted his details from her computer and mobile telephone and gave the letter to Sunny to post. She felt as if an invisible rope connecting them across the globe was now severed. Hugging her children was the greatest medicine for her injured heart. When she went into Isabel's room, she found her at her dressing table, applying makeup.

"Darling, look at you!" She laughed, putting her arms around her daughter from behind. "That's the reddest lipstick I've ever seen!"

"Kate left it behind," said Isabel nonchalantly. "I stole it." She grinned mischievously.

"Really? Today?"

"No, while you were away. She came to see Daddy."

Angelica's stomach cramped. "Did she?"

"Yes."

"Did you say hello?"

"No, we were meant to be in bed. But Joe and I watched from the top of the stairs."

"You spy!" she tried to sound lighthearted, but her instincts were screaming at her. "What were they talking about?"

"I don't know. They were having a glass of wine."

Angelica felt sick. Why hadn't Olivier told her? Or Kate, for that matter? She thought Olivier loathed Kate. She hurried from her daughter's bedroom to seek refuge in the bathroom. Leaning against the marble, she stared at her stricken face in the mirror. Little by little, comments that Kate had made, that had meant nothing at the time, now added up to something far more sinister. The fact that she knew his birthday, the time she had said how much she'd love to wake up to him every morning—and countless more. Was Olivier having an affair with Kate? Was Olivier the father of Kate's child? Was that why Kate was unable to name her lover? She sank onto the loo seat and put her face in her hands. It suddenly made an awful lot of sense. And she had been so smug in assuming that *her* husband was the last person in the world to whom Kate would turn for comfort.

Tormented by these thoughts, she muddled through the children's homework until the doorbell rang to relieve her. She opened it cautiously. On seeing Angie standing there wringing her hands, she fell into her mother's arms with a sob. Angie immediately grew in stature, responding to her daughter's need with efficiency and self-importance. She helped her into the kitchen, sent the children upstairs to watch television, and put the kettle on, taking down two cups and a teapot from the cupboard. It had been years since she had set foot in Angelica's house. She had forgotten how pretty it was.

"My life is unraveling," Angelica sniffed, slumping in her chair.

"I'm here now, love. Everything is going to be all right." Angie opened the fridge and took out a bottle of milk. "I want you to tell me exactly what happened. Get it all out. Cry as much as you need to. You'll feel so much better. A problem shared is a problem halved."

Angelica didn't have the heart to tell her that she'd already shared it with Candace, which must mean that it would now be quartered. She watched her mother bustle about and felt a surge of gratitude.

"Thank you for coming."

Angie placed the cups on the table. "I needed to make sure that you were all right." She narrowed her eyes and scrutinized her daughter's face as only a mother can. "Which, you clearly aren't. But you're going to be fine. We're going to discuss this until you feel strong again." She filled the teapot and placed it on the table, then sat down. "Nothing like a cup of tea to revive the spirits."

"You're so English, Mother."

"What do you expect?" She chuckled throatily. "So tell me, what happened?"

Angelica took a sip of tea, revived indeed by the hot liquid. Then she told her mother about the robbery. To her surprise, her mother listened without saying a word. Her face showed her horror, but she didn't interrupt, not once. Angelica felt the full force of her mother's attention and blossomed beneath it. Riding a wave of confidence, she confessed her adultery. Before she knew it, she was confiding everything, knowing that no one would understand like Angie. After all, Angie had just about done it all.

"I'm so sorry your heart has been broken, love," she said, her orange skin crinkling with compassion. She placed her pudgy hand on top of Angelica's and gave it a squeeze. "You think when you marry that broken hearts are a thing of the past, gone with your misguided youth. But the truth is, you're never too old to have your heart broken. I assume Olivier doesn't know?" Angelica nodded, blinking through tears. "Good. Don't tell him. Honesty is not always the best policy."

"Should I forgive Jack for betraying me?"

"He didn't betray you, love. He lost his heart to you and did all he could to protect it. There's nothing wrong with that. Don't feel aggrieved. Forgive him for being fallible, but don't blame him for being dishonest. You've lived a wonderful love affair, such as most people never experience in an entire lifetime. What a privilege to have loved like that. Denny and I had to sleep with other people to feel a sense of adventure."

Angelica wiped her face with her sleeve. "Don't you love each other enough?"

"We love each other enough to trust each other, if that's what you mean."

"I hated your swinging parties as a child. I felt they were more important than us."

"I know you did, love. That's why I wanted to come and see you today. I nearly lost you in South Africa, and that would have meant that I never had the opportunity to tell you how sorry I am that you felt like that. It's been bothering me for years, but I was too proud to talk to you about it. The robbery concentrated my thoughts. Life is too short to spend it with one's head under the carpet, avoiding the important things. The truth is that Denny and I were very selfish in those days. We let you down when you needed us most. I wanted to come now, because you're never too old to need your mother, and it's never too late for your mother to come to your aid."

Angelica took Angie's hand. "It's never too late, Mum."

When the doorbell rang again, Angelica looked confused.

"That'll be your sister, Angelica. She's come to pick me up. She also wanted to see you."

"You can stay here if you like," Angelica suggested.

"You need to be with your husband. I can't have two sons-in-law falling by the wayside. Go and open the door, love. Daisy's been worrying, too."

Angelica unbolted the door. Daisy stood on the doorstep looking pale and ashamed. Her big eyes shone with regret that so many years had been wasted in bitterness. Without a word they embraced. They understood each other without the need to articulate in syllables what they both felt in their hearts. Angie went to the cupboard and took down another cup.

After they had gone Angelica bathed the children and put them to bed. She lingered over their bedtime stories and smothered their smooth faces with kisses, taking pleasure from every moment, however small. She enjoyed the Full Joe and the Full Isabel, savoring the smell of their skin and the warm feel of their bodies as they wrapped themselves around her, begging her to stay just a little longer. She shoved Kate to the back of her mind as she made every effort to live in the present.

Downstairs, she poured herself a large glass of wine. She sat at the kitchen table and deliberated whether to confront Olivier. If he was innocent, wouldn't her suspicion lead him to suspect *her*? She was afraid even to mention adultery in case he questioned why she was considering it. Olivier was very astute and rarely missed a trick. It wasn't beyond the realm of possibility that he might start doing sums of his own.

As she prepared dinner, she thought of Anna, trying to channel some of her wisdom and tolerance. Say Olivier and Kate *had* slept together: Kate had said it was a one-night stand that had meant nothing, something they both regretted, it wasn't going to happen again, in which case it wasn't an *affair*, but a *mistake*. How could she pass judgment when she herself had fallen in love with Jack and had an affair lasting months? At least Kate and Olivier weren't in love with each other. She could forgive that. But what of Kate's baby? *Please God, let that baby belong to Pete.*

At last Olivier arrived. He swung open the door and called her name, a vast bouquet of lilies in his arms. "I thought these would make you feel better," he said. Angelica tried to behave normally and took them from him with a smile. *The actions of a guilty man?* she wondered.

"They're lovely, thank you."

He kissed her. "How are you feeling?"

"So much better. Mum came and we talked. Then Daisy joined us. It was good. We should have done it years ago."

"Sometimes it takes a scare to frighten everyone into realizing what's important." He looked at her intensely.

She returned his look, searching for any indication of *his* adultery. "You're so right."

"I bet the children were pleased to see you."

"So pleased."

"They missed you."

"And I missed them."

"Did you miss *me*?" he asked, pulling a sheepish face.

"Of course I did." She watched him take off his coat and hang it in the cupboard. In all his years of flirting she had never feared he'd leave her. Now she was no longer sure of him. "Would you like a glass of wine?"

"I'd love one." He followed her into the kitchen. "So what's up?"

"Kate has left Pete," she said, watching his reaction carefully.

"I'm surprised he didn't leap first." He shrugged. "It was always going to happen."

"I don't know. I thought they were trying to make it work."

"No one could possibly stay married to her."

She stood at the stove and stirred the tomato sauce for the pasta. "I thought the baby might help them patch it up."

"I did, too."

"It might not be Pete's."

He looked interested. "Really? Whose does she think it might be?"

"Someone she had a one-night stand with at the end of the summer."

He didn't look at all ruffled. "Does Pete know?"

"No, Pete thinks it's his, which, of course, it might be."

He shook his head and tutted disapprovingly. "She's a very careless girl."

"I'm not even sure that the man she slept with has a clue that he might have got her pregnant."

"Let's hope it *is* Pete's, then." He took a sip of wine. "Or someone is going to get a shock when the baby is born."

Angelica was confused. If Olivier was the man Kate had slept with, wouldn't he have been a little more flustered at the prospect that he might be the father of Kate's unborn child? Unless he already knew, in which case he would have had plenty of time to hatch a plan. Perhaps that was why Kate had come around. Maybe she had seized the moment, as Angelica was away, to confront him and tell him about his possible child. Still, he was remarkably cool for a man keeping such a terrible secret.

The following week, Angelica avoided Kate as much as she could. Every time she saw her belly she imagined Olivier's baby inside, looking just like Joe or Isabel. Her fear distracted her from thinking about Jack, but it inhibited her creativity. Much as she tried, she was unable to get back into her book, in spite of the flood of inspiration she had received in South Africa. To keep herself busy and away from her desk, she continued her Pilates classes three times a week and spent as much time as possible with Candace, for her friend confirmed over and again that she had done the right thing in cutting all contact with Jack, even though the absence of his texts and e-mails hurt her daily.

At the beginning of March, Kate invited Olivier and Angelica for dinner to meet Edmondo, the now infamous count. Diluted in the company of Art and Tod, Letizia and Gaitano, Candace and Harry, and Scarlet and William, Olivier gave no indication of intimacy with Kate, and Kate, all over Edmondo like a wiry octopus, barely tossed him a glance. If they shared a secret, they deserved Oscars for their ability to dissemble.

Edmondo was a central casting count: dark and handsome,

with thick glossy hair, smooth brown skin, and a large, sensual mouth, almost bruised from so much kissing. He spoke with a strong Italian accent that Angelica found as attractive as Olivier's French one, and he gesticulated with his hands. He was confident and funny and wild about Kate. Having expected an awkward evening pretending they all liked him, they were surprised to discover that no pretense was necessary.

Kate dragged the girls into her bedroom after dinner to discuss him. "I'm so grateful that he likes me, belly and all," she said. "I mean, he's never even had a child of his own, so having to put up with my two, and this one in here, is Herculean." She looked so pathetically grateful that even Candace was unable to find anything cynical to say.

It was only when Kate texted her friends in panic a week later that Angelica pushed aside her suspicions and ran to her aid, leaving the children to have tea with Sunny. Kate opened the door and grabbed her by the wrist. "You have to hear this. You won't believe it." She didn't look tearful and bedraggled like she had the day of the pregnancy test. Instead, she almost looked amused. The doorbell went again, and Candace walked in with Letizia. Angelica found Scarlet in a pair of black velvet hot pants drinking a cup of tea on the club fender. She beckoned her over with a wave of her hand, the rows of bracelets jingling on her arm like armor.

"Hi, doll. This is hilarious!" she said, flicking her blond bob.

"At least she hasn't split up with Edmondo."

"God, no, to the contrary, that seems to be rocking."

"So what's happened now?"

"I'm not going to spoil it. She has to tell you herself."

"Did we all need to schlep out to hear it?"

"Yes. Trust me, it'll be worth it."

Letizia and Candace came into the sitting room. "Tea, anyone?" asked Kate breezily.

"Yes, please," said Candace. "You can lace it with something stronger if you think we need fortification."

"I'm the one needing fortification, but I've given up booze."

"Really?" asked Letizia, sitting down on the sofa.

"Really. I've clearly got a problem, so I've joined AA. Edmondo is supporting me all the way."

"I'm impressed," said Candace. "Generous *and* sensible."

Kate knelt on the floor beside the coffee table and poured the tea into mugs. "Biscuit, anyone?"

"No, just tell us what this is all about," said Angelica, trying not to look too hard at her protruding belly.

"Okay, here, take your tea." She handed Angelica a mug.

"Are you going to tell us who the mystery man is?" Angelica hadn't meant her voice to sound so edgy.

"I wish I could say it was Edmondo's. I'd love a little Italian child."

"I highly recommend them," said Letizia cheerfully.

"So what is it, then?" Candace asked.

"So I'm called in to see Mrs. Moncrieff."

"She called you?" Letizia asked.

"The secretary did. I thought *I* was in trouble. I'm in my forties, and I felt like a schoolgirl again, called in to see the headmistress. So in I go. She asks me to sit. She's looking really embarrassed. Actually, I'm feeling sorry for her. She puts her elbows on the table and knits her fingers. "I'm very sorry to have to mention this, Mrs. Fox, but I feel I should explain before you see Amelia's form teacher. You see, Amelia brought something quite inappropriate for Show and Tell this morning." As you can imagine my mind was racing with all sorts of possibilities, but I could never have guessed it would be my vibrator!" She watched with pleasure as they all stared at her.

Finally, Candace shook her head and grinned. "How do you do it!" she exclaimed. "Just when I think you've exhausted every possible drama, you find another one even more entertaining than the last."

Kate giggled. "She pulled out the drawer and handed it to me in a bag, wrapped in paper. Can you imagine? It was horribly embarrassing. Someone had actually wrapped it up!"

"Did Amelia take it out and show everyone in assembly?" asked Scarlet.

"Thank God her teacher got to her before she got into assembly. As it is, I'm never going to live it down!"

"What did she say it was for?" Letizia added.

"Oh, I should think she thought it was a clever little massage device," said Candace with a cackle.

"Do you think Mrs. Moncrieff knew what it was?" asked Angelica.

"Oh yes," Kate replied. "She knew exactly what it was. She suggested I find a more suitable place to keep it. I wanted to die. I couldn't look at Amelia's class teacher. I couldn't look at anyone. You can bet the whole school knows about it by now."

"It's hilarious," said Scarlet.

"For you!" Kate reminded her. "For me, it's a nightmare."

"What are you going to say to Amelia?" Angelica asked.

"I'm going to tell her that she mustn't take Mummy's things into school."

"Tell me, what does the vibrator look like?" Candace asked.

"A rabbit," Kate replied.

Candace shrugged. "Easy mistake." She sipped her tea.

Scarlet grinned over her mug. "Tell me, does it rock?"

29

Surrender to the flow of life.

In Search of the Perfect Happiness

Angelica couldn't shake off her suspicion that Olivier was having an affair with Kate. She recognized the irony, but still, the idea that her husband had betrayed her with one of her closest friends was like a knife to her heart. She clung to him at night, wrapping her tentacles around him, waking in the early hours to check that he was still there. He assumed her neediness sprang from the robbery, not from her fear of losing him. The more she thought about it, the more she regretted her own affair and the more she realized how much she loved him.

Olivier started coming home earlier in the evenings, and they bathed the children together and took turns reading to them. She listened to his worries and tried to give advice, or at least support. He, in turn, went into her office and took down a paperback copy of *The Caves of Cold Konard*. At first he read a little every night, and she knew he was struggling, but she was grateful for his effort. But then he kept the light on later and later as it became harder to put it down. "I just have to find out what happens to Mart!" he exclaimed, without taking his eyes off the page. Angelica grinned into her own book with pride.

Then, on March 5, Olivier mentioned her birthday over supper. "I thought you'd forgotten," she said, pleased that he hadn't.

"I thought we could go out for dinner at Mr. Wing."

"Sure." She had rather hoped for something a little more exciting.

"I've been so busy I haven't had time to arrange anything better. Why don't we go and spend a weekend in Paris in spring? A kind of belated birthday weekend."

"I'd love that."

"We can go shopping, and you can choose something . . ."

"I don't need a present," she said humbly, knowing that now was no time for extravagance but disappointed all the same.

"We'll choose it together. Have the girls planned anything?"

"I haven't mentioned it. To be honest, I've been busy, too . . ." She thought of the book she had to write and the wasted hours staring at her e-mail, willing Jack to find a way of contacting her. Hoping he'd make the effort in spite of all the obstacles she had erected to stop him. "I wouldn't expect them to remember."

"Well, I've remembered, and the children have got something for you."

She smiled at the thought of Joe and Isabel's gifts. They'd be more precious than anything bought in a shop.

The following morning, the children woke her up to cries of "Happy birthday, Mummy." They had made cards and plates at the Pottery Café in Fulham. Isabel's was prettily painted in pinks and blues with butterflies and flowers around the edge and one glorious bumble bee in the middle. Joe's was a mess, but Angelica could make out a red train, puffing smoke. She cuddled both children, holding them for as long as possible before they wriggled away. Nothing could beat those delightful plates; she would hang them on the wall in her study.

Olivier was already dressed for work. He kissed her tenderly. "Be ready at seven-thirty. I'll come home early to change. I've reserved Mr. Wing for eight."

She walked the children to school, bumping into Candace as she left them at the door. "Happy birthday!" she said, Ralph straining at his lead as he attempted to follow a scruffy little bitch down the pavement.

"Thank you!" Angelica was surprised.

"So what's Olivier got you?"

"Oh, nothing yet. We're going to go to Paris in the spring. He's busy at the moment."

Candace pulled a face. "Too busy to buy you a present? Honey, there's a Tiffany in the City."

"Don't tell me!"

"Is he taking you somewhere nice tonight?"

"Mr. Wing."

"A Chinese?" Candace crinkled her nose in disgust. "I think he could do better than that."

"I love Mr. Wing."

"We *all* love Mr. Wing, but not on our birthday."

"Oh, it's fine," Angelica said, laughing it off. "Things are really good between us now—I shouldn't complain. At least he didn't forget."

"I'd take you out for lunch if I didn't have a meeting."

"I've got to get down to some writing anyway."

"Go have a massage or something."

"Not today. I'm not in the mood."

"I'll see you at pickup." Candace gave the lead a yank and Ralph loped back reluctantly.

Angelica returned home and took a cup of tea up to her office. Claudia called at nine to find out how the book was doing, impatient to see what she had written so far. Angelica lied and told her she was halfway through it. Her mother telephoned to wish her a happy birthday, and Daisy called, suggesting they have lunch together. Angelica didn't hesitate but invited her to Le Caprice, thrilled to be doing something exciting on her birthday.

She scanned down her e-mails, disappointed to find that Jack hadn't written. She couldn't remember whether or not he knew it was her birthday. She had asked him not to contact her, and he had obviously respected her wishes. She had to summon all her strength to restrain from e-mailing *him*. She longed to find out how he was. But he was dying, with Anna at his side, guiding him towards the last leg of his journey home. There was no room for her there. It was well and truly over.

She opened her novel about the greasy Troilers who live on the estuary, and turned on her iPod. Engulfed in grief, she channeled her feelings into her novel. Her resentment formed the ugly, slimy Troilers; her love, the weightless, phosphorescent Dazzlings. The story would be an allegory of her love for Jack, and no one would ever know that but her. The music carried her into her fantasy world, where she gave vent to her emotions and thus created a captivating story where love battles to save the world from evil. She knew her theme was not original, but equally no one else could write it like she could.

After an agreeable lunch with Daisy, during which they had laughed about their ludicrous botanical names and their parents' disastrous attempts to hold on to their youth, she picked up Joe and Isabel and brought them home for tea. She hadn't seen any of her other friends, and none of them had called, which surprised her. Kate had prided herself on remembering birthdays; after all, she had remembered

Olivier's, Angelica thought bitterly. The least she could have done is remember *hers*. Sunny bathed the children as she showered and slipped into a black Prada dress. As she applied makeup and sprayed herself with scent, she reminded herself that happiness was a state of mind. That the quality of her life depended on the quality of her thoughts. If she dwelled on the negative aspects of her day, they would only pull her down. Instead, she concentrated on the positive things: The fact that her children had gone to such trouble to make her cards and presents. The fact that Candace had remembered her birthday. The fact that she had made peace with Daisy. The fact that she was now close to her mother. The fact that Olivier hadn't found out about her affair. The fact that she had such good friends. The fact that her husband and children were healthy. The fact that she had so much to be grateful for. After a while it began to work. She lit her scented candles and played *Back to Black* by Amy Winehouse. Her spirits rose with the perfume and filled the room.

When Olivier appeared, he found her in the bathroom singing loudly. He came up behind her, pulled her hair aside, and kissed her nape. She laughed at him in the mirror. He was handsome in the golden glow of the candlelight. She was surprised when he placed a pendant there, fastening it at the back. The diamonds fell against her chest, glittering against the black of her dress. She gazed admiringly at the heart that rested behind the letters O, J, and I, dangling on the end of a thick white-gold chain. "You've been to Chopard," she said, astonished.

"Of course. I know that there is nothing that excites a woman more than diamonds."

"How very right you are," she replied, turning round to kiss him tenderly. "Thank you."

"You look more beautiful than I have ever seen you, my darling."

"I'm ready for Mr. Wing."

He scoffed. "As if I'd take you to Mr. Wing!"

She stared at him. "Where are you taking me?"

"A surprise."

"Oh my God. I'm already surprised!"

"You're going to love this one." He took off his jacket and tie. "Give me a few minutes to shower and change, and then we'll go. There's a car waiting for us outside. Tonight, I intend to party hard!"

So he had never intended to take her to Mr. Wing. It had all been a ruse. She couldn't wait to tell Candace.

Olivier appeared on the landing in a pair of jeans, a white shirt beneath his favorite gunmetal blue Gucci jacket. His skin was brown against the collar and his dark hair still wet and tousled, pushed off his forehead. He took her hand and they walked downstairs together. She decided that she would forget about his supposed affair with Kate and enjoy the evening. Tomorrow she would confront him and hopefully dispel her fear once and for all. If he admitted it, she would cope somehow. She would not let it destroy her marriage or her friendship with Kate. Anna had proved that was possible.

They climbed into the back of the car. It pulled out into the street. The trees were still bare but the park was full of crocuses and daffodils, the air warmer, the days longer and brighter. Angelica was exhilarated with the suspense. She smiled all the way down Kensington Church Street, trying to work out what restaurant he was taking her to from the direction of the car. When they turned into Thurloe Square, she realized they were headed to Kate's.

"What's going on?" she asked, narrowing her eyes suspiciously.

"I promised to pop into Kate's on the way. She's got a present for you."

"This is all very fishy."

"She's bought you something special. She called me tonight on my mobile. She said she hadn't seen you at school today."

"No, but she could have called me herself."

"You know Kate," he said. Angelica wondered whether he knew her better than any of them.

The car drew up outside the house, and they stepped onto the road. Kate had changed her window box, filling it with an elaborate display of red geraniums. Before Olivier had time to ring the bell, the door swung open. A uniformed butler stood at attention. "Good evening, sir," he said. "May I take your coat?" Angelica was more suspicious than ever. She slipped out of her sheepskin and handed it to the butler, who folded it over his arm. "Mrs. Fox is in the drawing room."

The house was strangely quiet. Angelica noticed that the double doors were closed. She could feel the silence of a room full of people seeping out from beneath them. The butler strode ahead and flung them wide to reveal a sea of faces before her, all smiling in the semidarkness. None was more radiant or triumphant than Kate's. "Darling! Happy birthday!" She waddled over in the sexiest little Miu Miu dress, her big stomach protruding like a globe, and embraced her affectionately. Angelica swept her eyes over her friends, all of them, even her parents, Daisy, and the terrible Jenna Elrich, who had somehow inveigled her way into the party. Kate had even found friends she had lost along the way. "Are you surprised?" Angelica nodded, dumbfounded. "I'm so pleased no one gave it away. Olivier and I have been planning this for weeks, tracking down your old friends. I had a horrible feeling Joe and Isabel might let the cat out of the bag. I could have sworn they were sitting on the landing listening to our secret meeting."

Angelica hugged Kate again, for the guilt of having doubted her and for the relief that now overpowered her. "I thought you had all forgotten."

"Good!"

"And it's not a big birthday, either."

"Every birthday is big in importance, and besides, this is my year of being generous. Make the most of it while it lasts. I'll be back to Selfish Me next year."

Angelica wrapped her arms around Olivier. "Thank you," she said. He would never know the depth of her gratitude.

Candace approached her with Letizia, Scarlet, and Tod. "Fooled ya!" she said, handing Angelica a glass of champagne.

"You guys!"

"As if we'd forget your birthday," said Letizia.

"I should have known," Angelica replied, taking a gulp of champagne.

"Honey, what's with the diamonds?"

"Olivier's present."

"Now we're talking," said Scarlet.

"They're way over the top!" Tod added. "I thought we were in the middle of a financial crisis."

"I know. I can't imagine what got into him," Angelica laughed, toying with the sparkly letters.

"Absence makes the heart grow fonder!" said Letizia.

"And I thought he was having an affair with Kate."

"What?"

"Isabel mentioned that Kate had come over while I was away. I just couldn't understand why they were meeting at all and why neither had bothered to tell me."

Candace put her arm around Angelica. "That's a stretch of the imagination too far!"

"Kate would never betray a friend," said Letizia.

"Only her husband!" Scarlet added.

"I thought that baby might be Olivier's." Angelica's relief made her almost delirious with happiness.

"Why wouldn't it be Pete's?" Tod asked, confused.

Angelica put her hand to her mouth. "You don't know?"

The three women looked at each other guiltily. "I would have thought she would have told *you!*" Angelica gasped.

"Told me what?" Tod's bewildered expression spoke volumes.

"Okay, here's the deal, but don't say a word." Candace looked at him steadily. "Kate had a one-night stand. The baby she's carrying might or might not be Pete's. There, I've let the great big jungle cat out of the bag. If it bites us, we'll blame you!"

"Christ! That's heavy," said Tod, scratching his head.

"Don't think you'll get a name out of her. She hasn't told a soul. But at least we can rule out Olivier," said Scarlet with a laugh.

"I won't breathe a word," he assured them. "For God's sake, don't let on that I know."

"Are you kidding me!"

"Happy birthday, darling," he added hastily, looking past her. "Now I've got to go and tell Art."

"We are in serious trouble," said Letizia anxiously.

"Can Art keep a secret?" Angelica asked.

"It's not Art I'm worried about," said Candace. "Tod clearly can't."

After the buffet, Kate stood on a chair and clapped her hands, demanding silence for her speech. The noise died down, and everyone waited. She stood there in the tightest jersey dress that barely reached midthigh and patted her pregnant belly fondly. "Good friends, old friends, new friends, special friends like you, Angelica, Scarlet, Letizia, and Candace, and family friends, Daisy and Angie. Welcome to my humble abode, and thank you for keeping the party a secret and making it fabulous with your glittering presence. Angelica, you're very dear to me. You're a *true* friend, so I wanted to return your kindness with a party to celebrate *you*. Your birthday is a good excuse, but frankly, I would have done it on any other day for the simple pleasure of honoring *you*. You're loyal, you're wise, and in spite of you being a little absentminded, you never forget your friends. Please, raise your glasses to Angelica!"

"To Angelica," they all repeated. Angelica blushed with pleasure.

Kate leaned over and took Edmondo's hand. "And just in case you think this isn't about me, you're wrong. I couldn't let an opportunity like this pass me by. Can you please raise your glasses to Edmondo and me, the future Contessa Edmondo Augustino Silviano di Napoli."

"Yes! Edmondo and I are getting married." She looked sheepish a moment and giggled. "Well, as soon as I'm divorced!"

"To my wife to be!" said Edmondo, raising his glass, and no one had any choice but to follow suit.

As soon as the speeches were over, the dancing began. Kate remained in the center of the dance floor, which had been set up downstairs in the children's playroom, swinging across the wooden floorboards with her count. Angelica drank too many cocktails in a bid to forget the last party she had attended here, when Jack had waited for her in a taxi down the road. In a blissful alcoholic haze she allowed Olivier to sweep her onto the dance floor. After one in the morning, when most of the guests had gone home, Art took to the karaoke machine, singing "Crazy." At least this time he didn't pull down his trousers to expose his strawberry.

At three o'clock Olivier took Angelica home. "That's the best party I've ever been to," she said, climbing unsteadily into the waiting car. "And it was all for me!"

"I'm happy you enjoyed it."

"I didn't think you liked Kate."

"It's not that I don't like her. Just that I find her dramas exhausting."

"She's a girls' girl."

"Clearly."

"But you got together to organize *this*."

"For you."

"You're so sweet, Olivier."

He kissed her as the car drove up Kensington Gore. "I love you, Angelica."

"And I love you, Olivier." She sighed dreamily as she realized how much she really did.

As the car drew onto the street a hunched figure lumbered drunkenly down the road, hugging his coat tight to keep out the cold. "Oh God!" Angelica gasped. "It's Pete." They both stared as they passed him, making his way to Kate's. "I'm so pleased we're not there to witness the scene."

"He really wants her back."

"If he hadn't been such an idiot, she would never have kicked him out."

"I think he'll find he's missed the boat."

"People make their lives so complicated."

Olivier took her hand. "I'm lucky to be married to you. I see shipwrecks all over the beach and thank God that we're still afloat, sails billowing."

Angelica snuggled up to him guiltily. "Still afloat," she replied. Closing her eyes, she envisaged the leak in the timber and mentally patched it over. If it remained below the water-line, he might never notice it.

30

All things happen at the perfect time.

In Search of the Perfect Happiness

The following morning Kate was on the telephone at dawn to report the arrival of Pete banging on her door, demanding to see the children, begging her to take him back. By the excited tone of her voice she was thrilled that he cared and triumphant that he had been brought to his knees. "Why would I want him back?" she asked. "When I have Edmondo, who worships me? Who would have thought that I'd walk down the aisle again, me of all people? The Vera Wang dress is just too beautiful to leave languishing in a cupboard." Angelica listened sadly, thinking of the children and the little one not yet born into the chaos of Kate's dramatic life. It didn't really matter who the father was, for Pete would gather him into his brood and give him his name and probably never suspect that he didn't belong to him. As for Edmondo, if he ever made it down the aisle, he'd find Pete standing between him and the altar. Angelica suspected that Kate still loved him and that she probably always would. Pete wasn't going to give her up without a fight.

At the end of March, the children broke up from school, and the friends dispersed across Europe for their Easter holiday. Olivier rented a chalet in Klosters, where Letizia and Gaitano had an apartment with a splendid view down the valley. Letizia had managed to bribe Scarlet's manny, Ben, to look after her boys for the fortnight, so while the children skied together with Ben and an instructor, Angelica and Letizia were able to enjoy long lunches on the Chesa terrace in the sunshine and gentle descents down the Klosters Path. Olivier was a powerful, experienced skier, but instead of disappearing with skins in his backpack to spend the morning climbing and the afternoon descending in untracked powder, he took time to ski with his wife and children and found, to his surprise, that the pleasure he derived from watching Joe and Isabel stem down the piste far exceeded the pleasure of yet another perfect turn of his own.

They dined at the Wynegg on snails and cheese fondue and discussed Kate and the count. Letizia and Gaitano had many friends in the village, and they swept Angelica and Olivier into their social whirl, dining at friends' chalets and dancing at the little Casa nightclub into the early hours of the morning. Angelica felt revitalized, her marriage rejuvenated, her memory of the robbery faded and shunted to the back of her sub-conscious. But her first waking thoughts were of Jack.

She dreamed of him often, always with the same sense of loss. Awake in bed, recapturing the sense of him, she'd re-member the sunset at Sir Lowry's Pass and the gentle way he had looked at her. Above all, she remembered the way he had made her feel. But that woman was gone forever now, along with the future they had embroidered with the fine threads of delusion. A future had never been in the stars for them. Although her life had returned to normal, she carried within her a small part of Jack, like a warm nugget against her heart, comforting and grazing her simultaneously.

The children returned to school at the end of April and the girls' lunches resumed. Angelica settled into her writing groove and inspiration flowed. Her Troilers and Dazzlings took on lives of their own beyond the pages and began to dominate her thoughts. Dreams of her book on happiness were forgotten in the flurry of her new fantasy. She didn't know what the secret was; if anything, her affair with Jack had left her more confused than ever. What she *did* know was that loving her work, her children, her husband, and her friends gave her a cozy sense of contentment. If it wasn't for the little nugget rubbing on the tender tissue of her flesh she would have believed herself as happy as any person could hope to be.

But then Anna gave her the news she had dreaded.

Angelica was alone at her desk. The children were at school, Olivier at work. She had felt uneasy all morning, unable to write for a heavy sense of foreboding that strained every nerve, unable to decipher why she felt so low and so flustered. When the telephone rang, she knew. Her throat had constricted with grief even before she heard Anna's voice.

"Angelica? It's Anna." Angelica sensed her sorrow bleeding down the line from Rosenbosch, and tears rose from behind her carefully constructed dam and spilled freely onto her cheeks. "Jack passed away this morning."

"Oh God." Angelica's hand shot to her heart.

"He was very calm and very submissive. I held one hand, the girls the other. We told him how much we loved him and that, although we wouldn't be able to see him anymore, we'd feel his spirit here among the vines and in the sunsets he so loved. He smiled. He had no strength left, but he smiled, and I saw our old familiar Jack there for the briefest moment. Then he took his last breath, peacefully, without any pain."

"I'm so sorry."

"It's worse for the girls. They loved their daddy so much. I knew you'd want to know."

"I should have called him . . ."

"Don't say that. Put your energy into positive things. Send him loving thoughts for he hasn't gone far, just out of sight."

"I deserted him at his most needy."

"He understood."

"I think of him every day, Anna."

"And he thought of you. He talked about you often, but never with regret. So you must do the same. Treasure the memories. Your short time together was precious. Love and longing will be the forces that reunite you one day. Don't worry about that. You *will* meet again." She laughed in that light, untroubled way of hers. "I hope *we* do, too, Angelica. You're more than welcome here at Rosenbosch whenever you feel ready. Jack would want you to come back."

She swallowed hard. "When's the funeral?"

"Tomorrow. We're going to bury him on the hillside above Rosenbosch."

She knew it was impossible for her to be there. "Will you do something for me, Anna?"

"Of course."

"Put a sprig of sage on his coffin." She closed her eyes. "With that I'll bid him good-bye."

Angelica spent the rest of the day crying into her pillow. She had accused him of selfishness, but her own selfishness was shameful. Would it really have hurt to have telephoned him once in a while and e-mailed her love? Surely, the wishes of a dying man were more important than her own. She had the rest of her life to give to Olivier and their children; Jack had had only months.

At three she went to pick up the children. Candace was standing talking to Scarlet and Letizia, waiting for the big doors to open and release their offspring into the bright spring sunshine.

Candace hurried over when she registered Angelica's

stricken face. "What's happened?" she demanded. "Who's died?"

"Jack . . ." Angelica could not speak.

"Oh my God. Jack's dead? Truly?"

Angelica nodded and fell against her, sobbing.

Letizia and Scarlet gathered round, concerned. "What's happened?"

"Jack Meyer has died," Candace replied, wrapping her arms around Angelica.

"Christ!" Scarlet swore, blanching. "I don't believe it."

"Who's Jack Meyer?" Letizia hissed.

"A South African friend of ours," said Scarlet. "The people Angelica stayed with on her book tour. I knew he'd had cancer, but I thought he was in remission."

"It came back," said Angelica, pulling away and wiping her eyes. "He died this morning."

"You remember, he had the hots for Angelica," Scarlet reminded Letizia.

"But of course," said Letizia emphatically, putting her hand on Angelica's shoulder. "Why don't you let me take Isabel and Joe?"

"Let's all go to tea at your house, the children can play downstairs and we can give Angelica a stiff drink in your sitting room," Candace suggested. Angelica nodded gratefully, feeling the warmth of friendship envelop her like a beloved old rug.

Candace gave Angelica, Joe, and Isabel a lift in her car, calling her housekeeper on her mobile to change the arrangements she had made for her own children's tea. When they arrived at Letizia's terraced house, Joe and Isabel were delighted to find themselves in the company of all their friends and rushed off in a rowdy gang to the playroom downstairs. Angelica flopped onto the sofa in the first-floor sitting room, curling her feet under her and hugging the mug of tea Letizia had laced with whiskey. Scarlet joined her on the sofa. Letizia was on the point of sitting down, having brought up tea and biscuits on a tray, when the doorbell rang. "That'll be Kate," she said, hurrying downstairs to open it. The girls glanced at one another in silence, listening to the slamming of the door and Kate and Letizia talking in low voices in the hall.

"Not me!" said Candace, raising her hands.

"Letizia, of course," said Scarlet with a chuckle. "She was texting in the car."

"If I'm going to pour out my soul, it might as well be to *all* of you," said Angelica, smiling feebly. "Save you from gossiping about it later."

"Don't bet on it, honey! What you're about to divulge will give us all months of gossip!"

"I'm so sorry about Jack!" Kate exclaimed as she rushed in on a wind of perfume, her pregnant belly stretching the fabric of her vintage Mary Quant minidress. Since her love affair with the count, her dress had got more lavish, her jewelry more brash, and her scent overpowering. She sat down and crossed her long legs so that the gold buckles on her Roger Vivier shoes glinted in the sunlight streaming through the tall sash windows. "So who is he?"

Angelica smiled through her tears. "He was my lover," she said simply, and for once there was nothing Kate could say to bring the conversation around to herself.

The girls listened, spellbound, as Angelica confessed to loving Jack. She told them the story from the very beginning. From the moment she had felt the frisson of attraction at Scarlet's dinner party to the telephone call that morning, ending it all. They asked questions, probed into her feelings and her thoughts, and the strange thing was that the more Angelica talked about him, the less she hurt. Sharing her pain reduced the inflammation. Sharing the memories filled her heart with joy, for the love they had forged and the fun they had had. She trusted them to keep her secret: after all, they only gossiped to one another.

"The irony is that my affair with Jack has made me appreciate Olivier more. Our marriage has been strengthened because of it, and I salute Jack for that. He taught me to live in the present, and that is what I'm trying to do. None of us knows what's around the corner." She looked at her closest friends sitting around her, listening without judgment, understanding with compassion, supporting with humor, and realized that there was nothing in the world more healing than friendship.

"Oh my God!" Kate cried, holding out her teacup and staring down at her lap. "My waters have broken."

"Really? Are you sure?" Letizia asked, horrified.

"I don't know why else a torrent of water would gush out of me!"

"I hope they haven't discontinued that fabric," said Candace, glancing at the William Yeoward armchair that was now drenched with Kate's fluids.

Angelica laughed at Kate's immaculate sense of timing. "I didn't think anything could upstage *my* story."

"Foolish woman, you should know better," said Candace. "The time of reckoning is now upon us."

"Darling, do you want me to call Pete?" Letizia asked.

"Do you have to?"

"I think I should. It's his baby, isn't it?"

Kate pulled an anxious face. "I'm still not sure."

Letizia shrugged helplessly. "Do you want me to call the *other* father?"

"No," Kate snapped. "I'll call Edmondo."

"You can't have Pete *and* Edmondo at the birth!" Candace exclaimed. "There'll be a god-awful fight."

"What shall I do?" Kate wailed, suddenly ashen with panic. She grabbed Letizia's arm. "You have to come with me. I'm not giving birth on my own. You must *all* come with me!" Kate demanded. Letizia pulled her up to stand shakily, holding on to Letizia's arm as if it were her lifeline.

"I'll take you to the hospital," Letizia volunteered. "Someone has to stay with the children."

"I'll stay!" Candace put up her hand. "I'm not very good at childbirth. I don't *do* pain."

"Pain? For God's sake get me to the hospital quick. If I'm too late for an epidural, I might die." Kate began to stagger down the stairs.

"Where's your overnight bag?" Scarlet asked, following after.

"It's in my bedroom. Take the key from my bag and let yourself in. Thank God my waters didn't break in the Chanel department at Selfridges."

Letizia rushed Kate to the Portland Hospital, where she gave birth to a baby boy. Letizia was pale, having held Kate's hand for the duration. "Now I know why husbands prefer to pace the corridor outside," she said when Candace, Scarlet, and Angelica arrived armed with flowers and White Company bags of presents. "It's a bloody battle scene!"

The girls crowded into the small room. Kate lay serenely in bed holding Hercules in her arms, the two looking like the Virgin and Child. They gathered around curiously and gazed into the small face, searching for Pete in the squashed pink features of the baby. "He looks like you," said Candace, disappointed.

"He looks *just* like Pete," Kate replied happily.

"No, I can't see Pete in there. He's totally you."

"I've called him. He's on his way."

"What about Edmondo?"

"As Hercules is Pete's, it's only right that he gets to hold him first. A son. Imagine that! I've given Pete a son."

"You sound like Anne Boleyn," said Angelica. The door swung open.

"Ah, here's King Henry," said Candace, stepping aside.

Pete walked through them to gaze at his child as if they weren't there. His face flushed with emotion. "A son!" he exclaimed proudly.

Kate handed him over. "Hercules," she said.

"Hercules?" Pete wasn't convinced.

"A suitably heroic name," said Kate.

"The poor little thing hasn't done anything yet," Pete argued.

"Oh yes, he has," said Candace under her breath, nudging Angelica. "I think now would be a good time to leave."

"Do you think it *is* Pete's?" Angelica asked Candace and Scarlet as they descended in the lift.

"Absolutely not," Candace replied.

"Oh, I think it probably is," said Scarlet.

"Doesn't look anything like him."

"But it doesn't look like anyone else," Scarlet reminded her.

"That's because we don't know what we're looking for. Give it time. The truth always comes out in the end."

The birth of Hercules changed nothing with respect to Kate and Pete's divorce. The lawyers fought it out, and Edmondo distracted Kate with promises of palaces and parties and a lavish wedding on the beaches of Mauritius, which had always been her dream. A year went by. Angelica finished her book and handed it in. Claudia called as soon as she had read it to say that it was even better than *The Silk Serpent*. Olivier read the manuscript and took her out for dinner to celebrate, raising his glass to his gifted, beautiful wife, and

Angelica realized that, with time and love, it was possible for emotional scars to heal. Life went on like a train that waits for no one; she couldn't alter its course, but she could alter the way she chose to travel.

Then, one spring evening, as Angelica sat in the garden watching the blue tits fly in and out of the feeding cage that swung from the magnolia tree, Olivier came out with two glasses of wine, having just returned from work. The children were playing on the painted wooden playhouse, jumping off the roof, frightening the squirrels away from the bird food with their noisy chatter.

"You're home early," she said, pleased.

"I want to spend more time with my family." He handed her the wine and a little blue book, the size of his hand.

"What's this?"

"I was in Waterstone's, buying a book on Roman emperors for Joe, when I saw a pile of these on the counter. The funny name and pretty cover caught my attention. When I read the title, I thought it was something you'd like."

She stared at the words, her eyes misting with the sudden cascade of memories. "Thank you, darling," she replied. "How thoughtful of you."

"Daddy, watch me!" shouted Joe, swinging from the branch. Olivier went over to help him down.

Angelica gazed at the words emblazoned in gold on the front of the little blue book:

In Search of the Perfect Happiness

by J. A. Braai

She ran her fingers over them, sure that she could smell the scent of camphor trees. Her heart pounding, she opened the first page to find a simple dedication:

To Sage
The only words that matter are
that I love you

She didn't cry. She was too full of happiness for tears. So he had written the book in the months before he died, for *her*. He had loved her after all. She flicked open to the first chapter and laughed to herself:

The quality of our life depends on the quality of our thoughts.

She was sure she could hear him laughing, too; his irreplaceable voice carried on the wind.

Epilogue

The small gathering of friends and family sat on white chairs on the fine, sandy beach, just below the Saint Géran Hotel in Mauritius. Palm trees rustled gently in the breeze that swept in off the calm, turquoise sea, and red and yellow flowers gave up their scent to mingle with the heady smell of ylang-ylang that characterized the island. The sun had set behind the hills inland, no longer visible to burn their skin, but it was still hot enough for the guests to sweat beneath their summer dresses and shirts and for the children to fidget in their bridesmaids' dresses and pages' shorts. The reef roared in the distance and purple clouds gathered dramatically above the horizon as Kate cantered down the beach on a gleaming white horse.

Candace, Scarlet, Letizia, and Angelica stood in simple ivory strapless dresses, holding bouquets of white flowers, watching Kate approach in her Vera Wang gown and veil.

"I still don't know how I got to be here, in this dress, watching this charade," hissed Candace.

"I can't believe they've made it down the aisle," said Angelica.

"The fat lady hasn't sung yet," Candace reminded her cynically.

"There's no stopping her now."

"She looks stunning," Letizia gushed, blinking away tears.

"You're not crying, are you, Letizia?" Scarlet was appalled.

She was even more appalled to be posing at the entrance to the aisle in a conventional white dress that reached her ankles. "I feel like crying," she muttered, shuffling uncomfortably. "But for an entirely different reason."

"Me, too," Candace agreed. "At which point did we actually agree to be maids of honor? But smile, for here she is, looking like an Estée Lauder advert."

Kate beamed down at her friends, her eyes glittering with happiness. She smiled at her audience, then slipped off the horse, allowing an attendant from the hotel to lead it away. The girls dutifully smoothed out the creases in her dress and shook her train. The children shuffled into position behind her, holding little baskets of shells and petals to throw on her as she walked back up the aisle with her husband. The girls followed. Only Letizia, eyes filled with tears, was unable to see the intricate detail on the back of the bride's dress. Linking her arm through Art's, Kate proceeded to walk down the aisle between the chairs, decorated with garlands of white flowers and lush green leaves, towards her count, who stood with his chest puffed out like a fine peacock. Tod sat in the front row with Kate's mother and siblings, little Hercules squirming on his knee in the heat in a white linen shirt and shorts from Marie Chantal. Art handed Kate over to Edmondo, and, after exchanging affectionate glances, they turned to the priest to make their vows.

Suddenly, there was a strong gust of wind and a wail from the beach. Kate glanced at Edmondo. Edmondo glanced behind him. His face fell. The wail had come from Pete—and he was coming their way. "Told you the fat lady hadn't sung," Candace hissed to Angelica as the wail turned into "Kate, I love you" and got louder as he staggered towards the wedding party.

"What's she going to do?"

Kate collapsed in tears. Then she lifted her beautiful dress, kicked off her elegant Louboutin shoes, and ran back up the aisle towards him with a melodramatic sob.

"Well, I've seen everything now!" Scarlet exclaimed, throwing her flowers to the sand.

"This is so moving," Letizia sniffed. "She's always loved Pete."

"Now's a really great time for a reconciliation," said Candace sarcastically.

"Should we just wait? Perhaps she'll exchange the count for Pete," Angelica suggested.

"This isn't *Mamma Mia*!" Candace retorted.

Art stood up and put his hands on his hips. "Why didn't we see this coming?" He turned to the girls. "I think Tod and I are in for another honeymoon!"

At that moment, Hercules wriggled off Tod's knee. While no one was paying him any attention, he pulled his shirt over his head and kicked off his shorts, then headed naked down to the sea.

"Oh God!" Candace exclaimed, noticing the little toddler.

"What?" Angelica followed the line of her vision. "Oh my God," she repeated in amazement. "Isn't that . . . ?"

One by one the girls turned away from the sight of Kate and Pete falling on each other like animals, and stared at the little boy's bottom as he trotted down the sand.

Art's jaw fell open. "Good Lord!" he exclaimed. "Well, I'll be damned."

On Hercules's right cheek was a big red birthmark, the shape of a strawberry.

Don't weep for the dead. Keep all your love for the living. As one grows older one should escape from the captivity of physical belongings, for all is lent to us: possessions, friends, loves, even time.

In Search of the Perfect Happiness by J. A. Braai

Acknowledgments

This novel was inspired by my book tour to South Africa a few years ago. I fell in love with the countryside that strangely reminded me of Argentina, perhaps because of the monumental skies and magnificent horizons. I met some wonderful people and visited a stunning Cape Dutch vineyard in Constantia. Having based my previous books in Latin America and Europe, I relished the change. So a big thank-you to all my dear South African friends who patiently answered my endless questions and showed me their beautiful country with such enthusiasm and generosity: Cyril and Beryl Burniston, Julia Twigg, Gary Searle, and Leighton McDonald. I also want to thank Pippa Clarke for being an inspiration in herself!

I took advantage of my cousin Katherine Palmer-Tomkinson, who went to Cape Town last Christmas. I wrote her a long list of questions about vineyards, and she very kindly came back with photographs plus almost an entire manuscript written by the sales and marketing manager of Warwick Estate, James Dare, about the harvest there. I can't thank him enough for going to such trouble. If I have brought that delightful season to life, it is only thanks to him.

I thank my father for setting such a fine example—wherever there's a wise character in my books, there's a little of him—and my mother for her perceptive editing and ideas.

Thanks to my agent, Sheila Crowley, at Curtis Brown and to my editor, Trish Todd, at Touchstone Fireside. It's a joy to be published in the United States, and I thank Trish Todd and her dynamic team for their enthusiasm and drive and for giving my books such stunning covers! It matters so much to me.

Most importantly, I'd like to thank my husband, Sebag, who not only helps me construct my plots but makes me laugh like no one else in the world!

The Perfect Happiness

Bestselling children's book author Angelica Lariviere lives in an upper-class neighborhood in London with her loving husband and two wonderful children. At first glance, Angelica seems to lead an idyllic life; but Angelica's routine is becoming mundane, and she realizes that she and her husband, Olivier, no longer feel the same passion they shared when they were courting. To top it off, Angelica cannot seem to find the inspiration to begin writing her newest children's book.

Enter Jack. What starts off as harmless flirtation at a party makes Angelica feel sexy and alive again. Despite the warnings of her friend Candace, Angelica begins a correspondence with Jack—after all, they're only friends. Angelica certainly would not risk everything she has for a little thrill and rests easy knowing Jack lives thousands of miles away in Cape Town.

When her book tour takes her to Cape Town, however, an affair with Jack begins in earnest. Angelica soon convinces herself that Jack is the man for her, and she will do everything in her power to be with him. Tragedy strikes on their last night together and Jack makes a shocking confession to Angelica. Now everything she thought she knew about love and passion, safety and experience, right and wrong are entirely upended once again.

FOR DISCUSSION

1. Olivier and Angelica's discussion about flirting reaches a one-sided conclusion: it is okay for a married man to flirt but not a married woman. Do you agree with this? Could this discussion be viewed as the catalyst for Angelica's continued flirtation with Jack?

2 Angelica repeatedly tells herself that her e-mail relationship with Jack is dangerous. Yet she manages to "convince herself that it was as much a game for him as it was for her" (page 63). Why do you think she ignores the warnings in her mind and from her friends?

3. One of the key themes in *The Perfect Happiness* is the search for perfect happiness. Talk about the many notions of perfect happiness that are discussed in the book. Does Angelica ever find perfect happiness? What about Olivier or Jack? Do you think it is obtainable at all?

4. Contrast the Angelica that Olivier knows with the Angelica that Jack knows. Do you agree with Angelica's notion that if both Angelica's were to meet, "neither would recognize the other" (page 169)? Do the two Angelica's ever come together?

5. Discuss Angelica's group of friends: Candace, Scarlet, Letizia, and Kate. What perspective does each of them bring to the table? Who is Angelica closest to and why? Have any of them found "perfect happiness"?

6. Each chapter from *The Perfect Happiness* begins with a quote from the book *In Search of the Perfect Happiness*.

Who wrote the book and what is its significance? How does it bridge Angelica's gap between Olivier and Jack?

7. Anna admits that she knows about Jack's other relationships, but they do not bother her. What are her reasons? Do you believe that such an open relationship could exist? How does Anna say that Angelica was different from any of the other women Jack had been with?

8. What might Angelica's life have been like if she remained in contact with Jack after their experience in Africa? Do you think she would have worked so hard to fix her life and relationships at home?

9. What do you think the final message of *The Perfect Happiness* is? Do couples need to go through what Angelica and Olivier did in order to find their happiness? Do people need to stray from what they know to realize that what they had was perfect?

10. Olivier comments: "No one's normal. People present as normal, but really everyone hides some sort of weirdness behind closed doors" (page 193). What sort of weirdness does each character in *The Perfect Happiness* hide? Are Angelica's parents the only normal ones?

11. Candace and Angie advise Angelica not to tell Olivier about the affair. Do you think Angelica should have? How do you think he would have reacted? How was your view of Angelica affected by her decision?

A Conversation with Santa Montefiore

What was the inspiration behind *The Perfect Happiness*? Was there a particular scene you envisioned first?

I'm forty years old myself, with two small children and a very happy married life. An attractive man flirted with me at a dinner and then found me on e-mail, through my author Web site—that part is taken from life. It was really a what if from there. I wanted to explore two things: One, is it possible to have a flirtation without it developing into a full-blown affair? And two, we belong to a generation that feels happiness is our birthright, at whatever cost. We want something, we buy it on credit; we break something, we don't mend it as our mothers did but chuck it away and buy a new one. Do we treat love in the same way?—and destroy any obstacle in our path, even if that obstacle is our own husband, children, or friends? Do we selfishly believe we can and should have everything we want? The first scene I thought of was the robbery and Jack's confession, so I always knew where I was going, although I wasn't sure how it would end—and, true to character, Kate took over the subplot, which was never my intention!

Angelica struggles in *The Perfect Happiness* to get inspiration for her new book. She believes: "There was nothing more disconcerting than a blank document with nothing to write on it" (page 55). What do you do when you get stuck with writer's block? Does your writing routine mimic Angelica's?

No, fortunately I never get writer's block. My trouble is finding time to get to my desk with all the domestic chores I have to do!

Shopping, brands, and couture are a big part of the ladies' lifestyle in *The Perfect Happiness*. Do you consider yourself a fashionista like Kate, Candace, and the others?

No, but my girlfriends are very fashion conscious. I love clothes and shopping, but I'm not very good at it. If I identify with any of the girls on that front, it would be Angelica.

You created quite the range of characters in Angelica, Kate, Candace, Letizia, and Scarlet. Are any of these women based upon people you know? Who do you think you are the most like and why?

I drew inspiration from my group of girlfriends. We meet weekly for lunch at one another's houses or restaurants, and daily at the school gates. Although I invented their characters, the lifestyle is very much taken from my life. There is a little of me in all of them, barring Kate, who is like no one I know (but would rather like to know, as she's funny!). I'm sure I subconsciously draw on people I know. I'd never do it consciously—basing characters on real people could get me into terrible trouble!

Your descriptions of London, Johannesburg, Cape Town, and the vineyards are exceptionally vivid. Do you frequent these locales? What kind of research, if any, did you have to do for this book?

I always write about what I know. So, yes, I live in Kensington, have been on book tour to Johannesburg and Cape Town, and visited a beautiful vineyard there. I draw inspiration from real places—this novel is the most realistic of all my books, because I usually invent my towns and villages. All the restaurants, streets, and shops in London are real. Warwick

Estate, where Jack and Angelica go for drinks, is a real place anyone can visit.

Was there ever a version in which Angelica and Jack wound up together? Or was she always meant to go back to Olivier?

Jack and Angelica were never going to end up together. I knew from the start that he was going to die and that Angelica would return and repair her marriage. I wanted the affair to be the catalyst that drives her to find happiness with Olivier.

Angelica's story highlights the hardships of maintaining both a happy personal life and a successful professional life. What advice would you offer to women who struggle to balance the two?

I think it's incredibly hard to juggle being a wife, mother, and working woman. There is no secret to making it work. You spread yourself very thinly and feel exhausted at the end of the day after everyone has wanted a piece of you. I meditate, try not to put too much in my appointments diary so I get my sleep, and spend quality time with my husband and children on weekends. I'm lucky: I'm self-employed and can run my own timetable. If I get stressed out I can go for a walk in the park! My husband and children come first, no matter what, so my life revolves around them—but my writing is always there for *me*. It's a hobby that I'm lucky enough to have as a job.

Angelica's marriage is arguably saved by the events that transpire in *The Perfect Happiness*. What do you want readers to take away from the book?

First, I would like my readers to enjoy it. It's a love story, with a little mystery thrown in. I enjoyed writing it and took great pleasure from the characters I invented. I'd like readers to laugh and cry a little but end up with a warm feeling that carries them through their day. If they want to derive anything further on a spiritual level, then they can read extracts from *In Search of the Perfect Happiness* at the top of each chapter and try to work them into their lives. I know all the theory, but it's difficult to live it, but I certainly try.

Your books have consistently been on the top of British and European bestseller lists and now you are starting to take the United States by storm. How do you make your books appealing to so many different audiences?

First, the U.S. book covers are beautiful, so that's a great start when trying to attract readers. Second, love is universal. We all want it, no matter who we are or what we do. We all want to be loved and to love in return. But we all suffer loss, setbacks, disappointment, and hurt—as do my characters. I explore love in every form in my novels because love is the most important thing in my life and, I believe, why we're all here on earth. The simple answer is that love appeals to everyone.

What's next for you? Will we be hearing from Angelica again?

The Perfect Happiness has already come out in the UK and I have had many requests to write a sequel. I rather enjoy the idea of picking another character, say Candice, and focusing on her life—or Kate. . . . Watch this space.

Right now, I'm writing my next novel, based in Tuscany in the late 1960s and Devon, England, in the present day. Another big love story with a whopping twist! I've just changed publishers in England and am now writing for Simon & Schuster UK, so I'm under the big Simon & Schuster umbrella, which is wonderful. I want my first novel for them to be bigger and better than all the other ones, so I'd better get back to it. . . .

Enhance Your Book Club

1. Jack's vineyard produces some of the world's most exquisite wines. Research your favorite wine and discuss it with your book club. Bring some to share!

2. Angelica is an acclaimed children's book author. Do you think you can be the next Angelica Garner? Write a chapter of your "new" children's novel and share with your book club.

3. Have you ever visited Cape Town? If so, bring in some photos to show your book club.

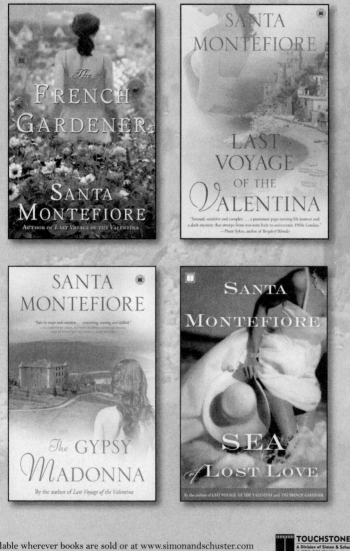